PIERS ANTHONY
SHADE OF THE TREE

A TOM DOHERTY ASSOCIATES BOOK

This is a work of fiction. All the characters and events portrayed in this book are fictional, and any resemblance to real people or incidents is purely coincidental.

SHADE OF THE TREE

A TOR Book

Published by Tom Doherty Associates
49 West 24 Street
New York, N.Y. 10010

Cover art by Linda Garland
Cover design by Carol Russo

ISBN: 0-312-93724-5

Library of Congress Catalog Card Number: 85-52252

Printed in the United States

0 9 8 7 6 5 4 3 2

Chapter 1

Josh heaved the microbus around the turn and angled it onto the sloping right shoulder of the road. The blacktop gave way immediately to deep grass, and the turf angled down to a crudely fenced pasture. The vehicle bumped to a halt under a hugely spreading live oak tree: a typically scenic Southern giant girt with hanging Spanish moss and arching branches.

He jabbed the seat belt release and climbed out, feeling his buttocks unkinking as his feet took the weight. Today's drive had been relatively brief: two hundred miles. But added to the thousand miles of the prior days, it was more than enough.

Quickly he unlocked the side door and slid it open. "Hold the dogs!" he snapped as the living cargo spilled out: two children, two dogs, and a toppling sweet potato plant. Others had asked him somewhat disapprovingly why he locked his family in; had they had a similar family, they would have known. The last thing he needed was a door opening and a dog leaping out while he drove at speed on the interstate highway.

"Let's go exploring!" Chris yelled, showing the way. His dog kept pace, putting his head down and hauling forward

1

with brute determination on the leash. Neither boy nor dog
envinced any interest in the pressing calls of nature they had
advertised for the last hour while Josh was trying to find his
way.

For a moment Josh felt light-headed. That happened sometimes, when he got to his feet too quickly after prolonged
driving. He was tired; he was glad the journey was almost
done. He leaned against the closed right-side door and stared
into the glass of the window.

His daughter moved in that reflection, a cute child almost
the image of her mother. Then his vision compensated for the
glass, and Josh saw the juxtaposed image of Mina as she
rummaged in her handbag for the map and directions. Mina
was a tall, slender woman, brown haired and brown eyed,
still attractive to him after eleven years of marriage. Their
years together had not all been easy, and there were problems
yet, but he still needed her. The most effective cure for love
was said to be marriage, but he had not found that to be true.
Wilhelmina—

Josh shook himself and the image vanished. No! He could
not allow himself to slide into that state again. Mina was not
there, had not been there for eight months. He squeezed his
eyes closed, hurting.

Suzanne came up behind him. "You aren't supposed to do
that, Daddy," she said solemnly. "You told us—"

She understood too much! Josh opened the door, reached
in, and lifted the paper from the seat. But his eyes were teary
and he could not read it.

The little girl took it from his hand and perused the directions with the intense concentration only a child could evince.
She looked up from the paper. "It says there's a railroad
crossing a mile west of the intersection of 480 and 581.
After that we turn north on Forest Drive." She looked up,
pleased that she had read it without a hitch, and brightened

further as she peered back at the intersection they had just passed. "Was that—?"

"Why do you think I stopped?" he inquired with an edge. Mina had a way of responding argumentatively like that, and it annoyed him. Now he was emulating her tone, and that annoyed him worse. In fact he realized he had picked up a number of Mina's mannerisms, perhaps as the visible manifestation of a suppressed obsession. Maybe it was simply a matter of fulfilling the role he had assumed: when the mother was absent, the father had to perform her functions, and the only model he had to follow was hers. This tedious, tiring journey had intensified it. It was impossible to be sure; he was no psychiatrist, and in any event he had a low opinion of the medics of the emotions. He was sure, however, that such mannerisms did not become more endearing in the course of a thousand mile drive.

He realized abruptly that the child was fighting off the hurt from his tone. "I'm sorry, honey," he said. "You're being very helpful, and I want you to sit up front with me and read the directions while I drive, so we don't get lost and drive into a swamp. Okay?"

Ray of sunshine through cloud. "Okay!"

Chris zoomed past, thrusting Pharaoh's leash into Josh's hand. "I'm hungry!" he exclaimed. He was hyperkinetic; he seldom stopped moving about. They had hoped he would outgrow it, but at age ten his energy was in its prime.

"Not until we get there," Josh said with the same edge he had used on Suzanne. But the boy was already gone.

Josh circled the bus to check the fish. Without electricity for the bubbler and filter, they had found it necessary to change the water frequently. The two goldfish were frightened by this, and none too partial to the constant vibration of the drive; they huddled together in the shadow. "There, there, Hammerhead, Nurse," he murmured, half smiling.

The fish were the pets of the children, so naturally these timid creatures had been afflicted with exorbitant nomenclature.

He moved back up front, hauling the balky dog along. It was hot even in the shade, for this was August in Florida. They had the vehicle's corner windows angled to blast air inside; now that the motion had stopped, sweat was flowing.

Suzanne was poring dutifully over the directions. "Is the road paved or guarded—*graded*?" she asked.

"How should I know?" Josh snapped, but caught himself immediately. He was a ragged edge, emotionally, and that was no good for the children. "One way to find out." He raised his voice. "Chris! Back in the bus!"

"Awww . . ." the boy complained routinely. He piled in.

Josh drove while Suzanne concentrated on the directions. "Kids, sing out when you spot the railroad tracks," he said.

"Will we see a train?" Sue inquired eagerly. She was seven, and somewhat disconcertingly bright. Josh had to keep reminding himself that though she looked and acted like a fourth grader, she was a second grader. He knew that he took such things as her reading too much for granted.

"Doubtful," he said, remembering her question. "It might see you first."

"Daddy!" she protested, with much the same edge as her mother, while Chris snickered. But she was joking; she was extremely cute when she tried. Unfortunately, she didn't always try. A bright child could be a joy—and a great aggravation. She could throw a tantrum that—

"Tracks! Tracks! Tracks! Tracks!" Chris chanted. "I saw them first!"

"So what?" Sue muttered, going into a pout. "They're rusty. Who wants rusty ol' tracks?"

Josh stared at the crossing, blinking. There were no tracks, though this was obviously the place. They had been paved over. Were the children playing a game?

Sue returned to the directions, her bastion of responsibility. "Next, Forest Drive taking off to the north," she announced, brightening. She pointed. "North is that way."

"Forest Drive! Forest Drive!" Chris screamed, causing the dogs to sit up and cast about for the source of excitement.

"Dummy," Sue retorted smugly. "That's just a car track."

So it was. But in a moment, just over the crest of a hill, a full-fledged gravel-and-shell road opened out. A huge sign proclaimed HEATHER HILLS, with two numbers for interested buyers to use. Neither number, Josh was later to discover, was current. Both children screamed glad recognition.

"Now we go north to Ridge Road," Sue said, squinting at the jiggling scrawl as the bus bumped onto the gravel. "Then on up—it looks like Forest Drive again."

"I'm hungry," Chris repeated.

"See if there's a cupcake left in the bag," Josh suggested. That distracted the boy, who was always hungry.

They navigated Ridge Road—all fifty feet of it, it seemed to Josh—and turned north on the renewed Forest Drive. There was a road sign that seemed to have a different name, but if Sue's sharp little eyes were satisfied, it was probably all right. He wondered what kind of a surveyor had laid out these back roads.

He found a growing apprehension instead of the expected relief. They were getting close to their destination, and that should be good—but he really did not know what to expect. His uncle, Elijah Pinson, had been an eccentric loner, prone to doing things his own eccentric way. Theoretically the man had had fair success—but the most tangible part of the estate Joshua had been able to assimilate was this property they were approaching. It was supposed to be thirty forest acres and a residence.

Uncle Elijah. Biblically named, as were all the males in the family up to his own generation, in a tradition extending back beyond the family records. But Elijah had broken free of the mold established for him, and gone off on his own, a black sheep. Joshua, a generation later, had followed his example. Perhaps that was the reason he had inherited Elijah's estate, though he had never met the man or even corresponded with him. Perhaps Elijah had seen in Joshua a fellow traveler. That seemed the most reasonable explanation for this windfall inheritance.

It also seemed that fate—Josh was unwilling to call so malignant an imperative God—had punished Elijah for his transgression, just as it had punished Josh himself. A one-two stroke, separated by a scant seven months—an eyeblink in the stern history of the family. Blood had flowed, abolishing first Joshua's wife, then his uncle. Who would be next?

"Not me, damn you!" he hissed through his teeth as though daring fate to take up the gauntlet. "I have committments—"

"What did you say, Daddy?" Sue asked with little-girl concern.

He should not have spoken aloud. His control was fraying again. Fortunately the noise of the moving bus had largely drowned him out. "Just thinking, honey."

"You shouldn't think, Daddy. It's bad for you."

Josh felt a surge of love and gratitude toward her. She was such a sweet child, when she wanted to be. "You're right, honey. What's the next landmark? We must be very close."

"The road dead-ends," she said. "Then turn right, no left, though a chap—chap—"

"Chaparral," he said. "That's a thicket of small oaks." He peered ahead. "I think we're coming to the dead end now."

"How can you keep driving past a dead end?" Chris demanded.

"Good question," Josh replied. "We'll just have to examine the situation at close range."

The scrawny oaks closed in, squeezing the road. The telephone line terminated in a pole set dead center of the right-of-way, which of course indicated that thereafter it was the wrong-of-way. There was space cleared to make a fifty-foot turning circle, and two desultory forest trails spun off from it, north and west. Beside one of them stood a mailbox on a post, with the name crudely printed on the side: PINSON 27P.

"This would seem to be it," Josh said as they drew to a halt.

"No house?" Sue asked blankly.

"There's a house," Josh assured her. "We just have to find it. Probably down one of these trails."

"The left," she said, remembering the directions. "Past the chap-ar-ral."

They piled out again. Bahia grass grew thickly in the road right-of-way, shifting abruptly to dry leaves a few feet beyond. Grass did not have much success in a thorough forest.

They followed the trail nearest the mailbox into the thicket. The path wound about, turning northwest, then southwest, finding its way through a wilderness of shrub and bramble, brushing by a thick-trunked pine tree here, a clump of palmetto there, and crowding blackberry bushes elsewhere. A bee flew up from a hole in the sand, startling the children. A bird flitted between branches, silently. Florida jungle, indeed.

Sue halted, afraid to pass the bee. Josh decided to experiment with a little psychology. "Known dangers can't hurt you," he explained. "The bugs aren't out to sting you; they're just minding their own business. All you need to do is understand them, and honor their home territory, and they will ignore you. Why don't you start a list of all the strange

bugs you see, and keep track of where they live? Then you'll
never be unpleasantly surprised."

She hesitated, and he wasn't certain she was buying it.
Then she smiled in that sudden way she had. "Okay, Daddy.
Can I have a notebook?"

"One notepad," Josh agreed. "First chance I get to buy
one."

"What about me?" Chris demanded. "How come *she* gets
to do everything?"

He should have known! "You can keep track of the birds,"
Josh said. "There should be many of them out here."

"Birds?" Chris asked, disappointed. "That's girl stuff."

"It is?" Sue asked hopefully. "I'll take them!"

"I didn't say you could have them!" Chris rapped. "It's
just that—"

"Birds do eat bugs," Josh reminded them.

"Yeah!" Chris said, suddenly more interested.

"Hey!" Sue protested. "Not *my* bugs!"

This was getting out of hand, as always. "Then there are
the other animals. The mammals and the reptiles. That is, the
rabbits and deer, and the snakes—"

"I got the snakes!" Chris cried.

"I wanted the rabbit anyway," Sue said. "Nyaa."

"Notepads for both of you," Josh said. "Now let's get on
with our business before darkness falls."

"Hey, this is sort of fun!" Chris exclaimed, running ahead
with Pharaoh on the leash. Sue followed more diffidently
with Nefertiti. Josh walked last. Another minor crisis navigated! Joy came so readily to children.

"Ooooo, a butterfly!" Sue exclaimed, abruptly halting.
"Pretty." Then, as an afterthought, "That puts me ahead of
Chris. Two for one."

It was a pretty butterfly, Josh had to agree. It was large
and striped with black and white, perched on a tall green

weed. He would have to buy some nature books so that the children could identify the creatures they "collected." This would be a positive way to commence their residence here, and it might help keep them from being frightened by the proximate wilderness.

"Oooo, pancakes!" Sue exclaimed, pointing to a clump of toadstools that did indeed resemble nicely browned pancakes. Then, before Josh could speak, she said: "I know, Daddy. Don't eat them. They're poison pancakes."

"The point is, we don't know," he said. "Some fungi are edible, and many are only mildly toxic, but—"

"Hey!" Chris called, out of sight ahead. "Come here!"

Trouble? Josh's heart jumped. He pressed on, reassuring himself that it had not been a cry of distress. Still, this *was* a kind of wilderness, and—

"Wait for me!" Sue pleaded. But Josh didn't wait. Unreasonable fear burgeoned: bear advancing on uncomprehending boy, hornet's nest jogged and stirring balefully, rotted-wood cover of some old deep well giving way slowly under feet . . .

He rounded the bend. Chris was all right. Josh relaxed, regretting the unreasonable fears. Normally he wasn't so reactive, but after the wearing drive—

"Oh! It got me!" Sue exclaimed.

Josh whirled, his fear exploding. Rattlesnake?

"With its thorn," Sue said, extricating herself from the encounter with a blackberry plant.

Josh relaxed, ashamed of his overreaction. He turned back to face the boy.

Chris was standing with the dog, looking ahead. "See the tree I found!" he exclaimed.

Josh looked south, humoring his son. And stood amazed.

The tree was monstrous. Perhaps seven feet thick at the base, it diverged immediately into three major trunks, each

about three feet through, that gnarled outward like the tenta-
cles of some giant squid. It was not tall—perhaps no more
than fifty feet at the highest—but it spread enormously, its
extremities reaching down almost to the ground in several
places as though resting. It stood in a hollow, so that the
ground was rising where the branches reached, making contact easier. Josh had never before seen a tree of this scale and
configuration.

"Oooo, what a pretty house!" Sue said, coming up behind
him.

House? Josh had been so absorbed by the tree that he had
not even noticed the house. It stood almost nestled within the
embrace of the tree, just east of it: a two-story wood-shingled
cube about twenty-five feet on a side. It had a bright metal
roof, a number of windows, a green-topped back porch, and
a front porch facing south with some apparatus on top. The
house seemed complete, yet looked unfinished. A power line
came to the southeast corner, evidently a devious offshoot
from the pole at the end of the main access drive.

"I believe we have found it," Josh said. He felt a gradual
and growing relief as his suppressed fears dissipated. There
was a house here; it was intact; it had electric power. They
would not have to camp out.

They advanced somewhat warily on the house. The dogs
sniffed the air, alert to something. Josh followed the line of
their attention. "Oh, no!"

"A horse!" Sue cried jubilantly. She was just coming up
on the age when all girls became aware of horses.

"That's a pony, dum-dum," Chris said witheringly.

There it was: a brown and white little equine tethered to a
smaller tree north of the great one. A female pony. She
neighed as the children approached.

"Wait!" Josh cried. "We don't know that animal. She
might not be friendly."

Indeed, as they drew closer the pony became uneasy, her ears tilting back. Josh remembered that this was a signal of warning. "Stay clear," he called.

He approached the animal himself. She had a water bucket that she had kicked over, and had grazed the grass down to bare ground in the circle the tether allowed her to reach. Josh knew he could not leave her there, but he didn't want to get bitten or kicked. He stood just out of range and extended one hand slowly.

The pony's ears angled forward. She sniffed his hand. He realized she thought he held feed; he was inadvertently teasing her. Still, she was reacting much more positively to him than to the children. Had she been mistreated by a child?

Josh patted her shoulder, then leaned down to pick up the water bucket. The pony nuzzled his hair. Her muzzle was velvety soft. "We'll see what we can do for you, pony," he said, taking the bucket.

Now he had to find water. He saw an external tap at the southwest corner of the house. He went to it, while the children and dogs exchanged wary glances with the pony. No question about it, she liked Josh, not the children. This was ironic, because he really was not partial to equines, while the children doted on any large animal.

The tap worked. He filled the bucket and hauled it back. The pony drank, then nosed the bucket over, spilling the rest. No foresight there.

Josh went to the small tree and worked at the knot. The rope had been wound several times around the trunk, and the knot had formed into a Gordian mass. He finally got it undone, while the pony nibbled on his hair. He walked to a tree with fresh grass and looped the frayed end of the rope about it and made a new knot.

The pony started grazing immediately—but tried to follow him when he left her. "Sorry, pony," he said. "I have other business at the moment." Inwardly he wondered how he was going to take care of a large animal like this. He had not had experience with equines for thirty years, and what experience he had had had had been bad.

Had had had been bad, he thought. *What a construction!* But it did not alleviate the complication. He had not anticipated animals with the property. The attorney for the estate had not mentioned this.

Now it was time to tackle the house. What other surprises awaited them?

The pony nickered, refusing to be forgotten. Was there hay or feed for her? Who had taken care of her for the month that Uncle Elijah had been dead? She was fairly well kept; obviously someone had been on duty.

He had better work this out now. It gave him a pretext to postpone entering the house for a few more minutes. Josh wasn't sure why he was not eager to check the house; perhaps it was merely a disinclination to have his preconceptions voided. "Let's check the shed for horse feed," he said.

The children were amenable. This was all one big adventure to them. *That was good*, he thought; he liked to see them relieved from the burden of grief, even if only temporarily. Children were not equipped to handle prolonged misery. That was one reason he had decided to make the move here: to establish a new setting, free from the associations of the old, with new stimulations and distractions. If it worked for the children, it would be worth it. Of course, eight months was a much greater span in their lives than in his; already they had rebounded better than he had, though for them the loss had been greater.

The dogs began acting strangely. Pharaoh, always aggressive in strange situations, was balking; Nefertiti, insatiably curious, was skulking, tail between her legs. This was atypical for them both. Though of similar breed—the supposedly

SHADE OF THE TREE   13

barkless basenji—they were as different as night from day in personality, but neither was cowardly. Yet both seemed to be extremely wary of this shed.

Curious, Josh went ahead. The shed was about eight by twelve feet, with a galvanized metal roof and no windows. Its walls were of one of the reconstituted woods, chips pressed together to form a new substance. Like metamorphosed rock, he thought, only less so. The whole thing was set on several three-by-five-inch timbers laid on the ground. A reasonably simple structure for someone who hadn't wanted complexity. And why not? Nothing frightening about this!

Why, then, did he feel nervous about opening the door? Why did the bold dogs hold back? The children, too, seemed reticent, their curiosity abruptly damped. Was there something *in* there? Surely not a moldering corpse!

Josh suppressed his inexplicable reservations and drew the door open and peered in, pretending unconcern. One shadowed section of his mind anticipated something dreadful, and he nerved himself not to flinch. Perhaps he was conscious of the report of Elijah's violent demise. The police had of course checked everything out, just to be sure it wasn't murder. It wasn't; it had been a freak accident. A chain saw had been involved—

His eye had been looking into the shed, picking things out of the relative gloom inside. Two bales of hay, a bag of horse feed, another of chicken feed, a round gasoline can—and a power saw.

Josh's eyes become riveted to that saw. He was no expert, but he had on occasion used a small gasoline chain saw. Such machines might weigh as little as ten pounds, these days, or even less, with twelve-inch bars to support the cutting chains, but they could do a surprising amount and were of course dangerous when mishandled. Thus he was aware that this one was a monster. Its bar was eighteen or twenty inches long and its engine section was compact but exceedingly solid. No toy; this was a machine a logger would use to handle the big timber.

Could it be the saw that had killed Elijah?

Josh closed the door, finding himself shuddering. "There's feed and hay," he reported.

"Daddy," Chris demanded. "Why are the dogs afraid of it?"

Not only the dogs, Josh was sure! Yet if the source of the fear was the saw, how could the dogs know? Was there blood on the chain? Was the smell of death associated with it? Surely the police would have disassembled it, wiped off all the blood, cleaned it—in fact, wouldn't the killer saw have been impounded as evidence? So this was probably not the one. Yet why would there be any other placed here, after Elijah's death?

"Maybe the dogs smell something," Josh said vaguely. He hadn't told the children how Uncle Elijah had died. In fact, he had never gotten too specific on how their mother had—

A mindless scream drowned the thought. The sheer horror—

Josh found himself leaning against the outer wall of the shed. It had been only a moment. But what a moment! He had been dipped in hell, and experienced a ferocity and desolation of emotion he hardly believed. He had thought he was becoming hardened, healed over, after all these months. Evidently he still had far to go. These brief sieges had been abating, but this one had seemed more intense. Was he backsliding? No, no, surely it was just the fatigue.

The children, preoccupied with the nervous dogs, had not noticed his lapse. He walked around the shed, and came across a covered machine. This turned out to be a small tractor, the kind used to haul a mowing rig, with small front wheels and big rear tires. It was clean and seemed to be in good condition. Well, it would no doubt be useful. He rejoined the children, and they went as a group toward the house. The dogs had no fear of this structure, at least.

The house faced south, but they were approaching from the northeast, circling the fantastic tree to reach the back porch. Josh could see that the house was as yet unfinished; boards and planks lay piled outside, and the porch was filled with four-by-eight-foot sheets of fiberboard, and stacks of one-foot-square floor tiles.

Josh tried his key, and the door unlocked. They stepped into the house proper.

It was certainly unfinished. There was no inside paneling on the walls. The paper backing of pink fiberglass insulation showed between the wooden studs, and the floor was bare concrete. Furniture stood lumped in the center of the main room, and the stairs were a ladder rising into a square hole.

"Gee, this is fun!" Chris exclaimed. "A haunted house!"

Now where had the boy gotten that notion? "Not haunted," Josh corrected him. "Deserted." But he was disturbed. Obviously this house was not in a fit state for occupancy. Where was his party to spend the night? They had camped in the bus on the wearisome drive down because of the cost of lodging and the need to stay with the animals; he had had enough of that. But unless the upstairs was a lot more finished than the ground floor—

He investigated. He climbed carefully up the ladder, through the six foot opening in the ceiling, and maneuvered his feet to the upper floor.

This level was worse than the one below. The plywood floors were bare, the rooms partitioned only by standing studs, no wallboard. There were no beds. Spiderwebs filled the corners and stretched across the gaunt trusses of the open ceiling. Nothing separated the attic from the second floor— except those wooden beams. Two huge galvanized tanks were perched in the attic, and copper pipes formed a spaghettilike tangle with extremities reaching from the solid brick chimney and from the south edge of the house. The plumber who installed this must have been drunk!

Closed cardboard cartons were stacked everywhere, marked in stencil OAT, MLK, NBN, PEA, POT, MAR, and APSL. Perplexed and distantly alarmed, Josh wrenched at the top of one of the POT cartons and got it open. It turned out to be filled with large metal cans of potato powder, evidently for mixing with water to make mashed potato. POTato, of course. The APSL was applesauce. These were assorted foods, canned in vacuum. Elijah must have bought food for a year ahead, this way, so that he never had to shop locally. Strange man!

Strange? No, upon reconsideration Josh found that he could see the sense in it. If a man felt no need for routine human interaction, why not simplify his existence in this manner? Elijah had probably saved considerable money and time. And if Josh ran low on money—which was by no means far-fetched!—he could use these staples to feed his family. So his uncle had already contributed materially to his security.

The rest of it Josh surveyed with dismay. This was the last week of August, Sunday the 26th. Tomorrow the children began school in Inverness, the nearest town. It would be all he could do to organize them for that, and have them neat and fed and ready by 7:45 Daylight Saving Time for the school bus that was supposed to come. Now it seemed he had no place to put them for the night.

He descended the ladder. He had understood Elijah had lived here. Evidently the man had not. But he, Joshua, would have to live here. He had made his commitment, put his own house up for sale in New Jersey, and found his way here with his family. It was reasonably final. They might have to lay their sleeping bags on the concrete, but they would sleep on this property tonight.

"Daddy, the lights don't work," Chris announced.

Josh checked. Sure enough, there was no power in the house. That was all he needed!

"How can we plug in the fishes?" Sue inquired.

"That's fish, not fishes, stupid," Chris said.

"The Bible says fishes," she retorted. "Isn't that right, Daddy?"

"It does, honey, but it means different species," Josh said quickly. "The normal plural for members of the same species is 'fish.' So you're both right, and don't fight."

He concentrated on the problem raised. There was a pump that circulated and aerated the water of the fish tank. After several hours in the car, that water had to be oxygenated or the fish would sicken and die by morning. What was he to do with an electric motor and no power?

Another man would say to hell with the fish, he thought. But he was not another man. He had no special brief for fish, but he was trying to bring his children up with a certain reverence for life and concern for the welfare of all creatures.

Reverence for life—in the midst of death.

And the fish were pets, important to the children on a personal basis. They had to be saved.

"We can dip some more cups of water and pour them back in," Josh said. But he knew that wouldn't be enough; it was only a stopgap oxygenation measure they had already used too much. Nature's ever-flowing rivers and ever-restless waves oxygenated the water continuously, but the tank did not work that way. They needed the motor running steadily, day and night.

The children looked as doubtful as he felt, but did not argue the case. Josh checked the rest of the house. Downstairs was structured in a rough U shape, the left side of the U to the north; that was the kitchen, with refrigerator, small electric stove, and a good double-sink/cabinet unit. He tried the tap, and water flowed—as of course it should, since the outdoor tap had worked. At least they had that! He presumed the water was brought from the well by an electric pump; it must have been necessary to connect that in order to build the house.

At the base of the downstairs U format, centered in the house, was a raised brick platform adjoining a handsome brick chimney. A crate sat there; he guessed it was a stove, as yet not connected because in this summer heat there was no need for it. The right side of the U seemed to be the living room area; large windows opened to the south.

Nefertiti barked. That set Pharaoh off, growling and squealing. He *could* bark, he just didn't deign to. Both dogs strained at their leashes, wanting to get outside. "Something's happening out there," Josh said.

Chapter 2

They allowed the dogs to drag them out. In a moment the distraction was apparent: they had a visitor.

It was an old man, tall and solid and slow. His face was wrinkled and weathered and his nondescript hair straggled out in diffuse whitening puffs. He supported himself in part with a gnarly cane, though he seemed capable of walking without it. He must have walked, for there was no vehicle in view.

"You're the nephew?" the man inquired.

"Joshua Pinson," Josh agreed guardedly. "You are a—neighbor?"

"Old Man Foster, half mile down the street. Nearest neighbor," he replied proudly. "You drove right past my place, never seen it. I knew your uncle."

"That's more than I did," Josh admitted. "I never met him."

"Never met him?" Foster asked, brow wrinkling impressively. "Why'd he give it to you, then? He set great store by this place."

Diplomacy was evidently not Foster's strong point. "I'm not sure myself. I think he figured I was the relative most likely to appreciate it—or perhaps least likely to liquidate it.'' Josh had spent a fair amount of private time in the past month laboring over this riddle. The Pinsons were a religious family, most of whose members were associated with a kind of farm commune system that had endured for generations. Few broke free of it—seldom more than one person in a given generation. Elijah had spun off as a young man, thirty years before, and gone into the mundane world of free enterprise and self-interest. Thus he was the pariah, used within the family as a bad example. He was rumored to have done quite well for himself. That was added to the tally against him, since it was presumed that an honest man could not succeed in business. Yet there had never been tangible proof of Elijah's (ill-gotten?) wealth, and there had been none coming from the mysteries of Elijah's will and the opaque process of probate. The attorney, Biggerton, had handled things by mail; closemouthed even on paper, he had let slip only that apart from the actual acreage of Willaurel Oaks there was little of substance to the estate. This thirty-acre tract was paid for, but other lots were encumbered by mortgages and liens and complex tax-shelter devices. It would, it seemed, be some time before probate was completed, and what little remained was duly taxed and released to the designated heir. Meanwhile, Josh was permitted to occupy the site, maintaining it. That last small favor was now becoming explicable: why hire someone by dint of great red tape to do a job the heir would do free?

Josh, in contrast to his uncle, had been lured out of the family system by a woman. Wilhelmina had been unacceptable to the family commune. She smoked cigarettes, she drank beer, she played cards, she wore lipstick, and she dressed in brightly feminine outfits: the very picture of the wanton woman. Since she could not be admitted to the family, Josh had departed the commune and joined her world of wider New York City. He had had considerable adjusting to do, but had survived it with her guidance. It had not been principle that moved him, but sex appeal. In that way he deemed himself inferior to his uncle, though he was not sure he approved whatever principle had governed Elijah.

Now that world of Mina's had destroyed her, and Josh was retreating to his own sort of commune. He had been too much infected with mundane values to return to his family, and had not wanted his children to become captive to the commune. Yet he had not wished to remain in the situation that had spawned the death of his wife. Elijah, by whatever fortuitous tragedy, had provided him with another option. Elijah must have wanted to keep his estate out of the commune, and had felt that Joshua was the relative most likely to be suitably corrupted by capitalism. Therefore the estate had been so designated, just in case anything should happen. And—it had happened.

This might not be the correct explanation, and was perhaps not truly germane to the occasion, but it was an operable rationale. Rationales were important to Josh; he could not relax with any situation unless it made sense to him. So he had dwelt upon the question that Old Man Foster asked, but he hardly cared to discuss it with a stranger.

If Foster noticed the long pause, he gave no sign. "He was a funny man," Foster said. "From a funny family, way I heard it. Communists—"

"Commune," Josh interjected. "There is a distinction."

"Oh, sure. Anyway, he was my kind of man. You wouldn't believe the doohinkeys he's built into this house."

"Doohinkeys?"

"He was a solar freak, don't you know! And a wood freak. Wouldn't waste anything at all. Said there was all that sunlight coming down, had to use it, and the whole dang house is made of wood. And he was a doomsday freak to boot."

"Doomsday?" Josh could only follow the man's lead, at the moment. What was wrong with a house made of wood? "He's got food and money and other stuff stashed away all over the place. He said the economic system was going to break down, what with inflation and war and the fuel shortages and dimwits in the government, so he wanted to be ready. But I reckon the end came sooner than he figured."

Josh wanted to question Foster more closely about the manner of Elijah's demise, but hesitated in the presence of the children. "We understood he lived here, but the house has no power."

Foster smiled confidentially. "He didn't have no permit to live in it. So he mostly camped out in the cabin. Cooked his meals on an open fire outside, even—and him with twice the money he'd need to buy out half the restaurants in the county! He never ate out anywhere, always made his own. Said all those places spiked their food with chemicals. Chemical feast, he called it. Can't think why."

Josh smiled. "Because virtually all commercial food is chemicalized for flavor and storage. Our family opposes the use of drugs and additives in all forms. Elijah was a renegade, but it seems he retained some of the fundamentals."

Foster's eyes widened as he assimilated this gossip. "You mean you're like him? Won't take aspirin, even?"

"True," Josh agreed. He had been through this before.

Foster leaned over far enough to slap his own knee, balancing precariously. "Don't that beat all! I liked that old kook. Gonna like you too, I reckon. I get along great with harmless eccentrics, being one myself."

Just so. "However, we do use electric power, and its absence here may cause our goldfish to die."

"Elijah had power," Foster confided. "The pump's connected, and there's plug-ins at the construction box. For the workmen to use, don't you know. Just run a line in for your refrigerator—but mind you unplug it when the inspector comes by.'' He screwed his face into a wink.

So that was it! ''I don't want to cheat the regulations, but our need is critical. Where is this cabin you mentioned?''

''Right up there beyond the tree,'' Foster said, pointing. ''You must of passed it on your way in.''

Josh looked, peering past the ponderous branches. There it was: a gambrel-roofed structure in plain sight to the northwest. How could he have missed it?

''Well, I'll be toddling off,'' Foster said. ''Don't want to get caught by the rain. Or the lightning. Central Florida's the lightning capital of the world, don't you know. More strikes here than anywhere. Take a look at all the thunder-struck pines. Watch out for the shade.''

''Shade?''

''The shade of the tree. At night, or whatever. I'll tell you about it tomorrow, maybe.'' And the old man was on his way, cheerily swiping at weeds with his cane.

''What does that mean, Daddy?'' Sue asked. ''How can there be shade at night?'' It was a good question, but he had no satisfactory answer. Was it some obscure joke?

''There are two meanings of the word shade,'' Josh said after a moment. ''Shade as in shadow, and shade as in spirit. Ghost.''

''Ghost!'' she exclaimed, pleased. She had no fear of the supernatural.

''See, it really is haunted!'' Chris agreed.

''I doubt it,'' Josh said, smiling. But he remembered the aura of fear around the feed shed that the dogs had scented. Elijah had died, and the saw was there. . . .

They circled the tree, admiring its huge trifurcation and angling trunks, and walked up to the cabin. The second key on the ring unlocked it.

It was an oven inside. There was a thermometer beside the

entrance that registered 110° Fahrenheit. There were boxes
stacked everywhere. A wooden ladder led up to a loft. Josh
started up it, but the temperature jumped at the higher level
and he quickly desisted. What heat would make 110° seem
cool in contrast? People had been known to die from taking
baths no hotter than this!

"Let's open the windows and let it start cooling," he said.
"Then we'll set the fish up at the house. Then—" He broke
off, finding himself suddenly too tired to work things out
more than one event at a time.

They drove the microbus in carefully, unloaded the fish,
located a fifty-foot extension cord, and got the aeration pump
going. The fish had been saved.

They unloaded the basic necessities into the cabin, which
was cooling with frustrating slowness. The house, in contrast, was relatively cool inside, as though an air conditioner
were operating. "The shade of the tree," Josh murmured.
"Keeps the heat of the sun from the house. Good arrangement."

"But we can't use the house?" Chris asked.

"That is the way I understand it."

"What's for supper?"

Was it that time already? How time passed where there
were too many things to do at once! Josh thought of making
another meal of crackers and candy bars, and rebelled; it was
time to have a decent supper. But how could they do it here?
Without electricity—he was not going to cheat on the ban
against the use of the house, apart from that minimum necessary to save the lives of the fish—what were they to do? Heat
a can of beans on the bus's motor?

"Let's have pancakes!" Sue exclaimed.

She was standing beside another pancake toadstool. Josh
had to laugh, but he was nervous too. In time, children could
experiment, and if those toadstools were poisonous—

"I think we'd better go into town and buy a meal," he

decided, conscious of his discussion with Old Man Foster. Unlike Elijah, Joshua did condescend to use commercial food; he regarded the additives as contaminants rather than drugs. He certainly preferred clean foods, but there were times when convenience overruled that preference. "Let's see if we can get halfway cleaned up."

"Milkshakes and French fries!" Chris said.

"No. Something halfway wholesome, this time. We'll go to a restaurant." He did not feel at ease in such establishments, his tolerance for the chemical feast notwithstanding, but this seemed the lesser of evils at the moment.

The children, of course, were enthusiastic; they liked eating out. "Will it have ice cream?" Sue inquired, just to make sure there would be something edible. She had very restrictive definitions, in contrast to Chris.

"Probably." He really didn't want to fight her.

They unloaded a few more items, lightening the bus, then put the two dogs in the cabin and shut the door. "I hate to do it, but we can't take them into a restaurant, and they should be safe here. I'm leaving the windows open so it'll keep cooling."

The dogs set up a chorus of yips and howls when they realized they were being left behind. But they had been through this before; Josh knew the animals would settle down and sleep in due course. He expected to return within two hours, so there should not be any serious problem.

Inverness was about ten miles away.

The scenery was beautiful. Huge old live oaks stood near the road, much lesser trees than the one that shaded the Pinson house but still substantial. They were interspersed with stands of pine and open pastures. Pretty horses stood watching the road, and large white birds stood near them, evidently seeking flies. On occasion there were small ponds and isolated farmsteads. This was, indeed, the country—a contrast to what he had become used to in the past decade.

The contrast was important. Wilhelmina had walked through metropolitan regions, and met her doom there. Josh wanted to get as far from that as possible. Crime in the streets—it was no idle catchphrase, for him.

"Hey, that's two for me!" Chris cried. "See those birds!"

"You can't count two birds," Sue protested. "They have to be different kinds."

"That's right," Josh interposed before an argument could develop. "Otherwise Sue could count a hundred flies in one room, and get way ahead. Keep track of each new species you spy."

"And that's my horse," Sue said. "A mammal."

The two craned their necks to spot more creatures, adding to their lists. Josh knew they were more interested in competition than in nature, but at least it kept them occupied.

The pony's ears perked up. The horsewoman was coming! The stranger had been all right, except for the children. Beauty didn't trust children, who were too apt to strike with sticks or throw stones. Adults were better. They brought feed. Soon she would have grain and some hay and more water. Beauty liked the horsewoman.

In a moment the mother hen appeared with her chicks. They liked to pick up the grain Beauty dropped. She didn't mind; the birds were the only company she had, except for the kittens and Horsewoman. And the Tree. Together, they awaited the arrival.

Nefertiti paced the cabin restlessly while Pharaoh snoozed. She did not like being left alone, and always tried to convey that to the human people, but not always successfully. But now, as she resigned herself to the inevitable, she became aware of another presence. Something was perceiving her, something very large and interesting. She was not after all quite alone, this time.

She turned her head about and sniffed the air, but could not locate the presence perfectly. It was in the general region of the larger house; that was all she knew. It had manifested only when things were quiet, after the stranger had gone away.

Nefertiti settled down, her nose pointed at the presence, tuning in. Reassured, she slept.

Dusk was closing as they arrived at the farmstead. The swath that was the main access was light, but the forest on either side darkened rapidly into gloom. The track beyond the mailbox seemed to have narrowed, the brush squeezing against the bus. What had been lovely by day seemed sinister by evening. Then the glade depression opened out, preternaturally lovely with the effect of night vision, the great tree dominating it, enclosing the house protectively. It was as pretty a sight as Josh could imagine, nature and civilization merged. Uncle Elijah had instituted this, and he had certainly had esthetic taste.

"Where's the pony?" Chris demanded.

Josh looked. The pony was gone. She hadn't pulled loose; the rope was neatly coiled and hung on a knob of the small tree. Someone had been here, and taken her.

They looked about. On the far side of the feed shed, west of the tree, they found a hen scratching about with a number of newly hatched chicks. Further along they found a pen formed of welded wire fence, which he hadn't noticed before, in which the pony was contentedly munching on hay.

"Someone has fed the animals," Josh said. "Perhaps Mr. Foster." But somehow he doubted it. Foster had said nothing about it, and had paid no attention to the animals. Why would he go away, then return in the family's absence to feed the stock?

They went to the cabin to let the dogs out. It was still over 90⁰ inside, but the dogs seemed to have adjusted. With no electricity to run fans, it was apt to be a bad night. The children were thrilled with the notion of camping out in the loft, though it was even hotter there. Josh hoped their attitude would remain positive until they slept.

The loft was about half filled with more cardboard boxes containing looseleaf binders, papers, and correspondence. Josh shoved them to either side to form barriers where the loft left off at either end. He didn't want anyone falling.

"Where's the bathroom?" Chris asked.

Josh had no idea. Wearily, he considered.

"I found it!" Chris cried, dragging the heavy unit from under a small table. It was an efficient portable toilet, with a button that made a minimal water flush and a pedal to open the lower chamber. It seemed to be watertight. Both children immediately had to use it, and pronounced it better than the real thing. Josh doubted that, but was sure it would do. He hoped it wouldn't smell.

They finished the leftover pizza by the light of a kerosene lantern. Josh spread their sleeping bags in layers on the floor of the loft. "Lay out your clothes for the morning," he said. "We'll be up early and won't have much time." Or convenience, he added mentally. Was this really better than civilized New Jersey?

At nine in the evening the temperature in the loft was 91°. They settled down and made the best of it. A fat roach came out and ran along a roof-support plank; the children refused to settle down until it was gone, so Josh had to swat it with a newspaper. Then it released an awful smell. Josh turned out the fluorescent lantern he'd brought up to the loft, so that no

more distractions could be seen. At least the children weren't
fighting or fussing about the heat.

"Do you think Mommy's in heaven?" Sue asked.

Oh, no! He had hoped they would escape this, this one
night. "I think she is beyond all suffering," Josh said.

To his surprise, Sue accepted this. She was silent, and he
knew that meant she was falling asleep. Chris seemed to be
drifting off too. Well, it had been a busy, tiring day.

They slept—but he did not. Damn that question about
heaven! Now it had *him* going! He, like the children, became
more vulnerable to pain and despair when tired. The recur-
ring nightmare of things lost—

Eight months ago. So short a time chronologically, yet an
eternity emotionally! Mina had gone shopping, taking the
commuter train into town, to catch a sale on Christmas toys.
She had always done well, shopping; she knew what she
wanted and what it was worth. Josh had always liked that in
her—the ability to obtain good merchandise at excellent prices.
It had helped immeasurably during their lean years. Josh
prided himself on having a methodical mind, but in the
wilderness of the shopping center he was largely helpless.
She had gone, as she had so often before, with a certain
bright expectation—

The rest was horror. Josh struggled with it, then drew
himself out of the sleeping bag. It was sweltering anyway, too
hot to sleep. He found his way down the ladder in the dark,
conscious of the danger of a child taking a fall from the
unguarded elevation despite the barricading cartons; he worried much more about such things now that he knew how
sudden and final death could be. A person did not have to be
evil to die; a person merely had to be in the wrong situation.

Below, he used his flashlight to locate the kerosene lamp.
He didn't want to bang its fragile glass chimney in the dark!
When he had the lamp lit, he unpacked his record books.

This was no formal document, but an informal manifestation of an orderly mind. Josh was so constituted that he liked to account for everything, especially his time. It was as though time unaccounted for was lost. As though it had never existed. That thought bothered him, so he noted briefly each day what he had accomplished, in business or in life, sometimes in more detail than in others. Over the years he had worked into a personal, private shorthand intelligible only to him, a bit like a computer flowchart. A single line summarized the events of a day, and sometimes a paragraph reviewed the thoughts. Thinking, too, was living. He had not had the chance to catch up on the past two days, and this was a therapy he needed.

Yesterday was easy: all day on the road. No significant thoughts. Today—road six hours, moving in—call it another six hours. Undifferentiated. But moving was a once-in-a-blue-moon endeavor, atypical. This date last year, in contrast—

He could not remember what he had done this date last year. That bothered him. He rummaged through his sheets to locate it, foolishly desperate that it not remain forgotten.

There it was. *Mem Hosp pqm 4, rsch 3; sup out 2.5; wgn; TV 2.* He remembered, now. He had labored weeks on that Memorial Hospital program, researching the facts, organizing, and at this point was into the system flowchart. Four hours on that, three more on continuing research. A system study could be a considerable education; in this case he had had to master the intricacies of the hospital situation and organize it in his mind so that he could set up the overall chart. Later he had gotten into the grind of the detail charts. It had been hard work, but he had set up a good system, and the hospital was using it today. The only thing that had bothered him about it was the necessity of working with some of the statistics relating to the drugs the hospital used. He had decided that it was not his place to impose his personal aversion to drugs on the institution, and he had done his job properly. In fact, it might not be an overstatement to say that his system had turned the corner for the hospital, increasing the administrative efficiency so that thereafter the institution operated marginally in the black instead of the red. A good computer system could do wonders, but it had to be properly programmed or it was useless. Josh was a good consultant. That system had been in effect, when Mina—

No! No! his mind cried. Blot it out, don't relive that awful experience yet again. Move on to the next thought. Supper out, two and a half hours, rather like today. There had been a malfunction in the electric stove, with the thermostat failing to operate, and Mina's roast had been burned. She had been ready to explode. He had acted quickly, bundling the family into the microbus and going to a restaurant to eat. It had taken time to find one that both adults and children liked, and when they did it had been crowded. It had taken the first hour for Mina to simmer down, but in the end she had enjoyed it. That evening they had gotten hooked on a TV movie, a romance whose title he couldn't remember, nothing special about it, but it had evolved a mood and they had made love—

Never again. Oh, God, he would give anything to relive that day, to have it just the way it was, tribulations and all. How trivial the burned supper seemed now. Had they known—

Josh closed the book. He could not escape his loss this way, and he needed sleep. He turned down the lamp, blew it out, and used the flash to make his way back to the loft.

The children remained dead to the world—bad phrasing, better make that "sound asleep"—as they usually did, once they nodded off. As he lay down between them, he remembered the other entry: *wgn*. What had that been? Oh, yes. While the supper was burning, unbeknownst to them, Chris had approached him for help with a wagon he was building. Josh had struggled with the homemade vehicle, trying to make it safe to ride, until Mina's explosion in the kitchen. At the time it seemed like one frustration after another; now in retrospect it seemed like bliss.

Josh finally sank into a troubled, sweaty sleep. Perspiration trickled down his back and sides, feeling like crawling bugs, causing him to stir nervously. Once he dreamed he heard crying. He woke and found it was true: Sue was sobbing in her sleep. So bright and cheerful by day, that little girl, never letting loose. It tore Josh's heart, but there was nothing he could do. She had to work it out herself, deep in her feeling mind, just as Josh had to do himself. Healing could be painful too.

Chapter 3

Josh's periods of wakefulness became more extended, and finally he realized that he was irrevocably conscious. He heard an airplane going overhead. Airplanes had little concern whom they disturbed. His watch said 5:05 A.M. The loft had cooled at last. He made sure the children were covered, then drew himself out and fumbled his way down the ladder.

The dogs were happy to see him and eager to be out. Last night they had been so quiet he never noticed them when he came down, but they had rebounded to normal now. Morning was a dog's time; new smells beckoned. And why not? This was a new situation, with many mysteries awaiting discovery, for human as well as canine being.

He put the leashes on them both and took them out. It was dark, but he trusted the dogs to keep him out of mischief, guide him around trees, and avoid holes. He could see a little as his eyes acclimatized. The dogs loved it; they sniffed and snuffled everywhere, jerking this way and that, threatening to wind the leashes about him. Finally he simply spread his legs and stood firm while they buzzed in small patterns.

Josh looked up and saw the stars beyond the curtain of the nearest trees. And was amazed.

The entire firmament of the heavens was spread out in the most splendid way he had ever seen. Each star was a burning pinprick of light, stabbingly clear. The great Milky Way wound across the nocturnal welkin, so clear it seemed he could see every mote in it. There were a phenomenal number of stars, more than he had imagined, each so pretty and precious that his mind balked at assimilating the entire display. The Milky Way—it had been years since he had seen it, for the background light pollution and vapors of the city had drowned it out. Only here in the country, where the air was clean and unspoiled, did the full magnitude of it manifest.

O wonder! O glory! It seemed he could perceive the depth of it, the stars beyond the stars. He seemed to become one with the universe, standing perched on this local ball of matter, wishing he could reach out and touch all the rest of it.

Had Mina gone to heaven? Surely yes! For the universe was heaven. . . .

The stars seemed to glow more brilliantly, moving toward him, gradually spreading apart as his perspective changed. Some expanded, others shrank, until they formed a dot picture of a person, a woman. It was Wilhelmina, there in the sky, ethereally lovely, at peace, happy.

The dogs were tugging impatiently, hauling him out of his reverie. "All right," he murmured. "We'll descend from heaven to earth." He let them tug him onward. But he felt better.

Slowly the realization came: he had suffered a hallucination. A pleasant one, to be sure, a wish fulfillment—but he had never done that before. It was disturbing. He knew, objectively, that his wife was not drifting contentedly in the night sky, and he believed, subjectively, that she had no consciousness in death. She was gone, completely, irrevocably. Only the memories of her remained, and for the sake of the children he had to minimize these. He could not lose his equilibrium, however painful it might be to maintain it. The children had no one else.

Meanwhile the dogs rushed on through the predawn, hunting things Josh could neither see nor hear. He gave them rein, but after fifteen minutes he began to draw back. They were tuned to exploration, and would keep ranging farther afield indefinitely if not curbed. Which was why he kept them leashed; neither one would come when called, if anything interesting beckoned elsewhere. Now he had to return to the cabin and organize the morning, getting the children up and fed and dressed.

But now the dogs shied away from something. This was unusual; Pharaoh hated all other animals, while Nefertiti loved the whole world.

Josh peered in the direction of the thing they were avoiding, suffering a certain nervousness himself. He made out the dark mass of the storage shed. The same one they had shied from before.

His chill became almost physical. This was beyond coincidence. He could not have transmitted any expectation of his own to the dogs, since he had not been aware they had circled back to this place. He knew what was wrong with that shed: the saw. Because he felt it too, now. A superstitious dread of the instrument that had killed his uncle. *Probably* had killed; he could not be sure. But why should the dogs feel it too? They knew nothing of what had happened here.

He circled the shed and the covered tractor, yielding to the dogs' concern, and moved on toward the cabin. He had been out longer than he had intended; wan illumination was showing in the east, masking the lesser stars. The matter of the saw still nagged him; he resolved to investigate more thoroughly when the children were safely off to school.

Inside it was still impenetrably dark. Josh lit the lamp. He had to get the children up and ready for school by seven forty-five. They needed their sleep, but he knew it would take twice as long to get everything done as any reasonable estimate would suggest. Mundane life, of course, defied reason. Half an hour for rising, toilet, and dressing; half an hour for eating; fifteen minutes for incidentals. Six-thirty should be early enough to get them up. So—make it six and hope for the best.

Before this year, Mina had always handled this sort of thing. Josh had learned a lot in the past months. Even if he had not loved her, he would have needed her.

He got out bowls and cups and miniature boxes of cereal. He had the milk stored in a cooler-chest. He would have to see about connecting the refrigerator in the house so as to be able to store food without spoilage. In fact, he would have to see about getting that house completed and approved for occupancy; this cabin was strictly a temporary expedient. So many things to do!

At six he roused the children, and the day began. They squabbled over who got to use the potty first. They knocked things over in the dark. Chris's underpants had somehow gotten misplaced, and Sue had lost one sock. Chris had been bitten by a mosquito and he remarked on the itch constantly, and Sue's hair was a mass of tangles that strenuously resisted combing out. Josh found himself yelling at them—something he did not like to do—and in the end they barely made it to the bus stop corner by seven forty-five. Par for the course.

And the bus did not come.

Josh had intended to drive in to the school anyway, to register the children properly. He had telephoned the school from New Jersey, but evidently no one had passed the word to the driver. But there was the usual paperwork to be done in person. He had shot records, birth certificates and such— all the data the schools seemed to want for their dead files. But he had wanted to put the children on the bus at this end and meet them at the other end, to be sure the system was in working order. Evidently it wasn't.

He drove them in. These things happened, he knew, but he wished this one hadn't. It was so important to establish confidence, in this new situation, to have nothing serious go wrong. If they could step into a stable situation here, put down new roots, grow strong, so as not to be permanently warped by the horror behind—

Nurse did not feel well. She swam listlessly, avoiding contact with Hammerhead. The past few days had been uncomfortable. The tank had been shaken continually, sometimes violently, and the water had slowly lost freshness, making her doubly sick. Just when it had seemed it would never end, things had settled down and freshness had been restored. But meals remained erratic; that was very bad. There really was not much to do except eat. The thing-figures that brought the fishfood appeared only seldom, and Hammerhead, more vigorous, got most of the food when it did come. That left a lot of boredom for Nurse. Once there had been steady light and activity beyond the boundary of the tank, always interesting to watch provided it did not approach too closely; now all was still.

Nurse did not like that stillness. The thing-figures had been familiar, now close, now absent, sometimes presenting their grotesque thing-faces for close inspection, sometimes merely cruising by like distant companions in their larger tank. This prolonged absence was ominous. Nurse began to suffer concern about disaster. It was as if some predator had frightened away the thing-figures, and now was orienting on the tank, the final bastion. Something huge, diffuse, and hungry, against which there was no defense. It had not moved up close, yet, but it was approaching, looming ever nearer. Hammerhead did not seem to mind it, but Nurse had a growing conviction of wrongness. She wished the thing-figures would remove the tank from this environment before it was too late—but she could not communicate this desire to her tankmate. The thing-figures, too, seemed unaware . . .

Josh came into the view of the tree and stopped the bus, awed. He had seen it before, of course; but each new approach, by new light, impressed him again. The tree was so enormous, so splendid in its enclosure of the house, so overwhelming! He sat there and looked at it, absorbed in the wonder of it. From up close it was just part of the environs; it was necessary to get a small distance away from it to appreciate it as a separate entity. He could just stay here and look . . .

Josh snapped out of it and looked at his watch. One-thirty already! Where had the time gone? He couldn't have consumed five hours in routine errands! How long had he been sitting here in the bus, gazing at the tree? Maybe he had snoozed. That happened to him sometimes these days, when fatigue got too bad. He could go for several days on short rations of sleep, then conk out when he least expected it. Mina had been more extreme in this regard; she could wash out for half a day at a time—

Josh started the motor and drew the bus up near the cabin. He got out, took the dogs out for a quick spin, then went inside. He was a methodical man, some said compulsive (*I am methodical*, he thought. *You are compulsive. He is obsessed!*) and this too had gotten worse recently. It was as though the stress of Mina's death had forced him to seek refuge in compulsion. His liking for accounting for his time had become necessity these last couple of days.

He had taken off in the bus at about eight-fifteen, once assured that the school bus was not coming. He was back

here at one-thirty. Just over five hours for the tour around the
county. He brought out his diary and entered that data.

That time factor bothered him. Five hours! Pen in hand, he
reviewed the details of his morning's excursion. It had taken
perhaps half an hour to deliver the children to their schools in
Inverness. He had gotten them duly registered, then gone on
a treasure-hunt type of chase to locate the party responsible
for school bus pickups. He finally got that straightened out:
the bus promised to come tomorrow. The school complex
was nice enough, neater and cleaner than the one the children
had attended in the larger metropolis.

Then he had gone shopping for the children's bug/bird
notepads and a turbine ventilator. He was not going to swelter another night in that cabin loft without some relief. And
he had looped on to the building department in the unincor-
porated town of Lecanto to ascertain the status of Elijah's
house. Ah, yes, that had turned out to be interesting.

A brief wait, then he was in the office of the head of the
building department. Josh was surprised at the relative infor-
mality of this region. Definitely small town—but he liked it.
He explained his problem.

The man summed it up for him nicely. "So your uncle
built the house, but died before completing it—and you're
stuck with it."

"Yes. I don't know who was working on it or how to get
it into shape to pass inspection. I'm willing to take whatever
steps . . ."

The man checked his records. "That's an interesting lot.
Were you aware that your uncle picked it up for taxes?"

"Taxes?" Josh asked blankly.

"The tax collector stages a sale of tax certificates every
year for delinquent taxes. People buy the certificates by
paying the taxes and penalties, with a good rate of interest. If
the property owner doesn't settle up in two years, the certifi-

cate holder can force the sale of the property. It is possible
for a patient and knowlegeable operator to pick up good
property at bargain prices. Your uncle was one of the canniest."
Josh glanced at him in surprise. "You know of him?"
"By reputation. He did quite well for himself by his
unorthodox dealings. He was honest, mind you; he was
just—different."
"It runs in the family," Josh said, smiling. "What was
different about the land he built on? It seems nice enough to
me."
"Oh, I understand it's beautiful land, in a nice location,
next to the state forest—"
"State forest?"
"Didn't you know? The Withlacoochee State Forest and
Citrus Wildlife Management Area. Lots backing on to that
forest command a premium price, normally."
"Except for this one?"
"Except for this one." The man seemed amused.
"What's different about this particular lot?"
"Well, for one thing it's got a handsome tree on it—"
"Beautiful. I should think it would enhance the value of
the property. It must be about the biggest oak tree in the
county."
"Must be," the man agreed. "I have seen bigger trees,
but they were banyans, and they don't grow here anyway.
Too cold for them."
"Too cold!" Josh exclaimed, remembering his stifling
night.
"It does get down to freezing here, on occasion," the man
said, smiling. "Into the low twenties, rarely. Teens, even, in
a blue moon. Banyans can't take that. I remember there used
to be this marvelous banyan down in St. Petersburg, with all
its secondary trunks, you know the way their branches send
shoots to the ground to form new trunks. A beautiful giant, a

real tourist attraction. But then came the freeze of '62, the all-time record low for that city, 22° above zero. Normally they fake their temperatures, recording them at Mirror Lake, the warmest spot in town, so the tourists won't know how cold it gets, but this time they played it straight for the sake of the record, and that banyan—" He shook his head sadly. "Actually it was so big it didn't freeze all that deep and it didn't quite die. It was starting to come back, but the yacht club there owned the land and they wanted a parking lot, so they quick declared it dead, you know, the way Rockefeller declared the Long Island Railroad to be the best in the world, knowing it was the worst in the world, and they cut it down and sawed it up and paved it over."

"The railroad?" Josh asked with a smile.

"The live banyan. The banyan is a protected species, you see. Can't just wipe one of those out without due process. But there's no protection in this world against greed for parking space! The whole sordid thing sickened me. I got out of there and moved up here, where they don't need so much parking. Yet."

He refocused on Josh. "Now I hope—"

"Don't worry! I have no intention of cutting down that tree! It's a monument as it stands."

The man nodded, satisfied. "No law against it, but it's the trees that make this country beautiful, what few are left."

"I agree. So what brings the value of the property down? I would consider it a bargain at any price."

The man took a breath. "It's haunted."

"By tax collectors?"

"That too. It has changed hands several times."

It occurred to Josh that the man was not joking. He had seemed so sensible; this new aspect seemed out of character. "How can land be haunted?"

"Well, that really isn't my department—"

"Oh—you mean there are rumors, a reputation that you can't repeat here? But surely you can tell me, in a business-like way, what specifically brought down the value of an excellent piece of land with a fine standing tree to no more than the amount of its taxes."

"There were awkward occurrences. Look, Mr. Pinson, this is way off the subject, and I have other business waiting. I'll send an inspector over, and he will explain to you, on the site, what needs doing. Will that be satisfactory?"

Josh saw that the man wasn't going to tell him any more about the haunted lot. "That will be just fine," he agreed. "When will he come?"

"This afternoon, if you're at home."

"Excellent! I'll be there." This was a refreshing change from the sort of bureaucracy he had known that usually managed to insert a delay of weeks between each motion.

Josh had left the office, shaking his head, bemused. A haunted lot! Naturally his uncle had risen to the challenge and made his residence right there in the shade of the tree.

And died there.

Coincidence, of course.

Allowing for driving time, adding up all his errands, he found himself short about half an hour. That was the time he had slept in the vicinity of that significant tree. He had it straight now.

Except for that business about the haunting. And a certain barely conscious feeling of being watched. They did seem to tie in together. Nefertiti, too, seemed to be trying to tune in on something. Perhaps a faint, subliminal smell.

It was two in the afternoon. The cabin had built up heat again. Josh took the dogs out and put them on long chains tied to nearby pine trees. He'd have to see about fencing in a yard for them to run in. He checked the other animals, and realized that someone had put out water for them. If this were a haunt, it was a beneficial one! Tonight he would watch and discover who it was.

He ate a quick lunch of bread and peanut butter and milk, then set about his main chore. He had installed a turbine ventilator before, so had a fair notion what he was doing. The hot air inside the building pushed up and out, making the ventilator vanes move. Wind outside also made it turn, adding to the suction. The device was a heat pump, constantly cooling the interior, with no electric power needed. Uncle Elijah would surely have approved.

The main problem was that he would have to cut a hole in the roof and fit the ventilator in. It was one of those do-it-yourself jobs best left to professional carpenters. But Josh did not intend to wait the week or so it would take to get a carpenter here; he wanted the ventilator in operation tonight. It should cool the loft appreciably, bringing the temperature down from swelter to merely hot. The difference between suffer and sleep.

He needed a ladder. Surely there was one around. Uncle Elijah, by all accounts, had been an independent cuss who never let others do work he could do himself. Since a ladder was essential to roof work, Elijah would have had one.

Josh looked around. He saw no ladder near the cabin, so walked down to the house. None there either. He approached the shed, and felt once more its dread. Not there either. At last he came back to the cabin, intending to bring out the indoor ladder after all—and found two fourteen-foot ladders stored underneath the building.

He hauled one out. It had a metal frame attached to one end; evidently these were the two halves of a double-length ladder. Good; he'd know where it was if he ever needed to mount the roof of the main house. For the cabin, one length would do nicely. He wrestled it around and leaned it against the northeast side of the cabin, where the slope of the ground provided extra height, and mounted to the roof.

The top of the gambrel seemed much less secure from above than it had looked from below. It seemed perilously easy to slide down it and fall off. He thought about bringing a heavy chain saw up here to cut the hole, and shuddered; that seemed far too dangerous.

Was he reacting to the insidious notion of a haunted machine, one that might somehow assume life of its own and turn against the man who wielded it? Elijah, the flesh of his leg ripped apart so that he bled to death . . . a victim of a malignant saw. The saw was passive now, but the moment he started it, it would be alive, in its fashion.

This was ridiculous! Others might be spooked by such beliefs, but he was hardly that credulous. If he feared something, he would meet it head-on and conquer it; that was his way. Still, he told himself, it needed no supernatural agency to make rooftop sawing dangerous; common sense advised him to stay clear.

He climbed down and went inside and up to the loft. The heat was high, already in the 110° range. It would have been worse, except for the open windows below and the small vents at either end of the cabin, near the peak. The turbine, of course, would greatly enhance the exchange of air.

From here the roof was readily accessible. The footing was secure, and he could see the nails coming through, so as to avoid them when cutting. This was definitely the preferred location.

Now for the saw. Josh had used one of these before, but never a monster like this. Elijah had gone first class on this machine, obviously. That seemed to be the man's way: top quality concealed beneath superficial indifference. Josh would rather have used a cheap, light chain saw. Still, he had a job to do, and he wanted to abate the nervousness this machine engendered. So he would master it now, before the children came home from school. Children around a running chain saw—*there* was a dangerous situation!

Josh nerved himself, opened the shed, and looked at the saw. It sat there somberly, massively, and passively menacing, like a sleeping rattlesnake. Truly, a thing that could cut off a hand or foot if misused.

Josh fought back his irrational fear and put his hand on the machine. The metal was cool, solid, firm, hard. The cutting chain projected forward like the snout of a vicious boar, the tusk points gleaming.

"Not dangerous if properly controlled," Josh said aloud, picking it up by the black handle that curved around side and top. He swung it into the light of day.

The saw was indeed hefty. It weighed a good twenty pounds—twice any saw he had used before. The foot-and-a-half long chain bar now most resembled a serrated sword. A deadly weapon, surely; and indeed it had killed. Yet it was basically a tool, the servant of man. He would make sure it remained that way.

He turned the monster around, inspecting it from differing angles. The brand name was clear: Sachs Dolmar. He didn't recognize the company; it looked German. Well, the best equipment was foreign-made these days; American companies, all too often, seemed far more interested in short-term profits than in long-term quality. Consequently, they were losing those profits along with their markets, purporting not to understand why. Josh regretted that trend, but had to go with the quality. As had his Uncle Elijah, evidently.

He set the monster down and went back into the shed for gasoline and oil. He felt no apprehension now about the shed; but when he picked up the gasoline mix and returned to the saw, he felt it again. It was definitely associated with the saw.

There was a plastic container of lubricating oil, and a wrapped toolkit. Josh unwrapped it, knowing that frequent adjustments were necessary to keep the chain tight. He found a screwdriver, round sharpening file, and a funny combination tool, like an old-fashioned corn cob pipe except that it was all metal. The stem was another screwdriver, and the bowl was a hexagonal socket wrench. He checked, and found that it was metric, and fitted the two nuts at the base of the bar; this was how the bar could be loosened for adjustment of chain tension.

Josh found himself hesitating. "Now let's analyze this," he said aloud. "I'm not even sure this is the saw that killed Uncle Elijah. But assuming that it is, as seems reasonable, it is still only a machine. It has no volition. It can do only what a man makes it do. So either Elijah was suicidally careless, or someone else—" He paused, the realization coming, "Or someone else wielded the saw."

He stood there, mulling it over. Murder? Then why had the death been listed as accidental? Incompetence in the coroner's office? Cover-up? Josh didn't believe that. His experience with local officials was quite limited, but the one had seemed quite normal and open, except for this business about haunting—and no one trying to hide a murder would seriously try to blame it on a haunt. Because a genuine haunt would arouse widespread curiosity, the last thing any guilty party would want. And what would be the motive for murder? Not acquisition of this property; that had descended routinely to Josh, who had not even known it was coming until it happened.

However, Josh realized he should make more of an investigation into the death of his uncle. He had not before sought the grisly details; they had not seemed necessary, and he had had more than enough of death. Mina—no, stifle that; he had thinking to do. Now he had discovered a need-to-know.

But for the moment, assuming the local coroner had known his business and that Elijah's death had been genuinely accidental—what could have accounted for such carelessness? It did not seem reasonable to suppose that an astute businessman would buy an inconveniently powerful saw, take excellent care of it, then use it in a manner that would cut himself up. That simply wasn't in character. What, then, could have induced the mishap?

The building department had said the land was haunted. Again, Josh found himself forced to consider this seriously. Could there really be a curse on the property that caused serious trouble, utilizing whatever instrument were available—such as a brute power saw? In that case, the curse would not be in the saw itself, but in the situation. Yet Josh and the dogs felt apprehension only about the saw. A curse did not make much sense, taking it in its own terms.

Josh shrugged. "It would be convenient at times to believe in the supernatural," he remarked. "Unfortunately, I do not."

Unfortunately? No, *fortunately*! Because a curse was operative only against those who believed in it. Josh believed in neither god nor devil, neither heaven nor hell—not fundamentally. That was part of what had set him apart from his family, even before he had left the commune. It was perhaps his most significant unity with Elijah: nonbelief. He talked of heaven with his children, and surely if there were a heaven his wife would be there, but he didn't really believe. He doubted that anyone who mourned the death of a loved one really believed; if they *knew* the departed lived eternally in bliss, why mourn?

Nonbelief destroyed the effectiveness of both the positive and negative aspects of the supernatural. A nonbeliever could not be helped by someone else's god, or harmed by anyone's devil. Scratch that notion completely. There could be no haunt.

Joshua was glad to dispense with this one. He had merely been examining all the possibilities, excluding none. What he wanted was not mere confirmation of his perceptions but the truth. It was a mental discipline with him to consider the irrational as well as the rational. That led to the extension of horizons, instead of to intellectual narrowing. His family-home-commune had tended to narrow the outlook and experience of the members; that too had militated against his satisfaction there.

To some people, even voting for the candidate of a different party was irrational. Such people could not see any virtues at all in anything outside their familiar mold. Josh hoped never to be like that. Still, the supernatural strained his tolerance, and he preferred to exclude it entirely from his outlook. If that made him narrow—well, no one was perfect.

Chapter 4

Josh filled the saw with the gasoline mix. Most of these small machines were two cycle, which meant that oil was added to the gasoline. He knew this had already been done because the container had crude numbers painted on it: 25–1. Twenty-five parts gas to one part oil.

Then he poured the chain-lubricating oil into its aperture. He saw with surprise that the oil was a deep red, apparently to distinguish it from automotive oil. All right; it was a sensible mechanism.

He checked the chain for tension. It was good, but he decided to adjust it anyway. He wanted to be properly conversant with this machine before using it.

He worked with it. This really was a well-constructed machine, with a good hand guard and an interlocking trigger mechanism. About as fail-safe as this sort of thing could be. A person should really have to work at it to hurt himself—which added to the mystery of Elijah's demise. The man would have had to draw hard on the trigger and rev up the engine while cutting his own leg. That was hard to believe.

Soon Josh had it adjusted. As far as he could tell, this saw was ready. He could delay no longer without accusing himself of stalling.

Now to start it. Again he felt nervous. Once he brought it to life, what then?

Only one way to find out. Josh set the trigger on half acceleration, pulled out the choke, set his left foot on the little plate provided, flicked the ignition switch to *ein*, and drew the starter cord with his right arm. The draw was smooth; no frozen motor here. He let it rewind, then drew again. The thing might not start at all.

The saw burst into life. Josh hastily put his finger on the trigger, revved up the motor, pushed in the choke so it wouldn't flood out, and hefted the saw. It ran beautifully. He let it run for fifteen seconds, then flicked the switch to *aus*.

The saw died immediately. It was in good condition, and obeyed directives well. No maverick, no demon loosed from the bottle. Had he anticipated otherwise?

Why, then, did he remain afraid of it?

Enough of this. Time was passing, and he had other things to do. He picked up the saw and carried it toward the cabin. Twenty pounds was not an undue burden to lift for a few seconds, but it quickly became arm deadening as he walked. He shifted the saw to his left hand, then back again before reaching the cabin. The dogs shied away as he approached, whimpering.

"Sorry—I've got a job to do," he told them. "After that I'll put the saw away. No fatal accidents for me. I promise!" But if he had believed he had any real choice, he would have put the saw aside.

It operated with the easy confidence of a dominant entity, one that knew its power and merely awaited its opportunity. Like a trained attack dog watching an intruder blunder nearer to the point of no return. Josh would have to be extremely careful; this was, he reminded himself strongly, a matter of common caution, not superstition. He had never liked taking risks, and since Mina had—

He hauled the saw on into the cabin and up the ladder to the loft. What ponderosity it assumed in this awkward maneuver!

Now the real trial was upon him. Josh marked a circle on the roof in crayon. The beautiful thing about a chain saw was that it could plunge cut. No preliminary drilling was necessary, no keyhole-saw maneuvers. Just set it at the spot and cut in.

He started the saw again. It roared into life on the first pull, loud in the confinement of the loft. He hefted it, muscling it up to head level, twisting it to angle the tip of the cutting bar at the slanting ceiling—and felt the machine wrench in his hands as though alive, the rushing chain tilting toward his face.

Startled, Josh paused, holding the saw halfway up. It ran smoothly, not fighting him. His grip must have slipped; the saw could not have jerked itself!

He lifted it again, bringing the bar up and around—and again it fought him, trying to free itself from his grip. Trying to—

To draw the fiercely cutting surface to his flesh?

Josh flicked the ignition switch to *aus* again, half afraid that this time it wouldn't work, that hours later his children would find him dead, his throat ripped out, his blood seeping through the crevices in the flooring of the loft to drip to—

The saw stopped immediately; his gruesome fantasy was meaningless and not at all his normal mode of thought. He set the machine down, shaken.

There was simply no serious place in his philosophy for a saw with a will of its own. He had considered the matter intellectually and come to a reasonable conclusion. But he was supremely skeptical of all supernatural phenomena, and that might have guided his thinking. Now he had felt that saw struggle in his grasp like a python trying to twist about to bring its fangs to bear. He could no longer dismiss his uncle's fate as a fluke. Obviously, Elijah had fallen prey to this same—

This same *what?*

Josh left the saw in the loft and descended the ladder. His knees felt weak. He passed the dogs, who greeted him with obvious relief, and returned to the shed. Somewhere there should be—yes, there it was. The instruction booklet. He should have looked at it at the outset. Not that he expected it to tell him anything about homicidal saws. . . .

He brought it out into the light and started reading—and discovered that this was a most unusual machine. It was not the normal reciprocal-piston deal; this one had a rotary Wankel engine. Thus, the booklet bragged in four languages, it had the equivalent of three cylinders, with a power stroke on every circuit and no energy-wasting reversals of piston. There was a set of diagrams showing the operating cycle.

Josh squinted at the illustrations, amazed. He had assumed that it was two cycle, because of the oil and gasoline mix, but this was at least three cycle. Was a three cycle, three cylinder motor possible? The rotary Wankel was a different breed, intriguing, mysterious.

It had, the booklet said, twice the power-to-mass ratio of conventional saws, and was the most powerful saw in its class: seven to eight horsepower.

One horsepower was plenty for a saw! This was truly a monster. It was the kind of saw professional loggers used to fell giant Douglas firs. In an automotive analogy, an ordinary chain saw was a four-passenger compact car. This was an eighteen-wheel semitrailer rig. What had possessed Uncle Elijah to buy a machine like this for household use?

Buy it? Elijah had probably traded it for six magic beans!

Rotary engine. Something nagged Josh's awareness. What

was there about that type? Like a gyroscope, it went round and round—

Aha! Precession! A sidewise torque developed when the gyroscope was tilted. A subtle, confusing but powerful force/counterforce that helped bicycles keep their balance, and made the planet Earth wobble in its rotation. Change the orientation of a running rotary-motor saw, and that force would manifest. The solider and faster turning the wheel, the more potent the reaction—and this was a heavy-duty machine. No haunt after all! All he had to do was refrain from twisting it against its axis of rotation, and there should be no trouble.

Heartened, he marched back to the cabin. A thing understood was a thing detoxified. He mounted the ladder. The saw was there, awaiting his convenience. It seemed less menacing now.

Once again he started the motor. He revved it up, then lifted the bar up toward the ceiling, careful not to twist the saw about. There was no trouble. He had eliminated this particular demon. He oriented on his crayon circle and touched the tip of the bar to the wood.

The saw kicked back violently. The hissing chain sliced toward his face. The speed and torque jammed his finger against the trigger, accelerating the chain velocity instead of diminishing it.

Josh's large muscles tensed reflexively, overwhelming the small muscles, shoving the whole saw back. His finger remained goosing the trigger, but now the chain was away from his face.

He set the saw down and switched it off again, shaking. An ordinary kickback, of course; he had been foolish not to anticipate it. The chain moved around the guidebar, away from the user on top, toward him on the bottom. In the ordinary sawing position, this tended to draw the saw into the wood. But when cutting from below, the saw tended to shove back. When the rounded end touched, it got pushed upward. Since a powerful motor drove the chain, this push could be violent—as it had been in this case.

Very well. He had figured it out. Still no haunt. Just a purely physical effect. He had been guilty of foolish amateurism. All he had to do was anticipate such things and be prepared.

If he held this saw upside down, it should not kick back. But it was so heavy! Maybe if he approached the ceiling at more of an angle, so that it would be impossible for the bar to swing toward him—yes, that should help. He wanted no more chains bouncing at his face! It was easy to see how a man could be maimed or killed that way.

Again he started the saw. He angled it up, braced himself, and touched it to the wood. This time it jerked and kicked but did not threaten him. The sharp teeth of the chain bit into the ceiling. A line appeared. Slowly it lengthened. Too slowly; the chain was ready, but he could not put it properly into the cut. The somewhat cramped space, his own hunched position, and the awkward angle of approach combined to make the operation inefficient. He needed more leverage than he had.

Now he became aware of the saw's exhaust. Hot fumes were shooting out, polluting the restricted air of the loft. Josh's face was near the vent. He was sweating profusely with the heat and exertion, and worried about the carbon monoxide. The molecules of that poison got into the system, prevented the uptake of oxygen, and caused painless death. It would be so easy to become dazed, let the saw slip, slice into his braced leg—

Had that happened to Uncle Elijah? He could readily see how—

Josh lowered the saw and flicked it off. He climbed down

the ladder and went outside to take deep breaths of clear air. What a job this was turning out to be!

But it had to be done. He headed back for another stint in the loft. This time the saw broke through, and the cut progressed rapidly. But sparks shot down, and Josh nervously halted again. The chain was burning hot, and bits of asphalt adhered. The roofing tiles—there was the culprit! All those bits of stone embedded in tar, tearing up the cutting edges of the chain. Brutal mistreatment of a fine edge. But now that he had punctured the roof, he had to finish the job.

He went at it again. More sparks flew, and a very faint haze of smoke appeared. The fumes became suffocating, but he held his breath, squinted against the particles and sawdust shooting into his face, and kept it going. His arms became tired, then more than tired as the saw bucked. It was difficult to cut in a circle, and he had to plunge cut several times to make the turn. The heat was terrible. His vision blurred, but still he pressed on.

"Stop, Josh!" a voice cried. Startled, he halted.

There was no one. It had been Mina's voice, crying out to him from memory. He tended to get embroiled in a task and bear down too hard, to the point of personal danger. She had always hauled him out of it, determined to protect him from himself. His mind, abetted by the awful fumes, had given him a warning from his own subconscious.

Josh got down and out, his head spinning, and gulped more fresh air. More and more he could appreciate how Uncle Elijah could have died. If he had become engrossed in his task and had been operating the saw in confined quarters, the fumes—yes, indeed.

What kind of a fool would Josh himself be, if, knowing that, he allowed the same fate to befall himself?

Well, the worst was over. He returned to the loft, ran the saw for one more burst, and finished the cut. He set down the saw, reached up, caught the edge of the disk and broke it out. The hole gaped, crudely cut but serviceable. Now he could breathe fresh air through it. Already the hot foul air of the cabin was coursing up and out, and that was the point of this effort, after all. He took a rasp and rounded the hole off.

The rest was comparatively easy. He took the ventilator up the outside ladder and oriented it, adjusting it to compensate for the inclination of the roof. He screwed in the flange and applied roofing cement. Already the vanes were turning, ushering the warm air out. They should cool the cabin dramatically by nightfall.

Tired but satisfied, he carried the saw down from the loft and out. It was a good machine. It had performed well in a difficult situation. All it had needed was understanding. He would have to sharpen and clean that chain before he used it again, of course.

Absolutely no haunt.

Yet his apprehension did not abate until he set the saw down in the shed. In fact it seemed to grow stronger until that moment.

As he closed the door and turned away, he saw Old Man Foster ambling up. "You weren't the one who watered the animals, were you?" Josh called.

Foster looked guilty. "Did I forget to feed my birds again?"

"I mean the animals here. The pony."

"Oh. Beauty? That's her name, don't you know. Not me. Why would I feed your animals? Got enough trouble remembering my own. I just came to tell you the building inspector's on his way. So if you got any guilty stuff to hide—"

"No guilty stuff. They promised to check the house today and let me know what's wrong with it."

"Can't fix what's wrong with it with a hammer, don't you know," Foster opined.

"You believe it's haunted?" Josh asked, smiling.

The old man did not return the smile. "I *know* it's haunted. You don't want to put those kids of yours in the shade of the tree."

"I don't believe in haunts, and I like the house," Josh said, somewhat defensively.

"All the same, be careful. Your uncle didn't take much stock in haunts either, but—you seen the saw?"

"Seen it and used it," Josh assured him. "It's an excellent machine."

"I'll say it is! It can cut—" But Foster did not complete his thought.

Now a car appeared on the access drive. "The building inspector!" Josh exclaimed.

"Told you," Foster agreed complacently.

They went up to meet the inspector. He was a tall, solid man with thinning hair and a somewhat florid face. "Donald Tempkin, Buildings," he said somewhat brusquely.

"Joshua Pinson," Josh said, shaking hands. The man's hand was large and strong. "And this is—"

"Old Man Foster," Tempkin said. "You're the one who discovered the body, aren't you?"

"Sure did!" Foster agreed zestfully. "And a grisly mess it was, too. You never seen so much blood—" Then he remembered Josh, and halted.

So Foster had found Elijah! Suddenly Josh had new questions for the old man. But right now he had to see to the house.

"Well, I'll be toddling on," Foster said, and started off up the road.

Josh looked after him. "Did he really find my uncle? It must have been quite a shock."

"So I understand. He's a nosy old codger, always poking around, but harmless. Knows all the gossip. It was a rather grisly accident; an artery in the thigh was severed, and he bled rapidly to death. Never had a chance, since he was alone.''

A cut like that would not be clean; flesh would have been ripped apart. Josh stifled a burgeoning image of Mina as she—*halt*.

They started toward the house. "Speaking of gossip—the man at the Buildings office said this place was haunted." Josh forced a chuckle.

"It does have that reputation," Tempkin agreed. "I don't hold with haunts, but I understand it dropped the bottom out of the value of the land. Now, with Mr. Pinson dead—" He shook his head. "I'm not superstitious, but I wouldn't care to live in the shade of the tree."

"Foster used a similar expression," Josh said. They were passing the tree now, and paused to survey it. The trunk seemed larger than before, massively corrugated, the crevices spiraling upward from the tremendous base. There were no signs of rot or infestation; it was a supremely healthy growth despite its evident age. "To me, the shade of a tree is the best air-conditioning there is. It is cool beneath a tree, the air is fresh, it costs nothing, and the branches protect you from the wind. Any tree is a miracle, and this is the most magnificent tree I've ever seen. I would have paid any fortune I had to buy a property like this. I think Elijah showed excellent taste, building here, and I intend to pick up where he left off."

"A commendable sentiment. No doubt he planned to improve the property's value tremendously by demonstrating the falsity of the haunt. He could have made a minor fortune, selling a house and tree like this as an escape retreat. Instead, he only augmented the grim reputation. The shade of the tree—there is a double entendre."

For a moment Josh paused, still contemplating the rising network of the tree, his eye tracing the crossing and recrossing branches as they disappeared into the canopy of small green leaves. From any angle it was impressive, moving, entrancing. "Oh—a shade as in spirit. We considered that. A haunted tree? A wood nymph who brings grief to intruders?"

"Not that literal, perhaps. Obviously the tree itself is harmless. But there has been an amazing concatenation of events in the vicinity of this tree. A hunter was shot to death here several years ago, and a railroad worker committed suicide here a decade or so back, and owners of the property have reported forebodings of evil. It's such nice land, many people have been attracted to it—but all have given it up, whether by choice or misfortune. Coincidence, probably— but it has lent a certain reputation to the region that has grown by hearsay. Elijah Pinson was merely the latest in an established line."

Josh was slightly discomfited. "Death requires no tree for its expression," he said, thinking of Mina. She had died on an open city street, no trees in sight, only blank pavement. He stopped that image before it got fully established. "Maybe people are attracted to the tree, especially when they are ill or depressed, so it's not surprising—"

Tempkin shrugged. "Possibly. It certainly is a handsome growth. I've seen some large live oaks—there's a hundred of them lining the main street in Floral City, that's the most beautiful road in the state—but I believe this is more impres- sive than any of them. Lot of firewood there!"

"Firewood!" Josh exclaimed, appalled. "I would never cut down a monarch like this! It must have stood for centu- ries, like that banyan in St. Petersburg—"

"I can guess who you talked with!"

"And will still be standing long after I am gone."

"Your uncle expressed the same sentiment—not two weeks before he died."

"Well, no superstition is going to make me harm this tree! The more I see of it, the more it grows on me."

Tempkin smiled, and Josh realized he had made a pun. It didn't matter; he liked the tree, shade and all.

They entered the house. Tempkin frowned. "No stairs?"

"No stairs," Josh agreed wanly, realizing that this meant no inspection approval at this time. But he had known there would be work to do yet.

"Need hurricane clips," Tempkin continued. "And beam hangers." He peered up the stairwell. "What's that up there?"

"Water storage tank," Josh said.

"Looks like about a hundred and twelve gallon capacity. You know how much one of them weighs, filled?"

Josh did a quick calculation. "Close to nine hundred pounds."

"Plus the weight of the tank itself. Half a ton, in a round figure. And it's just perched up there on the bottom beam of a roof truss. Those trusses aren't made to take that kind of strain; see, they're only tied together with metal patches pressed into the wood. That tank has got to be braced so it doesn't land in your living room one day."

"I'll see that it gets braced." He looked again. "Maybe it would be better to move the tank down to the basement."

Tempkin mounted the ladder. "Not unless you want to install a pump in what was designed as a pumpless system. Now I remember: Elijah Pinson was a solar buff. This is bound to be a self-powered solar water heating system. Also, there's no basement here. These Florida hills are basically dilapidated sand dunes; there aren't any true mountains in the state. Nothing but sand and more sand below. Some wells around here have to go down three hundred feet to lodge in hard rock. Good for drainage, not good for cellars."

No cellar? "I guess I have a lot to learn about this region," Josh said. "I can't make head or tail of all these pipes, either."

They walked around the second floor, tracing the pipes. "I'm no plumber," Tempkin said. "But I've seen these solar systems before. More of them being set up these days, as energy gets more expensive, and there's a lot of excellent sunlight here. There's the solar collector—see, out the window, on the roof of the front porch. About forty feet of copper tubing on a copper plate, convoluted under glass in the sun. Picks up the heat, transmits it to the water in the pipe, which rises up to the storage tank."

"Hot water rises," Josh agreed.

"So the storage tank has to be above the collector," Tempkin concluded. "This is a well-designed system; it operates without any circulating pump, any electric power. And the tank serves as a reserve in case of failure of your well pump. Water's a hundred feet deep, around here, not that much above sea level. So—"

"I thought you said the wells had to go three hundred feet deep."

"That's to find rock. Some do, some don't; it depends where the rock is. Wells that don't find rock are called dry holes."

"Now I'm really confused. Isn't it water they're drilling for, not rock?"

Tempkin smiled. "Of course. But the well caves in and can't be used without expensive work if it's in sand. So it needs rock as a basis. Then the water rises in the well to the level of the water table."

"Oh."

"Lightning takes out your pump, you just drain this tank, and you have enough for several days. You've got a similar cold water tank, too—that makes about two hundred fifty gallons storage in all. Your uncle really prepared for the worst.''

"Except for the very worst," Josh murmured.

"Yes. He failed to have the tanks properly braced. A set of two-by-fours here—oh, I see what you mean. He didn't count on dying early.''

"That's right. I never knew him personally, but everything I've seen here indicates he was a smart, careful, farsighted man. I can't see how he would walk into a careless accident with a saw.''

"Good question. I could feature a man like that dying of a heart attack or a lightning strike, but not from his own carelessness. I'd be curious about Old Man Foster. Oh, I don't mean he would have had anything to do with it; he's not that kind. But he must know more than he's telling. He poked around into—"

He was interrupted by the sound of a motor starting up. "Motorcycle?" Josh asked. But there was a disquieting familiarity about the sound.

"I saw a motorcycle parked a mile down the road," Tempkin said. "Yet this is more like a chain saw, over there by the tree, by the sound of it.''

"Chain saw!" Josh leaped to the nearest window on the north side.

Tempkin joined him. "I don't see anything."

Josh ran to the ladder and scrambled down. But by the time he cleared it and rushed outside, the noise had stopped.

There was no one by the tree. He went to the shed and opened the door. The saw sat there, undisturbed. Except—

Josh peered closely. Yes—a rivulet of red fluid was leaking from the saw. Blood—puddling on the floor beneath it.

Josh jerked back, overwhelmed by horror. How could there be—?

Tempkin came up, his face more flushed than usual from the exertion. "You look as if you've seen a ghost!"

"I thought someone—what we heard—I don't want anyone vandalizing that tree—so I checked, and—" Josh pointed. "Look at that." He half expected the blood to vanish when the man looked.

Tempkin squinted at the saw. He touched his finger to the red and brought it to his nose. "Oil," he said.

The colored lubricating oil! Josh had put it in himself, and forgotten. Now some had leaked from the saw, and his expectation had converted it to blood. "I must be more nervous about spooks than I thought," he said sheepishly.

Tempkin nodded. "Can't blame you. I see no footprints, no evidence anyone was here—yet the sound was plain enough. Could it be a practical joke?"

"Some joke!" But since no other explanation offered, it would have to do.

Tempkin returned to the house with Josh and identified its remaining deficiencies. The bathrooms would have to be walled in, and the stairwell at the upper level; certain supports were inadequate, and the windows were not well framed. "Will you be doing the work yourself or hiring a carpenter?"

"I'd better hire a carpenter. I don't know anything about carpentry, and it's all I can do to manage my family. I'll have to make a trip to New York—" He shrugged. "I gather you have been to this site before. Do you know whom my uncle hired to do the work?"

"As it happens, I do. Noel Carpenter, who worked along with your uncle. Good man; he certainly wasn't the one who framed those windows."

"He's a carpenter—and his name's Carpenter?"

"That's not as funny as it sounds. His family have been carpenters as far back as they can track the lineage. Must have taken the surname for that, and kept the trade. He does good work; I'm sure he intended to wrap this up properly, but lacked the authority when your uncle died."

"Do you have his address?"

"I don't recall it—but he's in the phone book."

"I don't have a—" Josh's eyes caught the phone on the west wall, beside the ladder. "At least I don't think I have—"

"Certainly you do. Haven't you made any calls? Maybe the company disconnected it, though I can't see them taking the trouble."

"But the house hasn't been occupied! How could the phone be connected?"

"The phone company knows no earthly law."

Josh lifted the receiver. He heard a dial tone. "It's operative! I never realized! I had a phone here all the time!"

"There seems to be considerable to discover," Tempkin said. He gave Josh his notes on the necessary work, and departed.

Chapter 5

It was now three-thirty, and Josh hardly seemed to have started his labors. Yet he had gotten a lot done today.

His first priority was to get the house in order for occupancy. His next—well, he had to make his trip to New York in the first week of September, so he had to arrange for a woman to stay with the children. He did not want to leave them with a stranger. They wouldn't have liked that in the best of circumstances, and sensitized as they were by their mother's loss—no. He had to phase this in carefully.

He approached the phone somewhat diffidently. Amazing that it had been here and operational all the time without his realizing—but of course he had only been here twenty-four hours. He had better make his first call to the phone company itself to verify the status of the account and make sure the instrument remained serviceable. There might be an intercept or something. Then the electric company; if they cut off the limited power, the two goldfish would die.

He got through to the service department. "Oh, sure, we knew Mr. Pinson was dead," the girl said. "That haunted lot got him. So we waited to see what you wanted to do. Biggerton, the lawyer, paid the bill for the estate. We'll just change it over to your name until you sell the house."

"I'm not selling the house," Josh protested.

"You're staying there?" He could almost see her shrugging. "It's your funeral." She laughed.

Josh kept being surprised by the small-town atmosphere here. Everything was personal; everyone seemed to know, or know of, everyone. He rather liked it, despite the occasional insensitivities. In the impersonal reaches of the large metropolis, much more unpleasant things could happen—

He blocked off the thought of Mina almost automatically. He was having an awful time with the memory, now! Had he suffered an abrupt enhancement of sensitivity? People got killed in the hinterland too; that was how he had inherited this property.

His next call was to Biggerton, the local lawyer who had managed the estate in the interim. He wanted it on record that he, Joshua Pinson, had arrived and would henceforth be resident here. Biggerton was out, so he left a message with the answering service. He hoped it would get through.

Then he looked up Carpenter in the book and called him. "This is Joshua Pinson, Elijah Pinson's nephew. I understand you were working on his house—"

"Not anymore," the man said quickly. "That house is haunted."

"What are you talking about?" Josh demanded, as if he didn't suspect. "This house has never been occupied! It hasn't even been completed. That's why I'm calling you!"

"Well, not the house exactly. But the ground around that tree. Been haunted for years. The skunk ape stalks there, and the spook train runs—"

"Spook train?"

"You listen, you'll hear it, especially at night in the rain. It's the ghost of the old mining train, used to run those tracks there. I didn't believe it either, but when I'd been working on that house a couple weeks, cleaning up the mess the prior contractor made, *then* I believed. Then when I was off, Mr. Pinson, he got caught—''

"Look, Mr. Carpenter. I'm his nephew. He willed the estate to me. I suspect this was because he knew I was the one relative who would try to take care of the premises in the way he wanted. I mean to live here; I'm already camped out in the cabin with my children, and we're sweltering, and we have no electric power there. We've got to get that house in shape for occupancy, and we need your help. It's not just that I want to finish whatever my uncle started; if anything untoward happened to him, whether natural or supernatural, I want to attend to it. If it's a matter of money—''

He let it lapse. There had not been any cash from Elijah's estate, and would not be until probate was completed, and it would probably not amount to much anyway. He was dependent on his own savings, and these were sufficient but not substantial. Once he got organized here and returned to work, his resources would be greater.

"Children, eh?" The man seemed to be wavering. "They shouldn't be out there without power.''

"All I'm asking is that you come in, just long enough to get the water tanks braced and the stairs installed and—''

"And the hurricane clips, and set up that wood stove and whatnot," Carpenter finished. "Got to box in those bathrooms and the stairwell, and build beds for you, and cupboards. I know the job.''

"You certainly do," Josh agreed. "I have to make a trip north in a few days, and I need to have the house straight before I go so I don't have to worry about the safety of my children.''

"Well, I can't say no to that," Carpenter said reluctantly. "I'll come in nine to three till it's done; that's all. Once you pass inspection, I'm through. Regular scale. I don't like leaving a job unfinished.''

"Thank you," Josh said gratefully. "I really appreciate it."

"Take care of yourself," Carpenter concluded sincerely. His genuine concern gave Josh a nervous feeling.

Next, Josh checked the ads in the local newspaper, the *Citrus County Chronicle*. The classified section was about two and a half pages long. He located the Help Available ads. There were ten entries, ranging from baby-sitting to room painting. Only one came close to his need: "Woman NEEDS work experience in housekeeping. Days, also baby-sitting evenings." And a phone number. He wasn't clear whether she needed work experience or needed work and had experience. Regardless, she would have to do. He knew he should have been asking for referrals from the people he had met here, but there was so much to do that this hadn't entered his mind, and he would have to make do this way. He hoped she had her own transportation.

He dialed the number. He got one Patience Brown, and no, she hadn't been hired elsewhere. Yes, she had experience, and yes, she was good with children. Ages seven and nine-going-on-ten? Just fine. Dishes, laundry, housework—certainly. Available to start any time.

This sounded good. Obviously, the woman wanted the job and seemed qualified. It might be that she was not as good as she thought, or would prove to be lazy, but at least it was a start. "But there are two problems," Josh said. "First, I have to make occasional trips to New York—there'll be one within the month—and I don't want to leave the children alone overnight—"

"I understand. Live-in while you're away." She accented the last three words slightly, making it clear that there would be no living-in when a man was present. Josh was satisfied with that distinction; he was not looking for anything more than housekeeping, and was happy to have that understood.

"And—there are stories that this place is haunted."

"Haunted!" she exclaimed, laughing. "There's no such thing!"

"I agree. But there *are* stories. I just wanted to mention it in case—"

"Mr. Pinson, if ever I see a ghost, I'll let you know. I'll charge extra if I have to baby-sit it."

Josh was developing a gut feeling that this was going to work out. He asked for references, and she gave him several names and numbers. They set it up. Josh wanted her to meet the children and get to know the family. She would come in Saturday, when the children were home, and get the feel of the premises. Once the house was occupied, she would come in daily.

Josh felt good as he hung up the phone. He had accomplished a lot in a short time. Now it was four o'clock, with the children due home on the bus within half an hour. He wanted to meet the bus just to be sure everything was now in order. That gave him a few minutes to himself.

The dogs were getting boisterous. They didn't like being chained for prolonged periods, and he could hardly blame them. "All right, canines," he said. "We'll all go for a walk."

That was met with enormous enthusiasm. Both animals pulled strongly forward on their leashes, their breaths rasping, and he simply followed where they led. They moved generally eastward, climbing out of the depression that surrounded tree and house, and snuffling through a field spotted with pine trees. This late on a hot day, the trees were fragrant with the aroma of sap; Josh loved it.

The dogs thought they spied something, and accelerated, Nefertiti yip-yipping. It was a false alarm that soon petered out beside the impressively standing column of a broken-off pine trunk. "Sunlight on a broken column," Josh murmured.

Wasn't that from Eliot's poem "The Hollow Men"? That pine column was so dramatically pretty in the slanting sunlight, and so suggestive of bygone glory and destruction, that it surely evoked an appropriate feeling in the beholder. Empires flourished and perished, often dramatically; likewise the great trees of the forest.

This was a wilderness, yet it was also the ideal locale for the dogs. When he knew the terrain better, he would let the dogs go, to romp to their hearts' content. They would come back to the house in due course, once they knew it was home. The same applied to the children. A wilderness life was a healthy one—so long as it was a reasonably tame wilderness.

Suddenly both dogs paused, ears perking. Then Josh heard the beat of horse's hooves. The dogs plunged forward, and this time Josh was as eager as they. The three of them tore through the brush, seeking the source of that fascinating sound.

Something pricked his leg while he was striving to keep his balance and avoid low branches. He braked the eager dogs and checked.

Burrs had gotten into his socks. He tried to brush them off with his free hand—and got stabbed in the finger. He brought his other hand to it and grabbed the burr just as the dogs yanked again on the leashes; suddenly his right hand was bleeding and his left one was punctured by the burr. What a little monster! Finally he got the thing off him, both hands smarting—but there were several more remaining on his socks, scratching through the material at his ankles.

The dogs were jerking him off balance again, and the unseen horse was close. Josh muttered a curse—and he was not a cursing man—and went on. But he was only in time to see the horse galloping away. He could not recognize the rider from the rear. He had delayed just that moment he couldn't afford.

Not that it really mattered. Quite possibly this was a regular horse trail, with people riding by often. He hardly needed to snoop on them.

They intersected a road and followed it east, curious to know where it went. This was of course the eastward extension of Pineleaf Lane that took off from Forest Drive. Josh was always curious about roads; he just had to know where they led. Perhaps this was a key to his personality, contributing to his success in computer organization. Merely another kind of path.

Within a quarter mile they came to Pineleaf's end, in another halfhearted turning circle. Another desultory trail meandered from it at an angle to the southeast, no more than parallel tracks pressed into the soft forest soil by passing vehicles.

It was time to turn back, but the dogs were both pulling steadily forward, down the trail, and Josh had not exhausted his urge to explore. So he yielded, going just a little farther.

The trail hit an intersection: another set of car tracks at right angles. My, my, he thought, smiling. Ought to be a traffic signal here. So the deer and the squirrels could establish the right-of-way.

The dogs bore left. He yielded again and let them pull him along. This new trail curved north. Then the dogs veered right, going east again, leaving the trail—and suddenly they were at the brink of the railroad track bed.

And brink it was. Josh stood amazed. The bed cut through the hill here, and great mounds of earth and sand had been thrown up on either side. Grass and brush and even trees now grew on these mounds, fixing them in place, an exaggerated example of the permanence of man's casual artifacts in the wilderness.

He approached. There were two sets of tracks, both quite rusty, overgrown by weeds. He blinked—no, no tracks, no ties, just the level channel where they had been; he had suffered a minor delusion of expectation. One channel was at approximately ground level, after allowing for the mounds of debris. The other was at a deeper level, twenty feet down. The slope was so steep that Josh shied back from the edge, knowing he would slide to the bottom if he overstepped. This was a man-made chasm.

No train had used this right-of-way in recent years, obviously. The tracks and ties had been taken up long since, and small trees were developing in the channel. Only the ghost train Carpenter had mentioned could travel here.

Ghost train! What wouldn't they think of next! If there could be such a thing, whom would it haunt? Who would be afraid of a train on its track, even if both train and track were ghosts? "There isn't a train I wouldn't take, no matter where it's going," he murmured. It was a line from an Emily Dickinson poem, he believed. Of course, the railroads had labored diligently for decades to degrade that mystique, charging ever-higher fares for ever-worse service, until the airlines siphoned off most of their business. Now the airlines seemed to be striving to compile a similar record. So this old bed was deserted, largely unlamented except for the efforts of nostalgia-prone oddballs like himself.

He looked at his watch. Twenty after four! He had to get back to the bus stop. He brought the dogs about firmly and hurried west, retracing their route.

He was winded, but he made it in time. Then the bus was late. Ever thus, he thought. He stood with the dogs, viewing the scenery. The road here at the corner/intersection had been mowed within a couple of weeks; the bahia grass was thick and even. He'd have to see about bringing the pony down here to graze one day; it should be all right if he kept a lead on her. At the fringe, the weeds grew taller, forming another layer. Then the leafy bushes and the small deciduous trees, and finally the stately pines. Layered habitats, ranging from grass for rabbits to the high branches for birds. He liked it.

Something stung his leg above the sock. It was a red ant. He swatted it off, but the sting kept hurting. He spied the burrs in his sock again, and reached carefully to remove them—but found it could not be done without further injury. What a monster variety of plant!

At last the bus came. Sue climbed down. "Gee, Daddy—you got sandspurs!" she exclaimed, admiring his socks.

"You can have them," he said, wondering how she had already learned about this local phenomenon. "If you were a good little girl today."

"Not good enough," she decided, watching while Chris disengaged himself from whatever tangle he had gotten into while the driver waited somewhat impatiently. The first day of school was always a hassle, anywhere.

"How was school?" Josh asked.

"Uh, okay," Sue said, disinterested. He knew that was all he was going to get. School was a different world, something children did not discuss with real people.

Chris at last extricated himself and joined them. He was as active as ever, charging down the step and out like a ball expelled from a toy gun. "I'm hungry!"

They waited while the bus cumbersomely maneuvered itself about. Several children waved, and Chris waved back. It seemed he had already made new friends. He was good at that; unfortunately they seldom lasted long.

They walked to the cabin. As they came in sight of the great tree, a horse galloped away, a flash of brown haunch and the red shirt of the rider. The one he had glimpsed before. The rider had been coming here!

The children chased after the horse, excited, but with no

hope of catching it. Josh checked the pony—and found she had been freshly fed. The hen and chicks were picking happily at seed put out for them. The kittens were chewing on their food.

This, then, was the mysterious feeder-of-animals.

Tomorrow, Josh promised himself, he would intercept the visitor.

He felt something at his ankle. One of the chicks was pecking at a sandspur. "Hey, that's not for you!" Josh protested. "It will hurt your little beak." But the chick persisted, and soon was joined by the mother hen, who quickly and neatly consumed all the burrs. What a convenient service!

A fly buzzed by. Hen and chicks watched it with such alertness that Josh was impressed. He had thought of chickens as clucks, but they had more personality than that.

The fly came too close; the hen leaped, spread her wings, and snapped it out of the air. She knew how to get what she wanted, and was teaching her brood.

Meanwhile, he had had his socks cleaned. "Thank you, Henrietta," he said.

The children returned. "What's for supper?" Chris called.

Josh hadn't thought of it. He had groceries but no way to fix a hot meal. "Sandspurs," he muttered.

"What?"

"We don't have any way to cook supper—unless we grill something outside."

"Hey, yeah!"

It was worth a try, perhaps. There was an impromptu outdoor fireplace formed from several chalky rocks near the cabin, and a small pile of dry logs and sticks. There was a rusty grill leaning against it. "We'll see whether we can cook here, tonight," Josh said. "It may not turn out well, though."

Both children exclaimed with joy. This was adventure to them. Josh hoped they still felt that way an hour from now.

He built the fire carefully, forming a crude pyramid of sticks over crumpled newspaper and lighting it at the base. The paper flared up briefly and went out. He tried again, blowing on it. The flame lasted longer but gave up the moment he did. He tried again. And again. Soon he was dizzy from blowing, and still had no self-sustaining fire.

Then there was a crack of thunder, startling them. Josh looked up and saw a great gray-black cloud looming from the south. Rain coming!

A gust of wind came, as if it felt free to express itself now that the secret was out. The storm was intensifying rapidly. But that wind fanned the paper into ambitious activity. *Now* it was willing to burn—when its future was hopeless.

Sue dashed into the cabin and emerged with their umbrella. "I'll keep the fire dry!" she exclaimed.

Josh laughed—then reconsidered. He didn't want to hurt his daughter's feelings. Maybe it would work, if the umbrella didn't just collect smoke.

They tried it. The fire, now fairly caught, blazed high with a fierce orange flame. There was some pine knot in it; that dense, fragrant wood was burning savagely, squirting out jets of fire like little blowtorches. A heavy pine branch was a center of conflagration; it was as though kerosene had been poured on it.

As he watched, Josh felt increasing unease. Fire was dangerous! A low grass fire could be tolerated, but when it came in dry season, igniting the trees—

Why was he worried about that? He was no tree, to be helpless against a forest fire! Yet for a moment he had almost felt like one.

Some highly flammable fluids came from wood. Turpentine, pitch—no wonder this stuff blazed! There was plenty of heat.

He put a pot of water on the grill, allowing the orange flames to engulf it, and it was soon boiling.

The storm wasted little time striking. The rain pelted down as Josh tried to cook hamburgers in a flat pan. Sue defended the fire valiantly with the umbrella, though she herself got soaked. Fortunately there was no lightning strike; it was only rain and wind. That was enough; every so often a swirling gust whipped the smoke through their locations, making them cough and close their watering eyes. It had a sweetish odor that somehow reminded Josh of the old steam engine trains he had known as a boy. He had always liked the soft smoke wafting from them. So, despite the present awkwardness, he liked this situation. Chris and the two dogs stood in the cabin doorway, not venturing into the sluice and smoke; they were more sensible than Josh and Sue, and perhaps less romantic.

The rain passed and the forest lightened. Tropical storms, he remembered now, tended to be energetic but brief. Sue, soaked but happy, folded the umbrella. She had proved herself; she had Been Useful and saved the fire.

They set up damp eighteen-inch-long pine logs as chairs and tables; these reminded Josh of huge marshmallows or stacked checkers. Each gust of wind caused little showers of droplets to fall from the trees of the vicinity, punctuating the occasion.

The meal, makeshift as it was, turned out delicious. But soon Sue was shivering, and Josh hastened to dry her off and get her changed. "Don't want you dying of pneumonia," he muttered. "That would be most inconvenient."

"Yeah," Chris agreed. "It would take a whole half hour to bury her so she wouldn't stink."

"Well, you stink already!" Sue retorted angrily, her brown eyes blazing through the bedraggled strands of her wet hair.

"Easy, kids," Josh warned. "Save your sibling rivalry for positive things, like schoolwork."

"Yeah," Sue agreed. She was the perfect student, while Chris was usually near the bottom of his class. He was bright enough but never paid attention.

Josh hauled another five-gallon container of water from the house, so they could wash the dishes, and finally poured the dishwater over the fire to extinguish it. He saved a thermos jug of hot water for the morning. A little foresight could lead to a great improvement in comfort.

As the landscape darkened, they saw little golden flashes of light. "Fireflies!" Josh exclaimed, delighted. "I didn't know they were in these parts!"

The children were fascinated. They chased after the flashes but were unable to catch any. Josh was pleased that they were taking to this life so well. It was indeed the change he had wanted.

At dusk the sunset came: a quiet, lovely show commencing a minute or two before eight P.M. and continuing for almost ten minutes. At first the white sides of the clouds turned orange: the western faces only of the ones to the south—and then they turned purple-red. The color showed in four widely separated places to west, southwest, and south. Gradually, the westernmost patch brightened and expanded, until it was a raging red inferno above a dark gray mountainscape of raincloud, making a silhouetted pine tree seem to be afire.

"Oooo, pretty!" Sue exclaimed. Josh could only agree.

At last the far-flung embers died, leaving only the sun's final redoubt, a patch of purple sinking behind the cloud barrier. The fireflies diminished also, as if afraid of the full night. To the south, silent flashes of lightning illuminated that particular cloud, showing that its internal fires had not died.

"I wish Mommy could see this," Chris said.

"It's like this all the time, where she is," Sue said. "She probably gets bored."

It would be all right, maybe, this time.

They went back into the cabin and prepared for sleep by the light of an old kerosene lamp with a circular wick and a fiber mantle that greatly enhanced the flame and converted it into something reminiscent of an electric bulb. The cabin was cooler tonight, perhaps because of the rain, but mostly, Josh trusted, because of the ventilator.

They settled down in their sleeping bags. Then Sue exclaimed in alarm. "A ghost bug!"

"There are no ghosts, dummy," Chris mumbled from the other side.

"Its eyes are glowing at me," she insisted.

"Oh—a firefly," Josh said. "It must have wandered in here when the door was open. Don't hurt it."

"Not a firefly. Its tail doesn't flash. Its eyes glow. Oooo, it's blinking at me!"

Josh hefted himself tiredly onto an elbow and peered in her direction. There was a bug there, not a firefly, and its two eyes did glow with green light. Josh had never heard of such a creature. As he watched, one eye slowly faded out in a ponderous wink, then glowed bright again. It was eerie.

Josh turned on the fluorescent lantern. Light flooded the loft. The bug was revealed as a long brown beetle—whose eyes still glowed hugely. He caught it under a glass. "We'll check it in the bug book—when I get a bug book," he said. "I'm sure it's harmless. Meanwhile, it is another creature for your collection. This and the fireflies."

"It's spooky," Sue said, pleased. "I like it. Can I keep it for a pet?"

"It'll die in a jar, dum-dum," Chris said. He was put out because he hadn't seen as many birds as she had bugs.

"No it won't! I'll feed it and care for it and teach it to come when I call—what do ghost bugs eat?"

"They eat little girls," Chris said.

"It's a wild creature," Josh said. "Like a firefly, it must be appreciated in the natural state."

"I appreciate it!" she said.

"He means you have to let it go, idjut," Chris said.

"No I don't, klutzhead!"

"We'll decide in the morning. Now sleep!"

"It's probably a mommy ghost bug," Chris said. "It has to go back to its family."

Josh kept silent. For once Chris had said the right thing. Sue did not want to keep the bug from its family.

They all settled down.

It seemed only an instant before Josh was roused by a commotion outside. A terrible squawking, as of a chicken getting chased. Henrietta.

Josh scrambled out of bed. He didn't take time to dress; his underclothes were enough in this warmth.

He grabbed the fluorescent lamp and hurried outside, galvanized by the awful chicken screeches. The moon was out, a fat crescent verging on a half disk, providing enough light for him to see beyond the lamp's range but not enough to make things clear. He caught a dim flash of white, and realized that it was the pony moving nervously about in her pen. She was colored broadly brown and white, and her brown sections disappeared in the night, so what remained looked amorphous and ghostly.

His bare foot snagged on something. He ripped it free. Now he saw the chicken—and realized she had abruptly become silent. A set of eyes glared at him, reflecting the light of his lamp. A wild cat?

Suddenly Josh was aware that he had no weapon. He cast

about, turning his light one way and another, but all he saw was a stack of wooden fence posts.

The eyes moved. Josh dived for the posts. His hands slid over them, the lamp bumping along, as he found and hefted the smallest. It was a generous six feet long and so solid he wasn't sure he could swing it effectively. The wood exuded a faint chemical smell: treated with creosote or something similar, no doubt resistant to rot and termites.

The animal growled and charged. Josh dropped the lamp, put both hands on the post, and jabbed it forward like a spear. It caught the animal on the chest. There was a yipe of pain; then the thing scrambled around and away.

A dog—only a dog! Of course!

Then another shape moved. "Daddy?" It was Sue. She had awakened and followed him outside.

But the voice was from the wrong direction. She was not the shape. There was another dog! "Get back in the cabin!" Josh cried, his alarm blossoming.

It was too late. The shape loomed over her, growling.

Then another shape hurtled forward with a snarl like a scream. It met the first, teeth flashing in the slanting moonlight, absolutely vicious. "Pharaoh!" Sue exclaimed.

As the two dogs growled and wrestled in the dark, Josh lurched around them and wrapped his right arm about Sue, picking her up while he balanced the post in his left. Then the strange dog yelped and fled. Pharaoh's single-minded attack had been too much for it, as Josh had anticipated. Yet Pharaoh, surprisingly, did not pursue.

Josh set Sue down and fetched the lamp. The fall had put it out, but it came on again when he shook it. The sudden bright light showed Sue's frightened face and the blood welling from the dog's shoulder.

Blood—déjà vu. Hadn't he had a premonition of that? Oh, yes, the bleeding saw. Irrelevant.

"Carry the light, honey," Josh told the child. "I'll carry Pharaoh."

They made their way back to the cabin. Chris, an extremely sound sleeper once he got to sleep, had not been roused.

Pharaoh's injury was ugly but not critical; it was a long slash, already matted with blood-soaked fur, surely painful. Dirt was ground into the wound. Pharaoh growled as Josh inspected it, and Josh decided to let the dog do it his own way. Pharaoh had always identified more with Mina, rather than with Josh himself, and at a time like this it showed. "Okay, boy. You clean it up and don't let it bleed too much, and we'll see you in the morning."

As Josh followed Sue up the ladder to the loft, he felt his own leg stinging. It had been scratched, and now that the excitement was over, it was really burning. He had salve in the bus; too much trouble to go out for it now.

The reaction set in. Those must have been wild dogs, marauding the nearest available farmstead. Sue, out there in her nightie—if Pharaoh hadn't been there, what might have happened to her? People were concerned about supernatural threats, but the natural ones were quite adequate to the need. This was an aspect he had not considered before moving here. He had thought of the forest animals as rabbit and deer, but there were also roving cats and dogs and poisonous snakes.

"Daddy, will Pharaoh get rabies?" Sue asked.

Those wild dogs—probably just a hunting party, but one *could* have been rabid. Pharaoh had had his shots, but they could not afford to take a chance. "I hope not, dear. But I suppose we'll have to quarantine him."

"What?"

"Quarantine. That means keeping him away from other

animals, not letting him loose for ten days, until we're sure he's not sick.''

"We do that anyway, don't we? Because he fights—''

Josh laughed somewhat uncomfortably. "It's not the same, but I suppose it will have to do.''

"He won't get sick,'' she said confidently.

But Josh, climbing back into bed, had a worse thought. He had no practical way to isolate Pharaoh from Nefertiti—or from the two children. Suppose the dog was infected with rabies and attacked Chris or Sue? Yet he couldn't callously dispatch the dog on suspicion—not after Pharaoh had saved Sue from a possible mauling or worse.

Chapter 6

In the morning Josh surveyed the damage.

Pharaoh's shoulder had been laid open, but the dog had assiduously licked it clean, and even taken care of the blood on the floor. Take him in for stitches? Not if it could be avoided, because Pharaoh would do himself more harm picking fights at the vet's office than any good the stitches would do. Josh took him out for a curtailed walk, missing the sunrise, though there was a layer of pretty fog, and the dog was happy to return to the cabin after doing his business.

Then Josh checked the outdoor animals. Henrietta was gone, her only trace a bloodstained feather. The six chicks were wandering about, peeping plaintively. The pony and kittens were all right.

This morning the children knew the way to the bus stop, so Josh watched them depart. He remained alert, however, and would not really relax until he heard the bus arrive.

He returned to the chicks. They were frightened of him at first, perhaps associating him with the event of the night, but when he remained stationary they slowly approached and pecked at his shoe laces. They had, after all, been friends yesterday. He squatted, and one bold one jumped up to perch unsteadily on his hand. It was his gold wedding band the

83

chick was orienting on; the bright metal attracted it. Soon the others were joining in, eagerly trying to harvest the morsel. Cute, he thought, though the ring reminded him of Mina, as did the death of the hen.

"I'll just have to bone up on chicken raising," he said, finding that he liked the little creatures. Yesterday he had become aware that the birds were by no means clumsy; they were alert and agile, and even at this size seemed to be able to fly a little. They were also good company. It did not matter that a chick could not do calculus or analyze Shakespeare; all it needed was the ability to catch a fly and peck up a seed. "If it is possible for you to survive without your mother, we'll pull you through. We know about that sort of thing."

Then he heard the beat of horse hooves. The phantom rider was coming!

Josh stayed where he was, chicks surrounding him, one perched on his forearm and climbing toward his elbow. He was afraid that if he moved, the horse and rider would disappear.

His ploy worked. The horse trotted right on in, all sleek muscle and sweat, stopped with a snort, and the rider dismounted even as the hooves settled.

Lo, it was a woman. Her dark hair was bound back in a bun, and her plaid shirt (it had been red yesterday) and her dungarees and farm boots tended to mask her femininity from a distance, deceiving him. She looked to be about thirty, of indeterminate height and weight, and wore no makeup, only a green stone on a necklace. A farmer's wife, most likely.

"Hello," Josh said, standing. The chick flew down from his arm, startled by his motion but not really alarmed.

The woman, however, jumped. She had not seen him at all—as he had halfway intended. "Oh—you must be the nephew."

"The same," Josh agreed. "And you must be the phantom feeder."

She laughed: an instant, pleasant sound, tinged by nervousness. He was, after all, an unfamiliar man she had come upon suddenly. "You may call me Philippa. Pip for short."

"Lover of horses," he said, remembering the derivation of the name. "That fits."

"Yes. My folks liked horses, and hoped I would too, and I do." She patted the shoulder of her steed. "I love animals."

"It seems we have both animals and children, here, now. Did my uncle make an arrangement with you to care for the farm?"

She considered, as though debating how much to tell him. "He did and he didn't. He expected to do it himself, but I checked on it during his absences. When he died—" She shrugged. "Someone had to feed the animals." She walked toward the feed shed—and the chicks and kittens converged, and the pony neighed. They knew her!

"Who paid for the feed?"

"There was some stored—"

"A month's worth?"

"No, not that much."

"What do I owe you?"

She glanced askance at him. "You're assuming Elijah's debts?"

"I inherited his estate. I have no idea what it may be worth or what debts he had, but yes, I'm assuming responsibility. Until the process of probate is complete, and then—" He shrugged. "Then I'm still responsible."

"I did it for the welfare of the animals. No charge for that. But it would help if you started buying your own feed."

"I will. Does it matter what kind?"

"Of course it matters! Animals get sick if you change feeds suddenly."

"Yes, of course," he agreed, taken aback by her emphasis. "Where's the hen?" She was getting out the chicken feed.

"She—I called her Henrietta—wild dogs raided here last night. We drove them off—too late. Will the chicks die?"

"The poor thing." There was genuine distress in her voice. "Elijah was going to fence the property, to keep the dogs and hunters out." She shrugged. "No, the chicks will survive nicely, if you give them feed and water and protect them from predators."

"I'll try." He realized that she had efficiently fed all the animals, and was about to mount her horse and ride away. "I appreciate your, uh, caretaking here. Are you a near neighbor?"

"Near enough. I live in Heatherwood One." She gestured east as she mounted. "This is Heatherwood Two. You can't get here from there."

Josh smiled, uncertain whether this were humor. "I gather you manage."

"Oh, I do, of course. I ride my horse. You ride your car. You can't get through." She slapped her mount's flank with the end of her reins, and the horse took off.

Josh watched them go, mildly bemused. At least he had abated the mystery of the phantom rider to some extent. A neighbor from across the tracks, feeding animals in need, as a favor to a dead man. He liked that sort of neighboring. Had that existed in the city when Mina—

Josh looked down at the chicks. They were happily scratching in the dirt between their peckings of seeds. One had uncovered something bright and was stabbing its cute little beak at it repeatedly. "What's this—found another wedding ring?"

He put his hand down and brushed the dirt aside with his fingers. The brightness increased. It was a fragment of metal, a disk about the size of a silver dollar but darker. A brass slug, perhaps. He picked it up and scraped more of the sand away.

The thing was surprisingly solid. In fact it was a medal or a coin—but not silver. It had such heft and luster that it had to be gold.

Gold—in the dirt where the chickens scratched? That hardly made sense!

Josh took the coin to the exterior tap and washed it carefully. Its shine brightened. Now he was able to see the pictures and read the lettering on the two sides of it. One face had an eagle and the words *Estados Unidos Mexicanos*.

This, then, was an old Mexican coin, probably gold of considerably purity. He would have to check it out.

Josh took the coin inside and weighed it on the postal scale in the kitchen. It hcftcd just about one and one third ounces. A good, solid coin indeed!

Then he heard a motor vehicle coming. That should be the carpenter. Josh dropped the heavy coin in his pocket and went out to meet the man.

Noel Carpenter was a small white-haired man in overalls and a battered pickup truck. He was all business. "I'll get right to it; know what I'm about," he said, and started moving tools to the house.

Josh followed after him somewhat helplessly. "You really believe this house is haunted? What evidence do you have? I mean, the house isn't even complete yet. How can a *new* house be haunted?"

"Someone dies in it, it can be haunted. You're telling me you ain't seen a ghost yet? Ain't heard nothing?"

Josh had to be fair. "I did hear a—a motor. But there wasn't anything—"

"Ayuh. Sound of the chain saw that killed Elijah. Listen close and you can hear the flesh ripping. How about the shots?"

"Shots?"

"Hunter shot himself right here, under the tree, 'bout five years ago. Dawn—that's when the shot was. When you hear it."

"I heard no shot this morning," Josh said. "Or yesterday morning. I was outside with my dogs then, so it should have been clear."

"It don't come every morning. Just some mornings. When the ghost's abroad. You keep listening, you'll hear it."

"I'll listen," Josh said. The notion intrigued him.

"Elijah really liked this tree," Carpenter observed as he hauled a four-by-eight fiberboard panel through the door and pushed it up through the stairwell hole. The panel was heavy, but the man seemed able to cope. "He wanted the house right by it, but he didn't want to hurt it. He was here all the time when the construction crew worked. No pesticides in the ground, because they might hurt the tree; don't know how he got around that law No roots cut; if a root was in the way, the foundation had to move, that was all. Drove the workers crazy. Couldn't trim any branches or dump wash water, because of that tree. Had to use a special lining for the concrete, so none of it would affect the soil. Even the septic tank had to be set well away, in case any sludge got to the tree roots—but in a hollow like this you can't drain away from the tree, so it's extra large and got extra filtration. Elijah was a fair man, but warped about that tree. Fetish, I guess it's called."

"I'll try to protect the tree the way he would have wanted," Josh said. "So much that is natural is wantonly destroyed—"

"You're his kin, all right; you sound just like him."

Carpenter was talking, but wasting no time. Soon he was hammering, measuring, and sawing. Josh was left more or less to his own devices. He fingered the coin in his pocket. It was additional evidence of Elijah's peculiarity.

In the afternoon the children were home. They paid solicitous attention to Pharaoh, who put up with it graciously, then admired the orphan chicks, stroked the kitties, and approached the pony, who laid her ears back at them. "Aw, come on, Beauty," Chris said. "That's your name, you know—the kids on the bus told us. We aren't like other children; we're nice. *I* am, anyway."

"So am I, big mouth!" Sue retorted. "Oh, I didn't mean you, Beauty!"

But the pony was unrelenting; she did not like children.

They descended on Josh: "Hey, Daddy—there's caves here. Can we go see them?"

Caves. Josh had always liked caves. "Do you know where they are?"

"In the state forest," Chris exclaimed.

"The state forest is several miles across. You will have to be more specific."

"Joey at school knows," Chris said.

"I am not Joey. You get me a map or detailed instructions, and we'll check it out this weekend. How's that?"

Sue jumped up and down, clapping her hands. "Oooo, goodie!"

Josh set out to feed the animals—and discovered that the horsewoman, Pip, had already been there and departed. The animals needed nothing. Evidently she hadn't trusted Josh to handle it correctly. Perplexing woman!

Carpenter worked well beyond the time he had specified, but wrapped up for the day and departed before dusk. The house was visibly changing; it was amazing what a single man who knew his business could do in a few hours. Josh was well satisfied.

Josh started the dinner fire outside the cabin with dry newspaper from inside, dry wood chips from Carpenter's exertions, and a topping of sodden outdoor wood. He put in a piece of pine—Carpenter had called it lighter knot—and that helped. The fire smoked awfully but deigned to continue burning.

He fried eggs somewhat clumsily, and the children attempted to toast slices of bread. None of it was very successful, but they ate it. The joys of camping out were wearing off.

They settled down for the night in the loft. The children seemed to be adjusting to this better than he was. Josh peered up at the ghostly flicker of light from the slowly turning turbine ventilator.

Ghostly—ghost—ghost bug. "The glowing bug!" he exclaimed. "I forgot all about it!"

"Don't worry, Daddy," Sue said sleepily. "It's a click beetle; the teacher knew. I let it go outside this morning. I wanted it to be happy."

Bless her! "You did the right thing," he told her. "We don't want to hurt any creature unnecessarily."

"Only bugs that bite, and wild dogs, and bad snakes," she agreed.

"Stay away from snakes! Most of them are good, so we don't need to hurt them, and the few that are poisonous are too dangerous for you to deal with."

"Okay, Daddy," she mumbled into the sleeping bag.

Josh returned his attention to the ventilator. That made a difference, but it remained hot here, interfering with his sleeping. The whirling pattern was hypnotic; he felt himself being drawn into it, not unwillingly. He began to remember, and then to dream, re-experiencing the happier moments of his life with Mina. Fortunately, he slept before reaching the tragedy.

*   *   *

Pharaoh was feeling better in the morning, and was beginning to pull in his normal fashion as Josh took the dogs out for the dawn run. This time they ranged north, to the boundary road that marked the edge of the Withlacoochee State Forest and Citrus Wildlife Management Area. There were several fallen strands of barbed wire that caused Josh to step carefully. As he elongated his stride to avoid the final barb, something shifted heavily in his pocket and clinked.

The gold coin, he remembered. The Mexican fifty-peso piece. He had forgotten it in the minor rush of events. Now it occurred to him that it might not be unique. Suppose there were several buried there in the dirt, the remnant of some ancient Spaniard's buried fortune? Spain had ruled Florida once. No—those had been doubloons; this coin was much more recent. Still, he would have to check that region carefully, or set the children to it.

He proceeded on up the hill to the east. Behind the trees he saw a huge burning red sheet, as though a forest fire raged. But it was too smooth, too even; it was in fact a potent sunrise, manifesting just before seven in the morning. As he came to the crest of the hill he was able to view it between and above the trees. In the course of four minutes it spread into a third of the sky, reaching upward as well as around. Clouds were scudding rapidly northward, providing excellent material for the nascent sun to work with; steadily they took fire. There were two darker layers, with blue sky between; the sunrise filled and overflowed that crevice.

Just when Josh thought he had seen the best of it, the effect expanded again. It encompassed the entire eastern half of the sky, from north to south and overhead, turning it all pale red. As it faded in the east, it progressed in the west, until the entire welkin glowed pale red and orange. In the end it resembled a sunset, the only remaining color tingeing the clouds to the west, though it was not as bright as a real sunset.

He had never seen a sunrise to match this. It awed him. Like life itself, beautiful in its blossoming, yet shaded already with the foreknowledge of the end.

A shot sounded from the direction of the house. Both dogs lifted their heads, their ears perking forward. Then, urged by a common imperative, the three hurdled the ramshackle barbed wire and charged back toward home. If some fool hunter had come—

Breathless, they drew up in sight of the tree. There was nothing untoward. All was in order. The farm animals were undisturbed. There was no sign of any intruder. No footprints, no smell of gunpowder.

Yet he and the dogs had heard the shot from a distance, definitely from this vicinity. Then Josh remembered Carpenter's comment: the ghost of the hunter. Was it possible?

No, it had probably been a branch snapping or falling. Such an event could be quite loud and sharp. Those turkey oaks were fragile weed trees; there were a number of topless trunks, snapped by high winds, still growing below the breaks. Pine trees died when they lost their tops, but the oaks lacked sense to quit.

Yet this was a fairly still morning, with only a mild surface wind beneath the stronger upper wind moving the clouds; insufficient to snap trees. And it had certainly sounded like a shot.

Josh retreated to the cabin, chained the dogs, and got the children up. He was running late now. The next forty-five minutes were taken by the usual rush to get ready for the school bus. Fortunately the children cooperated and offered a minimum of confusion and squabbling.

"Keep a sharp eye out for hunters," Josh cautioned them as they departed, only a few minutes late.

"It is hunting season?" Chris asked, interested.

"No. But I thought I heard a shot this morning. Maybe it was just an acorn falling on the metal roof of the main house."

"It sounded more like a gun," Sue said. "It was down by the tree."

"You heard it? I thought you were asleep."

"No, I woke up early. I just didn't get up right away." They rushed off toward the bus stop.

Josh considered. Down by the tree—where he had found nothing. And the farm animals had not reacted, though his two dogs had. Perhaps pony, cats and chicks were used to morning shots, and now ignored them, so long as there was no actual, physical presence.

He shrugged. Surely it was better to have a spectral gun going off here than a real one! Of course, there had been that chain saw sound the other afternoon, also near the tree—

But now he heard another sound. The beat of horse's hooves. That was one mystery he had laid to rest!

In moments she galloped up. "Hallo!" Josh called as the palomino steed chewed up turf in his stop. A full-sized horse, Josh realized, was an impressive animal—especially a fit creature like this.

"You haven't fed your animals!" Philippa exclaimed disapprovingly.

"Haven't had the chance. I just got my children off to school."

"You should have fed your animals first," she said sternly, making a smooth dismount.

"Before my children?"

She started busily on the chores, not meeting his eye. "Children can feed themselves."

He followed her somewhat helplessly. She was a well-constructed woman, and somehow this added to the awkwardness. "What do you have against children?"

"They're a bother, they mistreat animals—Beauty, here, can tell you about that—they're loud, they're full of mischief—"

"All children aren't alike." But he was learning things. If children had abused Beauty in the past, that accounted for the pony's attitude. "But are animals better?"

"Definitely. Haven't you noticed?"

"No," he said, getting warm. "I encountered some killer dogs the other night. I wouldn't want one of them—"

"Animals differ," she said defensively. "Had those dogs been treated properly, instead of being illegally dumped in the forest to fend for themselves, they would not have turned wild. Man is to blame. Probably somebody's children got tired of their pet, so—"

"You evidently have not had experience with good children," Josh said, showing his ire.

"Do good ones exist?"

"Children differ, as do animals. If a child is treated properly, not neglected—"

"Spoiled children are just as bad."

Why argue with her? "To each his own opinion," he said stiffly.

"I'll take horses any day." She mounted and galloped away, leaving him to shrug helplessly. He had never been at ease with assertive women.

Now he remembered the gold coin. He scratched in the dirt where he had found it yesterday. Almost immediately another coin turned up, and then a third.

Josh got down and sifted carefully through the dirt. In the course of half an hour he had built his collection up to six coins. Considering the price of gold, these might be worth a total of two or three thousand dollars, perhaps even more. That was food for thought.

The chicks were pecking avidly at the little stack of metal. Josh smiled. "That isn't chicken feed, you know."

He picked up the coins, took them to the tap for rinsing, and went back to the cabin, uncertain what to do with them. He couldn't keep all that weight in his pocket! He finally put them in a clean sock in his half-unpacked suitcase. He would be running out of clean clothes soon, and the children were dangerously near the brink; he hoped Mrs. Brown worked out as a housekeeper.

Josh poured the remaining hot water from the Thermos into the basin and set up his mirror for shaving. He did not bother with lather; it was too much trouble here. He just slapped the water on his face, waited two minutes, and started in. It was not the most comfortable shave he had had, but he didn't cut himself. Electricity would restore the electric shaver, in due course. He wished he could just quit shaving and grow a beard, but he had commitments in New York and had to maintain appearances. Maybe if he could manage a long enough break to get a beard properly established . . .

Next, he brought out his diary, intending to note the significant events of the past two days. But again he found himself leafing back, checking this date a year ago. It was a morbid exercise, only serving to freshen what should be allowed to fade, but he could not stop himself. *Only one entry*, he swore. There had to be limits to masochism.

He found the place. *Grueling day on the Donaldson program. Be glad to see this one done,* he read, automatically translating his shorthand into English. Ah, yes—that was the computerization of the Donaldson Chemical inventory. Josh had had to run down the nature of numerous obscure chemicals, their amounts and potencies and systems of refinement, grading, and pricing to formulate a program and a system that would enable the executives to maintain a cost-efficient ongoing inventory. The principle had been simple enough, but the details had been tedious. Josh was no chemist, so had had to pick his way tortoiselike through the maze of unfamiliar symbols. But he had done his homework, and it had worked well, in one step rendering the company's business procedure twelve percent more efficient (according to the projection; it would be at least another year before the final figures were in)—a quite significant gain. The job had paid well, though Josh considered it hackwork. He was supposed to be a systems engineer, not a mere programmer. But he had needed the money. The line between creativity and drudgery became fuzzy in a case like this. Josh was proud of the accomplishment and pleased about the improvement in their family life-style the increased income had enabled, but he wouldn't care to go through that experience again.

He lifted his eyes from his handwritten sheets. How small such concerns seemed now! If only she were with him again, there would be no—

He heard Carpenter's truck. Good; at this rate, the house would be ready for inspection in a few days. Josh liked the forest, but life would be more comfortable with electricity and the room and insulation of the house.

Hastily he put away his diary and trotted out and down to intercept Carpenter. "Hey, I heard that shot this morning!" he cried, as if this were positive news.

Carpenter squinted at him. "And you're not scared?"

"Of course not. I don't believe in ghosts. It's just another mystery to be resolved."

The man shook his head and went about his business.

In the afternoon Old Man Foster ambled by. "Did you hear about the big pot heist?" he asked, his eyes brightening with relish at the gossip.

"A broken pot? You dropped it?"

Foster peered at him. "The weed. In bales. Tons of it. Ol' boxcar came by the other night and dumped it in the woods, but the sheriff got there first, for once."

"I'm not sure I follow you," Josh said, perplexed. "We heard an airplane, but—"

"Marijuana," Foster clarified. "The big rage with the kids, at least the ones who can't afford the heavy stuff. Don't you know?"

"Oh. Drugs. The fact is, I don't know much about them."

"Not to know about pot," Foster said, shaking his head as though appalled. "Never thought I'd meet the man."

"Oh, I have heard of marijuana," Josh assured him. "I just don't happen to be informed about it."

"So you don't know about how the Zion Copts smoke it in their religion, and how they import it by the carload right through Citrus County here but they've never really been nailed?"

"I didn't know," Josh agreed. Then he turned to a subject of more immediate interest. "Foster, I think you knew my uncle better than I did. Was it possible he could have collected items of value and hidden them away?"

"Possible? Certain!" Foster said emphatically. "Elijah was a squirrel. He went to every auction, flea market, tax sale, bankruptcy liquidation, and barter in these parts, don't you know! He had a real eye for bargains. He watched the papers and pounced on anything he had a notion for. Antiques, broken stuff, out-of-season merchandise—"

"I haven't seen much of that around. Of course I haven't really looked—"

"He didn't keep it, mostly. He'd get it fixed and turn around and sell it for a fat profit—and the buyer knew it and was pleased. Elijah never cheated nobody; he could spot a bargain in a dunghill. There was this ol' no-'count oil lamp he picked up, had a circular wick and a cracked glass chimney. Well, he got a new chimney and wick and mantle—"

"Mantle?"

"Sort of a little tent made of net, fits over the flame and makes it glow real bright. Had 'em when I was a boy. Good lamps. They don't make 'em now."

"We have one of those in the cabin. You're right; it's a nice lamp."

"Sure is! Well, I guess he got several. Because after he fixed this one up he sold it to a fancy antique dealer for about ten times what he paid. Small potatoes, for him, but it shows how he was. Mighty canny businessman, your uncle. Didn't miss a bet, large or small. Must've built up a real fortune."

"According to the attorney for the estate, it doesn't amount to much aside from the land."

"Biggerton? That fathead don't know his ay from a dent in the sod. Elijah didn't trust to lawyers and banks. He bartered and traded on his own, mostly. No tax that way, don't you know. No capital gains."

"He had a safe, but that was impounded for the estate settlement," Josh said. "He might have had some stocks or cash in there."

"If he did, you'll never see 'em. The vultures'll take it all, and charge you for the service too. But Elijah didn't hold to them things. He said '29 could come again, only this time they'll call it '89, and he was going to be ready. He had some silver dollars, the kind with real silver and heft you could sink your teeth into. He showed me one, once. In fact he gave it to me. Sparkling shiny 1900 coin, pretty as you please. He said them Morgans were worth thirty times what they used to. I traded mine and got twenty for it, so it must've been worth forty, 'cause they always do cheat, don't you know."

"Silver dollars," Josh said, thinking of the gold coins he had found.

"I think he buried 'em. Got some kind of sealed cannister dingus from some company, airtight, to last a hundred years. Maybe he left a map, a treasure map. Most likely he just remembered where they were—and now no one knows. He just didn't figure on dying so soon."

"None of us do," Josh said, thinking of Wilhelmina.

"Well, I got to toddle on. My animals get lonely."

Foster toddled on. Josh was pleased with the visit. Now he had confirmation of his uncle's propensities. The gold coins were entirely in character. They had been carelessly hidden— but perhaps that had been a temporary expedient, done in haste by a busy man. Elijah could have planned to move them to a better location—but was overtaken by the unexpected.

Josh heard the clamor of a dog in the distance. The wild dogs—he had to keep them away from here, lest they raid again and do more damage. A fence—

He surveyed the fencing situation. There were several rolls of sturdy four-foot welded-wire fencing, together with a hundred or so six-and-a-half-foot treated posts and boxes of heavy staples. In the shed near the dread saw were a battered fence stretcher, a posthole digger, and a sledgehammer. That should be enough to do the job. He would get to work on it. At least it would solve the problem of vicious wildlife, and would provide an enclosure for Beauty to graze in without being constantly tethered.

He made a small tour of the immediate property to decide on the best siting for the fence. He should be able to do a lot with the trees, tacking the fence to them. That would make for a wiggly line, but he didn't care; he just wanted the job done quickly. He would travel a contour around the depression surrounding house and tree. This was nice terrain, with moderately sized pines and live oaks interspersed with fairly open ground. The turf was springy under the feet, as though he walked on a giant mattress.

Then he heard a rattle. Josh froze. It was a snake, large and black, with the trailing end becoming mottled and brownish. His eyes traced nervously to the tail—and found no rattle. This was not a rattlesnake; it looked more like a black racer. Yet the rattling continued.

A ghost rattler? This was getting ridiculous! Josh stayed well back, and the snake did not advance. It made the sound by vibrating its stiffened tail horizontally against the weeds and twigs surrounding it. Josh wasn't sure whether this was a deliberate imitation of a rattlesnake, or coincidence, or some intermediate evolution. But it had given him a start!

After another moment the snake gave up and undulated around and out of sight. Josh continued his tour, his adrenaline subsiding. He had been more nervous about the encounter than he had realized. He had never heard of a nonpoisonous snake acting like that, but it seemed like sensible protective mimicry.

He heard Carpenter's truck starting up. It was later than he had realized! Josh hurried onward, wanting to return before the children came home. For some reason he dreaded the prospect of them arriving at the property alone. Maybe the talk about ghosts and curses had gotten to him.

Chapter 7

The phone rang. It turned out to be Mrs. Bush, of the Inverness Middle School, fifth grade. She wanted a conference. She was polite but uncommunicative. Her final period was open today; if he could stop by—

Not one week in school, and Chris was a problem in class. It was the hyperactive syndrome, he knew; the boy's inability to sit still for five consecutive minutes, to pay attention, to be quiet, or to get his work done. Chris was bright enough, but absolutely inattentive in school. The result was teacher frustration and failing grades.

Josh agreed to go in for the conference in the afternoon. He knew the route. Most people were not aware that hyperactivity was not simply an accelerated motor, but was typically part of a complex that also included certain learning disabilities, aggressive personality traits, and extreme sensitivity. Such children needed special understanding, but their actions invited negative attention, so that they could be trapped in a descending spiral of negative feedback, especially at school. He would have to explain to the teacher that Chris was not deliberately obstructive, and no, absolutely no, on the drug therapy that some doctors liked to recommend for such children. "Speed" had the peculiar effect of slowing down such a child, but Josh was prepared to go to court to protect his family's freedom from drugs. So it would be a difficult session, but necessary. Educating teachers had become an annual event; they tended to have simplistic notions about children.

He would have to leave a note for Suzanne, so she wouldn't be alarmed if he didn't make it back home before her. The children rode the same bus, but were in different schools, Middle and Elementary, so it wasn't feasible to intercept her. Chris he would bring home himself. He still didn't like having Sue home alone, but he also didn't like the prospect of Chris failing school, which was what would happen if Josh did not get to that teacher. At least the dogs would be with Sue in the cabin; even a wounded Pharaoh represented considerable protection. Josh and Chris would soon rejoin her. So it should be all right. He hoped.

On future occasions there would be a housekeeper to bridge such gaps. That was one reason he needed that particular service: to cover the times he couldn't be in two places at once.

Sue was perplexed when her brother was not on the bus, but not unduly concerned. He had probably gotten in trouble at school, and been held for detention or whatever they did here. Daddy would check into it. Every year Daddy got into a big scene with a teacher about Chris.

She went to the cabin. It was closed, and hot, and the dogs were wild to see her. Nerfertiti jumped up and down, and Pharaoh made a rare woof. "But where's Daddy?" she asked.

Then she saw the note, weighted down by the lamp where she would see it. Daddy said he would be home soon; Chris *had* gotten into trouble, just as she thought. It made her a little nervous to be here alone, but of course she had the dogs for company.

Pharaoh was already scratching to go out. "Oh, all right," she said. "I guess you gotta go dog-do." Of course she couldn't take one dog out without the other, so she snapped the leashes on both and opened the door.

The dogs shoved out, dragging her along. She had to jump off the log step before she fell off. "Slow down!" she cried, but they only pulled harder, realizing they were making progress. They massed, together, more than she did, and they had eight legs to her two, and they didn't have to worry about falling over. So she was hauled along where they wanted to go.

Fortunately they didn't want to go far. They got into the big field area east of the tree. Here the sunlight was bright and the plants were thick and interesting and there was a pleasant pine smell and the ground was springy. She could just roll in it, if it wasn't for the dogs and the sandspurs and the itchy-plants. There were also a number of dirt piles, each a foot or so in diameter, as though some animal had been burrowing and throwing up the dirt behind, except that there were no burrows, just the piles. It was a mystery. She didn't want to roll in *that*. Not in her good school clothes, anyway.

As the dogs snuffled from tree to tree, dragging her under the hanging Spanish moss—which really wasn't very mossy from up close but more like tangles of string or fish line—she became absorbed in the variety and marvel of the flowers here.

The itchy-plants actually had some of the prettiest colors. Their leaves were green and pointy, the flowers petite and pure white. But one brush of a bare ankle or swipe of a forearm and ooooh, owww! it stung something fierce. So now she avoided them, and if she had a stick or a rock she bashed them, because they weren't very pleasant company. But other flowers were much better.

There were low places carpeted with little purple flowers on dark green creepers. What were these called? She didn't know, so she made up a descriptive name: carpet creepers. She had a methodical mind and liked to classify things. Farther along were off-white clusters of flowers on waist-high stalks; in the deep pine shadows they looked like little floating clouds, since the darker plant bottoms tended to disappear. So these were cluster clouds. Then there was a type whose real name she knew: dog fennel, standing head-high on her, just beginning to flower. The flowers were like microscopic daisies with yellow centers, maybe a dozen petals on each, and maybe a gross of flowers per plant. She knew what a gross was: twelve dozen. It was one of her favorite words, since it also meant supcryuck. Twelve dozen yucks. What could be better?

A train whistle blew to the southeast. Oh—was there a train in the forest? That would be fun! The dogs nosed on avidly in that direction, and she followed, now entirely distracted by the little wonders of nature and the vague background notion of a train. Here were round white flowers, purple in the centers, about an inch and a half in diameter, on climbing vines. She had heard these called greenbriars. And there were several variations of daisylike plants, and fernlike plants with buttercuplike flowers except for spots of red in the centers, like drops of blood. That bothered her, so she looked up at the passing pine trees for a while, noticing how pretty their green was against the deep blue of the sky, except for the one broken one that was like a windowless tower. It was dead, its whole top gone; she didn't like that either. Dead things made her nervous.

For a moment she paused, in thought if not in body, for the dogs were still hauling her along toward the train. She had the sudden feeling that someone or something was watching her. But she didn't see anything, and anyway the dogs would protect her, and there was no need to be afraid by day. So she shrugged it off.

There were cute cactuses, not in bloom and painful to touch, but they didn't bother her the way the itchy-plants did. There were baby pine trees, in their "pin cushion" stage; they bristled out all over before shooting up the way Daddy claimed children did. Actually, Sue had always been the same size; the world had become smaller.

She found herself cresting a bank—and there were the railroad tracks she had heard about. They had come a long way! These tracks represented the limit of this home as she knew it. She liked trains, but found she didn't like these tracks. Something about them made her nervous, and she had that "watching" feeling again. But the dogs were hauling her along relentlessly.

"Back!" she cried. "We can't go there!"

Still they hauled, intent on something in that great gully. To make it worse, she saw that this section was filled with the blood-center flowers. A bad omen! Did that mean that blood would be spilled?

Maybe she should call them railroad track plants, because they liked it here. That made them less frightening. But still she didn't want to wade among them. That blood—

She set her heels in the turf and leaned back, yanking on the leashes. Suddenly the stitching on the handle loop of Nefertiti's leash gave way. The loop broke open and the leash slipped from Sue's grasp. Nefertiti bounded into the track gully, dragging the leash chain behind.

"Oh, no!" she cried. She ran after the dog, half sliding down the steep bank and stirring up a cloud of dust. Pharaoh gladly kept pace; his healing injury bothered him less when he was doing something interesting. "Titi, come back!"

But the dog ran on down the track, and soon was out of sight. "Track her, Pharaoh!" Sue cried. And indeed the dog seemed to be doing that. They ran on down the tracks, heedless of the fact that they were going ever farther from home.

The chasm sides lowered; then the tracks actually rose above the surrounding landscape. They were on an elevated bed, a mound, and the ground on either side formed new gullies where the earth had been dug out to form this ridge.

On and on! She was tired now, breathing hard, her legs scratched. She was no longer sure Pharaoh knew where he was going. There was no sign of Nefertiti. Yet she had no better lead. She had to go on. Even though she still felt watched.

The tracks diverged. One set curved left into a new gully in a rising hill—and Pharaoh followed these. Sue plunged on, not wanting to admit that she thought she was in trouble.

A barbed wire fence crossed these tracks. "We have to stop!" Sue protested. "She can't be in there!"

But Pharaoh was insistent, as he was whenever his attention was caught by anything. Sue had either to drag him with four feet scraping furrows in the ground or go along with him. She really didn't have the strength to drag him all the way home, so she yielded. Eventually he would condescend to go back home, and maybe they would find Nefertiti. She climbed through the fence and threaded the leash through, and they went on into the new chasm.

Suddenly the tracks terminated. A huge pit opened out, hundreds of feet across, with a lake in the bottom. It was pretty in its fashion—but also scary, for the banks were really steep here, clifflike, with projecting rocks and sliding dirt, maybe fifty feet up and down from where she stood to the surface of the water. If she fell over that bank, she would slide and roll helplessly until she reached the water and drowned.

A pretty butterfly fluttered by, as if tempting her to make the misstep. She recognized it: a zebra swallowtail, according to her bug book, the prettiest of them all. Once she had identified a species, she knew it forever, and she had seen this one several times.

But now she had to go home, with or without Nefertiti. It was bad enough to lose one dog, but it would be worse to lose one little girl, especially in her school clothes. She turned. Pharaoh, getting tired too, was satisfied to come quietly now.

Then the dog growled. There, standing between them and the track chasm, was a monstrous, ugly, ferociously horned cow. It did not look friendly.

When Josh arrived home with Chris, there was no sign of Sue or the dogs. Immediately concerned, he set out to locate them. He called, but there was no answer. He checked the shed and the house, but they were not there.

Obviously the child had taken the dogs out on the leashes, and it had gotten out of hand. But where could they be? His concern was becoming alarm.

Then it seemed he was tuning in on something. He pictured a scene: two hands holding a rock, lifting it, throwing it down against another, making a silent sound. Then the hands taking hold again, lifting again, throwing down again. The hands were so dirty he could not tell much about them, but their proportions seemed to fit those of a child. Sue?

Why should he imagine a picture like this? It did not make sense.

The hands handled the rock again—and this time Josh thought he heard the sound. Really heard it—with his ears, not his imagination.

He closed his eyes, gesturing to Chris to be still. Once more he visualized the hands on the rock—and this time he was quite sure he heard the sound, though it was very faint. He pointed his finger at the direction of it, and opened his eyes.

He was pointing southeast. Toward the place on the map designated as the Story Mine.

He looked at Chris. "Did you—?"

"I heard it, Daddy," the boy agreed. "She's knocking rocks together to make a noise we'll hear."

So blithely the boy accepted the hardly possible!

"Let's go," Josh said, hoping he wasn't making a fool of himself in addition to losing his daughter.

They found her, perched on the top of a mountainous rock pile, the pile surrounded by cows. She had been afraid to get too near them, especially with Pharaoh eager for a fight, but had been unable to escape the mine area without doing so. So she had tried to summon help by making the loudest noise she could.

"Smart girl!" Josh agreed, picking her up while Chris walked Pharaoh home. "The sound carried all the way to the cabin, and we heard it when we listened." He tried to make it sound as if this were all routine, but his relief was tremendous.

But what accounted for his accurate vision of her hands manipulating the stone? Had he heard the sound subconsciously, and envisioned its likely mode of origin?

He shook his head. It really didn't matter. He had found Sue.

When they got home, Nefertiti was waiting for them, her tail wagging.

Saturday: no need to wake the children early. Josh took the

dogs on a longer walk through the forest but saw no sunrise. Instead there was fog, sifting in thin layers across the land, allowing the latest and brightest stars to shine through. He made out handsome Orion's belt directly overhead, three stars in a row, with scattered other pricks of light penetrating elsewhere. As he mounted the top of the hill he came above the mist. Then as he approached the railroad cut he saw that it was full of fog. So white, so soft, so silent; all the world seemed quiet, except for the gentle crackle of drops of water falling on the dry leaves of the forest floor.

Something jumped. Both dogs yanked, eager to pursue it, almost jerking Josh off his feet. It was a small brown deer with a white tail that flashed as it departed. Josh had not seen a deer since childhood. What a nice way to start the day!

Then home for the more mundane events. The children were intrigued when he reminded them that this was House-keeper Interviewing Day. Then they nagged him every fifteen minutes about when she was due to arrive.

Patience Brown arrived on schedule. Josh had the children cleaned up and on their reasonably good behavior to meet her. He certainly needed some help on these premises. He had phoned her references and had been assured of her competence, honesty, and reliability. "But she runs things," a former employer warned. He found that reassuring rather than alarming.

"If she's so good, why is she desperate for work?" he asked.

"She *is* good—but set in her ways. We outgrew her."

That seemed to him to be as good a recommendation as any.

Mrs. Brown drew up in a battered old car. She was not prepossessing. She seemed about fifty years of age, of ma-tronly mass, her hair converting from blond to gray without any particular grace, and her face weathered like that of a

farm laborer. She wore a clean but worn denim jumper and a
dark blouse. She might be competent; she was hardly attractive.

"I am Joshua Pinson," he said, stepping forward as she
emerged from her vehicle. "These are my children, Christopher and Suzanne." He gestured. Both children were abruptly
shy.

"Housework, cleaning, laundry, children, cooking, day-
times. Overnight in your absence," Patience Brown said
grimly, getting it quite straight at the outset. "Nothing else."

Josh was happy to agree. "At the prevailing wage, plus
whatever is needed for groceries and things. That does in-
clude shopping?" He paused awkwardly but saw her nod; her
"nothing else" was not referring to that sort of thing. "Um,
we prefer no smoking or drinking of alcoholic—"

"Of course. Let's see the house."

"I'm afraid we haven't moved in yet. The carpenter is
working on it so that we can get the final inspection passed.
Then we can move in."

Nevertheless she surveyed the house. "Stairs?"

"He expects to install them Monday."

"Those fish been fed?"

Chris jumped. "Oops." He hurried to do it.

Mrs. Brown nodded. "When does it start?"

"The job?" Josh asked, startled. This woman was certainly taking hold rapidly! "I have to make a trip to New
York this Wednesday. I'd prefer to get things straightened
out before this—but I can't guarantee the house will be
ready."

"I've handled worse." She located an extension cord and
plugged a portable lamp in at the kitchen counter where there
was an outlet on the cord running to the refrigerator. She
had caught on to that particular situation instantly. "Can't
use the stove—it's two-twenty—and it's too hot for the wood

stove." They had gotten that set up, but it was as yet untested. "Bring in the kerosene stove."

"Kerosene stove?" Josh asked blankly.

"On the back porch," she said. "Just bring it around inside so I can set it up. I think it has some kerosene."

Josh checked the porch. The stove was there, with the pale fuel in a glass jar. The woman certainly had a sharp eye; he hadn't noticed it at all. He hauled it awkwardly inside.

Soon Patience had the stove going. It stood about thirty inches high on a slender metal frame, with two burners shaped like coffeepots, fed by a line from the inverted jar of fuel to the side. Gravity brought the kerosene to the base of each burner, and the enclosure above the wick served to amplify the flame in much the manner of the mantle on the lamp, until it literally hummed. The half-pleasant odor of kerosene wafted through the kitchen. It was a good thing Mrs. Brown was familiar with this type of device; Josh wasn't sure he could have operated it alone.

She rummaged in the refrigerator and amid the stored cans and in due course produced excellent vegetable soup and hot cornbread in a frying pan. She handed steaming chunks of it around, with margarine sliding off the tops.

Chris tried his piece somewhat dubiously. "Hey—it's good!" he exclaimed with undiplomatic amazement.

Sue, who seldom liked anything new, was more cautious. She nibbled off a piece from a corner, no larger than a grain of rice. "Well—"

Josh tried his. It was excellent. "If you can do this in these conditions, you can do just about anything," he said.

"By daytime," she qualified. It was more than evident that she did not want a man getting in her way, but, true to her newspaper ad, she badly needed the work. "Now clear out of here so I can clean up."

They cleared out. "Let's take the dogs for a walk," Chris suggested. "We've hardly explored anything."

Sue was reluctant. "I explored before."

"And got lost, dum-dum," Chris retorted.

"Not your fault," Josh told her quickly. "Two dogs are too strong for you. Sometimes they almost yank me off my feet. However, I would like you to be familiar with the landscape so that if you are ever in that region again, you will know your way home. We don't want to lose any children. We've been fortunate so far, knock on wood." He tapped lightly on her head.

"Daddy!" she protested. But she was mollified.

First they followed Pineleaf Lane east to its end, tracing the chewed path of Philippa's horse. They continued to the track bed. "Say, great!" Chris cried. He had not seen the chasm of the cut before; they had crossed the tracks well south of this section when locating Sue.

They found a narrow, slanting ledge that slid down to the base of the cut, and another up the far side. But beyond the rim the trail soon petered out amid weeds and bushes. Seeds like black beanpods dangled from tall plants. They left black smears on the hands when touched. Sandspurs abounded, and prickly vines. "Let's leave this particular direction for another day," Josh suggested. "We can circle around south and see what neighbors we have."

They returned to the bed and walked south, toward the mine. "You see, Sue, all you have to do is follow the cut until you come to where the horse path crosses, then follow it home. Next time you get lost. Okay?"

"Okay," she agreed, faintly reassured. "But I'm not going back to the storybook mine."

"We won't go as far as the Story Mine," Josh agreed.

"Bet you can't balance on the rail," Chris said.

"Bet I *can*," Sue said, rising quickly to the challenge.

"What rail?" Josh asked.

"The track rails," Chris said.

"There are no tracks. They were taken up long ago."

The children exchanged glances. Then Sue pointed to the ground. "You don't see that track. Daddy?"

What was this, a game? He played along. "Oh, *that* track."

The children took turns walking along it, precariously balancing, pretending that there was a rail. Josh was disquieted because they were so serious about it. Could they actually believe that tracks remained? They had seemed to see them the first time they drove across, a mile south, he remembered now.

The dogs sniffed avidly at holes in the steep banks. Josh was nervous about what might lurk in such recesses but decided the dogs should be able to recognize any threat as well as he could. Pharaoh's injury was healing nicely, hardly slowing the dog at all. The wild dogs had not shown their snouts again; perhaps they had been permanently discouraged. This was not really a dangerous land—

Sue screamed. Then Josh became aware of the angry buzzing and the small flying shapes. They had blundered into a nest of wasps or bees!

"Get out of here!" he cried. But on either side the banks rose high, too steep to navigate swiftly. They were trapped.

"Run forward!" he cried. "Straight down the tracks. Just get away from here!"

The children started running, in their excitement releasing the dogs. Josh dashed to catch the leashes—and got stung on the right thumb. He never saw the bee that did it, but the pain was fierce. "Come *on*!" he yelled, half dragging the dogs.

The bees did not pursue. People and dogs found themselves where the banks had eased; it was now easy to climb out of the railroad bed. "How many stings?" Josh asked, as though assessing casualties on the battlefield.

Sue had been stung on the left thigh. Chris was scratched but not stung. Josh put his arms about them both, somewhat awkwardly because of the tugging of the dogs. "Bees," he said. "I never saw the nest. I know it hurts; I got stung too."

Sue's tears were already drying; it gave her comfort to share the pain with her father. "They just came out of the ground," she said. "Little holes in the ground."

Holes in the ground. "Could be. I seem to remember seeing one of those before."

"On the road from our mailbox," she said solemly. "There's a bee hole there."

"Oh, yes. So we can't tell a beehive from a hole in the ground. We won't go back to look." He gave her a parting squeeze, then concentrated on handling the dogs.

They found an old double-rut trail that cut west and followed that, not bothering to proceed on south. Maybe the mine just wasn't fated to be properly explored. There seemed to be a number of things out here that were best left alone.

The road terminated at a ramshackle farmstead. A house trailer was propped on cement blocks near hutches containing rabbits and a rickety chicken coop. Pharaoh winded the birds and strained at the leash.

A cat and several kittens appeared, by their coloration related to the two kittens at home. Josh had to choke up on the leash again to keep the dogs in order. "Oooo, kitty-cats!" Sue exclaimed, just as if she had seen none in years, and hastened to fondle them.

Three young dogs also appeared, barking while wagging their tails. They were all thin, their ribs showing. Yet again Josh tightened his grip on Pharaoh's leash. These half-grown pups did not deserve the treatment Pharaoh would give them.

No human proprietor was in evidence. Finally Josh spied

the mailbox: Foster 27F. So this was where Old Man Foster lived! Josh realized that he must have driven by it several times without ever seeing it.

One bird was wandering loose near the road. It was a somewhat bedraggled rooster, with brown and black feathers and a bare neck. Josh looked twice to make sure it wasn't a turkey. The birds ignored him, unafraid, pecking up items from the soil.

"That rooster should be in the coop," Josh said. "He can get run over out here." He turned the dogs over to the children, one to each, then went to shoo the bird toward the coop.

It didn't work. The motley rooster moved away from him, but not in the right direction. Josh tried to circle around him, but the bird only countercircled, getting them both into the brush. He simply refused to be herded.

"Well, you'll just have to take your chances, then," Josh said, irritated, and turned to go.

Suddenly the rooster was on him, flapping his wings, stabbing forward with his beak, plunging his claws into Josh's thigh. Josh reacted instinctively, smashing the bird with his forearm. "What *is* this?" he demanded.

The rooster ignored him, pecking innocently at the ground. Josh stood for a moment, then he turned away again—and the rooster attacked a second time.

Abrupt rage possessed Josh. The first time might have been confusion, but the second time was sheer malevolence. Josh's foot came up violently. It caught the bird in midair and sent him hurtling away.

The children hurried over with the dogs. "What happened, Daddy?" Chris demanded. "Why did you kick that chicken?"

"That chicken kicked me first!" Josh said hotly, massaging his punctured thigh muscle. He was shaken, both by the attacks and by the violence of his own reaction. He was not used to being attacked and did not like it at all. This rooster was evidently another of Pharaoh's type, hostile to all strangers.

"Pharaoh would chomp that mean rooster!" Chris said, his eyes bright with anticipation. Indeed, the dog was straining at the leash, hackles raised.

"Precisely. Hold him tight. We can't go around killing other people's animals."

"But—"

"Two wrongs don't make a right."

"But you kicked the rooster!"

"I seem to have been overreacting recently. The bird is not attacking me now, so I'll leave it alone."

"Oh." Chris shrugged, not quite understanding.

They moved on, Josh remaining ill at ease. He thought of himself as a man of peace, yet he had reacted with explosive violence. He was becoming like Pharaoh, indulging in unfettered animosity.

They followed the road until it intersected Forest Drive near the mailbox. From there it was a short walk north to their own mailbox, then on to the tree, and they were home. Patience Brown had made remarkable progress on the house. Boxes had been stacked in corners, and a living area had been cleaned up. "But you know we can't stay here until it passes inspection," Josh reminded her.

"You'll pass that on Tuesday," she assured him. "I'll be in Monday." She departed in her car.

She had, amazingly, done some more cooking during their absence, in addition to the formidable cleanup. A set of chocolate puddings sat cooling on the counter. "What do you think, children?" Josh asked. "Will Mrs. Brown make a good housekeeper?"

They contemplated the pudding. If there was one thing both children liked besides ice cream, it was chocolate pudding. "Will she make us take baths?" Chris asked.

"Yes. And she'll make you do your homework, and get off to school on time when I'm away, and go to bed on time."

Chris sighed. "I knew there was a catch to it. That pudding sure better be good!"

It was good. They all had some. Then Josh went out to survey his fencing situation again, telling the children to tackle their assignments—which meant one long quarrel with each other, since anything was better than homework.

The quiet of working alone didn't last, of course. It was always difficult to get much done when the children were home. "Daddy!" Sue cried, running up to him. "Chris's got a bad snake! Didn't you say to stay away from them?"

"I certainly did," he agreed. He had told her, but had made the mistake of not telling Chris directly; naturally the boy was getting into mischief instead of doing his homework.

"It's hissing and striking and it has a flat head and everything," Sue said, excited. "Bright colors."

Josh hurried back with her, hoping the boy had not been even more foolish than anticipated. "Does it have a rattle on its tail?"

"I don't think so."

No rattlesnake, then. "Does it have bright bands of color right around its body—yellow, red, black?" The coral snake was the prettiest little reptile extant, a magnet for a curious child—but also had the deadliest toxin.

"I think it's white underneath," she said.

Maybe it was all right. Now he spied Chris, squatting beside the house. The boy looked up tearfully as Josh approached. "It's dead," he wailed.

"Did it bite you?"

Sue found that uncontrollably funny. "It bit him and it died! No wonder!"

"No!" the boy said, glancing murderously at her. "It tried to, but I poked it with a stick, and it just died."

"Snakes don't just die," Joshua said. "You must have struck it pretty hard."

"No, I just poked it. Honest! I didn't hurt it! And it died."

"Oh, sure!" Sue said witheringly.

The snake lay belly-up, its jaws wide open, saliva forming a festoon to the ground. It was light below; no coral snake.

Josh went to the cabin and donned his heavy work gloves. He didn't like the notion of handling an unfamiliar snake, but he wanted to identify this one. If poisonous snakes lurked this close to the house—

He slid his gloved fingers under the snake and turned it over. Its topside was decorated with large brown patches, not true diamonds. Probably not a poisonous snake, though its head was flattened. What did a copperhead look like? He would have to get a good reptile book to match the bug and bird books.

"Hey, it's dead again," Chris said.

Josh looked down. The snake was bottom up, as before— but he had left it right-side up. "Did you—?" he asked, upset.

"I didn't touch it, honest!" Chris said. "And I didn't kill it before, either."

Josh gingerly turned the snake over again. Immediately it convoluted to turn itself upside down for the third time.

"Why you faker!" Josh exclaimed. "You're playing dead!" He picked it up again, this time holding it in his hands so that it couldn't turn over. Surely a poisonous reptile wouldn't have need of such a trick!

The snake struggled briefly, then gave up. It moved its head, studying him. Then it began to crawl up his arm.

"Is it going to bite you, Daddy?" Chris asked with a certain scientific detachment.

"I don't think so. I think this is a harmless snake, after all, who indulges in protective mimicry of one sort or another. When it couldn't frighten you away, it played dead instead. Now it is deciding we're no threat, so it is getting friendly."

"Can I hold it?" Chris asked eagerly.

Josh debated briefly with himself and decided that this risk was worth taking. He could rush the boy to town for emergency aid if he had to, and probably the snake was all right. He was becoming more certain that there was no danger here, without knowing why he felt that way. He handed the snake over. "But don't squeeze it hard, and if it should bite you, let me know immediately. And no, you can't keep it; just play with it gently, then let it go."

"Aww—"

"But you can count it on your list. It's a reptile."

"Say, yeah!"

Soon the boy had the snake climbing onto his shoulder. The snake seemed perfectly contented to be tamed. This struck Josh as unusual, but perhaps the wild creatures here had not had enough experience with man to be afraid of him. Nature largely unspoiled: it could be a dream come true. But Josh could not quite believe that, yet.

Chapter 8

Chris woke with a start. Shafts of moonlight slanted down from the turning ventilator. He had been dreaming of Mommy, going out shopping for a Christmas present for him, saying "Merry Christ-mas, Chris-topher," and "Good-bye, honey," and himself pretending not to hear because he felt a bit guilty. It was in his mind that he had not been doing well at school and didn't really deserve a good Christmas, yet he wanted that gift. So he was trying to suppress his own unworthiness, not trying to hurt her, but all the time it had seemed that if he had only spoken out, admitted his culpability, told her not to go shopping . . .

That little guilt had expanded monstrously thereafter, and now it had surfaced in his dreams. He had been punished for his neglect, crushingly punished. For that had been the morning Mommy had not returned.

Daddy lay sleeping beside him, and Sue was snoring gently beyond. Chris was the only one awake. That made him lonely. It was eerie to be conscious by oneself. He knew he should simply go back to sleep, but the feeling of guilt remained strong. For his punishment had been meted out not only to him, but to Daddy and Sue as well.

"Chris!"

120

His body stiffened. That was her voice, calling from out-side. Calling him!

Mommy was—was—yet he had *heard* it. If not his name, something else. It could have been a scream.

If Daddy woke, it would turn out to be nothing. It always did. Even though it was always definitely something when Daddy wasn't there.

"Chris!" There it was again! Mommy *was* out there!

Chris scrambled out of the makeshift bed and felt for the ladder. He thought of taking the fluorescent lamp, but knew Daddy wouldn't like it. Children, Daddy always said, knew how to turn things on but not how to turn them off, and batteries got upset about not being turned off: In fact, they just died, Daddy said. So no lamp. There would be moon-light outside.

The dogs were sound asleep. Some watchdogs! Chris thought of taking them along but wasn't sure he could handle them. So he felt his way around them and went out alone.

The moon was three-quarters full and strengthening into brilliant. He saw the ghastly face on it that seemed to gri-mace as a wisp of cloud passed it. Suddenly Chris was nervous.

But he had heard Mommy call. He marshaled his courage and stepped away from the cabin, into the clearing.

The main house came into view. It was embraced by the monstrous tree, like an elephant in the grip of a killer squid. By day he had liked the tree and eyed its hugely spreading limbs as prospects for grandiose tree houses, but this was eerie. What had been comforting then was now sinister.

The beams of moonlight bathing the open space between cabin and house were submerged in dappled deep shadow near the tree. In that shadow near the great trunk something moved. It was, he knew, Mommy. Frightened despite his certainty, Chris walked toward her.

Then he saw another figure in the shadow. It was large and gross and malignant, and it lurched in pursuit of the woman. "Watch out, Mommy!" Chris cried, terror and courage rising together. He looked for a weapon, but there were only splintery fence posts. Daddy had used one on the wild dogs; Sue had told him about it. Chris hauled one up and staggered toward the tree.

The woman screamed as the brute figure caught her. Chris lurched at them, trying to ram the end of his stake at the monster. Didn't they pound wooden stakes through the hearts of vampires? The woman lay on the ground, sobbing, hurt, helpless.

The post went right through the monster's body. There was nothing there! No brute—and no woman. Chris stood alone, panting, his hands hurting.

He dropped the post on the empty ground in the moonshade of the tree and trudged toward the cabin, not bothering to wipe the tears from his face. He should have realized. The nightmare was no dream; Mommy really was dead. She was beyond human help.

But as he passed close to the feed shed he heard a whimper. Chris paused, his fear building up again, and with it a feeble, futile hope. It could be a wild dog in there, or another ghost, or—something. Should he check? Curiosity warred with caution and fear.

He heard the sound again. This time it seemed like a woman crying.

Chris fumbled with the latch, then yanked the shed door open. Moonlight shone in.

There was no ghost. Only the great red saw, its bar and chain pointing forward like the muzzle of an alligator. Drops of dark fluid glistened on those teeth, and a black pool seeped into the floor beneath the squat body of it. Blood, of course; by daylight it would show red.

Suddenly Chris felt the immense, implacable menace of the brute machine. It was a killer of trees and men. He knew with intuitive certainty that it would kill again. Soon. The terrible threat of it radiated out like waves of heat. Grim, chilling heat.

Chris was so frightened that he could hardly think. He pushed closed the door and made his way back toward the cabin, full of a sick suspicion. The saw was waiting for Daddy. It had the patience of its kind. The time would come. It wanted Daddy, because if it took Chris himself or Sue first, Daddy would destroy it, but if it took Daddy first, he and Sue would not be able to stand against it. And Daddy could not be warned, because he pooh-poohed the supernatural. Probably Great-Uncle Elijah had not believed either.

If he told anyone, he would be branded a liar or a dope. He did not know whether he could stop the machine, but he had to try.

Monday was Labor Day: no school. Josh thought the children would be pleased, but Chris was strangely reticent. "What's the matter, son?" Josh asked.

"Daddy—can I watch you next time you saw?"

"Saw wood? I suppose so, one time or another, provided you stay clear."

"*Next* time. The very *next* time. Don't do it while I'm at school. Promise?"

Josh was surprised. What was bothering the boy? "All right. *Next* time. But I can't guarantee that will be very soon. I dulled the chain sawing through that roofing, and it will take me time to figure out how to sharpen it. Saw's not much use right now."

"That's okay," Chris said, seeming relieved. "No hurry."

Josh remained uneasy. Why this urgency to see the saw in use—but no hurry? On the morning run with the dogs he had noticed that the storage shed door had not been firmly closed. Someone had been there during the night. Had it been Chris?

Josh decided not to press; it would come clear in due course. There was indeed something about that saw; he had felt it himself, and so had the dogs. Chris might simply be reacting to Josh's own feelings. Josh would have to be more careful in the presence of the children; they were impressionable, and the grief of this family could sublimate readily into morbidity.

Patience Brown arrived promptly at eight, surprising him; he had assumed she would not work on Labor Day. "Had breakfast yet?" she inquired briskly.

"I'm afraid we slept late," Josh admitted.

She brought a grocery bag from her car. "Thought so. Come on in to the house."

"But we aren't supposed to use the house yet—"

She ignored him. Once in the house she unpacked crumb-buns and margarine and served them cold. They were nevertheless delicious.

"What do we owe you for this?" Josh asked.

Mrs. Brown handed him the cash register tape. It came to a hefty amount; she had evidently surveyed the family's haphazard stock and made a massive correction. Well, she knew her business. Josh wrote her a check without question.

At nine Carpenter arrived. Apparently nobody but the school and post office observed holidays locally. "Today should do it," he announced. "I've got the circular stairs in my truck. I'll phone in the inspector tomorrow morning."

Things were really moving along! "I wonder," Josh said to Mrs. Brown. "I daresay you have a lot of organizing left to do, and Carpenter is trying to wrap up his job—I suspect we'd just be in the way—"

"Yes," Patience agreed.

"Can you recommend somewhere we might go for the day?"

"Weekiwachee," she said, handing him a brochure. "Be back by six."

Josh turned to the children. "I think we have a big day coming up."

"Boy, she bosses you just like Mommy did," Chris muttered.

"It's her right," Sue said. "She's a woman."

Josh pondered whether to correct his daughter for such a remark, but reminded himself that she was only seven years old.

They piled into the bus and took off.

They made it home on time. Josh was tired; he had not enjoyed the excursion as much as the children had. He had seen bird shows before, and had taken boat tours before. The celebrated underwater mermaid show had contained only two mermaids, briefly, before lapsing into a rather corny skindiving skit.

But the trip had not been for his benefit but to amuse the children, and it seemed to have done that satisfactorily. He could not complain. In just two days he had to make a business trip north, and he wanted the children to have good associations here.

Meanwhile, Mrs. Brown had made giant strides in organizing the house and had an excellent supper ready, and Carpenter had installed beautiful circular stairs. The children were thrilled, and so, more sedately, was Josh.

Next day the County Building Department authorized a temporary permit for occupancy of the house. The following morning the power company connected full power. Mrs. Brown had already made up the beds Carpenter had fashioned from surplus plywood, and was ready to stay the night herself. Her competence was gratifying; he had made a fortunate choice.

Josh bid farewell to his children and the dogs in the morning, then went into the kitchen with his little tape recorder.

Mrs. Brown paused from her dishes to look askance at him. "I've made a recording for my children," he explained. "We always do it when I have to be away from them overnight. We don't like to be separated, since my wife died—"

"I know. I'm a widow."

"Yes. So we try to be together. One way or another. You can give the tape to them tonight."

She nodded and returned to her work. Evidently she was not much for modern gimmicks.

He had made the tape last night. "Hello, Chris. Hello, Sue," he had said. "I know you're feeling a bit lonely right about now. So am I. But I'll be back the day after tomorrow, and I'll bring you something nice. Now that we have power, I can set up the computer so you can play your games on it, too. So you two behave, and don't turn into little demons the way you usually do. Remember Mrs. Brown is only doing her job."

He paused. "What's that, Sue? Your teddy bear? All right, I'll try to bring that back with me. Chris, did you do your homework? Why not? Well, tomorrow you get it done, okay? Teachers are very fussy about that sort of thing, and you have to humor them. You may watch some TV tonight, but at nine you're through, no fussing."

He paused again. "Yes, I love you too. Here's a kiss. Don't fight over it. Remember how you fought over the last one and it landed on Pharaoh? The poor dog doesn't like kisses! Now get to bed and sleep." He knew they would be playing the tape again, at the appropriate hour, to make that part come out all right. And they would fight over that kiss, finally taking turns, taking it alternately as they replayed the tape.

"What's that? Oh, all right. Good night, Pharaoh. Good night, Nefertiti. Good night Hammerhead, good night Nurse—don't drink too much water."

He had stopped, smiling. That would cheer the children. Yet now he also felt tears in his eyes, and suddenly he wished passionately that he could stay here with them instead of going to New York.

He put the recorder on the kitchen counter. "That will do it, I think," he said. He fetched his small suitcase, went to the microbus, and drove south, toward the Tampa airport, away from house and tree.

Patience Brown was tackling the laundry. As with all disorganized households, this one was horribly backlogged on dirty clothes. Today the sun was coming out, after two days of disturbed weather. Hurricane D, the first really formidable one of the season, had missed Florida to the east; it had brushed Miami and cruised up the coast on its way to Georgia or Carolina. Here on the other side of the peninsula they had experienced only the outer fringe. Now, with luck, it would be possible to get a line of laundry dry.

Patience hauled the first load out to the yard where a nylon clothesline had been emplaced. Obviously a woman had been associated with these premises before, one who had planned to live here; the good washing machine and clothesline were evidences of that. Yes, the sun was emerging as the clouds cleared away. A gust of wind tugged playfully at her dress. It would be a good day. It needed to be, because hurricane F was on the way. Right now it was just a little tropical storm tagging along in the wake of D, like a child. No one was paying attention to it now, but Patience knew better than to ignore a child or a tropical storm. Either could mature rapidly into a robust adult, and if that storm landed here—

She paused, listening. Was that a train whistle? It certainly sounded like it. Too close to be from the line running through Floral City—but the old mining track that passed near here had been deserted and taken up. There couldn't be any train on that!

The whistle sounded again, louder. Definitely from the local track! Which was impossible. There were no rails at all. So there was no train.

Yet she had heard what she had heard. Her hair might be graying, but her hearing remained acute. Something had made that whistle, and that something was a train.

Patience experienced a prickle along her forearms. She had heard the wild stories of phantom trains but never credited them.

She could of course go down the tracks and check. Either something was there or it wasn't.

Patience shivered. No, she was not going down there! Better the mystery than the confirmation! She had a good job here, and she was not about to ruin it by getting spooked. She returned to her laundry with extra vigor.

Sue was lonely. It was not that Mrs. Brown was bad; she had fixed a pretty good dinner even if it did have yucky greens, and had made Chris do most of his homework, and had let them watch TV for an hour and bundled them off to bed and turned out the lights soon after nine. Sue knew that was what Mrs. Brown was paid to do, and she had done it letter perfect. She had even let them get away with quick washcloth washups instead of baths, because two days of cloud and one day of laundry had made the hot water too cold. She hadn't even yelled at them. No she didn't have any complaints there.

But Daddy was away. Mommy had gone and never returned. Sue knew that separation did not always mean loss, but she worried just the same. What would they do if they lost Daddy too? Daddy's tape was nice, but it wasn't enough. The bad fears always got worse when he was away. She should have told him to phone every night. Well, next time he went, she would. It was the kind of thing he didn't think of on his own.

Sue normally fell asleep early and slept soundly until dawn. Tonight, however, she came awake in the middle of the night. Something was bothering her, something she could not define.

Daddy was part of it; she had visions of the plane going down in storm, flames erupting, dropping into the ocean far from land, and oily bubbles coming up. She had seen scenes like that on TV, and they scared her. But no—Daddy could pretty much take care of himself.

Whatever it was, was closer to here. Something ugly and evil. She could almost smell it: dank, dark, pervading, yet not quite definable. Like fumes coming up from a graveyard. She had never actually sniffed such fumes, but she had a fair idea what they would be like, and this was it. The odor of death. Maybe.

Sue made her way quietly downstairs. She liked those spiral stairs; they were neat. Mrs. Brown had set little nightlights in the electric outlets, so that people wouldn't bump their toes into things. There was still a lot of junk around.

The dogs were sleeping on their cushions. They were supposed to be guard dogs, but a robber could come right in and they would snore right on. Unless the robber stumbled over Pharaoh in the dark. Then Pharaoh would bite him.

She glided carefully through the living room, trying to

orient on the wrongness, though it scared her. Better to find it—before it found her.

The feeling became stronger as she moved, until it was almost a mild burn on her skin, like a lighted match held too long.

She was standing before the fish tank. Sue could not see the two fish in the dark, only the outline of the aquarium, but the sound of the bubbler identified it for certain. The wrongness was inside it.

She could not prove it, but she knew for sure: one of the fish was going to die.

Patience was up early, as always. The two Pinson dogs looked at her, obviously expecting Mr. Pinson to appear and take them out for their constitutional. She opened the back door for them. Mr. Pinson had said to keep them always on the leash, but he was from the city. "You two don't need any supervisor out here in the forest," she told the dogs. "There aren't any cars to run you over. Get on out and do your stuff." They paused, hardly believing their fortune; then both launched themselves out the door.

Patience smiled. Dogs liked freedom to sniff about. They would be back in half an hour, satisfied, and probably sleep all day. She got to work on a pot of oatmeal for the children's breakfast and a cup of coffee for herself. She had brought her own; Mr. Pinson did not drink it. He didn't use aspirin either, or liquor, and he didn't smoke. *Really* didn't; there was nothing of that nature hidden about the house. Strange man! But that figured; by local accounts, his uncle had been much the same. The main distinction between them was that the uncle had been older and richer and hornier, with a kept woman. That was all she knew, but it was enough. It was hard to get authoritative gossip on short notice.

She roused the children. Both were logy, resisting the morning. She had understood that Suzanne, the little girl, was an early riser, bright and shining. Not this morning; she slept as if drugged. "Come on Sue—breakfast and school."

The girl groaned and turned over. Patience began to worry. "Are you sick, child?" She put her hand on the small forehead. It felt normal.

Suddenly Sue sat up, her eyes as round as those of a big doll. "Nurse!" she exclaimed.

"Nurse? I'm no nurse, child—"

But Sue scrambled up and ran for the stairs in her nightie. "My fish!" she called back by way of explanation.

Patience followed her down. The child had reached the goldfish tank.

The fish were all right. After a moment, Sue went back upstairs to get dressed. Patience decided that the child must have had a nightmare about her pet fish, and awakened to think it was true. That happened with children.

The boy bustled down. "Where's Pharaoh and Nefertiti?" he demanded.

Patience did not like such a tone from a child, but she repressed her irritation. "I let them out. Dogs need to get out."

"But Daddy said not to let them loose!"

"I'm sure they'll be all right," Patience said firmly.

Surprisingly, he said, "They won't run away. They like us. Only—"

Patience looked at him inquiringly, but he did not express his reservation.

After that, the morning was routine. Sue fussed over her oatmeal, but Patience was firm. The child pouted but obeyed.

The dogs had not reappeared by the time the children left for the school bus. Patience experienced a mild apprehension; could she have misjudged those animals?

She opened the back door. No dogs in evidence.

Lovebugs were clustered on the screen. Little black and red flying insects, mating on the wing, always flying in couples. They had a spring season and a fall season, and were usually worse in the spring, but there were more of them this fall than before. She closed the screen quickly. They were harmless, but a nuisance; they flew into everything and couldn't be shooed away.

Well, there was nothing she could do about them at the moment. She was sure the dogs would be all right. Dogs always came home in due course. Home was where the food was.

Let's see: she had dishes to do, and some more cleaning up. The house was not yet in proper shape. Packed cardboard boxes were littered all over the floor. She should check into some of those and see whether they could be moved outside. She did not like a cluttered house.

She got to it. The first box contained cans of whole wheat. Six five-pound cans, sealed. Now who in his right mind would want to can whole kernels of wheat? Curious, she read the label. Ninety-eight percent of the oxygen had been removed, it said. Ah—maybe this was vacuum packing. No air, no spoilage. That should keep a long time. But still— thirty pounds of it? Maybe the old man had been wholesaling it.

She checked another box. This one contained sealed cans of oats. Other boxes were stored under the couch. One box, however, was different. This one contained electronic things—a radio, a calculator, a watch, a funny flashlight, a thermometer with strange panels, assorted meters and things she could not define. These would have to be handled by Mr. Pinson.

She began to sweep. There was a commotion outside. She hurried out, broom in hand. The dogs were back—and were attacking the tethered pony. The female was just nipping at its heels, but the male was really vicious; he was leaping, trying to get his teeth into the throat. The pony was plunging about, trying to avoid them, but hampered by the rope.

"Stop that!" Patience cried, brandishing the broom, running toward them.

The dogs did not stop. By the time she got there, the pony had snapped the lead and was fighting back more effectively. The female dog yiped as a hoof clipped her glancingly, but the male dog would not give over. He was growling with a high tone, his fangs bared, charging in as though demonically inspired. Patience had never heard an uglier sound from an animal.

She waded in with her broom. Wham, wham! "Leave off! Leave off!" she cried, catching the dog on the flank. Surprised, he did so, retreating.

"Get on into the house!" she cried, advancing on him threateningly. "Move! Move!"

Both dogs, partially cowed by her tone and action, suffered themselves to be herded to the open door. At last they passed inside. She followed, closing the door firmly.

She was angry, but in control. "I won't punish you, because it's really my fault," she told the dogs. "I shouldn't have let you loose. But it'll be a cold day in hell before I let you loose again! Now you two settle down and stay out of trouble!"

The dogs took long drinks of water and settled down on their cushions, tired, as well they might be.

Chapter 9

Patience returned to her work, muttering. Whatever had possessed those dogs to act like that? Sand was all over the floor, tracked in by the animals and herself in her hurry. Lovebugs were flying in the kitchen, crawling over the clean dishes. Fornicating on the silverware.

That damned tree, she thought. That tree, growing so big, spreading its branches, cutting off the light, smothering out the grass, so there was nothing much but dirt left below, and shade for the bugs.

She swept the floor vigorously, wielding the broom as though it were a scythe. Chop down that tree, let the light in, let the grass grow, cut down the dirt, clear the bugs out. Take *that*, you infernal tree, and *that*! The dirt fairly flew.

The female dog watched. Nefertiti—that was her name. An Egyptian queen's name for an Egyptian breed of dog, though she was obviously a crossbreed, a mongrel. Normally alert and friendly.

She did not look friendly now. Slowly the dog's ears were tilting back, her eyes narrowing.

"What is it with you?" Patience snapped, swinging the broom near the dog. Nefertiti moved back, but her disquieting gaze remained fixed on the woman.

Patience continued sweeping, still cursing the tree. The
male dog, Pharaoh, was sleeping across a sandy patch of floor.
She had to sweep it. "Move it, mutt," Patience said,
nudging him with the broom.

Slowly the dog got up. That pony could have flattened him
with one good kick, had she had the freedom and the wit to
do it. But of course animals weren't smart. That was why
they were animals.

Pharaoh was now staring at her the same way as Nefertiti.
The look bothered Patience; it was no friendly or disinterested glance but a curiously hostile gaze. She had just seen
how savagely this animal could attack. She didn't want him
looking at her like that.

"Back off!" she snapped, gesturing at him with the broom.
The dog did, but only marginally. A meanness developed
about his muzzle.

Pharaoh made a small growl. He stepped toward her, his
legs stiff.

"Back!" she snapped, gripping the broom tightly with
both hands. The dog stopped, but did not move back.

Regular curs she could handle; there wasn't one of them
that a good smack with a broom wouldn't tame. But Pharaoh
frightened her.

Now Nefertiti moved, sidling around to the left. "You
too!" Patience cried desperately. "Keep clear!" These dogs
weren't acting natural. She did not like this at all.

Patience retreated—and both dogs advanced, stiff-legged.
Pharaoh's lip curled slightly, and his body lowered marginally as if preparing to spring. He was a lazy, somewhat fat
dog, but now he looked distressingly dynamic. Her broom
seemed inadequate. She might block off one of the animals
with it, but two—

Pharaoh nudged forward, his hackles rising. He whined,

almost like a child—but it was the whine of thwarted combat, not of pain or fear.

Patience stepped back again, broom held rigidly before her—and banged into the guardrail of the circular stair. Quickly she slipped around the rail and mounted the stair backward, not taking her eyes off the dogs.

The two animals lunged, perfectly coordinated. The stair was an open spiral, accessible from all sides; they could jump on under the rail. Hastily she backed up several more steps, avoiding the dogs.

But now they were scrambling to get on the stair. The dogs did not realize that it was easiest to go around to the lowest step; they were trying to climb directly onto the third step from either side. Patience swung the broom, not hard, because the rail interfered, and smacked Nefertiti on the nose. The dog yelped and dropped but immediately tried again, this time for the second step, squeezing up behind it, underneath the third step.

Patience turned and ran up all the way, grabbed the first cardboard box she saw, and shoved it to block off the top part of the spiral. It wasn't enough, so she took another, stacking it on top. And another. Soon she was panting from the exertion, but she had erected a waist-high barricade.

Pharaoh was having trouble navigating the stairs, but Nefertiti was working her way slowly up. She was evidently afraid of all the open gaps between steps, but gaining confidence each moment. Patience peeked over her barricade, finding this uncertain progress more alarming than a confident one would have been. It was as though the dog were possessed, her limbs operated by some alien will, making her clumsy but doubly dangerous.

Patience found her breath rasping, her heart thudding. Some of it was from the recent effort of lifting the heavy cases and shoving them into place, but more of it was from straight old-fashioned fear.

There was a whining beyond the barrier, and the sound of scratching. Patience found herself clenching her teeth. Why was she so desperate? All she had to do was reinforce the barrier; they would never be able to push through.

She moved boxes until her arms ached, trying to put the heaviest ones up high where they would anchor the light ones. Peas, beans, carrots, cheese, milk, their abbreviated labels said—food enough for a small army. The stair was now a dead end. She should be safe.

The phone rang downstairs. With dismay she listened to it ring itself out, the sounds becoming farther spaced as if getting tired, until at last they gave up. Who had it been? Mr. Pinson, calling to check on his family? What would he think, with no answer! Yet she did not dare remove her barricade. She would simply have to wait until help came. Maybe that nosy Old Man Foster—she could call to him from a window.

She went to the master bedroom. It overlooked the front porch, with the window casement solar collector on its roof, and it commanded a fair view south and west. The large south-leaning branch of the gross tree passed close to that collector, but did not interfere with the sunlight falling on it. In fact, it should be possible to climb out the window, onto the front porch roof, and step across to the branch and climb down it to where it came within three feet of the ground, south of the house. She was not eager to try that, however. In a real emergency she would do it—but not yet.

She sat on the bed, looking out. She knew she should do some housework up here, so as not to waste time—but if she did, she might miss Old Man Foster or whoever else came. Someone *had* to come!

For a long time she watched, tensely. The dogs scratched interminably on the stairs. No one came. Slowly her concentration diminished. She tried to remain alert, but something seemed to be putting her into a trance. As afternoon progressed, she fell asleep, her body sinking to the bed.

Beauty's ears perked up. She heard the sound of a distant motor, approaching. Still shaken from the attack by the dogs, she tried to hide from the sound, but the tether prevented her.

Then an old memory returned, evoked by the sound and the confinement. She was for the moment young again, just brought to a new and strange place, nervous about everything.

Children came, their voices shrill. "Lookit! A horse!" one boy cried.

"Not a horse, stupid!" a larger one said. "A pony!"

"Gee, let's ride it!"

They tried to scramble up on her back, but Beauty had not been broken for riding and did not understand. She shied away, and the smaller boy fell.

"Bad horse!" he screamed. He picked up a stick and struck her on the shoulder. The blow was not hard, but it did sting, and she squealed in protest.

"Oh, yeah?" the larger boy demanded. "We'll show *you!*" He fetched a stick himself and struck her across the nose. This blow was hard, and her nose was tender; the pain blinded her for an instant. She reared, seeking escape from it and her tormentors.

Then a motor sounded, loud and getting louder. It came close and a bigger boy jumped out. "What's happening?" he demanded.

"This horse's trying to kill us!" the smallest boy yelled.

"Yeah? Well, I'll fix that!" The newcomer jumped back into his motor and the sound of it became a roar. It started moving, and it turned to come right at Beauty. Not understanding, she stood there, and it banged into her flank and knocked her down. The pain was terrible.

The thing backed off, then came at her again as she scrambled back up. "Kill it! Kill it!" the smallest boy yelled gleefully. Desperate, afraid for her life, Beauty knew she could not escape. She had to fight. She reared, her front hooves coming down on the front of the motor. Glass flew, and there was new pain and now blood on her leg, but the motor stopped.

Now she was back in the present. The distant motor had faded; the threat was gone. There were prints in the ground where she had reared and struck in the course of her memory.

Calming, she remembered the rest of it. A man had come, an old man, and suddenly the boys and the motor were gone. The man had been angry, but not at her. He had taken her away and brought her to this place and taken care of her until she mended. She liked him. Then he had gone, and Horsewoman had come, and been kind too.

But still Beauty remembered the elements of her horror. Adults were nice, but children were not. If there was doubt about which kind a person was, there was one sure way to know: anyone who struck her on the nose was an enemy. Quiet motors were harmless, but loud ones were bad. The only way to stop them was to strike them with her hooves until they died.

But no one had done that, here. These children had not struck her, but she distrusted them. As long as the nice new man was here, she seemed to be safe from the children and from motors. He was like the one who had brought her here. But right now he wasn't here, and that made her nervous.

Chris banged into the house first. Both dogs charged forward to greet him. Nefertiti jumped up to lick his face, and Pharaoh made one of his rare barks. Chris put his arm around them both and hugged them. Then he headed upstairs, around the fun spiral of the new stairs, to dump his books on the bed.

There was a solid wall of boxes blocking the top. Amazed, Chris just stared at it. Then he yelled for Sue, just arriving.

She was as baffled as he. "Mrs. Brown must've done it," she said uncertainly. "But where is she?"

"Stuffed on canned food, maybe," he said, eyeing the titles on the cartons. "Hey, Mrs. Brown!" he yelled in a voice loud enough to rouse the vicinity. "Where are you?"

Then they heard her, stumbling on the far side of the barrier. "The dogs!" she cried. "Stay away from the dogs!"

The children exchanged glances on the stair. "What's wrong with the dogs?" Chris demanded.

"Don't let them—" There was a pause. "How did you get in? Where are the dogs?"

"They're right here. They're okay. We better take them for a walk and feed them supper, though."

"No walk!" Mrs. Brown pulled some of the boxes out of the way and came downstairs. Whatever malice had possessed the dogs had dissipated. She wouldn't say anything more about her reason for sealing herself off upstairs. Supper was late, but everything worked out well enough.

On Friday morning Patience nerved herself and took the dogs for their walk on their leashes. Both animals acted entirely normal. Today Mr. Pinson would return. She debated with herself whether to tell him about yesterday's episode. What could she say that wouldn't make her sound like a hysterical old woman? Better to keep silence.

One thing was sure: she would not again be bluffed by those animals.

Meanwhile, she thought as she and the dogs reentered the house, she had work to do. She would start by scouring out the sinks and toilets.

She did the bathroom first and paused at the fish tank as she headed for the kitchen. Nurse seemed to be ailing; there was discolor in her tail, changing it from gold to black. Probably not serious, but she would keep an eye on it. She knew Sue was concerned.

A linked pair of lovebugs flew down toward the surface of the water. She tried to shoo them away. but they landed in the tank, and before she could fish them out Hammerhead, in true sharkly fashion, snapped them up. Well, that probably didn't hurt; flies were the natural food of fish.

Patience moved on toward the kitchen—and froze. A woman was there, standing by the sink, pouring something into it.

Patience stared. The woman was not dressed for company; she was in a dull housedress, her hair bound back with a carelessly tied ribbon and bow, her feet in worn slippers. Just as though this were her own house.

Patience resumed her forward motion. "Who—?" she began peremptorily.

The woman looked up, turning at the sound. Her face was young and elegant. She did not seem surprised. Then she vanished.

Patience gaped. The kitchen was empty. The woman could not have walked out—yet she was gone.

Patience realized that she had seen a ghost.

Josh arrived home in mid-afternoon. Patience Brown met him outside. "This position is not for me," she said, tight-lipped.

Josh did not know how to deal with this. "Something's wrong?"

"No—no—I just feel it isn't right for me."

"Well, of course I can't hold you. Let's see what I owe you. Come on into the house and I'll make out a check."

"Not the house," she said instantly.

What *was* this? "Mrs. Brown, I assure you I will not harm

you. I just want to settle accounts." He looked at her. "Is it
something I have done?"

"No, you've been just fine, Mr. Pinson." She still was
not volunteering anything.

"The children? Did they misbehave?"

"No, nothing like that. You're a nice family. I just have to
go."

Josh went inside, set down his suitcase, and dug out his
checkbook. Everything seemed to be in order. He returned
outside and made out the check. "Look—there has to be
some reason. I thought you were working out well here. I
have certainly been satisfied, and if there is anything I have
said that suggested otherwise—"

"I said you're fine, Mr. Pinson."

"Then I think you owe it to me at least to tell me what
bothers you."

She sighed. "I'd better tell you, Mr. Pinson. It's only fair.
You'll think I'm crazy, and maybe I am, but—" She shrugged.

Josh began to have a premonition. He was tired from his
trip and realized he hadn't been fast on the uptake. "The
house—something about the house?"

"In a way. Mr. Pinson, remember when I said I'd believe
in ghosts when I saw one? Well, I saw one."

"Some trick of the light? I doubt—"

"This morning, in daylight. A woman in the kitchen—and
when I hailed her, she just—she was gone!"

"A woman," Josh repeated. "Maybe a neighbor?" Yet
the only neighboring female to come on the property was Pip
the horsewoman, and she would not enter the house unin-
vited. "You're sure she wasn't outside, with the animals?"

"Quite sure. She wasn't even dressed for outdoors. Young,
pretty, but not dressed. And I swear she just faded out like
smoke, not ten feet from me. Two days ago I heard the
phantom train. Yesterday the dogs treed me upstairs; some-

thing was *in* those animals, something that didn't like me. Today I saw a ghost. I don't know if it's me or the house— but Mr. Pinson, I've got to get out of here. It's not your fault at all. I like this job. I just have to go."

There was no arguing with superstition. "I understand. I'm sorry to lose you, Mrs. Brown, but I can't tell you that you didn't see what you saw. If you should change your mind—"

"I'm better off somewhere else." She went to her car. "I'm sorry, Mr. Pinson. I really am."

"I'm sorry too." Josh watched her drive away. No, he couldn't blame her. The stories about this place had gotten to her. Maybe Old Man Foster had spun her a lurid tale.

Josh had hardly started to unpack before Foster arrived. Think of the devil! Josh was tired, and uneasy about Mrs. Brown's abrupt departure; but he had to be polite. He went out to meet Foster. "Something up?"

"I seen Brown zoom by like a bat out of hell," Foster said with grim relish. "You fire her?"

"Of course not! Why should I fire her?"

"After the way she goofed off yesterday, sleeping upstairs instead of working."

"I didn't require her to work all the time! She was just here to keep the house in order and take care of the children." Then a tangent question occurred. "How did you know she was sleeping?"

"I came by, same's I always do. Knocked, and them dogs went crazy, but she never answered. Then your kids said she'd blocked off the stair with all them boxes so she could sleep in peace. Didn't you know about that?"

"I just got back. She told me the dogs had—I believe her expression was they had treed her."

"Them harmless mutts?" Foster asked derisively.

"Pharaoh is not harmless. He'll attack any other animal,

and sometimes a person. Nefertiti sometimes follows his lead. I can understand how Mrs. Brown could get concerned.''

"Same's Rooster Cockburn. That ol' bird goes after anything.''

"Rooster Cockburn? Apt name. I know how he is. I met him the other day.''

"He's been here? I've lost him. Been looking all over.''

"Why not let the ornery bird go?''

"Well, I let him be for a long time. Us tough old birds got to stick together, you know. But when he starts wandering, the neighbors start complaining. He speared a child yesterday; hand all bleeding, looked like a piece of shrapnel had hit that kid. So I got to put him away before the sheriff puts *me* away, don't you know.''

"I see. So that's why you're out today.''

"Yep. If you see Cockburn, give a holler. I'm going to make gristle soup out of him, more's the pity. Don't want him going after one of your kids.''

"I'll call you if I see him here. What's your phone number?''

"No phone. Just send a kid to yell. I'll hear. So why'd she leave?'' Foster asked abruptly, and Josh realized that curiosity had inspired Foster's visit as much as the business of the bird.

"She saw a ghost,'' Josh said with a straight face.

"That so? Which one?''

"A woman.'' Josh wasn't certain how seriously to take this.

"Must be that high school girl got raped here three years back. They say her ghost comes back under the tree—and gets raped again. Funny thing—'' He broke off.

"Funny?'' Josh prompted, finding this story unfunny.

"Sure. Because she ain't dead. You ever hear the like? Her ghost comes back, but she's alive. She moved out of town, of course, but—'' He shrugged.

The ghost of a *living* woman? "This ghost was a woman in the kitchen."

"Couldn't be. Weren't no house here when she got it. Man ran her down under the tree—" Foster broke off again, brightening. "Maybe it's still okay. Ghost is just where she always was, only the house was built around the spot."

"I had the impression this one was standing by the sink, not alarmed. Since the floor is above ground level—"

"Must be some other ghost, then."

Josh chuckled. "That must be it."

Old Man Foster toddled off. Josh went inside again. The dogs were glad to see him all over again, though he had been gone only a few minutes. They had driven Mrs. Brown upstairs? It must have been mostly her imagination. Dogs could be sensitive to human reactions. But she had seen a ghost in broad daylight. Perhaps there was an unstable streak in her. So Mrs. Brown's departure might after all have been for the best. But this was an uncertain conclusion.

Now he unpacked the six gold coins. He had had them checked by a reputable numismatist, who had informed him that each coin contained approximately 1.2 ounces of virtually pure gold worth several hundred dollars on the present bullion market; that these were not in good condition, but their special numismatic value would be much greater than that of their gold content alone.

Josh, taken aback, had decided not to market the coins. They were really part of Elijah's estate, and should be kept with it until settlement. But how had Elijah acquired them, and why had he hidden several thousand dollars worth of coins so carelessly? This find suggested that the man, whether sane or deranged, had had a good deal of money that the estate lawyer did not know about. Of course Old Man Foster had said Elijah avoided bankers. Still—

He heard the distant roar of the school bus. He put away

the coins and hurried out to meet his children. All else became unimportant in the face of that reunion.

Next morning Josh was out with the dogs as usual, enjoying what had begun to be a chore. A visit to the city really helped put the country in perspective. This forest took a certain getting used to, but this morning he liked it enormously. The grass was moist, gently soaking his feet as the dogs drew him through it. The dogs never wanted to stay on the neat, clear road, oh no! They had to plunge through the thickest of the thicket, entangling Josh in all sorts of inconvenience. On the other hand, it was pretty out here, and he might never have experienced the joy of such mornings unless the dog runs had brought him out. He hauled back on the leashes, slowing the pace to a walk.

Spiderwebs decorated the fields like so many six-inch dishes, outlined in detail by the condensed water droplets. Each had a tube forming in the center, going down, like a diagram of a black hole in space. By dry day not one of these networks was visible—which made sense, since what fly or bug would blunder into one of these traps if they were in plain sight? Though there were some little flying bugs these days, mating perpetually on the wing, that were stupid enough to go anywhere; their bodies were plastered all over the bus. Some predators Josh liked, and spiders were among that number: they preyed on bothersome insects. Except for the black widow spiders, which he understood were resident in these parts—but he doubted they would come seeking people to bite. He tried to avoid stepping on these pretty webs, though the dogs charged right through without noticing. There was one of the distinctions between dogs and men: the artistic or aesthetic awareness. Those webs were beautiful, and indirectly functional for man—but only man perceived this.

The sun cleared the obscured horizon. The light fell first

on the upper sections of the trees, illuminating the tops while leaving the bottoms shrouded. Down it crept, dropping inch by inch and foot by foot along the trunks of the trees, until at last the final vestige of night was vanquished and day reigned supreme. Lovely.

It was Saturday; no school, and they all could relax. Naturally, the children were up and about when he returned, more vigorous than on weekdays, eager to explore mysteries with him. They discovered the box of electronic items Mrs. Brown had set to one side.

The solar watch was not only running, but was right on time. It was one of the kind that shut down most operations when the light failed, while maintaining its time internally. That was pretty sophisticated; it had been months in that box. It was a calendar model, and it chimed on the hour. In short, it was a better watch than Josh had ever been able to afford. "Might as well use it," he said, putting it on his wrist. His regular watch was an old dial face windup that lost a minute a day; it could take a vacation.

The calculator also had a solar panel, and no ON/OFF switch. When the panel was shaded, the number display faded; when the light fell on it, the instrument functioned again. Such things had become commonplace, but this calculator seemed to be a fairly sophisticated one, with a number of special features. "To verify your homework," Josh said, passing it to Chris. The boy's eyes lit up.

The radio was another solar-battery item; it operated in and out of sunlight, but not when its panel was covered. It was FM; Josh located a classical music station and gave it to Sue, who liked music. She wrinkled her nose. "I like rock better."

"Rock!" Josh exclaimed with mock outrage. "This is for music!"

She turned the little dial until raucous strains emerged. "*That's* music, Daddy."

What a grab bag of trinkets Uncle Elijah had left here!
They quested on through the box. A solar-rechargeable
flashlight. A thermometer that flashed the current temperature—
75°—apparently by the device of individually attuned solar
panels. A translucent plastic rod that was warm—only slightly
warmer than the current ambience, yet it had to have been
dissipating heat all during the cooler night, too, which suggested considerable reserve capacity. Josh put it in the sun, to
see whether it would absorb more heat. It just might serve as
a footwarmer on cold nights. A light meter, self-powered. A
prism. Several items he could not yet identify.

The children were delighted, but Josh was pensive. All this
evidence of Elijah's hidden wealth—he hoped it had been
legitimately gained. Of course the man had been an extremely apt investor and trader. Had he not died prematurely,
he would have had an excellent life here. A person never
knew what fate had in store for him.

Chapter 10

In the afternoon Old Man Foster came. This time he was not toddling, he was lumbering, his cheeks red, his breath blowing. He was in pursuit of Rooster Cockburn, who arranged to remain just out of reach.

Josh moved out to intercept the rooster. The bird scurried back; he only attacked a person whose back was turned. Foster's left hand shot out and caught him about the neck. "Grab his feet!" Foster puffed.

Josh grabbed the rooster's feet, uncertain what the old man intended. Maybe a rope to tie the feet so the bird could not escape again. Now Rooster Cockburn was stretched out between the two men, wings flapping desperately, a half-strangled squawk escaping from his beak.

Then a wicked-looking knife was in Foster's right hand. He put it to the rooster's red-hued neck and sawed, heedless of the few feathers there. The bird jumped, wrenching one foot free of Josh's grasp, and made an awful shriek. Then blood spurted as the knife severed the artery.

Josh, appalled, let go of the other foot. Chris and Sue were standing nearby, their eyes wide with horror.

Old Man Foster dropped the body. The thing flapped madly, pumping blood, its head dangling crazily to the side.

It thrashed about on the ground, its wings catching and spattering the blood in a wide arc. Josh retreated squeamishly, but spots of red were already on his trousers. The bird seemed to take forever to die.

At last Foster carried his dripping prize away. "Come into the house," Josh said, herding the children before him. The two moved like little zombies.

"Did Mommy die like that?" Sue asked.

A new abyss opened beneath Josh. Mina had been killed by a bullet wound in the throat and had not lost consciousness instantly, according to the report. The rooster's demise—it was a closer analogy than Josh found tolerable.

"Mommy's death was a terrible thing," he said as calmly as he could. "There is no way I can hide that. But we are alive, and we knew she wanted us to keep going and to succeed. We have to try to forget. To remember her as she was in life, not as she died."

Damn that rooster, the highly visible and savage manner of his dying! Had Josh only realized what Foster had in mind, he would have insisted that the bird be taken home for the execution. To have it happen so brutally, with his children watching, and himself an accomplice!

"Did she run around and bleed with her head on sideways?" Chris asked, staring at nothing.

"No, no, of course not! Nothing like that!" Yet how could he be sure? Of all the things to happen here—!

The children, having made the nightmare transition from bird to Mommy, were both dissolving into tears. How could he shield them from that abyss, when it yawned just as compellingly for himself?

"Come on upstairs," he said. "We're in this together."

They went upstairs. Josh lay on his back in the center of the double bed, Chris on his right, Sue on his left. He drew them both in to him tightly. "Now we cry," he said.

They cried. The three of them lay close, hugging each other, and the tears washed across them all. They gave themselves up to unmitigated grief in a way they had not done before. It was not for the rooster, but for themselves and their loss. For Mina.

After a time they stopped. The children drifted to sleep, and Josh, pinned between them, slept too, but he did not wake refreshed. He felt logy, and his arms were hurting from the children's weight, and a pall of horror remained gripping his mind. A rooster, running about with its head half sawn off, pumping blood. A woman—

This was part of the necessary process, he thought with some other level of his attention. Shock had shielded them for a time, and then a kind of temporary expediency had taken over, tiding them through between crises for months. Then the move had taken their superficial attention. But now the relocation was complete and the tragedy remained unchanged, its horror spewing out anew, like dark blood. Its reality was infiltrating their few remaining bulwarks of resistance, soaking in, circling to the rear, enclosing them. The deep subconscious realization was rising like a dark tide, the ultimate knowledge that there was no mistake, no reprieve, no hope at all for redress or reversal. That there was to be no awakening from this nightmare. As with an alcoholic who had to admit he had a problem before he could be cured, the grieving had to accept the full extent of their loss before they could hope to recover from it. Somehow they had staved it off this long, this devastating reckoning—only to be caught off guard and dropped into the depths again. A necessary thing, perhaps, this final letting-go—but oh, it was a painful process! He had thought he had his emotions under control. Control? Obviously he had been fooling himself!

It was now late afternoon. Josh stirred. The dogs needed to be taken out, and he had to see about supper.

The children woke immediately. Josh hoped they would be refreshed, but again he was disappointed. The pall of gloom remained. It was as though some great storm system had moved in, chilling the air and dulling the sky and sinking its invisible fangs deep into the ground, freezing everything, refusing to pass on by.

"I feel like a plant with its stem cut off," Sue said. "The rot hasn't reached my head yet, but it's getting there."

Apt, awful image! Josh had seen such plants, still green and vigorous at the extremities, decaying at the base: dead without knowing it. "No rot for you, honey," he said firmly.

Josh got to his feet and limbered his arms. He started to fall and had to catch himself against the wall. He was dizzy, and it was no fun feeling.

He held tightly to the rail on the spiral stair, steadying himself as he tramped down. The dogs looked up; they too seemed listless and sad. Josh went around to the downstairs bathroom—and paused to look at the fish.

Hammerhead seemed to be his usually vigorous self. But Nurse seemed to be in trouble. There was a patch of dark brown on her tail that did not look natural, and another on her left fin. Some kind of fungus, he conjectured; and evidently it was sapping her vitality, for she seemed listless. He would have to get some medication to put in the water before the malady got worse.

He finished with the bathroom, then put the leashes on the dogs and took them out. They immediately headed for the spot where Rooster Cockburn had succumbed. Josh saw the scuffle marks and the dark spots where the blood had soaked into the dirt. Angrily he jerked the dogs away. But his eyes dropped to his own trousers, where similar spots remained. He would change clothing as soon as he got back to the house—but how could he clear the bloodspots from his soul?

In due course he returned. The children sat like mannequins on their chairs, staring at the table. They were taking this so hard! He wanted to cheer them but could think of no way.

Unless action would help. "Come on. Let's feed the animals."

"Pip does that," Chris said, uninterested.

"Who says she has to do it?" Josh demanded. "She just filled in while the farm was vacant. They're our animals now. We're taking care of them."

They went out. As it happened, the sound of horse's hooves was just becoming audible. Philippa was on her way. This was the second time that the thought of a person had seemed to bring that person. It was the kind of coincidence that seemed to be in vogue here.

"You folk look dreary indeed," Pip remarked as she dismounted.

"Old Man Foster slaughtered his rooster here," Josh explained. "It was an ugly scene."

"Rooster Cockburn? That old bird was overdue for it. He's attacked me several times."

"You feed Foster's animals too?"

"I check on them. He sometimes forgets. Animals can get by without feed for a while, but water is critical."

"But why? They're not your animals."

She furrowed a brow at him. "Would you want an animal to suffer?"

"No, of course not," he said. "Yet in the case of Rooster Cockburn—"

"Sometime remind me to bore you with my ponderous philosophy of animals," she said. "And reminiscences pertaining thereto. When you have a great deal of time to waste, because I'm a motor-mouth on the subject. I don't regret Cockburn's end, but I would not have allowed him to starve."

"I suppose not," Josh said uncomfortably.

"Funny things happen around here." She wrapped up the chores and mounted. Her gaze swept across the huge branching canopy above. "But what a lovely tree! That justifies it all. Bye." She was gone with the sound of galloping hooves.

"I should do my own chores," Josh muttered. Once again he had stood befuddled while she had done his work under his nose. He looked around, realizing that his children had disappeared. They were hiding behind the massive trunk of the tree. "What happened to you, kids?"

"We like the tree," Chris said, awkwardly. "It's friendly."

"Pip doesn't like us," Sue added.

"Has she ever said so?"

"She doesn't have to," Chris said. "She glares."

Josh returned to the house with the children. The gloom closed in again. It had abated briefly with the arrival of the horsewoman, as though a ray of sunshine had momentarily penetrated the encrouching clouds. He rummaged in the refrigerator and found the carefully packed remnants of several prior meals. Mrs. Brown had been fastidious, wasting nothing. If only she hadn't seen the ghost.

They ate reheated leftovers. The children did not complain; they consumed it mechanically, still brooding. The nature of the meal seemed in keeping with the mood.

After supper, Josh turned on the television set. Elijah had been no recluse from civilization; he had installed a forty-foot antenna tower with a rotor, and a citizen's band radio set with a call number and the "handle" pasted on it—the handle was "The Prophet"—and a shortwave radio as well. Josh was no authority on this sort of thing, but suspected that his uncle had been able to tune in the whole world at will and broadcast to it too. The lack of electricity had prevented Elijah from getting the equipment all operative at this site— unless he had sneaked in a line, a distinct possibility—but obviously he had been long conversant with communications.

This must have been handy for building his fortune—and Josh could only hope it was an honest fortune.

However, though the tower brought in twelve television stations, none of the programs seemed worthwhile to him or the children tonight. The gloom rendered everything drab. Finally, by common consent, they turned it off, went upstairs, and turned on a radio: a station with meaninglessly popular songs interspersed with ads that could be safely tuned out. That held the silence at bay but did not really cheer them.

This was awful. There seemed to be no way to fight out of the depression they were all mired in. Josh knew exactly how the children felt, and therefore could not disparage it.

"This is not considered good child management," Josh said. "But I know neither of you wants to sleep alone tonight, and neither do I. We're all suffering a reaction, and I guess we'll all just have to ride it out together. It's like a storm. It's terrible to be in, but may clear the air. Get changed to your nightclothes, and we'll sleep on my bed."

They scurried about and in seconds were ready. Yes, they did not want to be alone! The three of them settled on the bed.

"Daddy, tell us an imagination," Sue pleaded.

"I'll try," Josh said. Maybe that little game of theirs would work. "You see this bed?" he asked rhetorically, and both children nodded obediently. "See how it sort of floats in the room, with no visible support? Of course we know it's just two sections of heavy plywood that the carpenter set up on three little drawer sets, but right now we can think of that plywood as the bottom of our boat. Imagine it floating, rocking about on the gentle swell of a mighty ocean. Now we start the motor—it's a very quiet motor, you can't hear it at all, unless you really want to, and then it's just a little thrum-thrum way down under—and it starts our raft moving out into the middle of the room. Now we're going on out through the wall—this is a fun house, there are lots of things we don't know about it, and we've just discovered that the walls are only mirrors, not really there, so we're floating through the mirror like Alice in Wonderland, going on into a nice bright world outside where our night is their day and they have three brilliant suns, one blue for Chris's blue eyes, another brown for Sue's brown eyes, and the third just sort of bleary mottled red like my eyes.''

They chuckled dutifully. Josh's eyes, of course, were blue. Yet their hearts weren't in it; the gloom had not lifted.

''Now we're floating over seaweed flowers, all sparkling and pretty, and some of them have little flower faces, and when you listen you hear the sea inside them, because they grow out of shells. Some shells are very big and they have little puppy dogs inside; I think that's where we got Pharaoh and Nefertiti, only Pharaoh was too fat to fit and his tail got all jammed and never did uncurl.'' He took them on through his imaginary land, floating on the bed, a royal trip.

Almost, it worked. He did have the sensation of floating, but the images he described never came fully clear. The gloom retained its implacable grip, no matter where they traveled, and at last Josh brought the floating bed home, defeated. They slept, and he woke at odd times to hear little sobs in the night, and knew that a nightmare had pursued Sue in her dreams.

In the morning it still had not lifted. Josh made one more great effort: ''Where's a good place to visit on a Sunday?''

''The kids at school say Fort Cooper's fun,'' Chris said without enthusiasm.

Josh had seen it on the map. ''We'll go there. If it's no fun, we'll come back.''

They did not argue. They were well behaved, the way they had been in the first week after Mina's death. Little automatons, living strictly by the book, emotionally damped. Now the shadow was back in full force, Stygian, awful.

Josh plowed ahead. In due course they loaded into the bus and drove off.

Hammerhead was worried. Nurse was listless, refusing to play chase around the tank, leaving much of her food for him to scavenge. She had never been as lively as he, but now she was no fun at all. She just rested on the bottom and brooded.

But he was not feeling very spry himself. It had started yesterday with an awful feeling of destruction, as though Nurse had suddenly leaped out of the tank and drowned. She hadn't, but the mood had clung. All night there had been brooding horror, the incipience of death. The water tasted insipid, as though it had gone stale, though it really wasn't.

In the morning the shapes had come with the food—but even the shapes seemed repressed, moving slow, quiet. Soon they had gone, and the region was still. Sunlight streamed in, warming the water, but the gloom remained. The whole environment was stifling.

Then in the afternoon it became worse. Something really terrible loomed, something so awful that Hammerhead had to flee in terror—yet there was nowhere to flee. Nurse felt it too and sank to the lowest corner. They huddled together while the horror drew near outside, overwhelming—and abruptly burst.

It had after all been a good excursion. The gloom had lifted at Ft. Cooper park and they had all enjoyed themselves. There had been swimming and a beach and a nature trail that wound about the wilderness vegetation. A play ball had been lost out in a swampy region, and Josh waded out through the water grass to recover it, and then Sue had let the ball get carried too far out by the wind and it had been lost in the swamp again. This time they let it go.

They followed another road that led to the battlefield monument. It seemed Ft. Cooper had been used in the war with the Seminole Indians. Josh had been glad to fill in this bit of local history for himself and the children.

In December 1835, that lore went, the Seminoles had reacted against broken treaties and gone back to war against the United States government. They massacred over a hundred soldiers at Ocala, and held off the Florida Volunteers in the Battle of Withlacoochee.

"Withlacoochee!" Sue exclaimed. "Isn't that our forest?"

"Sure, dummy," Chris said. "And the Seminoles play football."

"Uh, yes," Josh agreed. The Seminoles were the Florida State team. "But these were the original Seminoles—the Amerind tribes who lived here."

"Hey! Maybe we'll find some arrowheads!"

"Maybe." He continued with the historical narrative. General Scott had marched on the Tsala Apopka lakes region to deal with the matter. But what had been anticipated as a brief campaign turned out otherwise, and the war stretched out seven years.

"Those Seminoles are tough," Chris remarked with satisfaction. Josh wasn't sure which ones the boy was thinking of.

In the course of this war, Fort Cooper was set up on the shore of Holathlikaha Lake for the care of the wounded. Chief Osceola was determined to annihilate this fort. Five hundred Indians stormed it unsuccessfully. The Indians shouted obscenities and bared their buttocks toward the fort, trying by these insults to make the soldiers waste cannon shots.

Chris and Sue thought this hilarious. "Let's play soldier and Indian," Chris suggested to his sister. "You be the Indian, and bare your butt, and I'll fire my cannonball up your—"

"Enough," Josh interposed, smiling. This was not precisely the aspect of history he had intended to impress on them, but it was wonderful to see them grinning.

Then they had driven back past Inverness, and Josh had mentioned that it had been named after Inverness, Scotland, near Loch Ness where the nefarious lake monster lurked. "Did the monster come over here too?" Chris asked.

"Well, I don't know about that, though the Tsala Apopka chain of lakes might be a good place for it. Of course they may not be deep enough—"

"Pop-pop-apop-ka! That's what the monster would say," Sue said brightly. "And it eats salad-pop. Salad-a-popka."

"That's Tsala-pop," Chris corrected her.

"Actually there may be something," Josh said. "I understand this is the home region of Bigfoot, or some similar monster. There are supposed to have been sightings. So if there doesn't happen to be an Apopka monster in the lake, you could keep a lookout for—"

"Yeah," Chris said zestfully. "The lake was too shallow, so it slogged out to the forest."

"Is that the monster that's around the house?" Sue asked.

Josh was startled. "What monster around what house?"

"The one we smell under the tree, sometimes," she said.

"My nose has clouded up pretty much since Friday," Josh said. "Have you smelled it, Chris?"

Soberly the boy nodded. "At night sometimes. It smells big and evil and awful."

Josh remembered the night the shed door had been unlatched. "You go out at night?"

"Only once, when I heard Mommy call. Only it wasn't Mommy, it was a ghost a man was chasing."

Josh remembered the story of the raped girl. "You saw this ghost?"

"Yes. But when I tried to help, there was nothing. Then I saw the saw bleeding—"

This was getting too serious. "Well, next time you smell the monster, tell me, and I'll go out and bop the creature on the snoot until it promises to take a bath."

"Okay, Daddy," Sue agreed, but she didn't smile.

They were now traveling north on Forest Drive, almost home. Tomorrow would be school again, back into the normal routine. Josh was glad he had taken them out to the park; it had done the job.

He threaded the access drive. The shadows were slanting longer, and the magnificent tree rose like a distant mountain, its leaves dense and dark.

"Daddy!" Chris screamed, pointing ahead.

Josh slammed on the brakes, throwing out his right hand automatically to protect the children, though of course the seat belts took care of that. The bus skidded, and the three of them were hurled against the restraining harnesses as their picnic basket slid forward.

Across the road was the prone body of a man.

"Stay in the bus," Josh snapped. He unbuckled and jumped out, alarmed. He hoped the body was a trick effect of the late afternoon light, that it would turn out to be a fallen log, an optical illusion, even another ghost. He became conscious of a faint unpleasant odor, as of something decaying. He put that aside, intent on the fallen man.

For it was indeed a man. It was Old Man Foster. His face was frozen in a rictus of horror, and there were scuff marks on the ground where he had evidently dragged himself along. He was dead.

Josh was in a shocked quandary. He should not disturb the body, but he did not want the children to see it up close. He could not drive around it, and if he had them walk to the house they would pass close by.

Well, his children were more important than the dead man. He got his fingers under Foster's shoulders and dragged him into the brush. The man was remarkably heavy: a literal deadweight.

Josh returned to the bus, rubbing his hands against his trousers. "I think it will be better if you don't look," he told the children. "It is Mr. Foster, and he—there is nothing we can do for him."

"Did Bigfoot kill him?" Chris asked.

"Of course not. He—he was an old man. When people get too old, they—wear out. It is a natural process." Then, to forestall the inevitable: "Not the way it was with your mother. She died out of turn. This is different. None of us need to fear death of old age." Yet the expression on Foster's face, as if he had glimpsed a demon from hell . . .

They were silent as he restarted the bus and drew it up to the house. Of all the times and places for the old man to die, this was the worst! What nightmares might the children suffer now?

As they got out of the bus beside the house, Josh saw that the feed shed door was hanging open. "Go on inside," he told the children. "I'll be right with you."

Foster's scuff marks had started here, as though his heart had begun its failure by the shed, and he had tried to stagger home before it finished him. It looked as though he had clung to the shed door, perhaps after opening it.

Inside the shed, the dread saw sat askew, its ugly and glinting chain pointing outward as if it had been reaching for something. More red oil was spilled on the floorboards.

A natural death?

Josh shoved the door closed and latched it. What he imagined was impossible, and he put it determinedly out of his mind.

Back in the house he phoned the sheriff. In half an hour a

crew arrived. Josh was glad to let them handle it, but he could not avoid the questioning or shield the children entirely. "Another victim of the shade of the tree," the sheriff remarked, as though this were commonplace.

The preliminary conclusion of the officials was that Foster had died of heart failure, exactly as Josh had conjectured. There was no question of physical foul play. Foster's fingerprints were on the shed door; he had opened it for a reason unknown (but easy enough to conjecture: to borrow feed for an animal), and at that moment nature had caught up with him.

Yet Josh could not escape from that one sight of Foster's dead face, lying sidewise in the dirt: that look of horror. Not pain, not worry, not even really fear. Just stark, absolute, mind-consuming horror. As though the man had seen something so awful it had stopped his heart, literally.

Suppose there *was* a monster, horrible beyond belief, and Foster had seen it, there by the shed? Now Josh remembered the smell he had encountered, there at the body, strong enough to penetrate his stuffed nose. It could have been from the body, of course, but somehow it had seemed more general, as though something foul had recently departed the vicinity. Bodies did not spoil that quickly, did they, even in this hot climate? So something else—

No, nonsense, he told himself angrily. His imagination was getting out of hand. The forest floor had an odor sometimes, as leaves and fallen wood rotted; Foster had merely scuffled this up in the course of his laborious progress.

What, then, of the saw? How had it moved? Had the old man tried to pick it up, and overstrained himself? Or had it moved toward him on its own? *That* could account for the man's fatal horror!

No, again. Of course not. Obviously Foster had started to pick up the saw, perhaps just to move it, then suffered some sort of shock. Perhaps the sight of the seeming blood under the saw—that certainly made sense. Yes, that had to be it. Foster would not have opened the shed for feed; he paid little attention to animals. He had wanted to borrow the saw. Nothing supernatural here. After all, the saw had not even been running.

Why, then, was there such an aura of menace about it, even when it was idle? Josh thought he had conquered that fear, but it now seemed it had only abated temporarily. The saw radiated renewed evil.

He was overreacting, he decided as the sheriff's men departed. That was to be expected. Sudden death was always upsetting.

Chapter 11

In the morning, Monday, Josh packed the children off to school as usual, except that this time he walked with them to meet the school bus. He did not say so, but he wanted to be quite sure that no more bodies lay in the road and that there was no ghost where Foster had been. Of course there was no such thing, but the children might think they saw it, without the steadying presence of an adult.

After the bus passed, Josh walked on south to Foster's farm. Sure enough, no one had fed his animals the prior night; probably no one had checked his premises at all. The caged rabbits were ravenous, and the cats fawned at him desperately. Josh poked about the feed shed and located chicken feed and dog food. He tried the latter on the cats and it seemed to do. It was certainly all right for the dogs.

There was a large fallen branch in the front yard, too big to haul away by hand. Obviously it would have to be sawed up—and probably Foster didn't have a saw. There was the motive for borrowing Josh's saw.

Then he heard approaching hooves. He knew whom that would be!

"Now you understand," Philippa said as she dismounted.

"Now I understand," Josh agreed. "The animals must not suffer neglect. Where were you yesterday?"

"Off on a business trip. I shouldn't have gone; it seems all hell broke loose. How did Foster die?"

"At my place. By the feed shed—well, he dragged himself up the road. Heart attack."

"I don't believe that. He was old, but I'm sure his heart was sound. He walked around a lot: good exercise."

"Maybe a monster scared him."

She burst out with that ready laugh. "Why don't you take the morning feeding, and I'll take the afternoon, until someone takes over here," she suggested.

Josh smiled. "I can see you've been through this before. Who'll buy the feed?"

"I'll do it," she decided. "I'll send the bill to Foster's estate."

"When do I get the bill for the Pinson estate?"

Again the laugh. That, it seemed, was all the answer he was going to get.

"Actually," Josh said, "I have to get moving on my next project, or I won't be able to afford much feed of any kind." He wasn't going to touch those six gold coins until he knew their origin.

"What is it that you do?" Pip inquired.

"Oh, didn't I tell you? I'm a free-lance computer systems consultant." He paused because a low-flying jet plane passed at this point, drowning out conversation. It was a swift swept-wing job, handsome enough, flying substantially ahead of its sound. "It's my job to select the best feasible computer system—that's hardware and software—for the particular application, and adapt it to the need, and get the regular company personnel started using it. I took a vacation while I was getting my family moved, but now I have accepted an assignment involving the payroll and inventory of a large merchandiser. I'm going to have to take a crash course in accounting procedures so I can organize it.''

"Accounting procedures," she repeated thoughtfully.

"Yes. Something new each time. That's the way I like it.''

"You can do that? Master an entire separate discipline for the sake of a single project? I should think you would go broke just getting through it."

"I *have* to do it. It's the only way to formulate a system efficient enough to make my fee become a bargain. I am not inexpensive." He smiled ruefully. "But when I made this contract, I did not anticipate having a man die virtually on my doorstep. I'm going to have trouble getting the necessary concentration."

"Maybe you need a good public accountant to help you get into it."

Josh considered. "Yes, maybe so. I had planned to hit the books—I mean, the interactive courses I can run on my computer. I'm a very quick study on such things. But now—"

"I happen to have the number of the best free-lance CPA in Inverness. Would you like it?"

"Yes. Yes I would," Josh said, brightening. "A person remains better than a computer, so far. It can't do any harm to check, and if it doesn't work out I can still research it on my own."

"It is P. Graham, at 726—"

"Wait, let me get that down!" Josh fished for his little notepad and pencil. She gave him the number, then mounted her steed and trotted off.

Josh walked home, considering. Sooner or later he would have to reach out, start finding local resources. Why not now?

At home he telephoned the number immediately. A man's gruff voice answered. "Graham."

"I'm looking for a CPA," Josh said. "Have I the right—?"

"Oh, sure," the man said. "Just a moment. Who is—?"

"The name is Pinson. I want to see about—"

"Right. Be right back." There was a click as the phone was set down.

There was a long pause. Then the man was back. "Can't make it to the phone right now. Appointment for Thursday?"

"Well, I just wanted to—"

"Ten A.M. do? Or later?"

"I really had in mind—"

"Ten, then. Got the address?"

"No, I—"

"It's tricky to find. Better jot down the directions."

Josh did so. These backroads developments seemed to be purposefully devious, with T intersections, dead ends on the main roads, and loops. At least it did not seem to be too far away; all these 726 prefix telephone numbers seemed to be in the same general area.

Meanwhile, he had the fencing to attend to. That look of horror on Old Man Foster's dead face still unnerved him. There was a feeling of security in a good fence that the children needed now. That *he* needed now.

Josh decided to begin at the south boundary, near the intersection of Forest Drive and Pineleaf Lane. First he cut a path through the palmetto thicket along that boundary, so that he had room to install the fence. Then he struggled with the posthole digger, trying to set the posts in more or less uniform manner along Forest Drive, from the bus stop north to the mailboxes, from which he could cut back west along the private drive, and so on around the house and eventually back along his new-cut path to the bus stop again, enclosing perhaps three acres. That should do for a start.

His arms quickly tired, and his first few posts were
not well aligned. Yet now that he was into it, he wasn't
satisfied just to string barbed wire around trees; a fence
was also a demarcation and needed to be somewhat aesthetic
in itself.

At last he gave it up for the day. He simply was not
acclimatized to such physical labor, and there was a lot more
work to such a fence than he had guessed. His arms and
shoulders were bone-weary. Time to go in and relax with
Mina for a while.

Mina. There he was, forgetting again. No one awaited him
inside. Not even a housekeeper. He would have to check the
ads and get on the phone and go through the whole tedious
process again, because in two weeks he had an update con-
sultation in New York that could not be missed. He had to
have someone reliable by then, and preferably well before
then. He should have gotten on the matter of the replace-
ment housekeeper the moment Mrs. Brown quit. He tended
to forget household details, since Mina had always taken
care of them, and this delay was bound to get him into
trouble.

Josh entered by the back porch. He was hot and thirsty; as
he passed through the back door he turned left toward the
kitchen.

There was a woman there. She was standing by the sink,
pouring something into it, facing away from him. She seemed
familiar.

"Mina!" Josh exclaimed, even as he realized that it was
impossible. Mina was dead. It had to be Patience Brown,
who had changed her mind and returned.

The woman turned. But as her face came into view, framed
by her fair hair, Josh saw that she was a stranger. She was a
well-endowed woman perhaps in her forties, in an ankle-
length skirt and a somewhat frowzy housecoat, with frown

lines about her mouth. In her youth she must have been beautiful, and she remained striking, but the flush was gone.

"Who are you?" Josh asked, taken aback.

She glanced up at him, possibly contemptuously. Then she faded.

Josh stood staring. In a moment the woman was gone. There was absolutely nothing there.

He had seen the ghost.

He went into the living room and sat down. The two dogs came up for petting, and Hammerhead eyed him curiously from the tank. "Did you see it too?" he asked the dogs. But he had no way to know. Pharaoh would have reacted angrily to any intrusion by a stranger, but Pharaoh had been asleep until Josh walked by him.

It had been a figment of his imagination. He was tired, and had been thinking about the need for a housekeeper, and his fancy had granted him a vision, a waking dream, a wish fulfillment of sorts: Mrs. Brown coming back.

But the woman had been different. She had resembled neither Mrs. Brown nor Mina. He had never seen her before.

Chris had reported seeing a woman in the night that he thought was his mother but had turned out to be a ghost. The ghost of the girl who had been raped, and who was not dead. A different ghost, but nevertheless a ghost. Mrs. Brown herself had seen the kitchen ghost. All three sightings here in the shade of the tree.

One thing about the ghost: she had not been malignant. She had seemed entirely innocent, unlike the chain saw. She had not been trying to frighten him. He had spun a fantasy, his suggestibility enhanced by fatigue.

He heard a clamor outside. It was after four, and the bus had roared away. The children were home.

Chris burst in. "Hey, Daddy—there's a new path in from the bus stop!" he exclaimed.

Sue went for the aquarium. "Nurse is worse!" she wailed. Josh had not thought to check the fish. He came wearily to look. Sure enough, most of her tail was brown, now, and the left fin, and a spot on her left side behind the gill. Hammerhead, in contrast, was his normal resplendent gold, and had more vigor. Sue was quite concerned, and Josh could hardly blame her. "I'll change the water and get some medicine," he said, and Sue responded with a fleeting waif-smile.

"Say, are we going to get another housekeeper?" Chris demanded as he served himself vanilla ice cream. The children's tastes in desserts matched their hair: Chris liked yellow, Sue liked brown. Josh liked to tell them that if they ever got confused, and reversed their ice creams, Chris's hair would turn chocolate brown and Sue's vanilla yellow. They affected horror at the notion, and confined themselves to their regular flavors.

Housekeeper. Josh sighed. "We'll have to. I can't guarantee that whoever I find will be as good as Mrs. Brown was, but we'll have to have someone."

"Aw, she was okay, but she got spooked too easy. She was scared of the dogs."

"Did she really see a ghost?" Sue asked. She had gotten out the chocolate ice cream. Josh didn't like the additives and things in commercial ice cream, but had realized long ago that he was apt to do more harm to his children by trying to keep them away from it than any additives could do.

"We can't be sure what Mrs. Brown saw. Certainly she believed she saw a ghost, and I can understand—"

"Daddy, I know someone who'd be great for a housekeeper," Chris said.

Josh smiled. "You know a housekeeper?"

"Well, I don't exactly know her, but Billy's big sister takes care of all six of them when their folks are away, and—"

"Who is Billy?"

"Billy—I don't guess I know his last name yet. He's in my class at school. His big sister's real old—seventeen or eighteen. She's out of school, even. She used to be a real good baby-sitter, but now she's not doing anything much. I bet she'd come if you asked her."

A classmate's big sister. Well, girls matured early these days. It was just possible she might do on an interim basis, until he found a competent woman. The children would be less likely to give her trouble if they were involved in the selection process. It might be considered part of growing up. "All right. Give Billy our number and tell him to have his sister call us if she's interested."

"She's real good," Chris assured him hopefully.

Josh tousled his son's hair. "She'd better be."

Hurricane D had been a bruiser, but had rolled up the east coast of the state. Little storm F had drifted in D's track, then fallen south and stumbled the entire length of Cuba, degrading itself below even storm status, so that it emerged into the Gulf of Mexico as a mere tropical depression. Chris had rooted for the underdog, hoping that little F would recover and become the worst hurricane of the century. Josh had told him jokingly that he identified too much with the letter F because of his grades in school. Heeding the boy's encouragement, F had responded; hourly it grew stronger, passing into storm status at 35 mph winds, then into hurricane status at 75 mph, then into major hurricane status at 130 mph. Chris was ecstatic, but Josh was concerned—for F was zeroing in on Citrus County, Florida. Already its perimeter circulation was gusting here, southeast winds just hinting at the power to come.

But Hurricane F seemed to be passing Florida to the west,

going north instead of recurving east. Now the Florida panhandle was bracing for its onslaught, while it seemed that charmed Citrus County would escape again. Somehow Josh got the feeling that every tropical storm had its violent, whirling eye focused on him personally and wanted to cut its terrible swath across his property. That was just his private paranoia about big storms, probably shared by every person in the state except those who foolishly lived on the beaches— the ones most likely to be wiped out. The "What—me worry?" kind.

This was Tuesday, September 11th: school picture-taking day, already. Josh had methodically posted all such events on his calendar, the way Mina used to, so as not to forget. In his day, school pictures had been taken at the end of the year; evidently it took much longer to process them now. He had made sure the children were properly dressed and coiffed this morning, hoping a gust of wind wouldn't mess them up just before the camera shutter clicked. He also hoped they didn't decide this was the occasion to play Picture, in which the object was to smile angelically until that fraction of a second when the shutter clicked, at which point the foulest of faces was substituted to be recorded for posterity. Then back again to angel face. Properly executed, this maneuver happened so quickly that the photographer never realized its significance— until the picture was developed.

Josh returned to work on the fence. The day was mostly overcast with layers of cloud scudding rapidly by, occasionally dropping small showers. His rain gauge indicated only two tenths of an inch all day, but it seemed like more when he was trying to set posts in it. Josh plodded on, his shoulder muscles hurting, and slowly the line of posts lengthened.

On Wednesday Hurricane F struck the Mississippi–Florida panhandle coast, wreaking the damage of the century. Chris's wish had been fulfilled, and for that Josh felt obscurely guilty.

There was more rain, and the local gusts became fiercer. At one in the afternoon a line of clouds charged by, and the wind turned ravenous. It stirred up dust devils and whorls of leaves and made the trees bend back and forth as if in agony. Josh hurried to get inside. A shower of pine needles blew down as he passed by the handsome pines, and a cone smashed into his shoulder with force enough to make him jump. These cones were big, solid things, seven or eight inches long, with cutting hooks around the surface: halfway formidable missiles.

There was something awesome about the strong wind; invisible yet making its effects highly visible. Josh found himself moved and even frightened by it. At the same time, he enjoyed it; the elemental power of it invigorated his spirit. To ride the wind . . .

As he approached the house he heard the phone ringing. How long had it been going? He hurried inside, afraid it would stop just before he got there. Phones enjoyed doing that.

He was in luck. "Mr. Pinson?" a dulcet female voice inquired. "I almost gave up on you. This is Brenna Sears. I understand you are looking for a housekeeper?"

Housekeeper. "You must be Billy's sister!"

"That, too," she agreed.

"I'm not sure what the kids told you," Josh said. She sounded so young! "I am a widower with two children, and—"

"I've got five younger siblings," she said. "They've already handed in their spy reports. They say the boy's hyperactive and the girl's a little genius."

Josh laughed a little uneasily. "Some intelligence system, your siblings! It's an overstatement, but Chris is hyperkinetic and Sue does do well in school. But what I really meant to say was—''

"That your house is haunted," she finished. "It sounds fascinating."

"It drove our first housekeeper away. She saw a ghost, and I have to confess that I—''

"A ghost! Wonderful! I've always wanted to meet a genuine live ghost."

"Well, ghosts are normally dead, though these ones—''

"Oh, sure. You know what I mean."

She might change her mind if she had an experience like his. But at least she had been warned. "Actually, there may be a question of propriety. You see, I work at home, and you're seventeen—''

"Nineteen, Mr. Pinson," she said firmly. "But don't worry. My mother thinks I'm still thirteen, so she looks out for me. She drives me to any jobs I get and brings me back. I've got my driving license, of course, but no car."

This promised to be even more awkward. "We're some distance from town—''

"Twelve miles. We're halfway there. It's not so bad. Mr. Pinson, I really need this job. I'm going stir-crazy at home. Let me come over and give it a try. I do know how to manage children; I've had a tremendous lot of experience there. I work hard—''

Josh was embarrassed. A young girl who wanted to get away from home and needed money: that hinted at all sorts of potential trouble. Yet she might be all right. He felt right about neither yes nor no. "Well—''

"I could come in tomorrow—''

She was certainly eager. "I have a prior appointment," he said, glancing at the calendar by the phone. That was his day for the accountant.

"Friday, then. If you don't like me, you can kick me out."

There were overtones of other than housekeeping here. Josh feared he was making a mistake, but he was a sucker for damsels in distress. Maybe her mother would veto the arrangement, getting him off the hook. "Friday," he agreed. "Uh, part time. Maybe three to seven? The children get home from school soon after four—"

"I know. I'll be there. Thanks, Mr. Pinson."

"You know the address?"

"Sure. You're on Box 27. The school bus goes by there."

"27P," Josh agreed. It seemed the development of Heatherwood had taken off from the spot on the main road where Box 27 was, so that had defined the entire settlement. "At the end of Forest Drive."

"Got it. Bye."

Her voice was so sweet! Well, the truth would be known on Friday. He would still have a week to find another housekeeper, if he needed to.

A fierce gust of wind rattled the windowpanes. More pine needles flew. Beauty the pony neighed outside, alarmed.

Was there any suitable cover for the animals? Josh had a vision of the chicks getting blown away. He hurried out. The back door almost yanked from his grasp as the wind caught it. The green roofing panels vibrated with a loud burr and seemed about to lift from the porch.

Outside it was worse. The pony had her posterior to the wind, her mane blown forward. Acorns descended like hail from a smaller tree to the side. Josh shielded his eyes with one hand. Where could he put the pony? There really did not seem to be any better place than where she was. "Sorry, girl," he told her. "Maybe one day I'll build a good shelter for you."

The chicks and kittens were huddled under the shed where

the wind hardly touched. They, at least, did not suffer from fear of ghosts! Now if only the shed were properly anchored—

The shed? What about the cabin? Josh angled his torso into the wind and navigated for the cabin, determined to verify its anchorage. There was nothing he could do if it blew loose, but he had to check.

The fury of the wind tormented the smaller trees. There was a crack as a turkey oak snapped. Half its length dangled, forming an inverted L. This was not the hurricane, but there seemed to be hurricane-force gusts here!

The cabin was all right. It was mounted on a dozen concrete blocks filled with cement, and metal bands extended from the cement to the wood. The building wouldn't blow away.

Now rain was sluicing down. Josh lumbered back toward the house.

There was a smell, dank yet warm, as of a wet, living body. Josh's nose remained allergically stuffed, but this was strong enough to taste. It suffused the air, cloying, awful. Like the odor that had been associated with Foster's death, but stronger. The children had mentioned—

Josh took momentary shelter by the northward-leaning trunk of the big tree. And recoiled.

It was hot. It was as though a fire had burned here recently, radiating into the trunk—but of course there had been no fire. Perhaps a lightning strike, though he had heard no crack of thunder. What was that Foster had said about the frequency of lightning strikes in this region?

The stench was intolerable. Burning garbage? Maybe ball lightning had incinerated the nearby leaves and fungus. He knew next to nothing about that phenomenon but understood that some strange effects were possible. The odor—if the

wood were scorched by the current, invisibly, deep down
inside—

More rain pelted down. There was a noise very like a
groan. The wind cutting past the branches, of course—but
suddenly Josh felt extremely uneasy. A monster, the children
said. Surely not, yet it became easy to believe in the midst of
the tempest. He ducked his head and hurried on to the house.

The storm abated before the school bus came, to Josh's
relief. The hurricane had vented its main force elsewhere;
this had only been an eddy.

Next day he drove to the other Heatherwood to see the
accountant. It was a fair labyrinth, but he followed the
instructions faithfully and located the address. He was right
on time, having allowed a margin for confusion. He usually
was prompt; it was part of his nature.

The house was a modern neat one-floor structure with a
tiled roof, reminiscent of the ones he was used to in the
north. Mr. Graham was surely a conventional man. Josh
hoped the accountant would be up to the challenge of educating an intruder from another discipline.

A woman answered the door. She was attractive in a light
print dress and shoulder-length brown hair. She glanced askance
at him.

"My name is Joshua Pinson. I'm here to see Mr. Graham
about a matter of accounting."

"Of course," she said. Her voice sounded familiar. "Come
in, Mr. Pinson."

Josh stepped in. He had not dressed formally; now, in this
tastefully neat house, he felt a bit out of place. He wondered
whether this quest was worthwhile. It really depended on the
accountant.

"Come to the office, please," the woman said, leading the
way. She was of medium height and well proportioned,

though somewhat beyond the bloom of youth. There seemed to be a touch of humor in her voice, though Josh could not place its reason.

The office was spare, with desk and chairs, and a certificate posted on the wall. "Have a seat, Mr. Pinson," she said, and took the desk herself.

Josh sat. "Oh—you're the CPA? I expected—"

She indicated the certificate. "Philippa Graham, CPA."

"Philippa?" He looked at her from a new mental alignment. "Oh, no! Not the horsewoman!"

She smiled. "I know, I know! You didn't recognize me in clothing."

"I didn't recognize you," he agreed ruefully. "You, in that dress—"

"Say what is on your mind, Mr. Pinson."

"Well, you're a comely woman."

"In contrast to my usual state?"

"I suspect I have dug myself in deep enough. Why didn't you tell me it was you?"

"I was disinclined to mix business with pleasure."

"This is business," he said. "I really do mean to explore the possibility of—"

"Certainly. And I believe we can do business. Otherwise I would not have given you my number. As it was, you caught my father by surprise."

Her father—the man who had answered the phone. "I assumed he was an associate," Josh admitted.

"Now I can provide you with the fundamentals—"

"Miss Graham, I am not certain I—"

"Oh, it's Miss Graham, now?"

"Pip," Josh said with difficulty. "I just don't think—"

"Oh? Changed your mind? Because I'm a woman—or because I'm a neighbor?"

"One or the other," Josh admitted.

"I trust you are aware this is fighting language?"

And she was a fighting woman. "Yes," Josh agreed. "I'm not saying no, I'm just saying I need to think about this. I'm just not certain I want to work with you in this capacity."

She frowned. "Now I don't really need the business, Mr. Pinson. I—"

"Mr. Pinson?"

She flashed a smile. "Touché, Josh. I don't have to trick anybody into hiring me. I *am* the best CPA in these parts. I'm not sure I even intended to charge you for this service. It intrigues me, that's all. It's a challenge. And perhaps I just want to find out how smart you are when you're learning. I get a little bit competitive about smart people, especially smart male-people. But I can do the job, and I resent—"

"Much as you would put a new horse through its paces," Josh said.

She paused, realizing that she had been scored upon again. "Touchy male ego. Very well. Let's think about it. I've got to shop for hay anyway. You need hay too."

"Hay?" This abrupt shift of subject disgruntled him.

"What horses eat. I saw an ad for hay in bulk at a good price, and thought I'd check it out. Callie. I usually stick to Coastal Bermuda, but one has to move with the times."

"I know nothing about hay," Josh protested.

"Then it must be time to learn. I understand you're a quick study. Come on." She bounced up and made for the door.

Josh shrugged and followed her. From accounting to hay, in almost a single thought. The way of women! But she was right. Since he now had a pony to care for, he did need to learn about hay, even though he would never arrange a computer system for it. She was also, he realized, letting him off the hook about the accounting by so effectively changing the subject.

Pip led him to the rear of the house, where three horses stood in a fenced pasture. The pasture had been eaten down to bare dirt. Obviously hay was vital.

"I give them hay at noon," she said. "It entertains them and gives their systems something to work on. Horses are designed to process a great deal of roughage. Coastal Bermuda is good hay, but it is expensive. Callie is moving into the area; if it's suitable, I wouldn't mind changing over. What I need to do is look at it, see whether there are weeds in the bales, how it smells, find out whether the horses like it." She dumped flakes of hay before the horses, who began munching contentedy. "This is early, but you never can tell how long these exploration trips will take," she explained.

She had a pickup truck. Josh joined her in the front seat and they took off. "I usually exercise them now, but I can't be a slave to a schedule. You know, according to the book you should exercise a horse two and a half hours each day—but that would take me seven and a half hours for my three, and I wouldn't have time for anything else. The same book says it is unhealthy to maintain a horse in top fitness for too long a period. Does that make sense to you?"

"No," Josh answered. She was right: she was a motor-mouth about horses.

"I mean, fitness is fitness; you can't have too much of it. I try to keep fit myself." She patted her abdomen, which was lean; she was indeed fit. "I suppose they mean overdevelopment, forcing a horse to perform beyond its natural capacity. Too much muscle, straining the rest of the system. That, I agree, is nonsensical. No person or animal should push beyond its nature. I try to tell my father that, when he starts driving himself too hard, but he tells me that if I want to boss a man around I should get married. He doesn't understand female independence.''

"What man does?" Josh asked, smiling.

She hardly heard him. "And of course all the racing animals are on drugs, legal, illegal, and in-between. That's what they call fitness? I would never drug an animal.''

"I agree.''

But she was already off and running, proceeding from thought to thought at breakneck pace. "You know, I entered my gelding Danny Boy in a fifteen-mile endurance meet last month, and he did really well. He had good wind and pacing, and he finished third overall, and he was in much better shape than some of them. He wasn't falling or bleeding at the nose, certainly! And do you know what?''

"What?" Josh asked dutifully, resigning himself to the fact that he was merely a bystander to this monologue, not a true participant. He had no knowledge of endurance meets and did not like to imagine a horse ridden so hard that it bled from the nose.

"They disqualified him," she said indignantly. "Because he didn't have papers. But it was supposed to be an open meet. *An open meet.* Can you imagine that? The hypocrisy of it! An open meet.''

She was still talking nonstop about horses as they returned two hours later. They had had a difficult trip, getting lost on back roads blocked by grazing cows, fiercely barking dogs, and mud puddles, because of a confusion in the directions. At one point the truck's wheels started skidding in sugar sand, and Josh wondered what Pip would do if they got stuck. Her pretty dress was quite unsuitable for dirty excavations. But she drove with nerve and panache, and finally they had located the hay farm.

Callie hay, it turned out, was coarse yellow sweet-smelling

stuff, the kind one could imagine sleeping on. Pip had bought ten bales to try out on a sample basis, and Josh had helped load them into the truck. Each bale weighed about fifty pounds and was bound by two strings; it took him a while to get the hang of heaving it, and his hands hurt and his forearms got scratched, but he had been embarrassed to let Pip do it all in her good clothing. Now they both had strands of hay on them, and the whole truck smelled pleasantly of it. It really had been a worthwhile experience.

She parked the truck and turned to him as a horse neighed welcome. "Take two bales for Beauty. Let me know how she likes them."

Josh got out and transferred two fragrant bales to his microbus.

"Now," Pip said, smiling. "About that accounting instruction—"

"I have decided to handle it on my own," Josh said. "Now I'll pay you for the hay."

Wordlessly, tight-lipped, she accepted the money. Josh went to his bus and drove away.

Now why had he done that? Josh asked himself.

At the moment, he had no answers.

That evening when he fed the animals, giving a nice flake of the new hay to Beauty, he heard the beat of horse's hooves and knew that Philippa was on her way to Foster's farm, as agreed. He felt guilty.

He distracted himself by counting the chicks who came out to peck the seeds he scattered for them. There were only five. He peered under the shed, but could not find the sixth. At length, regretfully, he concluded that a member of this farm community had fallen prey to a predator. He wished he knew whether it had been a ground creature who might have been fenced out, or an air creature who would have struck anyway.

His guilt expanded. Could this be taken as divine punishment for his rejection of the horsewoman? No, of course not; his guilt was giving a rationale to mere coincidence.

But the children would notice as soon as they checked the chicks, for periodically they liked to play with the little birds. Josh encouraged this, for chickens were not after all dumpy clucks; they made excellent outdoor pets, and when these were grown they would be accustomed to human contact. But this loss—Sue, especially, would take it hard. Her fish was ill, and the loss of a chick would double the burden. She was as yet too young to accommodate the harsh reality of death.

Chapter 12

Friday morning there was no sunrise; day simply forced itself into place. The horsewoman came riding again, and Josh had to meet her.

Pip wasted no time in circumlocution. "It may be that I deceived you the other day. It was not maliciously intended, and I apologize."

"It's not that," Josh said, wishing he were elsewhere. "The joke was on me. I just don't feel—"

"It may be that I talk too much about horses. I thought you were interested, but I certainly don't *have* to go on about—and I *don't*, when doing business."

"Please," Josh said. "It is no fault in you. You're an intelligent, attractive woman. I just—" He paused, sensing that she did not appreciate this compliment. She was a woman of achievement who wanted to be known for her ability, not for any accident of appearance. "It just isn't the kind of relationship I feel comfortable with."

"It would have been comfortable with a man?" she inquired grimly.

"I don't know. I don't think it's a sexist thing." On the other hand, he wasn't sure that it wasn't. She, for all her talk about the idiocy of driving too hard, was a driven woman. "I

just—think of you as the horsewoman. The good neighbor. I
prefer to leave it that way."

"Of course." She departed, subdued. Josh shook his head.
What was wrong with him? He had not had difficulty doing
business with women before. But he simply did not want to
work with this one. Not on accounting.

The day had started bleak, and grew bleaker. Rain fell
intermittently. It was not cold at all, but Josh felt cold
emotionally. He worked on the fence some more, but it did
not go well; soreness manifested in his shoulder muscles
immediately and his palms wanted to blister despite the
gloves, and the posts seemed determined to misalign. He got
caught by a surprise shower and felt cold though the temperature was 85°F.

Through it all he brooded about the horsewoman. He really
had had no call to turn her off like that. As far as he knew,
he had nothing against her; in fact he respected her independent mode. Why, then, was he alienating her?

Was there something about the premises that made him
react in a manner contrary to his nature? Such as a haunt?
No, he hoped not—yet how could he explain his irrational-
ity? He could at least have found a diplomatic way to turn
down her offer. He hadn't even searched for that.

He re-entered the house, afraid he might see the ghost
again, but this time the kitchen was clear. Nevertheless, he
was uncomfortable. He knew he ought to get down to work
on the research for that program, wrestling with the intricacies of accounting, but he was unable to concentrate. He
needed to get dry and comfortable.

The stove! It was time he tried it out, so as to be familiar
with its mechanism when the cold weather came. There was
dry wood stacked on the porch in a ring-shaped holder. Uncle
Elijah had evidently been preparing for winter when he—

Josh's discomfort intensified. Suddenly the stove seemed

as menacing as the chain saw. Therefore he had to tackle it and overcome his strange reluctance. No machine could hurt a careful man. Was the stove a machine? Yes, indeed; it took in fuel and delivered its product: heat. Allowed to operate uncontrolled, it could start a fire that would destroy a house. But correctly operated, it could convert a cold house into a pleasantly warm house. Man's use of tools and machines had made him supreme on earth—and no machine was going to be this man's master.

The phone rang. Josh jumped—and realized how nervous he was. He chided himself and lifted the receiver.

"Mr. Pinson? This is Brenna Sears," the dulcet voice said. "Mom says it's going to rain canines and felines at seven tonight, and you're on a dirt drive so a car will get mired, so she won't let me come today. I'm very sorry, but—"

"Quite all right," Josh said. Maybe this would free him to locate a more professional housekeeper without hurting anyone's feelings. The notion of a teenage girl in the house still bothered him. Why hadn't he had the sense to tell her no, just as he had told Pip no? Maybe he was learning from experience.

"But I can come in Monday," Brenna continued brightly. "Mom says there'll be a downpour tonight, moderate rain tomorrow afternoon, a little Sunday evening, and then clear for most of the week."

"Your mother is quite a meteorologist."

"Pardon?"

"She knows her weather."

"Oh, sure. The weather people always give the wrong temperatures and things, so Mom had to do it herself. So I'll be seeing you Monday at three."

"Yes, of course," Josh said with resignation. This would give him less time to verify her suitability, but there seemed to be no preferable course. She sounded so infernally sweet! He felt like a monster already.

Josh returned his attention to the stove. He brought an armful of split wood. He found a bucket of twigs and chips and dry-rotten sticks. He had read somewhere that all wood had similar heating value, weight for weight, even rotten wood; it was simply that it was necessary to burn a larger volume to obtain that weight or heat. Presumably that meant seasoned wood; green wood would weigh more and burn less well. This wood, at any rate, was good and dry.

The stove was solid cast iron. That meant he had to be careful about warming it up, because of uneven expansion caused by sudden heating. He would have to start with a small fire, and build it up gradually. There should be no trouble, if the chimney and flue were open. Carpenter had assured him that they were.

Josh opened the side door and peered inside the stove. The bottom was bare and ridged—and an instruction booklet lay there. Carpenter had thoughtfully left the booklet where it would be found upon need.

Josh checked it. It seemed that the stove's own ashes became the insulation that prevented the fire from burning out the bottom. At the start it was necessary to put sand in it; this could be shoveled out later when there were ashes. Clever!

Josh went back out into the drizzle and dug a hole in the ground, going deep enough to reach the golden dirt sand below. A kitten came out to supervise, perhaps hoping he would uncover a succulent mouse or mole.

He brought the sand in and spread it appropriately. Josh appreciated a nice design, and was getting to like the niceties of this stove.

He built what amounted to an outdoor fire on the sand; a little teepee of chips and twigs, with balled-up paper inside.

He would add larger pieces as the first burned down, gradually expanding the blaze until the stove became hot throughout. There should be no problem.

Why, then, did he feel so apprehensive? There was a rising foreboding in him, a feeling of impending calamity. A horror—of what?

Of fire. Fire, raging, coursing through the forest, consuming everything in its path, causing the leaves of oaks to blacken and curl, the trunks of pines to smoke and gutter, the terrible heat of it—

Josh shook his head. For a moment it had almost seemed he stood there, rooted, unable to avoid the onrushing blaze. Yet he had never seen a forest fire. Only the clips on television news, and perhaps descriptions he had read. This vision had been far more immediate and personal, a direct experience.

How could that be? Was he losing his sanity?

Some believed in the afterlife, in reincarnation. Could he have experienced something like this in a prior life, and—?

No. Most likely he had simply recalled some motion-picture scene, reviving it from dormancy. Like hypnotic recall.

And what could account for such recall at this moment, when he had never been subject to such a thing before?

Josh fully intended to light a fire in this stove. He discovered that a handle above the door operated the main baffle, the one that could route the smoke circuitously around inside the stove for greatest heating efficiency. He set it open, so that the draft was direct; it was necessary to get the fire established and the flue hot before getting fancy about smoke routing.

He struck a match, lighted a twist of paper, fought off another surge of foreboding, and poked the torch into his teepee.

The fire blazed up immediately. His concern made his heart pound, but he stifled it—and suddenly the foreboding passed. As with the dread saw, he had conquered his own foolishness.

Or had he? On another level it almost felt as if something were watching him, ready to intervene if he threatened it, but relaxing when it saw that he was doing no harm. A ridiculous notion, of course. Yet—

He closed the stove door. Now he noted the thermostatic mechanism, a wire handle on the back of the stove that could be set at any level. He wasn't clear exactly how it regulated the air vent, but would find out as the stove heated.

Josh got up and faced the kitchen. The ghost was not there. He relaxed. There was really no reason to think anything was watching, especially not a ghost!

In the course of the next half hour the stove warmed up. Josh fed pieces of wood in until it was up to normal-sized chunks. The twin copper pipes leading to the stovepipe began to function, the lower one cool, the upper one hot. The heat of the smoke was passing into the water within the coiled pipe inside the smoke column, and the hot water was rising in the system exactly as it was supposed to. This was another heat collector, like the solar unit on the front porch roof, only inside the flue. Elijah had really worked things out!

This loop operated more forcefully than the solar loop, though; the "hot" pipe was soon untouchable. It took a really compact, potent heat source to make the water move like that. The stove was such a source, and the water was certainly moving now.

The two dogs caught on to the heat source and settled down blissfully before it. When winter came, they would love this stove!

Then Josh thought of something. He went to the sink and turned on the hot water. Sure enough, there was a rush, tapering quickly to normal flow. The heating water was expanding, or more probably it was the air trapped in the big storage tank, putting pressure on the system; he would have to remember to keep letting off the excess until the temperature stabilized. He didn't want to blow out the relief valve.

In the afternoon the children straggled in, damp and grouchy. "Hey—it's warm in here!" Chris cried.

They stood beside the stove, pleased. Josh was gratified.

In the evening, not long after seven, a downpour commenced. Josh, intrigued, went out after an hour with the lamp and checked the rain gauge: two inches had descended in that hour, bringing the day's total up to 2.6 inches. The entire forest floor was awash and gullied. He could not see the road from here but was certain it was partially flooded. Driving would have been extremely awkward. Brenna's mom had been correct.

Beauty, the pony, stretched on her tether to the extreme limit, trying to reach the succulent grass beyond. Suddenly the rope snapped, as it sometimes did; she had learned not to give up too readily. Delighted, she ranged outward, eating along the way. The loose rope dragged behind her, sometimes getting underfoot; she was used to that and merely stepped over it and went on.

In due course she grazed her way to the fifty foot wide swath of bahia grass that was the main drive. This was wonderful! For the first time in months she was getting her fill of the good stuff.

There was a glint of light from the south. Something was moving, coming toward her. Beauty froze, her eyes oriented on the thing; now she heard the machine. It was forging rapidly nearer.

She bolted. She charged north, her initial leap converting to a gallop. As she ran, her alarm increased. It was as though a metal monster were pursuing her alone, bent on unimaginable mischief. In terror, now, she raced for home, for the familiar Tree.

The trailing rope dangled under her front feet. One hoof came down on it. Suddenly her neck was wrenched. She veered, caromed off a tree, and took a forward tumble. Her body plowed into the ground.

For a moment she lay still. Then, laboriously, she climbed to her feet. One leg was hurting, and her shoulder had been scraped and bruised, and there was internal discomfort. But she could walk.

Beauty made her way back to the Tree, limping. She no longer felt like grazing far afield. The region beyond the Tree frightened her.

Later in the afternoon the horsewoman came by. She saw the pony and immediately recognized her distress. "Oh, Beauty—you've broken your tether and taken a fall! Did a car spook you? I saw car tracks; must have been a lost tourist."

She examined the scraped shoulder and the sore leg. "No bones broken, fortunately. You'll heal. But I'm going to tie you again so that you'll stay out of trouble. I'll give you some hay to take your mind off your problems. Do you like callie? Oh, I do so hate to see an animal suffer!"

She went on to the Foster farm after tending to Beauty, ill at ease. Strange things were happening around here these days. Oddities were a matter of course in Withlacoochee; not all of the hunters' bizarre tales were false. Things as yet unknown to man were reputed to lurk in the scant remaining wilderness of Florida's heartland; that was part of what fascinated her about it. She would give up her career for one real encounter with the Citrus County skunk ape! Some day, riding through the forest, she hoped to spot that creature.

But this matter of phantom trains and household ghosts and mysterious deaths—that was sinister. She had heard the train whistle on occasion herself, but presumed it was a trick of the weather. Sound could carry in odd ways when conditions were right. Certainly there could be no train on the trackless railroad cut, whatever the sound! And anyone who actually saw a ghost had to be deluded.

But the death of Elijah Pinson had been no delusion. Elijah had been a marvelous old codger, remarkably canny about hidden values, yet with a half-masked softheartedness about creatures in need. He had taken in Beauty because she had been ill and was slated for the slaughterhouse. With regular feeding and care she had been considerably restored, though she still was a bit crazy at times. Soon Elijah would have found a good home for her, and probably have turned a neat profit on the deal—but it was really the pony's interest he had had at heart. The acquisition of wealth had been a challenge to him, not an imperative, though it often concealed from others his more fundamental nature.

Then Elijah had died in what the police termed an accident. Pip didn't believe that, but had no better explanation. She could not claim it was murder; where was the motive? No one knew how rich the man had been, not even his lawyer. Especially not his lawyer!

She reflected on that, in a momentary diversion from her main chain of thought. She had a motor-mind as well as a motor-mouth, and tended to think more than was good for her. She, like others, had assumed that Elijah was a harmless eccentric, much the same as Old Man Foster. Until the day Elijah had taken her partway into his confidence and shown her his collection of stones. "I'm asking you to keep an eye on my place when I'm gone," he had told her candidly. They had had no personal or professional connection before; they had merely exchanged greetings when she rode by. But somehow he had known. "Of all the people here, you *care* about creatures. I can see right through you, and you refract like a jewel. Genuine, unpretentious. So I'll give you this bauble, and you wear it when you have a mind, and we're even." He opened a small cloth bag and poured several tens of bright colored stones into his palm. They reminded her of the bits of glass she had liked to collect at the beach as a child, except that these had not been rounded off by the action of the waves and abrasive sand. They were not jewels, because they were irregular, but they might be semiprecious stones.

"This one, blue as the welkin, perhaps," he said, picking it out between thumb and forefinger. His hands were mottled and calloused, but his touch on the stones was sure. He held the bit up before her, his eyes darting from it to her face and back again as though seeking a matchup. "No, not quite right; I see your eyes are green. This one, then." He dropped the blue fragment and chose another and held it up. The sunlight caught it, and it radiated an intense, breathtakingly lovely green. "Yes, this is you. Foolish of me not to know it before. A nothing, really, but a memento, a private appreciation to one who deserves better from one who has nothing better to offer. Sentiment gives it value." She tried to demur, taken aback by this sudden familiarity, not wanting to accept something from a relative stranger, but he forced it on her. Thus Philippa, bemused, had taken the bit of glass with solemnity, oddly touched.

That had been months ago. She had taken it to a jeweler to have it mounted in a necklace because she did not want to hurt Elijah's feelings by not wearing it. She had inquired, just in case, whether it had any value, and the jeweler told her that he didn't recognize it as any precious stone. "But there are a great many semiprecious stones, and this is very pretty," he told her. "It could be worth twenty or thirty dollars.'' "It's priceless," she replied with a smile, knowing that there was no way to value such a token of respect. Beauty was so very much in the eye of the beholder.

In a week she had returned to pick up the necklace. The jeweler had done an excellent job, forming a frame around the irregularity of the green stone so that it put its best facets forward. But the metal of the chain—"What is this?" she had demanded. "It looks like gold!" Soberly the jeweler nodded. "But I can't afford gold for a bit of glass!" she protested. "There will be no charge," the jeweler said. "No charge?" she asked blankly. "If you wish," the man said, "I will purchase that stone from you at a fair price." She frowned, becoming suspicious. "A fair price?" she asked, hoping she had misunderstood. "I must explain," he said. *You bet!* she thought, but made no overt reaction. "I did not recognize this stone, before, but my curiosity was piqued," he continued. "I did some research, and verified it with an expert. This is a modern stone, coming into popularity in the past decade. I will offer you six thousand dollars for it."

Now she paused in mid-reflection to lift the stone from her breast and glance at it. That scene with the jeweler still overwhelmed her in retrospect. The stone had turned out to be a tsavorite garnet, about two and a half carats, irregular but of perfect quality. Retail it might be worth eight thousand dollars; the jeweler admitted he would charge more because he had taken some trouble with the setting, so he was offering her what might be a fair middleman price, well above wholesale.

Amazed, she had turned it down, and paid for the setting; thus Elijah's gift had actually cost her a fair amount. She had worn the necklace prominently the next time she encountered Elijah, showing him that she valued the bauble, but had not mentioned its monetary value. She knew the canny old man knew it! He had told her he had nothing better to offer, as though the stone were worthless, but in fact the gem was such a fine specimen of its kind that it must have been the best anyone could offer. And he had a bag of perhaps thirty similar stones. What were they—diamonds, sapphires, rubies, all irregular, not worth the separate fortunes that large, perfectly cut stones would have been, but still a good deal more precious than gold? "Just you keep an eye on things while I'm gone," he reminded her. "I don't want my animals hungry, and I don't want strangers snooping." She had understood why, at this point; there was no telling how much of value he had squirreled away here.

Elijah had been absent frequently, usually without notice, and she had kept the requisite eye on the premises, and never mentioned the jewels to anyone else. She was concerned that someone could rob or hurt the man, if news of that wealth got out. Elijah had trusted her, in his subtle way, with information vital to his welfare; the least she could do was protect his secret.

Then Elijah had died, and she had feared that someone had discovered his wealth and killed him for it. But apparently it had been an accident. She had continued to watch the property. Elijah had certainly paid for that service, as much by his trust as by the value of the garnet he had given her.

Then the nephew had inherited, and her position had become awkward. Joshua was mildly reminiscent of Elijah, being clean-living and intelligent. By this time he must have caught on that there was considerably more to this estate than a pony and some chicks. She had felt a kind of responsibility to keep an eye on Josh, too, for in a fashion he was now part of the estate. She had debated with herself whether to tell him about the precious stones, but his abrupt limiting of relations had squelched the opportunity. And, perhaps, the desire; it had stung.

Why had Josh done it? She had no designs on Elijah's

wealth; she could have robbed the house at any time in the month after Elijah's death and no one would have known the difference. She was only keeping the covenant, as Elijah had known she would. The old man really *had* her heart in his odd and forceful manner.

Meanwhile, Old Man Foster had died, in almost the same spot as Elijah, and as mysteriously. Now something had really frightened Beauty, though that had probably been coincidence.

Who would be the next to die? For now she strongly feared that the fabled haunt of the property had not finished its rampage. Elijah had pooh-poohed the notion of a curse on the land, and built directly under the haunted tree to prove it—and had died there.

She dismounted at Foster's place and set about feeding the animals. She would leave Joshua Pinson alone, since he wanted it that way, but she would not relinquish her tacit commitment to Elijah.

Late Saturday afternoon they arrived back from their cele-bration of their near-completion of three weeks here. They had driven to Homosassa Springs, another resort attraction, and were satisfied. The children reiterated the high points: monkeys coming on the boat to be fed, fish viewed from an underwater station, a huge marshmallow-eating hippopota-mus, and a bird walk. Chris had tried to note all the birds for his bird list, but had given up; there were too many, and his handwriting was too awkward.

"What was your favorite thing today?" Josh asked Sue as they turned onto Forest Drive.

"Buying a wooden nickel for five cents," she responded promptly.

"Hey, they didn't have those wooden nickels at Homosas-sa," Josh said. "They were at Weekiwachee."

"I know," Sue replied smugly.

On Sunday they had a picnic in the Withlacoochee State Forest. They walked about a mile up the forest road, north, found a nice live oak tree, and spread out an old bedspread and ate peanut butter sandwiches that Sue had meticulously assembled with her very own smudgy little fingers. They had the dogs along, who sniffed everything in the vicinity with fascination, and it was all very pleasant. Josh felt a bit wistful; next weekend he would have to leave them again.

"This is a live oak tree?" Chris asked.

"It isn't a dead one," Sue replied with a smirk.

"Shut up, fertilizer-face. How come this tree is different from our big tree at home?"

"Is it?" Josh asked. "I never paid attention."

"Sure." Chris pulled off a leaf. "See—this is spoon-shaped. Our tree's leaves are flat."

"Well, there are several species of oaks," Josh said. "Maybe you should research the subject and do a report for school. You just might prove that our tree is of a species unknown to man."

"Say, yeah!" Chris agreed, lighting up.

Josh was pleased. His son was seldom motivated toward scholastic things. If he followed through—

Rain threatened, and they wrapped up their picnic and got home. So far, Brenna Sears' mother had been a perfect predictor. Several clear days should be coming up.

Promptly at three in the afternoon Monday an old car pulled in. Two females got out, one a somewhat worn, graying woman in a conservative dark dress, the other a striking black-haired girl in a yellow blouse and culottes. The mother, in appearance, was very much the kind of person Josh had had in mind for the job—but he knew it was the daughter he had to deal with. Well, that was his penalty for allowing his children to set it up.

The girl came forward, her hair swirling voluptuously about her startlingly pretty face. She had an easy stride and was excellently put together. Josh felt increasingly uneasy. This was not merely a teenage girl; this was—what was the appropriate term?—a creature. The female of the species at the precise moment of devastating bloom.

"Mr. Pinson? I am Brenna," she said, smiling. She had, of course, perfect teeth and a mirror-clear complexion. "This is my mother, Mrs. Sears." She shrugged, her excellent bosom moving.

Josh wrenched his eyes to the older woman, embarrassed by the details he was noticing in the younger one. His wife was now nine months dead. The inherent sex appeal of the young woman was an imposition. He simply did not want that sort of thing in his vicinity. Not this year.

Both women were looking at him expectantly. "Ah, yes," he said. "My children will be home in an hour. The house—it isn't really finished, and things are disorganized. I had a housekeeper, but—"

"But she saw a ghost," Brenna finished, and laughed. Girls like that, he thought, should not laugh in public; it was too distracting. "I wish *I* could see a ghost: It would make my whole day. May we come in?"

"Yes, of course." Josh awkwardly ushered the two of them into the house. He hoped the ghost had the sense not to manifest right now. "As you can see, I'm not much for housekeeping myself, which is why I need . . ."

"Let's see what we can do," Brenna said.

"Well, it may be more than you really care to—"

"No, I'm used to it," she assured him. "Mom can tell you."

Josh glanced at Mrs. Sears, but the older woman was

silent. She had not spoken since their arrival. Josh could not be certain whether this was a positive, negative, or opinion-withheld reaction. "I thought—well, I was paying Mrs. Brown by the hour and she did the shopping herself and I paid for that directly—if you don't have a car—"

"Mom will take me," Brenna said easily, examining the kitchen cupboards. "We'll make up a list and bring the stuff tomorrow, if that's all right with you."

"Of course." It seemed impossible to discourage her. But perhaps her mother would have something to say privately, after this session. A flat veto was not impossible.

He showed them the rest of the house, embarrassed again by its unfinished state, by the dust that had accumulated in the absence of Mrs. Brown, the new spiderwebs in the window—they left the spiders deliberately because they helped cut down on the lovebugs that kept getting in—and the boxes of canned food stacked in odd places. "This house uses solar power for the hot water, so on cloudy days it's not much. And a wood stove for space heating. It's not exactly—"

"It certainly seems like fun," Brenna said.

Fun, he thought sourly. What would she do after the first day or so, when it became dull? Was this just a game to her, a way to pass the time between boyfriends?

Now the distant, awesome roar of the bus came through the forest. "My children will be home in a minute," Josh said. How the hour had flown! He felt as though he were on a high trestle, unwilling to remain but unable to step off. What would he do when the older woman departed, leaving him alone with this self-possessed bomb? What would people think? If the horsewoman rode by and saw Brenna, or if Old Man Foster—

Foster! He was forgetting that the man was dead! Amazing how the shock had faded, in just one week. He had continued feeding Foster's animals in the mornings, yet somehow the significance of the man's absence had not completely pene-trated. Still, Foster just might be useful, even in death.

"I should advise you that my nearest neighbor died here last week. He was old, and it was a heart attack, but—"

"My grandfather died two months ago," Brenna said, evidently unshaken.

The children arrived. "Hi, Billy's big sister!" Chris ex-claimed. "Hi, Billy's mother!" Both women smiled.

"I suppose that's it," Josh said. "Now you've met them. If you think you can handle—"

"Sure can," Brenna said. "Kids, get into jeans before you start playing in the sand. If you don't want to play, you can watch the catoons on TV, but after that you have to give equal time to homework. Supper at six, take it or leave it. Any questions?"

Chris paused, gazing at her. "Gee, you're pretty," he said. "Billy said—"

"I know what Billy says. You'll say the same when I make you wash behind your ears. Now go get changed."

Chris ran upstairs. Sue lingered. "Will there be peas for supper?"

"Not this time," Brenna said.

"Good!" Sue headed for the stairs. "I hate peas." Then she paused again. "Beans?"

"Canned beans. That's most of what we've got to work with today."

"Yuck!" Sue exclaimed with satisfaction, and went on up.

Brenna and her mother began bustling about the kitchen, putting things in order. Josh felt out of place, so he went out to set a few more posts. Soon the children joined him. "What do you think?" he asked them.

"Can't we get ice cream instead of beans," Sue inquired wistfully. "I couldn't get my ice cream today, because they were in the kitchen."

"We all must make sacrifices," Josh said. "If they have supper on schedule, you won't need a snack. But what I really meant to ask was do you think Billy's sister will be all right for a housekeeper?"

Sue considered, cocking her head judiciously. "She's awful pretty."

Josh wasn't certain whether Sue intended this to be positive or negative, and decided not to pursue the matter. Until the mother departed, they would not know how the daughter was at the job, anyway. They worked on the fence, the children patting dirt in around the placed posts, until Brenna called them in.

It was a good supper, fashioned from the meager supplies remaining in the house. Josh had never been an apt grocery shopper, and things had backslided in the absence of a housekeeper. He had forgotten to point out all the boxes of vacuum-canned food, but wasn't sure how adequate or adaptable those were anyway.

He was glad when it was over and they were gone. Josh hoped that the mother would let the daughter work alone next time, so that he could verify how apt she was at the job.

It was not to be. All week long mother backstopped daughter, not bothering to drive home when she would only have to return within four hours. Brenna only took money for one. Apparently her mother's services were unofficial.

If only there were some convenient way to have the mother take the housekeeping position, letting the daughter go home! But there did not seem to be. Was Brenna competent? What would happen when it was just Brenna and the children?

What choice did he have? With luck Mrs. Sears would check frequently on her daughter, in person or by phone, and tide her through. He would cut his trip as short as he could. Two days, most of which time the children would be either asleep or in school. They might get away with a number of ice-cream meals, but that was not any major disaster. Not too much chance for anything critical to go wrong.

Why, then, did he feel so apprehensive? It was more than the notion of having a careless girl in charge of his children. He feared something worse. Something like another death. Could he cancel the trip? No, not if he wanted to deliver on his contract. There were people he had to consult with, key references he had to check.

He had his airplane round trip reservation, and the closing on the sale of his old house in New Jersey had been fixed. He had to be there!

"Pray that it be all right," he told himself.

Chapter 13

Brenna Sears relaxed at last. Joshua Pinson had driven off at noon to catch his plane in Tampa, and Mom had driven home an hour later, assured that no daughter of hers would remain one minute alone in a house with a strange man. This overprotectiveness had cost Brenna jobs before, and it had really looked as if Mr. Pinson was getting fed up, understandably, but they had hung firm and held the job. It was hard for Brenna to blame her well-meaning parent, though. Mom had had to marry in a hurry—that was back before abortions were easy, and it seemed she had been criminally ignorant of contraceptive measures—and she just didn't want her daughter to repeat. Since Brenna herself had been the cause of that swift marriage, by getting herself conceived, she could hardly fault her mother's concern. Had Mom decided otherwise, Brenna would have been in a bad way.

Women simply hadn't known very much, in Mom's day. They still didn't; Mom was grossly out of touch with today's realities. Brenna had exceptional physical resources, and knew it; once she had made a game of counting the number of male heads that turned as she passed. She had given that up; they *all* turned, in one fashion or another. She had managed a good deal more experience than Mom's generation dreamed

of. It was simply a matter of knowing the worth of one's
hand, and how to play it. But that was no topic for discussion
at home. As far as Mom was concerned, Brenna would
remain an innocent child until she somehow got married and
moved away. Mom figured that the right age for a girl to
marry was about twenty-five—which was another signal of
her naivete.

Since Brenna did understand Mom's attitude, she did not
make any overt objection. She hoped to find herself a good
situation despite Mom's "help" and go from there—carefully,
without emotional violence. It was too soon to tell whether
this Pinson residence was what she was looking for; it had
fallen into her lap by pure chance, by way of her little brother
Billy, of all things. Maybe Billy had just wanted to get her
out of the house so that he could run wild, since Mom didn't
worry about boys the way she did about girls. But it did seem
promising. Joshua was a nice man, even if he was closer to
Mom's generation than to her own, and Chris and Sue were
nice children, and this was a pretty nice farm, if a little far
out from town.

Now, with Mom out of the way, Brenna could do things
her own way. There were new recipes she wanted to perfect,
new games for children, new schedules for accomplishing
housework. It was a pleasant challenge, all hers to organize.
Brenna, unlike other girls her age, really liked housework; it
had its own special rewards, and was not intellectually de-
manding. The sight of a freshly clean and shining floor sent a
thrill through her, especially when she had cleaned it herself.
Friends had tried to tell her she should be trying to get into
acting or motion pictures because of her appearance, but she
knew that sort of constant hassle was not her style. She didn't
want to fight for recognition; she just wanted to be part of a
good household, secure and appreciated. She knew her liabil-
ities as well as her assets, and so she knew that in the world

of motion pictures she would be cast as ordinary. How much better to be outstanding in a single household!

And, despite their aggravations, she liked children too. She would have to see what they could do together. Right now Chris and Sue were out with the pony and the chicks, but they'd soon get tired of that and come in. She could read the signs: they were afraid for their father, afraid he wouldn't come home, as their mother had not come home. They needed special support right now.

She saw a bug sitting on a curtain. It was roachlike, but no roach. In fact it was an assassin bug. One of her brothers collected bugs, and was especially proud of the worst ones. Such as hornets and scorpions and swollen ticks. Once he had heard the tick-sick joke and pulled it on Mom: "Mom, I've been eating the grapes off the dog!" Mom had screamed, then spanked him when he dissolved into laughter. He didn't really eat bugs; they were too valuable as grotesqueries. One of the prides of his collection was the Mexican bedbug, or bloodsucking cone-nose of the family of assassin bugs. Its name, especially, fascinated him. She had come to know it well, every time he got mad at her, which was often enough, he would bring the dead thing out and pretend it was going to suck her dry. He invented marvelously lascivious details. The bug actually was fairly pretty, with a fringe of barber-pole orange striping around its oval edge—but its bite was said to cause some people real agony. The bites could swell up on the arms and legs as though half eggs were buried under the skin, and even moderate bites had an intolerable itch that lasted for days.

Brenna grabbed an old copy of *Scientific American* from a box of magazines and slammed that bug so hard that it perished instantly. She recovered the little corpse and flushed it down the toilet. They certainly didn't need any assassins here! It bothered her to realize that this house wasn't tight enough to keep them out; such bugs could be really bad at night, when people were sleeping.

She was cleaning out the downstairs bathroom. Boxes were piled in the unfinished shower stall. No point in moving them until that shower stall was complete. This house had only a temporary occupancy permit; a lot of work remained before it would be pronounced fit for permanent occupancy. That didn't bother her; it was part of the challenge.

Curious, she opened one box. It contained several worn brown albums. But instead of pictures they contained old stamps. Brenna had no interest in stamps, but another brother did; she knew they could be fascinating for the right child.

As if on cue, the children burst into the house. "Look what I found!" Chris cried. "A gold medal!"

Brenna looked. "That's no medal," she said. "That's a coin." She took it and rinsed it off in the sink. "Looks Spanish to me. Maybe it's a doubloon, like the ones in *Treasure Island.*" How many adventures she had read to her brothers!

"It was near the shed," Chris said, properly awed. "Right in the dirt. The chicks scratched it out. Can I keep it?"

"It sure isn't mine!" Brenna said. "Why don't you start a coin collection? It might be very rare."

"Yeah!" Chris agreed, and dashed off with his prize. "Maybe I can find more, and get rich!"

Sue lingered, clouding up. Brenna knew the signs: sibling jealousy. "What can *I* collect?" Sue asked plaintively.

"Stamps!" Brenna exclaimed, and hauled out the box.

That scored. In moments the little girl was deep in the albums, exclaiming over what she found. "Here's a stamp a hundred years old! It says so right under it. Is it worth as much as Chris's ol' coin?"

"It could be," Brenna agreed. "I'll ask my brother when I get home; he knows about that sort of thing." The important thing was that the child was happy. Happy children meant better job security for Brenna.

"Can I keep these?" Sue asked, excited. "All for my own?"

"Well, you'll have to ask your father. But you might say you've inherited these stamps from your uncle. Is your father the sort of man who lets you have things like that?"

"Well, I guess, if I take care of it," Sue decided. "Daddy wants us to be happy without being spoiled, but he spoils us a little. I wish he was here."

Mr. Pinson did seem like a nice man. A good one to work for regularly, or even—she caught herself, then decided to think it through carefully—even to live with regularly. He was mature; she liked that. He was nice; she liked that too. And he might not know it yet, but he might have more wealth in this property than showed at first. That made him a reasonably secure provider.

Brenna was no gold digger, but she had schooled herself to be aware of the realities of life. Mom would not protect her forever; she had to look forward to the time when she would have to make it on her own, all the way. She could not do odd jobs indefinitely. Ultimately she wanted a home of her own; all her baby-sitting and light housekeeping jobs were practice for this. This Pinson household kept looking better.

She fixed the children a good supper in the evening, made sure they had done their homework, and let them watch television. It was a quality color set, and that big antenna could bring in just about any station in Florida. There were a lot of things about this house that were quality, though they didn't look it at first, like the red cedar siding that never needed painting and the stainless steel roof that would probably last forever and the solar hot water system that used no other power at all, except for the pipes running to the wood stove for winter. She was not fooled by dust and cobwebs and unfinished paneling. The old man Uncle Pinson must have sunk a quiet fortune into it, and deliberately left it unfinished so nobody else would notice. Funny man!

The children liked to be read to sleep, so Brenna did that after they listened to their father's taped message. They could read themselves, of course, but there was a different, special quality to reading aloud. She had brought a book her brothers loved, *How to Eat Fried Worms*, and read to them from that. It was a big success, as she had anticipated.

She had them safely asleep by 9:30. All was going well. Satisfied, Brenna changed into her nightie and got into the double bed in the master bedroom. This was where Joshua Pinson slept, she thought. It gave her a peculiar, pleasant feeling to imagine him lying there. If—but speculation was premature. First she had to prove herself.

Brenna woke abruptly in the night. The illuminated clock radio said 2:34 A.M. Something alarmed her, but she could not place it. She had been dreaming about assassin bugs.

There was a rustle. Quickly, silently, she reached up to press on the fluorescent light above the headboard. This bed was made out of drawers and a sheet of plywood, but it had a headboard, somehow. Actually it was a separate standing unit. But why not? It would be the easiest bed in the world to move, since it was completely disassemble-able. She squeezed her eyes closed as the light came on. In a moment she had adjusted to the brilliance and looked about.

A roach was running across the floor. A big, fat, glossy black wood roach, the kind that usually stayed outdoors. Not the common kind they called palmetto bugs, but the sturdier, handsome wild breed. Brenna hated roaches of any breed, but she didn't know where the bug spray was. In fact, she hadn't seen any chemicals around this house. Odd.

Well, there were other ways. She found an old section of

newspaper, *The Wall Street Journal*—what was a sheet like that doing in a place like this?—rolled it up and stalked the roach.

She paused, hearing a faint moan. For an instant she felt fear swelling up, but she suppressed it; she did not believe in ghosts, especially not the kind that groaned. Poltergeists, they were called: literally, "noisy ghosts." Her pesky brother had tried to spook her often enough with that sort of thing! But she listened carefully.

It came again: half discomfort, half sigh. From Sue Pinson's room. Something was wrong with the child!

Brenna hurried in, rolled newspaper in hand. She turned on the light.

The child was half buried in assassin bugs. Orange-striped cone-noses sucked the blood of her two little arms and one exposed leg, gorging. The welts and agony that would leave—!

Brenna screamed with sheer horror and leaped forward, the newspaper swinging. Frantically she swept the bugs off the leg and then the arms, swishing back and forth in her desperate effort to clear away every last one instantly. She had never seen a more horrible sight.

Sue woke, shrieking in terror. "Don't kill me! Don't kill me!"

Brenna froze, newspaper lifted. The bugs were gone, not squashed, not swept away, just gone as though they had never existed—and the child thought Brenna was attacking *her*.

She dropped the newspaper. "No, no, Sue! There were bugs, horrible bugs biting you! I was swiping them off!"

Sue was understandably wary. "Where? I don't see any."

"All over you! They might be in the bed—"

Sue scrambled out with the alacrity of revulsion. "I dreamed about them. They were hurting me—"

Brenna threw back the sheet. The bed was clean and clear;

no bugs of any kind. Not even lovebugs. "But they were here! Bloodsucking cone-noses, the worst kind!"

Sue was staring at her unbelievingly. "Where?" she repeated.

Had she lost her mind? Frantically Brenna ripped the sheet out the rest of the way, then turned over the pillow. Nothing. Now her horror of *not* finding a bug was becoming worse than her horror of finding it. How could the little girl ever trust her again, if—?

Could she have seen the bugs the child was dreaming of? A true nightmare? No, impossible!

Brenna picked up the pillowcase by two corners, and shook out the cushion inside. Then at last a bug appeared.

It was a bloodsucking cone-nose.

Now Sue believed her. "You stopped it from biting me!"

"Yes," Brenna agreed with enormous relief. She slammed at it with the newspaper, again and again, making absolutely sure the awful thing was dead.

"Maybe that's why I've been having bad dreams and feeling sick," Sue said.

Now Brenna felt a different concern for the child. "You're sick?"

"Sometimes. It comes and goes. But it's mostly my fish, Nurse. She's getting real bad."

Oh. "You're not sick now, then?"

"Not right now. You stopped the bug."

Brenna squeezed her about the shoulders. "I'm sorry I scared you, honey. I thought there was more than one. I guess I scared myself."

"Yeah." Sue found that funny. "Ghost bugs."

They checked the whole bed again, and the floor beneath it, but found no more bugs. At last Sue settled back to sleep, and Brenna returned to the master bedroom.

As she got onto the bed, another thought occurred. She

jumped off and hurried to Chris's room. Why hadn't there been any sound from him during the whole noisy scene?

The boy was blissfully asleep, head buried under his pillow. Obviously he hadn't heard a thing.

What an experience that had been, with Sue! Brenna decided she must have had a hallucination. The sight of the assassin bug downstairs earlier in the day had set her up for it, made her exaggerate the threat, for where there was one such bug there could be others, and they usually struck at night. Yet she had never suffered such a vision before, though her brothers had surely given her reason. This whole thing made her extremely uncomfortable, and it took her a long time to get back to sleep. This time she left the light on.

In the later wee hours of the morning Nurse stirred nervously in the fish tank. She was feeling ill, and having difficulty getting enough oxygen from the tepid water. She moved nearer the bubbler, but it hardly helped. She simply lacked the vitality she once had had, and it was getting worse.

The specter of nonexistence was looming like a cloud of stirred-up sediment, becoming slowly comprehensible. She could not swim fast enough or far enough to escape it.

Monday passed well. Brenna, a bit tired from her loss of sleep of the night, got the children up and dressed and fed and off to the school bus on schedule; this was a long-familiar routine. Then she set about cleaning the whole house, taking apart every bed, changing every sheet and pillowcase, checking under every mattress. She flushed a number of roaches which she swept into oblivion, and caught several pairs of lovebugs which she let go outside, not liking to kill creatures who were in the act of making love. But she found no more cone-noses. At last, satisfied, she relaxed. She wanted no repeat of the horror of the night.

The afternoon was routine, except for three things. First, she felt as if she were being watched. That she shrugged off, as there seemed to be no reason for it. Second, she found a little bag of colored stones, hidden in a sock drawer. They were very pretty baubles, probably of no value, but she did not take chances; she put them carefully back where she had found them and made a mental note to tell Mr. Pinson.

Third, a woman came by on horseback, looking for Joshua Pinson. "He's on a trip to New York," Brenna told her. "I'm housekeeping while he's gone."

The woman eyed her. "I should hope so."

"Beg pardon?"

The woman seemed to change the subject. "That's why Foster's animals didn't get fed."

"What?"

"Never mind. Not your fault. I'll take care of it."

Brenna didn't understand what this was all about, but didn't worry about it. "I'm feeding the pony and chicks and kittens," she said. "Or the kids are. They know what to do. That's a nice horse you have."

The woman decided to smile. "Yes, I like him, myself." She touched the stone on a necklace she wore, in momentary thought, then clicked to her steed and galloped off.

Brenna had heard a horse going by in the afternoons last week, but it had never stopped here. That might be the one. She would have to ask the children if they knew the horse-woman. Strange, that green stone she wore; it reminded Brenna of the stones she had seen in the bag. Did Joshua Pinson have some personal connection with the woman? That might explain the woman's reaction to the sight of Brenna herself. She had been wondering if Brenna was more than a housekeeper. Well, that just might become the case.

But in the rush of homecoming, homework, supper, and television, she forgot to mention the matter to the children.

They had a good evening, until there was a sound outside. "Oh, nobody moved the pony to the pen for the night!" Brenna exclaimed, remembering.

"I'll do it!" Chris volunteered. He hurled himself out into the dark, taking the lantern. Brenna saw the shadows leaping as the light moved. She also heard the noise of a motor, some loud car or truck lost on Forest Drive.

After a moment there was a cry. Brenna went to the door and peered into the night. The lamp had gone out; only the porch light illuminated the yard. "What's the matter?" she called.

"Beauty's acting funny!" Chris called back. "She knocked out the light."

"I'll help," Brenna said, striding out. "You just hold the gate till I lead her in."

But the pony was not to be led. She yanked her head about as though trying to escape, breathing in snorts. She was much smaller than a horse, but she still weighed about seven hundred pounds.

Then Beauty tried to bite. "Stop that!" Brenna snapped, slapping the pony on the nose. She did not take that sort of thing from animals or from children.

Beauty reacted ferociously. She reared, jerking her head free. Brenna, startled by the violence of this response, stepped back. She tripped over a dirt mound and fell. She saw the pony's forehooves flashing in the wan light, and for a moment thought they were going to come down on her.

But Beauty came down to the side, coincidentally, and danced away, squealing. Brenna didn't like that sound at all; it was ugly, menacing. She scrambled to her feet, unhurt but quite alarmed, and retreated to the house.

"Something's wrong, Chris!" she called. "Get inside. We'll have to let her quiet down a while."

Chris, shaken, scooted inside. Brenna followed him, carefully closing the screen door. Her heart was pounding, and now she was beginning to feel small bruises about her body. She wasn't used to having an animal turn on her like that. What had gotten into that pony?

"Animals have been acting real funny," Chris said, breathless himself. "Mrs. Brown got treed by the dogs, and a chick disappeared, and Sue's fish is having trouble, and now this—"

"Something's funny about this whole place!" Brenna agreed. She remembered the phantom bugs of last night, but decided not to mention them. "I don't believe in spooks, but—"

She stopped. They all listened. The two dogs perked up their ears.

The sound of hooves was coming toward the house. Pounding, as of a charge.

Then there was a thump as the pony struck the wall. The light cedar shingles cracked. Inside, the big hanging clock shuddered, and a calendar fell to the floor. "What's she trying to *do*?" Brenna cried. "She acts like she's crazy!"

Chris went to the dining room window to look out. Suddenly a head rose up, framed by that window, eerie in the partial light. The round white-rimmed eye of the pony stared in.

"Get back!" Brenna cried with sudden premonition. When Chris didn't move, she leaned forward, caught him by the collar, and hauled him back.

Beauty screamed. It was a completely alien sound, unequine, horrible. Her front hooves came up, smashing against the window. The screen separated; glass shattered, spraying into the room. Brenna closed her eyes and covered Chris's face with her hands, protecting him from the shrapnel-like fragments. She hoped Sue was far enough out of the way.

They shook themselves off. Powdered glass drifted to the floor. They seemed to be all right. The boy got back away from the window, his mouth slack with amazement.

Again the pony struck, her feet projecting into the house. *She was trying to climb inside!*

Brenna was too desperate to be afraid. She picked up a chair and swung it violently at those horribly intruding legs. The pony screamed again, plunging her head forward, eyes glaring, lips pulled far back from the huge discolored teeth, ears flat back against her neck. Her disheveled mane stood up in spokes like horns. Creature of hell!

The dog Pharaoh growled and leaped, his own teeth bared. He caught the lip of the pony. Flesh tore as the dog dropped to the floor. Blood dripped.

The pony heaved—and fell back outside. The dog scrambled for the window, but Chris dashed up and caught him around the middle. Pharaoh cried, humanlike, in frustration at not being able to re-enter the fray, but submitted to the restraint.

The pony's hooves knocked loudly against the wall. They heard wood splintering. There was a strangled squeal, then silence.

They waited for the next move, but none came. All was eerily quiet outside.

"She's up to something!" Brenna gasped. "I didn't hear her leave. She's still there, right by the window, waiting. Barricade the doors!"

They propped chairs up against the doorknobs, bracing the entrances against the possible attack of hooves. Brenna cut out cardboard and set it in the broken window so that the night bugs would not fly in. She swept up the broken glass. The pony remained silent, invisible in the dark. They dared not go out to check; that might be what the creature was waiting for.

They went upstairs. "The dogs will let us know if anything happens," Brenna said. "We can sleep." She didn't quite believe that, though.

"Treed by a pony," Chris muttered, awed.

"Can we sleep with you?" Sue asked hopefully. She was trying to be brave, but her features were drawn and pale.

Brenna didn't know what the Pinson family policy was, but she had been severely shaken herself. "We'd better," she said.

What a conclusion to what had been such a peaceful day!

The night was quiet. They slept huddled together on the double bed, afraid of what never materialized. In the morning they got up, girded themselves, and went down.

Beauty was lying beneath the window she had broken in, blood on her front legs where the glass had cut deeply and her lip torn open. She was dead, her body stretched out and cold. She must have bled to death after she fell back from the window. There was something painfully moving about the stiff, still form.

Brenna phoned her mother, who phoned a man she knew who always needed meat for animal food. He normally came and winched up the body and left a pair of leather gloves in token payment.

But when the man learned from Brenna of the circumstances of the animal's demise, he refused to come. "Can't risk one that sick," he explained gruffly. "No telling what's in that meat!"

So they arranged for a man with a bulldozer to come instead. He efficiently dozed out a great hole in the ground of the pasture south of the house, then used his blade to shove the pony into it, and dozed it over so that it was practically level.

Tomorrow, thank God, Joshua Pinson was coming back.

Chapter 14

Josh felt it as he neared the tree: an ambience of family, home and goodwill. The tensions of the trip had begun to loosen as he entered Citrus County. Now they were dissolving, falling away in irregular chunks, leaving a bruised core of positive feeling.

It was dusk as he turned onto Forest Drive and drove the last little stretch north. The surrounding landscape assumed the preternatural beauty of its hour. The trees were darkening green, the pines poking into the white sky. The nether foliage seemed to draw in closer than it did by full daylight, and looked thicker and softer. Perhaps this was the result of the recent rain. He had passed through a stiff shower on the way, and at one point the road had been awash. He had been lucky there had been an opening for the plane to come in; as it was, it had been worrisomely delayed. This region seemed to be having a great deal of precipitation for September. He had read that the fundamental weather patterns of the world were changing, becoming more extreme, less predictable; so far that did seem to be the case.

He bumped around the jag that was Ridge Road and swerved north again on Forest Drive, splashing out soupy mud. Then on up over the hill, down again, and past Old

Man Foster's place, and down into the final declivity. The feeling of homecoming grew stronger.

On past the turnoff, and the mailbox, and into the narrow canyon of the access drive. Then at last the tree hove into view, great and green, embracing the house protectively. Home!

Already the children were charging out, having heard the car. Sue flung herself into his arms as though tackling a quarterback. Josh reached out and pulled Chris in too. "It's great to be back," Josh said. "I brought something for you." Then, as they looked up eagerly, he amended: "In my suitcase. Let me get inside and I'll open it."

The children insisted on helping him carry his bags, which slowed things somewhat. As they hauled themselves up to the door, Josh spied Brenna. She stood at the back porch, breathtakingly pretty in a dark skirt and white blouse, her midnight hair flowing down across her shoulders like a soft shawl. For an instant the sight stopped him short; he had almost forgotten what it was like to approach a lovely woman. Woman? Girl, he corrected himself. She was a teenager.

"How's everything been going?" he inquired to them all as he approached. "Any ghosts?"

He had intended it lightly, but immediately the children sobered and Brenna frowned. "Beauty died!" Chris exclaimed.

"I'll tell him in a little while," Brenna said quickly. "Get your presents now."

"Yes," Josh agreed, grateful for the respite she provided.

They piled inside. There was no sign of Brenna's mother, and Josh remembered that her car was not here. The daughter had finally been allowed to fly alone.

Josh opened the case and bestowed his prizes: a model rocket kit for Chris, perfume in an ornate tiny bottle for Sue, and of course another prized doll from the other house. They had had similar gifts many times before, but always wanted more of the same. Chris had a collection of model aircraft, watercraft and spacecraft, and Sue had a row of little colored bottles on her dresser. She seldom used the perfume on herself, but was content merely to sniff it on occasion, and sometimes put a drop on a favored doll. On very rare occasions one of the dogs was honored, but they usually did not show sufficient appreciation. In a moment both children had disappeared with their treasures, leaving him to settle accounts with Brenna.

"I apologize for being late," he said. "The weather delayed my flight—"

"I understand," she said softly as she took his coat. "Mom said it would. You must be tired. May I bring you something to eat?"

"Hey, you don't have to baby-sit me!" he exclaimed, laughing, conscious of her near presence. "I have to settle accounts with you and take you home before your folks worry."

"I've already phoned," she said. "We were afraid you'd be later than you were."

Josh moved to the kitchen to fetch himself a cup of milk— and noticed that the counters were clean, the dishes washed, and a pan of something good was simmering on the electric stove. "You haven't eaten yet?"

"Chris and Sue kept hoping you would join us, so we waited," she explained. "They snacked a little to stave off their hunger pangs, but they wanted to save their main appetite for you."

"They do that," he agreed, touched. "Well, if you don't mind getting home late—"

"I don't mind," she said, flashing him an oblique glance and an enchanting smile.

Suddenly the children were downstairs again, in the midst

of an argument about whose gift was better. "I see they're back to normal," Josh said, with a small sigh.

"They were very good. Now the tension has been released. They really missed you."

"I missed them too. I wish I hadn't had to leave." He shrugged. "But I have commitments." Why did he feel he had to explain to her?

They sat down to supper. Brenna served an elegant cheese soufflé, hot rolls, a tossed green salad, and milk. She gave Sue a large roll and a very small portion of salad. "You can choke down that much," she said firmly. She evidently had child management down to a fine science.

The soufflé was delicious. "Have you been eating like this all the time?" Josh inquired, smiling, knowing that this had to be a special effort.

"Better, mostly," Chris said around his mouthful of soufflé. "Yesterday we had rice pudding."

"And French toast," Sue added. "Yum."

"Yum?" Josh asked with mock seriousness. "To you, ninety percent of all food is yuck, isn't it?"

Sue made a moue. "Well, I don't like all those dumb salads."

"Salad's good!" Chris exclaimed argumentatively. "You need green stuff."

"*I* don't. I need brown ice cream."

"Can't win 'em all," Brenna said, shrugging. "Close your eyes, Sue, hold your nose, make a face and eat your lettuce leaf. Pretend you're a bunny."

Josh's brow furrowed. "You've been fixing meals like this—throughout?" he asked.

"Oh, sure," Brenna said. "Balanced meals are important. I do most of the cooking at home."

"It is a trade you seem to have mastered," Josh said sincerely. He had assumed that her mother had done the real cooking; evidently he had gotten it backwards. "I thought you'd be opening cans, serving hot dogs and pizzas."

"And eating off paper plates so as not to wash dishes," she agreed, laughing. "No such luck, mister. I happen to like homemaking."

He had, it seemed, haphazardly stumbled on a jewel.

There was custard for dessert. Then Brenna shooed them out of the house while she washed the dishes. Bemused, Josh took a walk around the premises with the children.

The pony was gone, and there was a big new patch of bare sand in the south pasture, but he made no comment; he would find out in due course. The chicks appeared to be a size larger, and healthy, and still reasonably tame.

It was now fairly dark, and he did not feel inclined to go farther afield. He paused by the storage shed. "How did you kids get along with Brenna, really?" he asked.

"She's great, Dad," Chris said enthusiastically. Sue nodded agreement.

"Would you like her to baby-sit you again some time?"

Both agreed emphatically.

Josh shook his head. "When you two agree on anything, it's either very true or very big trouble!"

"But it was scary without you, Daddy," Sue said. "When you came back, it all got nice again. Don't go away again soon."

"No sooner than I have to," Josh agreed. "Now we'd better get back and take Brenna home."

"Can't she stay?" Chris asked. "She's neat."

"She can't stay the night while I'm home," Josh said. "That would be an impropriety. Do you know what that means?"

"It means people'd say you were smooching," Chris said.

"Close enough," Josh agreed.

"What's wrong with smooching?" Sue asked. "She's real pretty, isn't she?"

Josh always tried to be candid with his children. Sometimes it was a challenge. "It is not wise for a man to—uh—smooch unless he's ready to get married. Since I'm not—"

"Married?" Sue asked. "Like with Mommy?"

"As I was married to your mother, yes. So you see, I can't—"

"Mommy is gone," she said gravely. "Brenna would make a good pretend-Mommy, even if she's only Billy's big sister."

"She might at that. But it is hardly that simple. She—"

"Would she have to die, too?"

Josh felt like a torpedoed ship. "Death has nothing to do with that! But the matter is academic. I was just explaining why we have to take Brenna home now."

"It's just 'bout clear as mud," Sue said.

"Brenna is little more than a child herself. She—"

"She's as old as both of us put together."

How had they gotten locked into this subject? "And I'm as old as all three of you put together. Anyway, end of discussion. We're taking her home before her mother worries, and next time I go to New York we'll have her here again."

They returned to the house, buffeted by abrupt wind. "More rain coming up," Josh remarked, holding firmly to the door so it wouldn't slam into the children.

"Wettest September in years," Brenna said, emerging from the kitchen. "Good for the pastures. Last year we had a drought."

"All right. Let's pile in the bus and take you home," Josh said. "The kids are well satisfied, and so am I. Do you want cash or check?"

"Check," she said. "It's safer."

"Now I know we had agreed on a figure. But I was late

getting back, and you've done a better job than I anticipated. So I think an increase is in order. Apart from expenses, of course; I gather you had to hire a tractor for the, er, pasture?"

"No, the first figure is fine," she demurred. "And the 'dozer man left a bill for you to pay." She shrugged. "I enjoyed it, really I did."

"You can't appreciate how important it is to me to have my children well cared for. Call it a bonus for good performance. Shall we say an extra twenty-five dollars?"

"Mister Pinson, I had food and lodging and the kids were great," she protested. "I'm almost embarrassed to take money for it, and I don't need any bonus. I'd have done it for nothing."

"Nice of you to say so. Very well—I'll add the twenty-five." He began to make out the check.

Brenna put her hand on his, preventing him from writing. "No."

Sue looked at them, wide-eyed. "Are you having a quarrel?"

Both Josh and Brenna burst out laughing. "We are indeed," Josh agreed.

"For a moment I thought maybe you were holding hands," Chris said with a smirk.

"Here," Josh said quickly. "Kids, is Brenna worth more or less than what I'm paying her for taking care of you two?"

"More!" they chorused.

"They don't even know the figure!" Brenna protested.

"See? I have well-trained children." Josh glanced at them. "How much more?"

"Twenty-five dollars," Chris said promptly.

"Plus two cents more for holding hands," Sue amended.

Josh smiled at Brenna. "See? They know what's what. You're overruled."

Brenna smiled, and something seemed to melt in her. She

lifted her hand and turned away. "You're an awful nice family. I can't tell you no."

Josh made out the check, conscious now of the impression her hand had made on his own. There was something special about such contact. That fine-fingered, firm extremity! Too bad it was no longer fashionable for people really to hold hands. A lot could be conveyed or shared by such contact.

Josh passed across the check. Brenna took it, her eyes flicking down to read the figure. "You put in the two cents!" she exclaimed. "How will I explain that to Mom?"

"Tell her the truth."

"I will not! She'd never believe—"

"That the children insisted on a bonus."

She deflated. "Oh. Yes, sure. Two cents from the children." She smiled again. "Thanks, children. I'll try not to spend it all in one place." They laughed happily.

Brenna went upstairs to fetch her things. Chris opened the door—and a lurking gust of wind blew in. "Hey—it's raining!" he exclaimed, as if this were something new and wonderful.

"Fetch the umbrellas," Josh said.

They scrambled for the closet, routing out umbrellas. Each member of the family had his own, to minimize quarreling. Josh found his—then realized there was none for Brenna. "Well, she can borrow mine," he decided.

Brenna came down with her suitcase. Her legs were very shapely as they tripped down the circular stair. Josh felt guilty for looking. What business did he have, noticing a girl's legs, as though he weren't a married man?

Again that small shock of realization. He was not a married man anymore. Since Rooster Cockburn's demise, when he and the children had suffered so mutually and terribly, his emotional tie to Mina had lessened. It was as though she had completed her dying, then, by some devious alchemy, and set him free to reconstitute his family whatever way he could. Perhaps it had only been a matter of time. Eight months spent in mourning, the ninth month in returning to the world. At any rate, he was for the first time emotionally ready to consider another woman.

All of which did not mean he was looking for girls half his age. He didn't care to be a middle-aged fool.

They were now clustered by the porch door. "It's raining," Josh said to Brenna. "Take my umbrella—"

"Then you'll get wet, and you're already tired," she said. "Come on—we'll share."

"Oooo!" Sue said in little-girl scandal tones.

Josh ignored her as well as he could. He held the umbrella, and Brenna moved in close. There was a softness about her like that of a purring cat, and the faintest suggestion of some spring fragrance. They followed the children out to the sheltered porch, Brenna keeping pace with him well.

The rain was blasting down now, sheets of it illuminated by the door light. Why did rain always get worse when it was necessary to go out into it? Even the protection of the canopy of the tree did not seem to help; there was too much blowing in from the side.

"All right, let's make this efficient," Josh said. "You kids go out first and pile in the back seats and stand by the side door to let us in after you. Got that?"

"You're standing awful close to her, Daddy," Sue said. "Are you going to smoo—"

"Move!" he said quickly.

"Got it," Chris exclaimed happily. "Into the breach!" He charged into the night. Sue followed, her red umbrella catching the light.

"Our turn," Josh said as he heard the thunk of a closing car door. They stepped down to the ground, and the rain caught them, sluicing in around the perimeter of the umbrella. Josh got wet on the left side, Brenna on the right. His elbow was separating them.

"We're too far apart," Brenna said. "Here, move your arm around me." She guided his elbow up until she could duck under. His arm now encircled her shoulders so that he could hold the umbrella before them. She put her left arm around his waist. "Now let's keep in step, and we should make it without quite drowning."

They moved out in step, her left thigh against his right, as though in a three-legged race. The rain blasted at the umbrella, but for the moment the wind had subsided. Josh was fully conscious of her, of the lithe body, the luxuriant fall of hair, and the faint female fragrance of her. She moved so easily that she seemed to have no mass at all. It was like dancing. It was as if the two of them were in an isolated capsule, a miniature world apart, while the universe raged in its chaos beyond that fragile bubble. He had not been this close to a girl like this for some time; he had forgotten the magic of it.

Remember—she's only nineteen, he thought. *Not for the likes of me.* Yet now he wished that were not so. Mina had been nineteen when he married her . . .

They made it to the bus and piled in as the side door slid open. Josh felt cold water on his back. There was some awkwardness as they got the umbrella folded and found their places and strapped themselves in. Then Josh turned the ignition key.

The motor wouldn't start. The moisture had drowned it out. This happened on occasion, especially when the engine had been hot and then cooled. They would simply have to wait until the rain stopped and the vapors stopped interfering with the ignition system. Josh muttered an imprecation under his breath.

"Oh, goody!" Sue exclaimed. "Now Brenna will have to stay the night!"

"No—it'll start when the rain abates," Josh said, hoping that it would. "But we might as well wait in the house. I'll phone the Sears' house and explain."

"*I'll* phone," Brenna said firmly. "They're my folks."

They made it back to the house, increasingly wet around the edges. Josh found himself secretly happy with the situation. He condemned himself again. He was old enough, and experienced enough, to know better than to get romantic delusions about attractive young women. She probably was not aware of him as a man at all.

Inside, they set the open wet umbrellas on the porch, where the rain thudded on the green plastic roof like a waterfall, which of course it was, and got themselves in in damp order. Brenna's wet blouse clung to her breasts translucently. Josh thought for a shocked moment that she was of the no-bra school, then saw the straps faintly outlined. He forced himself to turn away.

Brenna dialed her home. "Sissy? Bren here. Let me talk to Mom, okay?"

"That rain's going to delay us past your bedtime, and you have school tomorrow, right?" Josh asked the children rhetorically. "It's—my gosh, it's past eight-thirty now!"

"We'll watch TV," Chris said.

"Until nine!" Brenna called from the phone. "No later!"

"Until nine," Josh echoed, while Sue muttered, "Awww . . ." routinely.

"Mom?" Brenna said into the receiver. "Still tied up—the rain, you know. Canines and felines, like you said. Could be several hours more. Don't wait up for me, okay? Sure, we're fine—no trouble at all. I've got the kids watching TV till nine." She paused, listening. "Yes, sure, Mom. I know. See you when. Don't worry." She hung up.

"You might as well watch TV too," Josh suggested. "I hope you'll excuse me while I wash my hair. My scalp's itching, and I want it dry before I turn in."

"I'm expert at washing hair," Brenna said. "Ask the children."

"Say, yeah, Dad," Chris said brightly. "She did mine, and I never got a blink of soap in my eye. Let her do yours."

A hair wash without soap in the eyes? Chris? He'd never managed that. "At ease, soldier," Josh said, smiling. "Baby-sitters don't—"

"No, really, I like washing hair, and I really am good at it," Brenna insisted. "I'll show you."

"No, I couldn't think of—"

"Brenna's going to do Daddy!" Sue exclaimed, losing interest in the television. "This'll be fun!"

Josh started to demur more strongly, then realized that this would be asking for real child problems. They were so glad to see him home, he hated to disrupt the mood. "All right. She'll help me wash my hair. While *you* two watch your TV show."

"Aww," Sue said. But she was mollified.

Josh moved into the bathroom. Brenna came with him. "Take off your shirt," she murmured. "We don't want to get it wetter than it already is."

He removed his shirt, feeling embarrassed and titillatingly naughty. It was, for all his reservations, fun having this most attractive young woman fussing over him. Was it really wrong to enjoy it, so long as he did not lose sight of the reality? Brenna was doing her job, and knew she was good at it; she was showing off (possibly in more than one manner), and he was no more to her than a paying audience.

"Bend over the set-tub," she directed. This bathroom had a large double tub for old fashioned laundry, and an extra sprayer on a hose. "Close your eyes."

"I thought you said no soap in the—"

She ran the water for a moment, and he decided to close his eyes as directed. The warmth came, and she played the water over his head. "That's cool," he said.

"Sounds funny to hear you talk that way."

"I mean the water isn't hot."

"I know," she said, chuckling as she put her hands on his head, moving it to a better centering over the tub. Some portion of her anatomy nudged his shoulder, and he hesitated to conjecture what that might be, but it certainly was soft. "That's par, today. There's a big branch shading the collector in the afternoon, and then there's fog in the morning and rain in the day, so the sun doesn't have much chance."

"A branch?" He puffed air from his lips to clear the water that tried to run into his mouth. "I've seen it, but didn't realize it interfered with the sunlight."

"Maybe it didn't, in summer. But this is fall. The sun's lower and weaker and has less time. That branch really makes a difference, now."

"You've been doing the dishes in lukewarm water?"

"And washing the kids. It's not bad, really. At least there's plenty of it."

"A hundred and twelve gallons," he said. "I agree—it isn't bad. I'm not suffering. But the situation will only get worse in winter, whenever it's not cold enough to run the stove. I'll take a look at that branch tomorrow, soon's I sharpen the chain on the saw. I'd hate to saw off a beautiful limb like that, but we do need that sunlight." As he spoke he experienced an odd twinge, as though glimpsing some distant horror, but the distraction of the hair washing and her proximate anatomy overrode it.

"That should help. Now hold still. Soap's coming. It does stay clear of your eyes, if you don't move." Josh held still, but her torso moved against him, and this time he was sure he felt the silken contour of her blouse. He didn't dare open his eyes. She poured shampoo on him, then worked it into a lather with her fingers. Her hands were gentle yet skilled, traveling about his head almost caressingly. There were, he realized, soothable nerves in the scalp, and his were being invoked.

Brenna rinsed him, then lathered him again, and rinsed again. He could not remember when such a chore had been a more pleasant experience. Then she wrapped his head in a towel and fashioned the towel into a neat turban. Josh felt extremely clean.

"You *are* good at it," he said, thinking about the way her fingers had kneaded his scalp. There had been magic there.

The TV program went into its terminal flurry of commercials. "Washup and bedtime," Brenna said briskly.

"Awww . . ." Chris protested in knee-jerk reaction. Brenna shot him a look, and he hastened to comply.

"Now you don't have to—" Josh began. "Your job is over, and—"

" 'Sokay," Brenna said. "It's still raining."

It was indeed. Josh stood at the window and listened. The initial torrent had settled down to a steady downpour. The light from the house glistened in reflections from the drippings from the eaves and from the liquid coursing along the ground. When it rained here, it really rained! He hoped the chicks had found suitable cover.

He felt a draft. It had been there before, but only now had he become consciously aware of it on his bare skin. He was alone for the moment; the sounds of Brenna bustling the children to bed wafted down from upstairs. He checked the nearest window to the south, but it was closed. Curious, he checked the front door, but it too was tight.

Josh went to the kitchen and found a match. He returned to the window, struck the match, and held it up, burning. Yes, there was definitely a draft, a chill, moist breath from out-doors. He followed that current upstream, hoping to zero in on its source before the match expired.

It turned out to be the north window on the west side of the house. It was covered over by cardboard, but now a shift of wind was blowing that aside and bringing the air in. The window was not open; it was completely broken, as if some-one had attacked it with a sledgehammer.

"That must have been some accident!" Josh murmured. He had sat right beside that window for supper, and not noticed. Of course it was partly concealed by a curtain, but he should have been more observant. His lapse was a signal of his fatigue, and of the distraction his children and Brenna's good food provided. Well, he would ascertain the facts in due course. At least no one had been hurt.

The pony, however, had died. That was another matter he would have to learn about. The children would tell him everything, if Brenna didn't.

He remembered the way she had given him the shampoo, her body so close. Lukewarm water? Who cared! But he would definitely have to investigate that branch in the morn-ing, because in winter that water could be cold, and no pretty young woman to go with it.

Again he felt an odd disquiet, but he could not locate its source. Because this was not a physical thing, he could not trace it by the smoke of a lighted match.

His towel turban was coming apart. Brenna had formed it well—her experience in such things manifested in so many little ways!—but he had been moving about, tilting his head, jogging the material loose. He unwound it and combed out his half-dry hair. He certainly felt better; his scalp itch was gone. But it wasn't only that. He felt better just because he was back with his family. And, he had to admit, because he liked being attended to by the fairest of young women.

The sounds continued upstairs: of water running, of mislaid nighttime items being located, and of lights' curfews being renegotiated. Brenna certainly knew her business; with her here, he had no bother at all. Yet something bothered him about that, and in a moment he isolated it. "*I* should put my children to bed," he said under his breath. "I cannot allow my unity with them to be compromised."

Josh marched upstairs. He discovered the three of them in Chris's room, seated on the bed, talking in low tones. "Hey, I thought this was sleep time," he exclaimed gruffly.

All three jumped as if guilty. "We were just talking," Brenna said. "We do that at night, when we don't read."

Josh saw that the faces of his children were drawn, despite their attempt to be casual. "Is something the matter?" he asked.

Brenna shrugged. "We didn't want to burden you."

"Burden me! Has it anything to do with the broken window downstairs?"

"Beauty did it," Sue said.

"And the pony is dead," Josh said, experiencing a chill.

"Don't leave us alone, Dad!" Chris cried.

"I have no intention of leaving you here alone. Why do you think I had Brenna come here during my absence?"

"When you take her home."

"Oh. I hadn't thought that far ahead. Of course you shouldn't stay here alone. But you do need your sleep."

"Then she's staying the night?" Chris asked hopefully.

"Of course not. Her folks would have my hide if I kept her here."

"My folks don't know," Brenna murmured.

"Of course they do! You phoned."

"I only told them the rain was delaying me. I didn't tell Mom you were back."

Josh stared at her, astonished. "But I *am* back! We had a clear understanding—"

"You want she should worry, knowing you're back, while the car won't start, and sit up all night for nothing?"

"What's the matter with your being here?" Chris asked Brenna, interested.

Josh sighed. He returned to Chris. "Brenna is an attractive young woman. In our society it is not considered proper for such a person to be alone with an older man. Her reputation could suffer. I tried to explain that to you before."

"No you didn't," the boy asserted.

"I certainly did!"

"It was me you explained it to," Sue said.

"At any rate, now you understand, don't you? And you, Brenna—I can't condone—"

"Look, Mr. Pinson, times have changed. My mom doesn't know you like I do. She—"

"You don't know me at all! Now you call your mother back, or I will."

"I know you well enough," Brenna insisted. "I talked to Mrs. Brown last week, and she said you wouldn't hurt a fly, not like that, you know what I mean."

"What *do* you mean?" Chris asked, his antennae tuning in.

She ignored him. "And Chris and Sue have told me about you and"—she hesitated—"and Mrs. Pinson. So I'm not afraid to be here with you. But Mom—she's more like your generation, out of touch. Believe me, only mischief could come of that phone call. Especially if that car won't start until morning."

"Gee, this is a pretty good argument," Sue said appreciatively.

Josh looked out the bedroom window. Water still sounded on the porch roof beyond it. He knew the bus would not start.

He changed the subject. "What were you three talking about, just now? What has Beauty to do with that broken window? How did she die?"

"Bigfoot did it," Sue said fearfully.

"That's the skunk ape, dummy," Chris corrected her. "Bigfoot doesn't come this far south. He's only in the snows. So he can leave his footprints."

"Thank you," Josh said dryly. "Considering that both creatures are mythical—"

"No, the skunk ape lives here, right here in Withlacoochee," Chris said. "He killed Old Man Foster—"

"Foster died of a heart attack."

"He died of fright," Chris insisted. "Because he saw the skunk ape chasing him."

Josh's eyes narrowed. "Who was the author of that fiction?"

Brenna raised her right hand as though in a classroom. "Everyone knows the skunk ape lives in the State Forest. People have seen it. Mostly it doesn't bother people; it's sort of shy. Except maybe when it gets hurt or mad."

"I'm sure it doesn't," Josh agreed. "How does this relate to the pony?"

"It scared Beauty, and she tried to jump through the window," Sue said. The horror of the memory showed on her face. "And then the skunk ape killed her, and she died."

"But you never actually saw the skunk ape?"

She nodded gravely: no.

"I doubt you ever will," Josh said. "Especially not if it sees you first."

Sue smiled dutifully.

"But I'm not about to leave you here alone," Josh said. "When it's time to go, I'll carry you both down and strap you in your seats and take you along. You won't even need to wake up. You can dream about being on the magic bed, traveling through the forest. Out of reach of the skunk ape. So you can relax now. Deal?''

"Deal!" they chorused.

Soon Josh and Brenna were downstairs. He found himself feeling awkward. He had not felt awkward with Patience Brown—but she had been a middle-aged woman. Brenna was a stunning *young* woman.

"I don't believe the bus will start yet," he said. "It's still raining. If I run down the battery by trying too soon—"

"I'm sorry," she said. "You're tired, and you need to rest, and I'm preventing you."

"The *rain* is preventing me. Are you sure you shouldn't call your folks?"

"I'm sure," she said seriously. "You know, the kids really brightened up when you came home. They were so tense before, especially after what happened to the pony. We had her buried down in the pasture; couldn't just let her lie by the house. But when you drove in, it all changed. The fear just went."

"The fear," he repeated, not trusting this. "Of the skunk ape?"

"Maybe. There's something about this place. It's a nice place, don't get me wrong, a very nice place, but sometimes strange. It's easier to focus on the skunk ape. At least that's outside."

He began to see the rationale. A horror inside could not be escaped, but one outside was relatively harmless—as long as a person remained inside. "You saw the ghost?"

"Not exactly. I saw ghost bugs, though."

"Ghost bugs?" This was a new one.

"They were biting Sue in the night. She felt them; she was whimpering in her sleep. But when I swatted them, they vanished."

Shadows might account for that. "Did you look for the ghost in the kitchen?"

"No. I didn't think of it. But I never saw it."

"I looked," he said gravely.

"And you saw it? Really?"

"I saw it. Mrs. Brown was right. There was a ghost—or something. I thought it might be a hallucination."

"And you don't believe in the skunk ape?"

"I don't believe in the ghost either."

"But you just said—"

Josh paced the floor. "Look, Brenna—I'm tired. It—gets complicated. It really wouldn't be fair to you to listen to—"

"Tell me," she said. "I really want to know."

"You asked for it. My wife Mina—Wilhelmina—it has been only nine months—sometimes I forget she's dead, and I think she's just in the next room, and that I'll see her in a moment. Then she doesn't come, and reality returns with double force."

"That's awful," Brenna murmured.

"No. I only wish she *were* there. Her loss, and the manner of it—how I wish it were the bad dream I sometimes dream it is. I have no fear of Mina's ghost. That would never hurt me or the children. If only she could visit us! So when I saw that woman in the kitchen—"

"You thought it was your wife?"

"Not quite. I'd never seen this woman before. But I thought she could be a figment of my imagination, an attempt to recreate my wife—an attempt that failed because I really know she is dead."

"A ghost you *wanted* to see," she said. "That's sweet."

"Also not to be trusted. I don't believe in the supernatural or the hereafter. If I see my wife as a ghost, it is not evidence of the reality of ghosts, but rather of the imbalance of my emotion. So that sighting—"

"If I lost someone I love, I'd want to see him any way I could," Brenna said. "But I guess I see your point. Mrs. Brown saw that ghost, but she's superstitious anyway. You took the suggestion and saw it yourself, but you had an ulterior motive. So someone else'll have to nail that particular ghost."

"That's about it," he agreed. His eye fell on a pile of mail by the front door, and he went to pick it up. "It certainly didn't take long for the sucker list to tune in on a new address."

"I think it's been piling up," she said. "You probably haven't been checking your mailbox. This is more than there should be for just Monday. Anyway, I saved it all for you. One of them's from a bank. Maybe you'd better check that first."

Josh looked at the letter. It was addressed to E. Pinson, with the *E* smudged. Probably the post office had mistaken it for a *J*. His uncle's business mail was supposed to feed into the attorney's office so that the estate could be properly set in order. When the complex business of probate was completed, Josh would get what remained after taxes. This letter had slipped through. It was probably routine. He opened it.

He frowned. "This says the term of a money market certificate has expired; I need either to take out a new certificate at the prevailing interest rate for another six months, or let it lapse into a regular low-interest account. The amount of the certificate is ten thousand dollars." He paused. "Can that be true? Ten thousand dollars, just like that?"

"Oh, sure," Brenna said. "I've seen the ads in the paper. That's the standard amount for that sort of thing. They go six months and quit. If I had money like that, I'd sure buy one. It beats getting no interest and paying a dime a check on what I've got in the bank."

"But ten thousand dollars—I understood Uncle Elijah didn't put money in banks!"

"I heard he was a funny sort of man, but very canny. He could have made some real money in his time."

"Obviously so. The estate still hasn't been settled, but I thought I'd have to pay off some of its debts myself, actually. Now—" He shook his head. He would turn this statement over to Biggerton, of course.

"Say, that reminds me," Brenna said. "He had a stamp collection too. I told Sue she could have it, since Chris had the coin—"

"Coin?"

"A nice gold coin he found outside, so now he's collecting coins. And Sue has stamps. If it's okay with you."

"A money market certificate reminds you of a stamp collection?" he asked, bothered by the seeming discontinuity.

"Sure. Bits of paper worth money, both of them. I don't know much about stamps, but my little brother had a collection, and he's always drooling over the pictures of the old stamps in his books. He says there's an 1847 dime stamp that's worth a thousand dollars now. And—" She paused.

"Are you suggesting there's such a stamp in Elijah's collection?"

"Well, I don't know, but I sure wonder. What my brother says isn't necessarily reliable, but it bears checking out. And there sure enough is a dime stamp dated 1847 in that collection; Sue spotted it on the first page of the album, the oldest stamp there. She said it might be even older than you." She smiled.

Josh had to smile too. "She just might be right, give or take a century. Show me that stamp."

She went to the bathroom and reached into the unused shower. She hauled forth a cardboard box, opened it, and drew out a sheaf of old binders. "See—here."

Josh looked. Sure enough, the yellowing page had half a dozen old postmarked stamps on it. The first was marked 5¢, the second 10¢. Both were dated 1847, in crude black pen lettering on the album paper.

"Well over a century old," Josh murmured, impressed. "Assuming these marked-in dates are accurate, and I really don't have grounds to doubt them."

Brenna shrugged. "They just might be worth an awful lot of money."

They just might, he agreed mentally. It was evidently Elijah's way. To hide value in an unfinished shower stall, where no lawyer had thought to look. There had been a safe, but that had been emptied by the lawyer: the *un*safest place in the house, as Elijah had obviously known. His uncle had indeed been a funny sort of man—but more and more, the methodology of his madness was coming through. Josh liked his uncle better as he came to know him, posthumously.

"I'll see what I can do," he said. He glanced at Brenna with a new appraisal. She could easily have taken this entire collection home to her brother. Instead she had called Josh's attention to the collection's existence and potential value. He liked that.

"I wonder what else remains to be found around here," he commented.

"The skunk ape," she said, and they both laughed.

Chapter 15

Josh looked out the window again. The rain had slacked down, but had not stopped. "I'm sorry to hold you like this," he said again.

"Mr. Pinson, I don't mind being held. You just take it easy."

Unconscious double entendre? "I'm afraid to rest; I might conk out and leave you stranded."

"Sure, you're tired," she said sympathetically. "Maybe I can help you, long's we're caught here anyway. Let me give you a massage."

"A massage!" he exclaimed. "Oh, no, that's not—"

She laughed. "I mean a back rub. I do it for my brothers and sisters, and it really makes them feel better when they're tired or worked up. I'm good at it, honest I am, Mr. Pinson. You've been sitting up in airplanes, and driving, all tense—it will relax you. Let me show you."

"It isn't appropriate."

"Oh come on now!"

He spread his hands. "You have already done too much."

"I like doing for people. I was never much in school; I got by mostly on my legs."

"Legs?"

240

She smiled. "A girl can get by if she keeps her mouth shut and looks decorative in class. I know I'll never be a scientist, but I am pretty good around the house, so I work on that. I like doing what I'm good at." She reached up and kneaded his shoulders, and to Josh it felt extraordinarily good. His muscles *were* tight; now he was aware of that.

"All right," he said. "I have the feeling I shouldn't—but I *am* tired, and we *are* stuck here, and unless you want to watch TV—"

"Lie down on the couch," she said briskly. "Might as well take off your shirt; it's better that way."

Josh acquiesced; he really didn't have the strength to refuse. She perched beside him, her solid upper thigh warm against his side, and kneaded his back. Her hands were gentle but firm and sure, as they had been for the shampoo. They fashioned a spell of good feeling that spread throughout his body.

"You're a marvel," Josh murmured. "You will make an excellent homemaker, when you're ready for that."

"I'm ready now," she said. "I just haven't found the right home yet."

"You surely will," he said, intrigued by the way she had said "home" instead of "man." "With hands like these—"

"Half my school class is married already," she said. "I guess I could have been, but—well, the boys my age seem so immature."

"They do catch up in due course," Josh said.

"By the time they're your age, I suppose. That's a long wait."

"A lifetime's wait, by your reckoning," he agreed. "When you were born, I was your age now."

"Fascinating," she said indifferently.

That was not quite the reaction he had anticipated. But her

hands kept on working, reducing his muscles and spine to blissful relaxation. "That reminds me of a riddle about age."

"I like riddles."

"Mary is twenty-four. Mary is twice as old as Ann was, when Mary was as old as Ann is now."

Her hands tensed, then relaxed. "I thought you meant pun riddles. I can't make head or tail of that, Mr. Pinson."

"Few people can. That's why it's fun. It can be cracked algebraically, of course, though some consider that to be unsportsmanlike. Let X equal Ann's age now, and Y equal the difference between them. Thus twenty-four minus Y equals X, and X minus Y equals twelve. That is, twice as old as Ann was. It becomes a simple problem in addition: X plus Y equals twenty-four, X minus Y equals twelve. The Y's cancel out, and—"

"Mr. Pinson, please! I'm just no good at higher math. I use a pocket calculator to add up my groceries. I don't know X from Y."

Her tone alerted him. She was upset. She had indeed warned him that she had not been an apt student in school. "I'm sorry, Brenna. I'm a computer systems man; this sort of thing comes naturally to me. I didn't mean to—"

"It's all right," she said quickly.

Josh twisted around on the couch to face her. "Look, I'm embarrassed. I didn't mean to get off on something technical. You impress me tremendously. The way you took care of my children—"

"They're great kids. I'll be glad to stay with them again, any time. And of course I want to come in daytime and keep house and cook for you—and just be here, you know."

Josh looked at her face, as he sat up, and suddenly he was aware of the tremendous aloneness that had closed in about him and his children in these recent months. At first there had been the shock of Wilhelmina's death, alternately numbing and devastating them all. They had gone through the stages of adjustment together: denial, anger, bargaining with God, depression, acceptance. The last two had really occurred since they moved here. Yet as that sequence passed, the fundamental loss remained. They were a family, with one vital element missing. They were lonely, they needed the companionship and services Mina had provided. They needed—a woman.

Brenna was very close, and infernally lovely. Josh slowly leaned forward and kissed her.

Her lips, like her hands, were firm and gentle. She was good at this, too.

Josh drew back, abruptly appalled at himself. But she anticipated him. "Don't say a word, Mr. Pinson. I know what you're thinking. You're thirty-eight years old and I'm nineteen, and you're taking advantage of an innocent girl and you feel quilty and you didn't mean to do it and it will never happen again. Right?"

Dumbly, he nodded.

"I have news for you," she continued. "I may not be able to figure out about Mary and Ann or X and Y, but I'm past the age of consent and I do have a pretty good notion what *that's* all about. Maybe in your day boys took girls on dates and kissed them and took them home and said good night and figured they were well off. Today boys expect more, and girls give more, and it's no big thing, usually. I've been the route. I know about VD and pregnancy and who and when are safe. You and now are safe. I know what family life is like and what makes a household operate and about men and women too."

"Evidently so," he agreed, still numbed.

"I think you're coming into a lot of money, Mr. Pinson. I'm mentioning that because I want you to know I was turned on to you before I realized that. You've got nice children and you're a nice man and you may not realize it yet but you can't go on like this. You need someone to run your house and do for you, and I know you think I'm young but I'd really like to try for it. Because you're the kind of man I've been looking for. It's not just because you're mature, though that certainly helps. I like a smart man who can handle the sort of thing I can't, like mortgage interest rates and income tax forms, and who cares about people. I'd like you any age, but this age is fine. We don't know each other well enough yet to be sure, so we have to talk more and be together, and maybe it won't work out and if it doesn't then I'll be sorry, but I'll never be sorry for trying. Mr. Pinson, I want to show you what I can do for you, so you can decide."

Josh felt a little like having been hit by an avalanche. "Brenna, this—you're right, this isn't the way my generation does it. I can't just—I wouldn't—sometimes young women get unrealistic notions—"

"Mr. Pinson, I'm about as realistic as they come. If your wife were alive, believe me, I'd never make a move on you. But you need someone—maybe not me, but someone—and I want to try out for the part. Now, tonight, before the rain stops."

Her implication was absolutely clear, but he couldn't believe it.

"Mr. Pinson, I want to make it with you."

His mind balked. She was not about to let him hem and haw and stall while he made up his mind. It was make or break, on the spot, the way the modern generation did it. "You planned on this all along?"

"No, of course not. I was ready to go home, tonight, and see how things worked out. This could've come next week or next month, when it seemed right. But the car wouldn't start, and I got to know you more and more, and rain sort of turns me on, you know, it's so wet, and I do believe a little in fate.

I guess I didn't know I was going to put it to you so fast—there's something about this house that hypes me up. Anyway, maybe the car won't start until we do what we're here for. We'll never have a better chance. I'm willing."

Josh shook his head. "Brenna, I believe you believe what you're saying, at this moment, but I can't take a girl to—to bed just because she's curious how it would be. I don't—I wouldn't—unless I were prepared to marry—"

"That's the leading option," she agreed.

She was serious! She had found a house she liked, and she was ready to marry into it. Yet she made a compelling case, and he wanted her more then he dared show. In fact, he was amazed at the emotion she had roused in him. *No fool like a middle-aged fool!*

"I just don't want to risk—hurting you," he said inadequately.

"I wish you would risk it," Brenna said. "I'm sort of going out on a branch, telling you like this. It hurts to get rejected."

"Don't think of it as a rejection. I just—don't operate that way. My generation—I—"

He paused. She was sitting there gazing at him, her expression unchanged—but a tear was starting down her left cheek.

"Oh, now, don't do that," he protested. He put his arm around her shoulders, and she turned her face to him and kissed him, her way.

It was as though a dam inside him cracked and then burst apart. The emotion came out in a torrent. He kissed her repeatedly, holding her close, and she responded warmly. The time for excuses and protestations had passed; there was no longer any question where they were going.

"Upstairs is better," she said. "The kids sleep like logs, once they're down."

"Yes." He followed her up the spiral, this time not ashamed to look at her shapely legs and derriere. *If this be sin*, he thought, *so let it be*. If she got to know him as thoroughly as she was about to, and still wanted to make it permanent, she just might after all be the one to fill his need, despite the age differential. He did need a woman, for all the things a woman did. Love did not have to be a part of it. He was not ready for love, not while the memory and hurt of Wilhelmina remained strong. But Brenna understood that—and in time there could be love for her, too.

She paused at the upper landing, by the night-light. "But maybe—no lights," she murmured. "Just in case."

"Yes."

They stood at the foot of the bed, disrobing. In the wan glow of the hall's night-light he saw the obscure highlights of her breast and flank. She was a completely endowed woman, fuller and firmer than Mina had been. In fact she had the kind of body normally photographed for male magazines.

That daunted him somewhat; he was not used to sex appeal of that potency. Not in the flesh. He began to feel guilty—he found this woman more attractive than his wife. Even than his wife as she had been at nineteen. A less attractive or accommodating woman would have produced less guilt; with her he would have known that he would never have taken her in preference to his wife, had he been in a position to make that choice. That would have been better, in its way. But he also knew that this entire attitude was foolishness.

She moved into his arms and kissed him standing, and she was like a goddess in the night, all sleek and full and desirable. Yet he thought of her still as a neighboring adolescent, and he worried about hurting her. He ran his right hand down her bare back, gently drawing her in to him.

She shuddered. She had been so positive up till this point, but now she seemed to hesitate.

They were standing there embracing, his hand slowly stroking her smooth back and buttock. "Oh, that feels so good," she whispered.

Good? He had hardly started! He really had been marking time while he got his thoughts settled. Evidently there had been very little closeness or delay when she removed her clothes for her young boyfriends, assuming they had taken the time to remove them all. No time to work up to it, to savor the process, to shape it to its ultimate. That was another thing that came more readily with age. She thought she was experienced, but she must really have been an acquiescent object, hardly sharing the real experience.

Silently he guided her onto the bed. They lay down, side by side, and the plywood board beneath squeaked, causing them both to stiffen momentarily with alarm, then relax. He lifted his head and shoulders to kiss her, this time running his left hand down along the front of her torso.

"You have a beautiful body, Brenna," he murmured, caressing the fullness of her right breast.

She reacted as though she had never been complimented before. Her arms came up to draw him in close, and she moved her mouth against his. It was still a normal kiss, a good one but not special. She did not seem to know the deep kiss. Yes—slow and gentle would do it, for this young woman who thought she was more liberated than she was. Like a fine animal that had been neglected, she had positive reactions but negative expectations.

He realized he was analyzing. It was his nature; it was one reason he was good at his job. He seldom accepted a system as it was; he was compelled to review it, study it, verify his prior understanding of it and seek improvement. Often this was wasted effort—but often it wasn't. Josh made very few mistakes, once he had analyzed a situation to his satisfaction. Of course Brenna might not appreciate it if she knew—and then again, she might not care. She was a pretty fair hand at analysis herself, of the practical kind.

Yet he knew that if this had been Mina, he would not have thought about it like this. He would have proceeded with the confidence of long familiarity and let it happen. Here, it was as if he were on stage, being judged for his performance, representing his generation. Generation: possible pun there! He did not desire gratification of a bodily urge so much as of an emotional one. He wanted to give this beautiful young woman a better experience than she had had before, or was likely to have elsewhere. Once he was assured that this was the case, he would be able to let himself go. He would have proven himself in a way more fundamental than sex.

Or was he fooling himself? He might really be stalling, giving her a chance to change her mind. Her? He was giving *himself* that chance! Brenna knew what she wanted.

Wilhelmina had been nineteen when he married her. Younger during their first intimacies. It was old enough.

He turned Brenna to her side, facing away from him.

"I don't think it can be done this way," she said uncertainly.

How little she knew! "I want you to look at something," he said, moving in close so that his body cupped hers, his right arm raised, his hand coming down to clasp her left shoulder.

"I don't think we should turn on the light right now."

"You don't need light. Just your mind's eye. Picture the sky."

"The *sky*?" This was not sex as she knew it.

"The great welkin, the dome of the heavens. Deep blue, with white clouds, the sunlight slanting in from a forty-five-degree angle west. Quite pretty, nice."

"You know, I can see it," she said, surprised. "But what has this to do with—?"

"With love? Let's just call it my kind of trip. Try it with

me; I think you'll like it." He, too, was beginning to see it. He had played this game before, in variants; most recently with the children and the floating bed. Then it had not really gotten off the ground, but this time it was really working, and he saw the sky and clouds and slanting sunlight.

"I have to admit this is different," she said. "Like a dream, only—"

"Imagine the sky, so bright and lovely." His hands were busy as he talked, working with her body, his right sliding from her shoulder to her breast, his left stroking her flank, her belly, her thighs. Slowly, gently, evoking the responses of her body while his words diverted her mind. She had been tense; she was relaxing. "The clouds float so low and firm that you'd think you could sit on them. If you could just spread your wings and fly up there—"

"It reminds me of a song I heard once, dreaming a dream," she murmured. "Is it all right to talk? I mean—"

"It is all right to say anything that pleases you," he assured her, his fingers brushing across her nipple, feeling it react. Did young folk believe that love and sex had to be silent?

" 'I dreamed a dream the other night. I saw my love dressed all in white.' "

"Dressed all in white," he agreed. "You can wear anything you want, in this vision. Just take a little leap and float up into the sky, your skirts spreading diaphanously. I'm doing it with you."

"I guess you are," she agreed, for now his left hand was helping her thighs to part, facilitating a closer contact from behind. "But I'm a little bit afraid of heights. I don't like flying. In airplanes, I mean. I'm afraid the motor will fall off or something."

"No motors here. Just us. I'll hold your hand."

"More than that!" she agreed, laughing. "You sure know how to—I mean it doesn't even hurt, and—"

"It never is going to hurt."

"I'll try to remember the rest of that song. It's about this man who dreams about the girl he loves."

"So I gathered. Men do that. Sometimes they even get close to the girls, and still dream. Now picture that sky, and jump."

"Jump!" she agreed tremulously. "Oh, I'm nervous!"

As he had known. "I'm holding you close, Brenna. We're sailing up to that nearest cloud. See it there, like a floating fleece."

"Oh, yes!" Her legs moved a little, with the suggestion of jumping. "Say, I never did this before. Flying. Like this, I mean. But if only I could remember. 'She came to me by my bedside, dressed all in white like some fair bride.' Only there's more."

"Now the ground is dropping away below. We are going up, up to the level of the highest clouds." His left hand caressed the most intimate region.

She shuddered, the last of her apprehension dissipating as the pleasure began to take her. "Oh, it's fun, but I've never been this high before. I—oh, now I've got it. 'And proudly in her bosom there, a red red rose my love did wear.' "

"Yes, bring your rose along. We are becoming one with the heavens, merging with the sky. Now we are rising even higher, flying free in the sky—" He saw it literally, and knew she did too, as their bodies became warm. When he stroked her, now, she shuddered from breast to buttock, unconsciously.

" 'She made no sound, no word she said—' That's all I can remember." Brenna inhaled, realizing. "Oh, I really *am* flying! I've never been so—oh!"

The blue sky converted to a nova-burst sunset, the culmi-

nation of their steady ascent. Josh experienced it as vividly as
she did, he was sure. They had found a momentary place in
the sun. Red suffused the blue, brightening into gold, sending bright rays out from the great disk of Sol, now hidden by
a huge cloudbank ahead of them. Embraced, entranced, as
close as man and woman could be, they shot toward it,
striking the clouds, entering them, becoming surrounded by
colored fog. Moisture coalesced about them, precipitation,
the formation of raindrops. Then the rain itself, bursting from
a thunderhead, washing past them as it had under the umbrella, but this time it coursed all along their bodies, causing
them to cling more tightly to each other. The storm winds
buffeted them, rocked them, threw them about, tossed them
high into the sky, up above the cloudbank, pulse after pulse,
and into the blinding effulgence of the sun, heating them to
incandescence. The pleasure was indescribable.

Now they sank slowly down. The storm was gone, the sun
had set, and shadow closed in. They descended through the
night until at last they came to rest back on the bed, their
embrace finally changed, he on his back, she sprawled half
over him as if flung there by the violence of the storm, her
legs separated and twined around his, her arms clasping him
with a desperate, joyous force. "Oh, Josh, I never—never
knew what it could be," she whispered. "I never really knew
when you—I never felt—that was the climax, wasn't it! You
brought me to it, with your hands, your words, and I never
realized—I thought it was only the man who ever—it's a
whole new dimension!"

"A shared experience," he agreed. "The way it should be."

"I told you I knew what it was all about, about men and
women. I didn't know anything! *Now* I know! You took me
there—"

"We went together," he said. "If you hadn't been ready
to travel—"

She kissed him, this time without either art or passion, just gratitude, and that was the best of all. Then she disengaged and lay on her back beside him, unspeaking. But she found his hand and hung on to it with a kind of little-girl intensity, still experiencing the fading wonder of the experience.

Now the sounds of the night became audible. External things had faded from awareness during the excitement of their excursion; that was a measure of its power.

A clock was ticking. Some distant night creature was sounding off. A pipe was creaking. Across the room was a faint scratching, as of a roach burrowing under papers. The rain had stopped at last, outside; there was only the occasional dripping of leftovers from the trees. It was all wonderfully pleasant, at the moment. Josh knew that it had been many years since he had had as satisfactory an experience, and he was privately amazed at its success. They really had been flying!

There was a *pop*! and a terrible hissing almost over their heads. Brenna rolled over to clutch his arm. "What's that?"

"Sounds like steam," Josh said, sitting up so suddenly that the blood drained from his head, making him dizzy. "Or water—a leak in a pipe—"

"There's something outside!" she cried. "Listen!"

He heard it. It sounded like rain—but it fell only on the west side of the house, beyond their window. Near the hissing.

"What *is* it?" Brenna demanded, her voice hysterical.

Josh reached up and turned on the light. It came on blindingly, like the sun they had so recently imagined, but not pleasant; it stopped further investigation for the moment while their eyes adjusted painfully. Josh shaded his face with one hand, and saw Brenna lying beside him, her body splendid.

He climbed off the bed and got into his shorts and trousers, hastily, trying to locate the source of the noise more specifically.

The hissing abruptly stopped. But Josh had identified it: "The pressure-release valve!" he exclaimed. "On the hot water tank! The water was shooting out, dropping to the ground—that's what sounded like rain."

"Oh, yes," she agreed, relaxing. "My folks' old gas heater does that." She tittered. "*It* blows off steam. Right when we're—"

"A neat analogy," he agreed. It did seem funny, as if the water tank had worked up a romantic heat and—

Heat? That water was barely lukewarm! He had commented on it while Brenna was washing his hair. He had not started the stove, and the solar collector was of course inoperative at night. How had the water gotten hot enough to blow the safety valve?

"What's the matter?" Brenna asked, stirring. She got gracefully off the bed and headed for the bathroom, her breasts bouncing, unself-conscious.

"Where's the heat source?" Josh asked. "Water doesn't just heat up by itself, and this system has no gas or oil or electric heater. That tank should be cooler than it was this afternoon."

"Say, yes!" she agreed from the bathroom. "Here, let me check the hot water." There was the sound of water gushing into the sink.

"It's burning hot!" Brenna exclaimed.

"That's impossible." Josh joined her and put his hand in the flow. He jerked it back. The water was a good 130°F!

"I thought it was impossible to fly, too," she said, smiling, as she used a washcloth.

Josh rather wished he could stay and watch her wash, but the mystery bothered him. There was definitely something wrong here. He could not abide a seeming violation of a law of physics—even in the company of a nude and lovely girl.

Josh traced the pipes with his eyes. The loop to the stove-pipe downstairs traveled along the brick chimney; he touched each pipe and both were cold. No fire in the stove.

If not the stove, it had to be the solar collector. Which it couldn't be. The collector would not operate in the absence of sunlight, and even in the strongest light it was unlikely to blow out the safety valve. Nevertheless, he climbed on the bed and reached up past the trusses to touch the collector access pipes.

One was lukewarm. The other was painfully hot. The water was definitely circulating here. That meant the heat was coming from the collector. The source was outside—and must have been operating for some time to elevate the full storage tank that way. Probably even the "cold" pipe would have been hot, if Brenna hadn't just run a lot of hot water, bringing in fresh cold water to replace it in the tank.

He peered out the window to the south. The collector was there, faintly visible in the light from the window. There was nothing there. What, then, was applying the heat?

"I'm going out there," Josh said, shrugging into his shirt and poking his bare feet into his shoes. "I'm going to find out where that heat is coming from."

"Be careful," she said from the bathroom.

"There's no danger. Just a mystery." He paused, unable to keep his eyes from that divine body of hers as he passed. He chided himself as no better than a gawking adolescent and turned to the stairs.

But as he went down the stair spiral, he wondered: there had been strange things around this house, and this was one of the strangest. A ghost could be a trick of vision or hallucination of the mind; a sound could be the effect of the wind. But water could only be heated by the application of considerable energy. Spooks and poltergeists were intangible; hot water was supremely tangible. It could be measured and traced. So—suppose the heat source could not be traced? What then?

Heat. Now he remembered how the trunk of the tree had been hot, during the storm. He had thought it to be the result of ball lightning, but now found that harder to believe. Lightning could account for a temporary heat, but not for the sustained temperature required to heat a hundred gallons of water.

Josh felt a chill at his spine. It was impossible to explain away hot water! He *had* to locate the source of heat.

He picked up the fluorescent lantern and turned it on. The white light flickered, then spread out strongly. He had not been able to see *under* the collector from the upstairs window— and the front door opened immediately under it. Whatever it was could be there. Right by the front door. He preferred to check that region from a safe distance, to start. He stepped onto the back porch, then on outside beside the tree.

It was cool and quiet outside. The earth was matted with the refuse of spot flooding, but had firmed as the waters subsided. The ground here was porous, since these Florida hills were in fact overgrown sand dunes. This was a hollow, but still there was plenty of sand. Real flooding was impossible here—but the local storms certainly tried!

Then the smell hit him. It was a dank, close, awful odor of—of something like rotting wood, spoiling garbage, and decomposing animal flesh.

It was overpowering. Yet there was a sweetish tinge too, cloying, as though citrus peels had been incinerated. He expelled his breath, not wanting this stench in his lungs—but of course he had to breathe. Had the rain flooded out poor Beauty's grave?

He moved out from the house, beyond the horizontal

branch. Then he followed the branch south to the southwest corner of the house. A gust of wind set off a minor shower: drops shaken loose from the leaves above. Farther to the west an owl hooted.

He was startled by a sharp *crack* at the front of the house, as though a branch of the tree had broken. Josh whirled to face it, aiming the lamp—but saw nothing. He approached the collector nervously; if something had fallen on it—

Everything seemed to be in order. The porch roof was intact, the collector pipes emerging from the house and passing near the huge branch before entering the collector. He doubted that anything had broken the collector's glass, because he had not heard any tinkle of fragments and it had looked intact from above. But it wouldn't hurt to check. He could climb up on the rail of the porch, put a foot on the branch, and hoist himself up high enough to see.

Now he felt the heat. It seemed to be radiating from the porch and the branch, steaming up from the ground. It was as though a furnace were operating, sending its calories out six feet in every direction, causing the wet surfaces to fog— but there was no furnace. There was nothing. Just the porch, the branch, and the heat.

Heat—enough to activate the collector, sending hot water coursing up the pipe, bringing cool water down. Josh knew from his experience with the wood stove that the transfer could be rapid, depending on the intensity of the heat source. But because only a small amount of water was in the pipe at any one time, the temperature had to be maintained for an hour or more to do much good for the household supply. Sunlight was not as intense as the fire in the stove, but it endured all day and got the job done. Again he had to conclude that this mystery heat source had to have continued for some time to elevate the tank pressure to the point of blowout.

Heat without light. Fireflies had light without heat; this was the opposite. Yet it was eerie.

Josh squatted and put his palm to the ground. Yes, it was warm. He touched the corner of the house: warmer. The higher he went, the warmer it got. Then he tried the corner post of the porch: hot! And the nearest surface of the branch, passing here at just about the level of the porch: burning!

He walked a few paces north and reached up to touch the branch again. Warm. He reversed course and walked south, next to the branch. Slowly the branch descended, as though too heavy to hold itself aloft, until at last the leafy extremity rested on the ground. It was easy to reach here—and it became cooler. So the source of heat had been right at the corner of the porch.

The smell was strongest here, too: less rotten and more like burning, though there was no scorch mark on the wood or bark. It was not, then, a fire. Something of boiling-water temperature.

Still no identifiable heat source! There might have been something here, right between branch and collector, heating the branch until it cracked and the collector until the valve blew. A silent, potent, and enduring radiator. But it was gone.

Something between branch and collector? It would have had to be seven feet high to rest on the ground and heat these surfaces like that. Something like a wood stove, with the flame roaring up a vertical flue that passed right here. Yet of course there had been no stove; there were no marks of it on the ground, and how could it have come and gone like that? Unless it were a ghost stove—

Josh smiled. He had not yet accepted the kitchen ghost; he was certainly not ready for a ghost wood stove! More likely the heat source had not rested on the ground at all, but squatted on the big branch, one foot on the collector—

Squatting? Feet? Was he thinking of a living creature? Such as the skunk ape? The foul-smelling monster!

He shook his head ruefully. Sheer fantasy!

Whatever had been here was here no longer; perhaps that crack had been the sound of its departure. His lamplight could have frightened it away. Certainly it had been here until a moment ago; already the heat was fading, though it would take hours for the massive branch to cool to normal. Perhaps it was just as well he had come out when he did because surely such heat was not good for the tree.

Josh made one further check, for footprints. There were none except his own. But of course an hour ago it had still been raining, so those prints could have been washed out. When departing, the thing could have traveled along the branch, and jumped off near the ground. The release of weight could have accounted for the crack, as the branch sprang back into place. He had seen no footprints at the extremity either—but that was wilder terrain where they wouldn't show anyway. He was no Indian scout, to track a beast by its spoor.

Josh headed back inside, suddenly nervous about remaining outside. His heart was beating hard; fear had been building up in him and now threatened to dominate. He cursed himself for being unduly emotional, but now he almost ran.

Brenna met him at the back door, now fully dressed. She remained startlingly lovely. "That smell!" she explained. "What is out there? I got so afraid for you—"

"It's gone." He went to the couch and sat down, suddenly weary.

"*What's* gone?"

"Well, you might as well call it the skunk ape." He had thought to make a joke of it, but his body was shivering.

"The skunk ape!" She was horrified. "Here? Now?"

"Not really. But there was a heat source out by the solar

collector. It must have been on the branch by the corner, the one you say shades the porch, and jumped off when I came out. Something similar may have been here before, when—"

"Jumped off. Then it *was* the skunk ape! Sitting there outside the window, looking in while we—"

"It was dark inside," he said, smiling at her sudden modesty. "Nobody could see a thing."

"I mean it was trying to get in the window!" she cried hysterically. "Climbing up on the house, coming after me—"

"Why should it come after you," he demanded, irritated by her extreme reaction. "Despite the comics showing monsters carrying away maidens, it would not be interested in—"

"Because I have sinned!"

This set him back. *Now* she was suffering guilt? "There is no sin in love," he said gently, though now he felt a strong undertow of guilt himself. "What we did was beautiful."

"Yes! I *liked* it!" she said accusingly.

So the sin was in enjoying it! Complex and contrasting currents running beneath the superficial simplicity. "I *wanted* you to like it."

"But you're a married man! The ghost of your wife—"

What a reversal! "There are no ghosts," he said, but with less certainty than he would have had a month ago. "Yet if there were, and my wife was one, she would not have to climb in any window. I would welcome her in the door."

"But I was here, in your bed—"

She was getting farther and farther out, and his reasonableness was mere papering over his own abyss of doubt, fear, and guilt. "Brenna, get this straight. If Mina came back, it would be only to assure herself that the children and I were safe and happy. She was never the jealous or vindictive type. There is no way she would seek to hurt me or anyone with me. That is not the person I married! She would not generate any spectral heat. And she would absolutely never be associ-

ated with a smell like that one outside. Whatever that thing
was, it was not my wife.''

"Yes, you're right," she agreed, visibly pulling herself
together. "She would not—not manifest like that. It must be
some demon. Maybe the one that killed her. And wants to
kill me.''

"I don't believe in demons either." But it was becoming
apparent that Brenna did.

"But all that—oh, I'll never touch hot water again!''

"Let's just stick with the skunk ape. It's the most reasonable explanation." He found it hard to believe it was himself
talking! "Except for a man with a portable furnace. No
actual threat to us.''

"No! I *washed* in it! It's doom for me! I know it!''

Josh stared into her face. It was drawn and pale. She was
really frightened. Her self-assurance had been totally under-
mined. "How can you 'know' a thing like that? Assuming
this is some sort of inimical monster, why should it be after
you instead of me?''

"You belong here. You own this house. It likes you.
Nothing bad ever happens when you're here. Terrible things
happen when you're away. I'm an intruder. It hates me!''

"You're being irrational," he warned her. This was a side
of her he had not seen before, and he did not like it.

"I'm scared out of my skull!" she cried.

"Because something inexplicable happened? I'm right here
with you, and it doesn't scare me." But he realized as he
said it that this was bravado; a core of apprehension verging
on panic was expanding in him.

"If you hadn't been here, it would have come right in after
me! Like the pony tried to!''

The pony had tried to? There was evidently a lot remaining
for him to discover! "If I had not been here, there could have

been no 'sin,' either, so no reason for it to come in. You have to have more reason to fear it than that.''

"Don't yell at me!'' she yelled.

"I'm not!'' he shouted. Then, shocked at himself for being drawn into hysteria, he wrestled his emotion back into control. Certainly he knew better than to allow himself to be embroiled in that sort of argument. Like a drowning person, she flailed at her rescuer. "Just tell me what really set you off.''

Her shrill defiance collapsed. "You're such a nice man, so strong and smart. Not like the jerks my age. I wish it had worked out better. But I can't stay here.''

Josh was coming to the same conclusion, for his own reasons. But he felt she was holding something back from him. "Why can't you stay?''

"Oh, God, I'll have to tell you,'' she said. "I didn't want to.''

"Tell me,'' he agreed.

"I finally remembered the end of that song. The one I was—while we were—you know. While you were outside, it came to me.''

Josh was becoming impatient. How trivial could she get? "What is it, then? I remember that he saw her by his bed, all dressed in white, with a red, red rose in her bosom. Delightful male fantasy, and you filled the role nicely.''

" 'She made no sound, no word she said. And then I knew my love was dead.' ''

Josh was silent a moment, feeling an ugly chill.

This was obviously a foolish fear on her part, but nonetheless devastating. He knew he should talk to her, persuade her to stay—

But he felt it too. There *was* something out there, and the mystery of it shook him as it did her, and he could not truly deny her concern. Maybe it *was* out to get her. Or any other woman who tried to reside in this haunted house.

Yet to admit that, even privately, was to accept something that he would not accept. What was he to do?

"I'll see if the bus will start now," he said.

"Don't go out there!" she cried, clutching his arm.

"Well, the bus won't come in here . . ."

"I know you think I'm crazy, but the skunk ape—I thought the bad things had stopped when you came back, but really they didn't, and this is only a warning, more animals and people will die, like Beauty and Old Man Foster and your uncle—"

"Coincidence," he said weakly.

"And that skunk ape skulking out there now—oh, please don't go out again!"

If he listened to her any more, his own fear would get the better of him. "Brenna, I have to take you home now. Why don't you go up and organize the children, and I'll bring the bus in as close to the house as I can. That way we'll all be out of here efficiently."

She hesitated, then turned and hurried upstairs. Josh watched her with a certain nostalgia, already; never again would he have a body like that in his bed. Whatever they might have had together was finished, thanks to the skunk ape. *Damn you*! he thought at it ferociously, his fear turning briefly to rage.

Chapter 16

Nerved by that, he went out to the bus. The very night seemed eerie, now. Mysterious heat—Foster's death of fright—a dead pony—ghosts—what did he have to explain these phenomena except the supernatural?

The motor started on the third try, to his immense relief. He warmed it up, then maneuvered the vehicle around the massive trunk of the tree and as close to the back door as possible. He put it in neutral, set the hand brake, and left the motor running while he went back in the house.

Brenna had both children down already, bundled in blankets, virtually asleep on their feet. Josh picked Sue up like a big package and carried her out. Brenna and Chris followed, the two dogs eagerly coming along. In a moment they were all safely ensconced.

Josh guided the bus out along the narrow road. The wheels spun and the vehicle skewed in the moisture, but did not mire. The headlights cut through the night. They showed the still trees, casting tremendously long and shifting double shadows. Ahead the tracks became white sand, and to the sides the bushes glistened. There was no sign of the skunk ape.

The skunk ape. Could there really be such a thing? A

creature undiscovered by science or taxonomy, roaming the depths of the Withlacoochee forest preserve? Josh found it difficult to credit. Yet what could possibly account for that phenomenal source of heat in the night? *Something* had certainly been there! It was easiest to label that unknown, much as he had labeled the unknowns in the Mary-and-Ann problem, for ready manipulation and solution. So why not call it the skunk ape, until the truth could be ascertained?

Was it malignant? That was doubtful. A thing of that mass and heat—it would have to have an extraordinary metabolism, like none known to present science. How could it have sat still for an hour, maintaining that level of energy output? Why hadn't it simply broken into the house? Had it in fact been spying on them? If not visually—though who could say what such a thing's vision might be like!—then perhaps emotionally, sopping up the strong feelings of their lovemaking? Was it curious about human reproduction? How did *it* reproduce? Was it male or female? Could a monster without a mate be jealous of—

No! There was a much less fantastic explanation, he realized as he negotiated the road and emerged at the mailbox. He glanced at Brenna, huddled beside him, and decided not to voice this new thought to her.

·The creature had been running hard in the forest, hunting, getting really hot with its exertions. The way a horse or a man did. It was hard for a large mass to dissipate excess heat quickly, especially in wet weather when the high humidity interfered with the effectiveness of sweating. Radiation was about the only way, and that could take an hour or more. So the skunk ape had stopped at last to rest, perching safely at a convenient place just off the ground. The kind an ape would prefer. A solid, level place sturdy enough to support considerable mass. On the horizontal branch of the tree, beside the solar collector, cooling off. The solar collector would be useful as a cooling apparatus, for it was moving hot water up and bringing cool water down to replace it. That could really help a hot foot, like an icepack on a fevered brow. Thus the monster's heat had dissipated into tree and collector by no coincidence; it had found the ideal place to cool itself. The creature could have discovered this a few months ago, so came here by night when hot, not moving until threatened discovery forced it away.

Thus Josh's endeavors with Brenna in the bedroom had been coincidental. It must have seemed, from the outside, that the house was closing down for the night, as it usually did, so the vicinity was safe. But the secretive creature did watch, of course, just in case, for it feared direct contact with man. Men were liable to carry guns and to drive loud machines. When Josh had come out with the lamp, the thing had spooked and fled. Size did not necessarily make it savage. Though of course if such a creature were trapped and in fear for its life, it could certainly be dangerous.

Old Man Foster—suppose he had come upon the skunk ape by surprise, and opened the shed and grabbed for the saw, hoping to use it as a weapon against the monster? The skunk ape might have taken a swipe at him and fled. Even a missed swipe could have been too much for the old man's heart.

And the pony, Beauty, smelling the ape—that horrendous stench!—reacting in natural animal terror, smashing into the side of the house, hurting herself, dying. Other episodes could be similarly explained. The huge old tree could be the natural home of the huge shy skunk ape, from before the time the house was built. No wonder strange things happened!

Yet there were holes in this rationale. Uncle Elijah would not have attacked the skunk ape; he would have regarded the monster as an invaluable discovery. Yet if he had started the chain saw for some routine work, and frightened the ape, and it had taken a swipe at him, knocking the moving chain into his leg . . .

What of the ghosts? Josh had *seen* the one in the kitchen, and she did not fit into this pattern. So he hadn't worked it all out yet. But he was making progress, and now was satisfied that there was no proper reason for fear. As with fire, the skunk ape had to be treated with caution, respect, and understanding. . . .

Josh woke much refreshed as the sunlight spattered down through the branches overhanging the house.

The children were already bustling about, getting ready for school. He was concerned that they would have trouble managing, after the rigors of the prior night, then remembered that they really hadn't been involved. They had ridden in the car when he took Brenna home; that was all. Should he tell them about the skunk ape?

"Hey, the water's hot!" Chris exclaimed.

"That's impossible, dum-dum," Sue retorted. "It was lukewarm yesterday, and the sun doesn't shine at night."

Josh decided he had better tell them.

So as they ate a patchwork breakfast, they exchanged stories. Josh learned surprising details about the manner of Beauty's death, and told them about the nocturnal visit of the skunk ape. "That's why Brenna had to leave so abruptly," he concluded. "That ape terrified her."

"Well, she was just waiting for the rain to stop," Chris said.

"That, too," Josh agreed, feeling a touch dishonest.

"Maybe footprints!" Sue exclaimed. "I'll look!"

"After school," Josh told her sternly. "Meanwhile I'll check around; if I see any, I'll save them for you."

She grimaced, disappointed, but did not protest.

Josh walked with the children to the road to wait for the

school bus. The ground was glistening, and myriad little bowls were suspended in weeds along the path: the globular webs of small spiders, made visible by the moisture.

After the bus roared in and away, its wheels spewing out gouts of mud, he returned to make a serious exploration of the vicinity. He wanted to find the spoor of the skunk ape, not merely to verify that it had departed, but that it had existed. He had worked out a perfect explanation for the mysteriously heated water; he wanted to be sure it was the correct one. He could live with the concept of a huge, hot, and shy forest creature; he was not sure he could live with the other, spectral explanations for such a phenomenon.

He checked all around the house, especially on the south side. His own tracks remained; the rain had abated, leaving them in place. Surely it had also left whatever other tracks there were. But he found none.

He checked closely about the end of the great horizontal branch, where it touched the ground. This was where the creature would have jumped off. The ground was too grassy here to show much, but still, a creature of that mass—there should be something.

There was nothing. Even after all reasonable allowances were made, there was no evidence that any large creature had passed here. No tracks, no indentations, no broken branches. Even the little spider nests were generally undisturbed. Those last could have been spun later in the night; still—

Josh shook his head and went on to the next chore. He had to saw off this branch, to clear the way for the sunshine to strike the solar collector all day. It was a step he did not like taking, but—

That saw. He felt increasing dread of it, despite his understanding of its nature. He imagined it sitting there in the shed, waiting, a trace of red oil glinting on one of its teeth. He had promised Chris to allow the boy to watch, the next time he used that saw; now that seemed like an excellent notion. So he wouldn't saw now; he would wait until the children were home. That postponement was a relief.

He surveyed the situation, assessing exactly where to make the cut, when he *did* make it. This was a giant branch; it would not be easy to sever at the base, but farther out there should be no trouble. Also, he did not want to take off any more than necessary; it was a shame to disfigure the magnificent tree at all. Unfortunately it was not feasible to move the solar collector; the south side of the house was the only place for it, and low enough so that the hot water could rise to the storage tank. Elijah had designed this farmstead as a whole, and changing any part of it was endlessly complicated.

A picture came into Josh's mind of a paper. It seemed to be a treasure map. The locations of valuable things were marked on it, such as precious stones, gold coins, the stamp collection, a cache of "junk" silver under the front porch.

How his imagination wandered! Josh glanced at the porch.

He shrugged. He got down on hands and knees and scraped at the dirt where the map indicated, just to prove it a fantasy.

Eight inches down he encountered something hard. Part of the foundation, probably. But he excavated further, just to be sure.

It was a metal cannister, very solidly emplanted, as though it contained fifty pounds of silver.

Suddenly Josh knew that his vision was accurate. Elijah had deposited worn silver coins there—dimes, quarters, and dollars. Better just to leave them, so that he wouldn't have to explain them to anyone—himself especially.

He returned his attention to the big lateral branch. Strange that the old man had not foreseen the problem with it! It was obvious that the shade—

Josh paused. Obvious? Not that he could see at the moment! The branch started out extending toward the collector, but then angled away from it, and the subsidiary branches spread from the opposite side. The solar collector was given a clear field of sunlight.

How could this be? Brenna had told him how the branch interfered, in the fall when the sun was lower, and that had made sense to him. But the branch did not interfere; there was a perfect channel for the sunlight.

Why, then, was the water lukewarm? This might be fall, but this was Florida; there was plenty of sun remaining. Of course a rainy day made a difference. Still, he had been gone several days, and it surely hadn't rained the entire time!

He contemplated the branch, thinking of his visit here during the night. Here was where the monster had stood, one foot on the branch, the other on the collector, so that—

No, it couldn't have. The branch was too far from the collector. The thing would have had to do a split of a good six feet, and anyway, the branch dipped considerably below the level of the collector at this point, further complicating any such position.

But last night he had stood and looked up, assessing the position of the branch. His memory was quite clear: The branch had passed within a yard of the corner of the porch where the collector was, and had been at the same level.

Now that was not the case. The branch dipped away from the porch.

Had he suffered a confusion of perspective in the night? He would not have thought so, but certainly there was no call to saw off the branch; it was not interfering with the solar collector.

Maybe the skunk ape had returned while they were delivering Brenna home, and stood on the branch again, and borne it down so that it no longer interfered with the collector. A crazy notion—yet easier to accept than questioning his own clear image of a different position for that massive branch. At any rate, it would have to do for now.

With a silent sigh of relief, Josh moved on, satisfied that he did not have to mutilate any part of the wonderful tree. It seemed that the skunk ape had managed to do him a favor.

Now he had to check the pasture region where the children had told him Beauty was buried. That was another peculiar occurrence! Whatever had possessed the pony to attack the house? And what had killed her? There should have been an autopsy. That smell—it was gone now, but if that grave had been disturbed . . .

And that story about the bugs on Suzanne. Children were imaginative creatures, but to have dreamed of being attacked by a bug, and to have had Brenna actually see them on her—except that they were phantom bugs that vanished without trace. None of this was to be believed—but neither was it exactly to be doubted. There were too many strange things occurring.

Josh had struggled on the new project for days, but his concentration was not good. The mastery of the details and principles of accounting, he saw, would have been a challenge when he was in full command of his faculties; now it was more than a challenge. He was distracted by the mystery of the skunk ape and the other unnatural phenomena. The rain continued on and off every remaining day of the month, with an inch on Saturday, keeping the children mostly in and the water mostly lukewarm, and his concentration mostly null. Sue's fish, Nurse, was definitely ill, with the blight spreading across her body and resistive to the medication they put in the water. Sue was distraught, and Josh couldn't blame her; that fish was one of the dwindling legacies of Mina, and the loss would carry more than ordinary significance to the child. It was so difficult to watch the progress of the inevitable so helplessly.

Monday, the first of October, the rain cleared. But not Josh's incapacity. He took a walk around the premises, once again admiring the private prettiness of the yellow fall blooms. Weeds, perhaps, to others, but to him no flower was a weed. Why was yellow so prominent this season? Was there a procreative advantage to that color as the land gradually cooled? Nature surely had good reason for everything, could man but fathom it. Man, unlike nature, could operate on an unreasonable basis.

And was he any exception? Here he had a good project to work on, and he was frittering away his time instead of getting down to it. What was the matter with him?

He stopped there, beside the broken column of the dead pine tree, and considered. What *was* wrong with him? This was not his normal state. He was normally an efficient worker, and if he had a problem, he focused on it and solved it.

Well, he was without his wife. That had thrown him out of kilter, to put it indelicately. He had learned to cope with such chores as the shopping and the laundry, and had gotten help with the children. But that was not enough. A woman was more than household help. A woman was—

Was, among other things, Brenna. Company, flattery, and delight in bed. He had not looked for anyone to replace Mina, but Brenna had shown him that it was time to consider that. Too bad it hadn't worked out with Brenna herself. But she had been too young. She lacked the stability to handle a thing like fear in the night, or the guilt for what should not have been a guilty matter.

Yet the appeal of her presence remained. If he could just fathom what was going on here, so as to eliminate its terror, perhaps she would reconsider, and—

Suddenly it burst upon him: why he had refused to work with Philippa. He had begun to see her as a woman who might replace Mina, and had recoiled. He had not wanted any such relationship, so had cut it off the moment the prospect manifested.

But nature did not cease her course merely because a man was a fool. Brenna had arrived on the scene, and cut through his reticence in minutes. It was no affront to Mina that he needed a whole woman; Mina had made him that way.

Josh strode back to the house. As he approached the porch door he saw a lovely young woman standing in it. Brenna!

But as he blinked and looked again, she was gone. He hurried inside, looking about, but there was no sign of her. He even looked upstairs—and saw her standing naked in the bathroom, washing. He opened his mouth—and she vanished.

He staggered to the bedroom and threw himself on the bed. *Brenna had become a ghost!*

He rolled over—and felt her body beside him. But now he knew it wasn't there. Yet he experienced the bliss of recent, perfect sexual satisfaction, as if they had just made love.

Was he losing his mind? He *had* to act.

But he couldn't call Brenna. Not to tell her that she had become a living ghost!

He picked up the phone and called Pip's number.

"Hello?"

At the sound of her voice, he had a confusion of second thoughts. What was he looking for?

"Hello?" she repeated.

"Josh Pinson here."

"Yes," she agreed cautiously.

"I—about that business association—I—is it too late to reconsider?"

"I'll be right over."

"Oh, you don't have to—"

"I prefer to discuss it in person."

"Yes, of course," he said somewhat lamely.

In due course the sound of hoofbeats signaled Pip's approach. He went out to meet her.

She dismounted and led her horse to Beauty's old enclosure, then turned to face Josh. She was dressed for riding, with jeans and a long-sleeved plaid shirt, and her hair was bound back.

"First, I want to apologize," Josh said, as he began walking with her away from the house.

"No need," she said. "You changed your mind. That happens to the best of us."

"When I saw you in your dress, looking very attractive, it wasn't just that I was embarrassed about not recognizing you," he said. "It was that I abruptly saw you as a woman. I—as a recent widower, I just wasn't able to handle—"

"Then perhaps it is I who owe you the apology. I should not have—"

"Oh, no! No, you were not at fault. I should have explained before. I just wasn't ready to face—" The memory of what he didn't want to face struck him with full force now, and he felt his eyes stinging. *He didn't want to let go of Mina.*

Yet he had to, to this extent. He had to fashion a life for himself and the children, a stable life that looked toward the future, not the past.

He fished a tissue from his pocket and dabbed at his eyes, embarrassed. Pip gave no sign of noticing: a gesture he appreciated.

"So I apologize for allowing a nonbusiness consideration to prejudice my judgment," he said. "I do need help on the accounting, and I would like to work with you on the project. I assure you that there is no—that it is strictly business."

"Strictly business," she repeated without emphasis.

"Completely professional. I will pay your normal fee."

"Yes, of course," she agreed.

"One other thing," he said, surprising himself.

"Yes?"

"Mary is twenty-four. Mary is twice as old as Ann was, when Mary was as old as Ann is now. How old—"

She laughed. "Eighteen, of course."

Why had he asked it? He had not intended to, and had not known that he would—until it had happened.

Again he had to ask himself: was he losing control?

They set their first meeting for Wednesday, as Josh had a number of chores to catch up on first. He would go to her house and she would learn enough of his project to discover how her expertise could apply. It was all very straightforward.

Josh was sure that the professional association would work out. But even as they agreed on it, he felt discomfort, because that wasn't what he really wanted.

So, dissatisfied, he watched her ride away. At least he would get the project moving.

He returned to the house. With luck, he'd see the living ghost of Brenna again.

Sue found no footprints either, that afternoon, but she found something almost as good, by her definition: a clump of toadstools. She screamed with delight.

In a moment both Josh and Chris were there, half in alarm. She was standing just southwest of the monstrous main trunk of the tree, pointing to the clump. "Aren't they pretty!" she exclaimed.

Chris opened his mouth, surely about to say something caustic, but Josh intercepted that with a warning look. Too many negative things had happened; if toadstools were a source of momentary joy, it was best to encourage it.

Josh squatted beside the clump. "That is indeed pretty," he agreed. "I've never seen that type before."

Chris decided to be positive. "They look like little houses," he said.

Josh knew what he meant. They had once been to an entertainment park where some elven scenes had been set up, with the houses resembling giant toadstools with little doors in the stems. These did seem to be that type.

Sue got down close. "I wonder . . ." she said, intrigued.

Then the clump seemed to expand, so that they could see every detail clearly. Sure enough, there were doors in the stems, and windows. The toadstools were so close together that their tops overlapped, forming a common roof, and the spaces between the stems became narrow alleys. It was a miniature village.

A door opened and an elf came out. He wore comically bright clothing and a tall pointed cap, and his beard trailed almost to the ground. He walked across the ground to a fallen twig, picked it up like a log, and carried it back inside. The door closed. Then a puff of smoke emerged from a stovepipe poking through the roof.

"Must be nice and warm in there," Sue murmured.

"Wish I was in there," Chris said.

"We can go in and light our own stove," Josh reminded them.

"Gee, yeah!" Chris agreed brightly.

They got up and headed for the house.

"I didn't know elves had stoves," Sue said.

Only then did Josh realize what had happened. *They had shared a vision.* Not a talk-through vision, such as with the floating bed, but a real one. They had all seen an elf and a puff of smoke. Perhaps it wasn't much as such things went, but it had brought them abruptly together in a way they desperately needed.

Was he crazy, to accept such a thing? No crazier than he had to be to believe that a massive branch could change its position by several feet overnight without breaking, or that a huge hot forest creature could be prowling in the vicinity.

It was of course not nearly cool enough to warrant it, but Josh lit the stove, making a token fire, and once it was burning well enough to establish a proper chimney draft, he opened the side doors, rendering the stove into a kind of fireplace. That was the way it was designed. They brought cushions and sat on the floor before it with the dogs, and used sticks to spear marshmallows that Brenna had left and toast them against the flames. Josh had never felt closer to his children, and he delighted in it. Who could have believed that such a positive experience could result from a little clump of toadstools!

Tuesday morning Pip rode in. Joshua Pinson was away; he was probably in town shopping. She should have phoned. She checked the kittens and chicks, then paused, looking at the huge Tree.

She had always liked the Tree. For her it was a living creature of considerable beauty and a certain personality. She had come to it before old Elijah Pinson built the house, and continued thereafter. The Tree was the best place she knew of for the sorting out of feelings.

She let the horse graze while she climbed up on the big lateral branch. It was like a highway, one she had always liked to mount to the region where it humped and started back down toward the ground, sending out its lesser branches. A highway? More like a bridge over some unseen river.

But the branch had changed. She paused, staring at it, to make sure this wasn't a confusion of perspective. It no longer passed close to the porch roof; now it veered away, as if giving the porch a wide berth. How could that be?

She walked on to the end, satisfying herself that the branch was now entirely low-lying, never rising more than a yard from the ground. Its own weight must have borne it down. Odd!

She returned to the center, where the hump had been, and inspected it closely. Now she saw serrations in the bark that she was sure had not been there before, and a faint, dank odor clung to it. Odd, indeed! What had happened here? Obviously the wood had not been damaged, for the leaves of the branch remained healthy, though of course it took a while for live oak to show damage. This species of tree was deciduous, but only barely; it dropped its tough little leaves in the spring as the new ones were growing out, so that it was never without greenery. Those leaves cascaded down like rainfall in the wind, in spring.

She sat on the branch, letting her legs dangle. It had been possible, before, to see into the upper bedroom window from here, not that she had sought to do so. But no longer; the branch was now too low, so the porch got in the way. Not that there would be anything worth a voyeur's while, for Josh was a sedate man. But could he possibly have ignored the beautiful young woman who had baby-sat for him during his last absence?

She closed her eyes, taken by an unusual sensation. She felt a brush of wind against her skin, and felt a pleasant darkness surrounding her. She saw the window, and though it was not lighted, she saw within. The young woman was there—Brenna, that was her name—innocent of clothing, with the kind of body that only the young could even aspire to. And Joshua Pinson was there too, naked, and the two were on the bed, seeming to float, riding some pleasant current, most intimately coupled. The sensation of that union seemed virtually to radiate out, wholly wonderful, wholly fulfilling, wholly—

Pip's eyes snapped open. The vision faded. What sinister bypath had her fancy taken her? She had never been given to casually lascivious thoughts!

Yet she felt a flush, and knew, without knowing how she knew, that it had been a true vision. *They had been intimate.* In the early night, waiting for the rain to abate.

Well, what business of hers was it? Josh was his own man, and the girl was of age. She, Pip, had no reason to object. She had made a mistake by approaching him in an unprofessional manner about a business relationship and alienated him; that still embarrassed her. It was not a mistake she would make again. She would complete her undertaking to acquaint him with what he needed to know of accounting, and then settle back into the role of good neighbor. Though Josh was paying for it, she regarded the accounting training as an extension of her commitment to Elijah: watching out for the man's estate.

Still, she was curious.

If the stunning teenager had indulged in voluntary sexual intimacy, why had she departed? Evidently Brenna had wanted to move in more substantially, then abruptly changed her mind. What had caused that change?

Perhaps there had been an argument, or maybe the girl had been daunted at the end by the magnitude of the commitment. The young were apt to get into things without properly understanding their extent. Yet the grapevine had it that the girl had been savvy enough about her prospects. Could there have been something about Joshua himself that reversed her attitude the moment she learned of it?

Now she remembered the way he had abruptly posed a mathematical riddle to her. She had encountered the Mary and Ann problem before, the first time as a child, and had found it devilishly tricky to handle. It had taken her a good fifteen minutes to solve. But perhaps it had stimulated her to play with numbers further, leading eventually to her present career. But why should Joshua have posed it at that moment?

Had he expected her to fluff it? He seemed to have a funny attitude about intelligence in women. Probably he would be best off to settle down with a woman without too much of a mind of her own. That teenager, perhaps. So why hadn't he?

She looked about, nagged by something. Now she realized what it was: there were no wild creatures here. No birds, no squirrels. No nests in the Tree. There never had been, though she had never thought about it before. How odd!

Pip jumped off the branch and went looking for her horse. It was time to move on, for she had the growing feeling that she was somehow being watched—by something very large, silent, and patient. She remembered how Old Man Foster had died, and shivered.

Chapter 17

Pharaoh woke, smelling something. Nefertiti remained snoozing on the other rug. He stood under the broken window, catching an interesting whiff.

Things had been quiet for several days, with the children away by day, and the Master gone most of the time too. Pharaoh didn't like being alone so much; Nefertiti didn't count as company, of course. But normally a good long nap sufficed to bring someone home.

He sniffed again. Yes—that was definitely the odor of Pony. The one he had gotten a good chomp of when she tried to climb into the house. The creature had had no business intruding in Dog Domain! He had thought she was gone, but that odor could not be doubted.

As he thought of it, the smell grew stronger. Now he heard the hooves. That stupid horse was coming again!

Pharaoh knew his duty. He leaped at the window. His solid body crashed through the cardboard blocking it. He fell straddling the sill, and scrambled on out, falling to the ground.

Whomp! The landing was jarring. Dazed, he lay for a moment, panting. His bad leg hurt.

Then the smell came again, and he roused himself. That

pony had to be chomped! He got to his feet and stood for a moment, swaying, again sniffing the air.

The problem with odor was that while it was excellent for identification, it wasn't much for location. But he heard the hooves drumming the ground a short distance from the house. He set off in pursuit.

The presence seemed to retreat as he approached it. That was natural; it was fleeing his righteous determination. He broke into a run, his bad leg hampering him less as he worked into it.

Now he was in the forest pasture, and the smell was stronger. But also different. Not exactly Pony. Not Wild Dog either. He didn't quite recognize it, but he was sure it needed chomping. Most things did. He charged on.

Now the thing turned at bay. Certainly no Pony! It was larger, and stranger, and worse. It definitely needed to be chomped!

Pharaoh charged, growling. The huge shape turned to face him. Pharaoh leaped, mouth opening.

The thing caught him in midair. Pain lanced through him as the blow smashed him to the side. His neck was broken by the first blow. But as he fell helplessly to the ground, the thing came down on him savagely. He hardly had time to scream with agony before his consciousness fled.

Chris jumped down from the bus, swinging his books about. It was only two more days till his birthday. Columbus Day, October twelfth—that was why he had been named Christopher.

Sue followed, more sedately. They waited for the bus to turn about in its lumbering fashion and crank up for the return trip, leaving its noxious cloud of dusty exhaust. Then they set off down the path to the house. They no longer used the driveway; they preferred the more recent path that wound directly down into the hollow, coming to the house from the southeast. Originally this had been cleared to make room for the fence, and the posts were there, but no wire.

They passed the big oaks near the road, then walked on through the big region of palmetto. They were always careful here because there were probably rattlesnakes in it. But Dad had cut the path wide enough to allow room to see, and the truth was that the average snake really wasn't looking for trouble. Not even a rattlesnake. If they gave it time, and didn't chase it or poke it with a stick, it would just disappear into the brush and not bother them. Anyway, they had never seen a rattlesnake here.

Once they cleared the palmetto, Chris broke into a run. He was too exuberant to move slowly. He just had to get where he was going—even if he had nowhere to go but home.

He detoured to loop by the place in the pasture where Beauty had been buried. He liked to make sure nothing had been disturbing the site. They didn't want any bones being dragged out, after all.

He skidded to a halt. The site *had* been disturbed! The dirt had been scuffled and shoved about, as if some large animal had tracked through it. And there was a smell.

Chris backed away, then turned and ran back to the path. "Something's been at the grave!" he cried.

"We'd better tell Daddy!" Sue said, concerned.

"Aw, he's not home yet. He's over at the horsewoman's."

"How do you know?" she asked challengingly. "He's supposed to be home before us."

"But he always runs late."

She nodded, agreeing. "Chris, do you think—?"

"They're smooching?" he finished.

"Or something," she agreed, embarrassed. "What if they got married?"

"If Daddy wants to get married, what's wrong with Brenna?" he demanded.

"You know Brenna's not interested. The skunk ape scared her, and she's not coming here anymore."

"Do you think it's still around?" he asked. "Maybe if—"

"Daddy says there's no such thing," she reminded him.

"Then what scared Brenna?"

She shook her head, unable to answer.

They entered the house. Nefertiti was just inside the door, wagging her tail frantically.

"Where's Pharaoh?" Chris asked. They had to take the dogs out on the leashes first thing when they got home so there wouldn't be any messes in the house. Chris normally took the male dog.

They looked, but there was no sign of Pharaoh. They spied the unblocked window. "He jumped out!" Chris exclaimed.

"Why would he do that?" Sue asked with annoying reasonableness. "He's lazy and fat; he wouldn't care enough to scramble out that way."

"Unless maybe there was something out there to bite."

Sure enough, the dog's prints were in the dirt near the house. Sue checked for the chicks, but they were all right.

"The grave!" Chris said. "Maybe Pharaoh—"

"Maybe," Sue agreed, relieved. She had Nefertiti on the leash, so was restricted, but Chris dashed back down to the pony's grave to see whether there were dog tracks there.

There were not. Whatever had disturbed the site seemed to have been considerably larger and clumsier than a dog.

There was a funny smell, too. Chris walked around the site, making a large circle, trying to track down whatever it was. "Pharaoh!" he called.

Then, in a small declivity that partially concealed it from view at any distance, he found the body.

For a moment he stared, unbelieving. He had never seen anything as horrible in his life.

Chris screamed, and ran.

* * *

Josh returned to find chaos. Both children seemed to be half in shock, and soon he learned why: Pharaoh had been killed.

In that waning evening light, Josh went to bury the animal. He was appalled when he saw the carcass; the death had been brutal. Blood was spattered about, and it seemed that just about every bone in the animal's body had been broken. It looked as if he had been savagely gored and trampled. What kind of a creature could have done this?

He could not afford to be carried away by the horror. He had to come up with a rational explanation. Surely there was one! If he let himself be ruled by emotion instead of common sense, what would he tell the children?

There were hoofprints all about. A bull, or even a cow. Such animals ranged these pastures, occasionally straying from their own herds. They were generally harmless, but they were big, and horned, and probably somewhat ornery about dogs. Pharaoh might well have been foolish enough to attack one.

He buried the dog near the burial site of the pony, and returned to the house as darkness closed.

The children were nervously awaiting his return. "You saw?" Chris asked, almost as if hoping that Josh would have found nothing.

"I buried him," Josh said. "You did the right thing."

"He—Pharaoh was really dead?"

"He really was," Josh agreed.

"And you aren't scared?"

Josh paused. Suddenly he felt a surge of fear. He fought it down. "Why should I be scared? I am very sad about this, of course, but these things do happen."

"Like with Mommy!" Sue said faintly.

Oh-oh. "Why do you feel that way?"

"Pharaoh went out—and something killed him," Chris said.

Which was exactly what had happened to Mina. "What do you think killed him?"

"The Skunk Ape," Chris said, and Sue nodded agreement. Josh forced a laugh. "There is no skunk ape!"

"But if it came again," Sue said, "and Pharaoh went out to bite it, and—"

"It looked to me as though Pharaoh was gored and trampled by a roving cow," he said. "You know how he is about animals. Those cows are pretty big, and they have horns and hooves. If he attacked such an animal, the result—" He shrugged. "I believe that is what happened."

"Then what about the Skunk Ape?" Chris asked.

"I don't think it killed Pharaoh." That much was true. Yet he remained appalled by the evidence of sheer ferocity. A cow should have gored defensively and fled; this creature had mauled the carcass savagely.

"What about the grave?" the boy persisted. "Something was trying to get at Beauty's bones!"

"The cow tracked through," Josh said.

The boy didn't seem entirely satisfied, but he didn't argue. Josh wasn't entirely satisfied himself, but he didn't care to argue either.

It just kept reaching, reaching, and finally she could flee it no longer. When she realized that there was no escape, she gave herself up to it, and the ugly darkness claimed her.

This time Josh was first to return. He saw the fish, Nurse, floating at the top of the aquarium, and knew it was over. He dreaded having to tell Sue.

He used the little net to lift the fish out of the water. He could bury her before the children got home from school—no. It would be better to let the child know the full truth at once. To get it over with.

When they arrived, he was waiting. He nerved himself and addressed his daughter. "Sue, you know your fish was sick. She—"

Then, to his complete surprise, he choked up. He was unable to say the word. The loss of the little fish overwhelmed him.

"Give her to me, Daddy," Sue said. "I'll bury her."

What was this? Josh, who had hardly noticed the fish while it lived, was suddenly all broken up—while the child, whose life had been devoted to that pet, was acting dispassionately.

Sue took the dead fish and a trowel and went outside. Josh saw her walking down toward the burial region in the pasture, chin up. She was doing the job.

Seven years old, and standing up so well! Josh was amazed and gratified. He was also extraordinarily proud of his daughter. She was already growing into a woman like her mother.

With that thought, he felt better.

The next morning Sue was ill. She got up and tried to get ready for school, but she was lagging. Josh checked her temperature, but she had no fever. Still—

"If you aren't feeling well, you should stay home," he told her. Sue was no laggard; she was not one to pretend illness.

"I don't feel well, Daddy," she agreed with a wan smile.

So she remained home and in bed, while Chris went alone to the school bus. Josh brought her chocolate milk, but she sipped it more from duty than pleasure. She seemed satisfied just to lie there and listen to the music on the little radio.

At nine o'clock he normally walked across the tracks to Philippa's house to work on the accounting program. That work had been going well, and his project was almost complete. It was also true that he liked working with Pip, and was casting about for some legitimate way to extend the association when the accounting was done. But today, with his daughter sick—

He checked with Sue. "I have been working on a project with—"

"Go ahead, Daddy," Sue said. "I'll be all right."

"But I don't want to leave you—"

"You need to get your work done, Daddy. I'll just sleep."

"But if anything—"

"I have the number. I'll call you there."

Certainly she looked all right, apart from listlessness and pallor. Whatever ailment she had seemed to be low grade, not life threatening. "You're sure you don't mind?"

She flashed a wan smile. "I'm sure, Daddy."

"I'll be back at noon."

"Noon," she agreed.

Heartened, he set off for Philippa's house.

When she was sure she was alone, Suzanne pushed back the cover and lifted her legs so that she could see them. She wore woolen socks to keep her cold toes warm. Slowly she drew off the right one, inspecting her foot closely. It was all right.

Then she removed the left sock. There, above her big toe, was a patch of discolor. It looked very like the one that had started on Nurse's tail.

Sue nodded to herself. She knew what that meant.

But she wouldn't tell Daddy. She didn't want him to worry.

Next week Sue was still sick. She had smiled for her father, and assured him that she was getting better, but her strength had continued to ebb. The dark patch had started on Wednesday, and had been larger Thursday. Friday the nineteenth had been a student holiday, so she didn't have to worry about missing school. But she had had to don heavier, longer socks to cover the patch, and she stayed in bed and kept her legs out of sight as much as possible. She had gone to the bathroom only when no one else had been near.

Now the long weekend was over, and Chris was at school, and Daddy was across the tracks, and she could relax. For three hours, anyway.

She got up and headed for the bathroom. She didn't think it would work, but she had to try: a shower. Maybe she could scrub off the bad patch.

She removed her nightie and stood naked, looking herself over. Her left leg was discolored almost to the knee, and a patch the size of a silver dollar had started on her right foot.

She took her shower, and scrubbed her legs, but the discoloration remained. It wouldn't come off. She knew why: it was because it wasn't paint on the outside, it was rot on the inside. Just as it had been with Nurse. There was no way to stop it; it would just keep spreading until finally she died.

She sighed. What had to be, had to be, because that was the way it was. But she wished she could have had more time. She knew that Daddy and Chris would be unhappy when she died. At least they could be happy a few more days—just as long as the patches didn't show.

She dried and put on a clean nightie and clean socks. She still had over an hour before Daddy returned. She could use that time to make a collection of the longer socks, so she wouldn't run out.

She went to the drawer, but all the balls of socks there were short. But there should be some in the laundry basket downstairs; she could wash them out herself, and hang them in her room to dry, and they would be ready by tomorrow.

She stepped down the spiral staircase, clinging tightly to the rail because she felt a bit dizzy and weak. She made it down safely, and made her way to the basket. On the way she glanced into the kitchen, and saw the ghost. That didn't bother her; that ghost never moved from the kitchen, and never stayed long, and didn't mean any harm anyway.

Nefertiti roused and looked at her.

There was something strange about the way the dog stared. Sue remembered how the old housekeeper, Mrs. Brown, had hidden from the dogs. They had started looking strangely at her—the way Nefertiti was looking now.

The dog stepped forward. Sue retreated. Nefertiti took another step. There was definitely something wrong with her!

Sue found herself at the porch door, blocked off from the downstairs bathroom and the laundry basket. And from the stairs. She could not get to safety. Still the dog advanced, slowly, tail held low, staring at her from eyes that seemed to be set low on the sides of her head.

Sue turned, grabbed the knob, and opened the door. She squeezed through, closing it quickly behind her, shutting the dog in.

But now she was shut out, in her nightie, socks, and slippers. She didn't dare go back in. Not till Daddy returned. She couldn't even phone him, without exposing herself to the dog! The ghost wouldn't hurt her, because ghosts didn't really exist, but the dog was real.

But maybe she could just go to Daddy. She knew where the horsewoman's house was. There was a path to it, across the tracks, for the horse. She and Chris had used it, exploring.

She started walking along the path to the school bus stop. She had a long way to go beyond that, but she could get there. She *had* to get there! There wasn't anything else to do.

But she was ill and weak, and she found herself rapidly tiring. As she passed the region of the three burials, she staggered, feeling faint. She had to stop, leaning against a tree, pausing to regain her strength.

She was near Nurse's grave. She could see the bared ground. She knew she had caught Nurse's disease. How she wished they had been able to cure the fish! She had been strong, so as not to worry Daddy, who already had enough problems of his own, but it was getting so hard to keep up the front. In her secret heart she was crying and crying, sorry for herself because she didn't want to die, and for how Daddy would miss her. He had always told her she was just like her mother, and he had loved her mother. Now, of course, he was getting interested in the horsewoman, and forgetting Mommy, and that was his business, but still it hurt.

Her tearing gaze focused on the fish's grave. Something was moving there!

She concentrated, alarm thrilling through her, and now it was definite: the loose sand was pushing up, as if something below were rising.

There was only one thing below that sand: Nurse. *The fish was coming up!*

Horrified, Sue ran back away from it. But she staggered, in her weakness wandering from the path and through the tall old grass. Her legs did not work as well as they should, because of the blight. Her left slipper caught on a root, and she almost fell. She caught herself, but lost her slipper.

Now she was at the brink of the largest grave: Beauty's. It, too, was stirring. The sand erupted and cascaded to the sides as a great dark shape thrust up.

Sue tried to flee, but her clumsy legs got tangled with each other and she fell. The thing from the sand drew itself up and loomed over her, parts of it gleaming moistly. She screamed.

Josh heard the scream as he came back along the path. He recognized it instantly. "Sue!" he cried, breaking into a run.

He charged down the road, past the mailbox, and down into the hollow. What had happened? He should never have been leaving her alone while she was ill! His breath was rasping as he covered the distance, but he hardly noticed. If anything had happened—! He pounded on toward the graves.

Sue was there on the ground, in her nightie, cowering,

terrified—and some huge and awful shape was looming over her. The thing was shedding sand, and in the sunlight its bones glistened.

"What the hell is that?" he cried, appalled.

"Beauty!" Sue cried.

Now he saw the shape of it—and it was the dead pony. The bones of it were walking, closing in on Sue.

He charged to her rescue, arriving just as the bones did. The equine skull bone was reaching down to touch her, but his shoulder intercepted it. He felt the cold contact of the bare teeth; then his hands grasped the little girl. He grabbed her—but the walking skeleton was shoving at him, trying to bear him down.

Josh held Sue with his left arm, and swung out with his right. His wrist banged into the ridged column of the neck.

He ducked down and shouldered into the thing's foreleg. The leg gave way, and the foresection collapsed. Bones showered down around Josh's head and rattled to the ground. He lurched on through, his knees snagging on a tendon; then he was free. But he could tell by the sound that the thing remained mobile, and was coming after him.

He staggered to a pine tree and set the child against it, then heaved up a large dead pine branch. He swung it at the pursuing thing.

The branch knocked the bones apart. The skeleton collapsed. Josh paused, panting—and saw the bones begin to move, forming back into the skeleton.

He dropped the branch, turned again, and seized his daughter. He carried her to the house and set her down at the porch door. The bones had not followed.

Now at last he took a good look at her. She was bedraggled and covered with dirt. She had on a nightie and long socks, nothing else. Her hair was a tangled mess, matted with dirt.

"Daddy, I took a shower," she said.

He had to smile at the incongruity. "So I see."

"But then Nefertiti started looking funny."

"So you got nervous and went outside?"

"And started walking to where you were. But—"

"But I was already on my way back. Fortunately."

"Those bones—"

"You want me to tell you they were all in your imagination?"

She smiled tremulously. "Yes."

He sighed. "I can't tell you that. I saw them too. I fought them. For all I know, they may still be out there shambling about."

She was silent. He looked at her again, this time noting how pallid she was under the dirt. She was shivering though it was not cold. He realized that he was not helping her. She needed reassurance and comfort now, not uncertainty.

"But isn't that impossible, Daddy?" she asked after a moment.

He put his arm around her and squeezed. She was trying so hard to be reasonable and brave! "Of course it's impossible!" he agreed. "Dead animals don't come back to life like that, and if they did, they wouldn't be able to move that way. There has to be flesh and muscle to pull the bones about."

"Then how could it be?"

He was still unable to give her the kind of answer she needed. "Either they were propelled by some other agency, such as—"

"The skunk ape?"

"Or it was hallucination," he concluded.

"We'd better go in," she said. Now she was starting to cry, her fright finally taking over now that she was safe.

Here he was, theorizing on what they might have seen, instead of getting the sick child back into bed where she belonged! Josh opened the door.

Nefertiti greeted them eagerly, tail wagging.

But the dog had seemed strange. This was the second time that had happened. He was disinclined to dismiss it as the confusion of a child. Too much of a pattern was forming: when he was away, strange things happened, and more than one of those episodes had resulted in death. This one, he was sickly certain, would have seen the death of his daughter, had he not returned in time to break it up. The dog, driving her out; the illness, weakening her. The bones, attacking her.

Had Suzanne escaped the bones, and told the story, he would hardly have believed it. But he had returned too soon, and battled those bones himself. Now he believed.

Something supernatural was stalking his family.

But he didn't want to alarm Sue. "Let's get you cleaned up and back into bed," he said.

"I'll do it myself, Daddy," she said quickly.

"But you're ill!"

"I can do it," she insisted, hiking up one of her socks.

Josh sighed. Modesty, surely, beating back both her illness and her fear. "Then you get yourself organized, and I'll fix your lunch."

"I'll be all right," she said. "You can take Nefertiti out, Daddy."

She wanted to be sure of her privacy! "Very well; we'll be back in ten minutes."

He leashed the dog, and they went out and down the path toward the burial sites. As Josh had suspected, there was no sign of disturbance here now. The bones were gone. Beauty's grave had been tracked up—but he had done that himself. It was obvious that nothing significant had come up out of that hole.

But he had bruises on his arms where he had struck those bones. He would have doubted another person's story about this event, but he did not doubt his own experience. Perhaps he had bashed his arms against the branch of some tree, while his mind conjured up the phantasm. But he still believed that he had saved his daughter from violent death. Now that he was alone, he could afford to shudder and react to that horror.

Something was leading them into mischief. Now he could see a pattern in it: the deaths of animals, and of Old Man Foster. The way the saw had seemed to attack him. The way it had succeeded in attacking Uncle Elijah. The events were generally based on natural things, so that they could be explained—but that seemed to be camouflage. There was an *un*natural imperative operating here in the shade of the tree. He had been trying to explain it all away—and that had been his error. No problem could be solved until the solver was ready to accept the nature of it.

He returned with the dog to the house. He would just have to talk it over with the children and do what was best.

Sue was clean and in bed. He joined her in her room, bringing her milk and a peanut butter and jelly sandwich. "Tonight, when your brother is here, we'll have to have a talk," he said. "You know I don't want you getting tangled up with any more bones."

She smiled weakly. "I'll try not to, Daddy."

"I wonder if I should take you to the doctor? I don't like having you mysteriously sick."

"No doctor, please, Daddy!" she pleaded.

He shrugged. "No doctor," he agreed. But he didn't like her nagging ailment. If she didn't mend soon, he would have to force the issue.

One week later Suzanne was no better; in fact she remained in bed and covered up even when too warm. This was no ordinary illness! But she remained adamant about not seeing the doctor.

Then he got a phone call. His new accounting program

was beautiful, and it seemed that the company was planning to implement it. But their engineers were confused about some of the details. He would have to go north and straighten them out personally, if the system were to be properly set up. Tomorrow.

"But I can't go on such short notice!" he protested. "I have a sick child—"

But it had to be. There was a lot of money involved, and the entire system could be fouled up if he was not right on the scene. He had to go.

Josh put down the phone. He could not afford to have that accounting system thrown out now. He had paid Pip her fee, and that had depleted his ready cash; he needed the money.

He would have to make the trip. That meant a baby-sitter. Whom could he get? He didn't want to trust his children to a stranger—not with Sue sick and with the type of things that had been happening here.

He would have to ask the horsewoman. He knew she wouldn't like it.

He phoned. "Pip, I need you—"

"Yes?"

"To baby-sit the children while I go north."

"What?"

"It's an emergency. I have to go tomorrow, and I have no one—"

"Josh, I am no—"

"I'll be glad to pay—"

"I'm not talking about money!" she said furiously. "By what nerve do you ask *me* to—"

"I just don't have anyone else I can—"

"To *baby-sit*?!"

Josh saw that this was not to be worked out. Of course she was a professional woman, and she had never deceived him about her attitude toward children.

"I'm sorry," he said. "I know I presumed too much on our acquaintance."

"You did indeed! Whatever possessed you to suppose that—"

"Yes, I can be very foolish," he said heavily. He felt a lump in his throat. Not only had he failed to get the help he needed, he had alienated Pip. "I'll find someone else."

"Perhaps that teenaged paramour?" she suggested.

About to hang up the phone, he stared at it. "What?"

"I shouldn't have said that. I apologize."

"Uh, yes," he agreed faintly. *How had she known?*

"Look, Josh, if you really can't—"

"That's all right," he said, embarrassed, and hung up.

Teenaged paramour. Had news gotten around? He had never imagined that Brenna would tell.

What did it matter? Brenna would never return.

Or *would* she? His need for a baby-sitter was desperate, and she was the best possible one. She had been terrified by the hot water, but she was young; perhaps . . .

Josh forced himself to face his true motive. He wanted to see her again. He had not intended to get involved with her, but it had not been by his choice that she departed. If he could possibly persuade her . . .

He dialed her number. He had, after all, a legitimate need. It made sense to ask her, quite apart from his personal feeling for her.

"Hello." It was Brenna's dulcet voice, sending an almost adolescent quiver through him.

"Josh Pinson. Please don't hang up, Brenna."

She laughed, sounding uncertain. "I wouldn't do that, Mr. Pinson. But if you want me to baby-sit—"

"That, too," he said, surprising himself. Oh, this was going to be awkward!

"What?"

"I mean, I have an emergency trip north, and I just can't leave the children—"

"Mr. Pinson, we've been over that. I like your children, but that monster—"

"Brenna, I understand. But I'm desperate. I don't want to leave them with a stranger. Could—could I bring them to your house?"

"Oh, no, that would be—we're overcrowded as it is, and—"

"If it's money—double the rates? I have to—"

"No, Mr. Pinson, it's not that! But—"

"Brenna, I'm pleading with you! Sue's ill, and if there's any way, any way at all—"

"Oh, darn it!" she exclaimed. "You're not playing fair, Mr. Pinson."

"I know it," he agreed wretchedly. "I—I understand. I'll try to get someone else. I shouldn't have called you."

"I'll do it."

"What?"

"Mom will drive me down. When do you need me?"

"Uh, tomorrow, if it's possible. Noon. But look, I didn't mean to—"

"I know you didn't, Mr. Pinson. But you're right. Those kids—what's Sue got?"

"I don't know. She won't let me take her to the doctor."

"She wouldn't," she agreed. "All right. Mom will drive me down. I'm afraid I'm going to regret this."

Josh was afraid so too. But he could not tell her no. Feeling guilty, he closed the conversation and disconnected.

Chapter 18

At noon, October 30, Brenna commenced her second stint as baby-sitter. Joshua left for the Tampa airport and would not return until Friday, the second of November. She had three days to get through.

Why had she agreed to do it? She made it a point not to fool herself. She had told her mother that it was an emergency, and that was true, but she had wanted to do it despite her fear. What she had had with Joshua Pinson had been very good, until the skunk ape had driven her away. Better than anything else she was likely to find. If she allowed herself to be driven from this, what future was there for her? So when Josh had called, she had been at war with herself. Desire versus fear. Which did she want to govern her?

Also, he had asked her, and it was not in her to turn him down. She liked him, liked him a lot, quite apart from his situation. When he begged her to do it, she had melted.

But mostly, it was just the children. They were more important to him than anything, and she liked them too, and they liked her. That counted for a lot. When she had heard that Sue was sick . . .

First, she had to make sure Suzanne was all right. As it turned out, the child had been home sick for almost two weeks, and she wasn't sure whether this was a genuine illness or a feigned one. Why hadn't Josh taken the girl to a doctor? Because she didn't want to go? No parent accepted that! She went upstairs.

She knocked on the child's bedroom door. "May I come in, Sue?"

"I guess," the little girl replied without enthusiasm.

That was odd. Sue had always been companionable before. Now she sounded like a stranger.

Brenna entered. The child was so still and pale she was shocked; this hardly seemed to be a feigned ailment!

"What's wrong with you, Sue?" she asked, not really expecting a sensible answer. "Why don't you let your dad take you to the doctor?"

Sue merely shrugged.

Brenna had dealt with uncommunicative children before. "Let's play a game," she said.

"I don't want to—"

"It's not exactly a fun game. It's a let's-see-what-might-happen game. I'll be the State Social Worker, and you'll be the Child at Home. Now I've just come in and I see you, and I say: 'What have we here? A truant child? Why aren't you in school?' "

Sue smiled weakly. "No, Miss Social Worker. I'm just sick."

"Then why haven't you seen the doctor?"

Sue was silent again.

"Uh-uh," Brenna reproved her. "This is a game. You have to answer, or maybe your dad will be thrown in jail for Contributing to Delinquincy in a Minor."

Again Sue forced a smile. "Maybe it's the ghosts," she offered.

"Ghosts?" Brenna said with mock severity. "Surely you don't believe in them!"

"We're not supposed to. But when they come in the house—"

"Are you telling me you've actually seen a ghost here?"

"Oh, sure," Sue said, getting into it. She knew that Brenna believed in some scary things, so this *was* a game. "But they don't do any harm, they just fade in and out. Mostly. It's when they take over the animals I get scared."

Brenna remembered the way the pony had acted. She permitted herself a private shiver. But she continued to play her part. "Suzanne, do you mean that you can—can evoke a ghost? When you choose to?"

The girl retreated back under her covers. "Is that wrong, Miss Social Worker?"

Brenna had to laugh. "If you weren't ill, I would ask you to show me a ghost right now!"

"I can show you now," the child said, almost eagerly.

This was a game, but it was getting serious, as it was supposed to. Still, this was an odd twist. She did not want to aggravate the child's condition, but was quite curious where this was leading. "What, here? Now?"

"No, she's downstairs, in the kitchen. But I can show you!"

"Sue, I would very much like to see that ghost! But I don't want you to make yourself worse than you are."

The child was struggling into her bathrobe. "It won't take long, honest, Brenna! We can just go down, and I'll show you, and then I'll go back to bed."

So positive! But better this than listlessness.

The girl got out of the bed, stood in robe, nightie, and long, heavy socks, and swayed. Brenna put out a hand to steady her. "You really should see a doctor, Sue! You are very weak."

"No, no doctor!"

There it was: the girl was adamant. No sense in pushing it, yet, until she understood why.

Sue started for the door. She swayed again, almost falling, and Brenna had to hold her steady.

They navigated the spiral stairs together, somewhat awkwardly, and stood at last facing the kitchen. "Now—think of drain cleaner," Suzanne said, clinging to the stair rail. "Think real hard."

"Think hard of drain cleaner?" Well, it was important to play fair. She closed her eyes and concentrated.

"There!" the child exclaimed.

Brenna looked. There by the kitchen sink was a woman in a frowzy housecoat, pouring something into the sink. She finished, and set the can down on the counter, and turned to face the two by the stair. Her mouth opened as if in surprise. Then she vanished.

Brenna felt faint herself. Not only had that been a ghost—but she recognized the woman! "That was Irma Pease!" she whispered.

"You know her?" the child asked, impressed.

"Not well. But she isn't dead! How can she be a ghost?"

"There're ghost sounds, too, and the zombie bones."

Brenna's mind was racing. Irma Pease—she remembered now. The woman had hired out as a housekeeper—and Elijah had hired her for a time. She had learned this when she researched about this place. *The woman had been here!* And now her ghost haunted the kitchen, even though she wasn't dead. This made little sense, even in supernatural terms.

"Let's get you back to bed, Sue. Then we'll talk about ghosts."

They returned to the bedroom, and talked about ghosts. Brenna, in the guise of Miss Social Worker, learned about the sounds: a gunshot, a power saw, stray growls around the house. And the outdoor ghosts, of the woman who was attacked by the bad man, and a hunter who built a fire nearby. Sue had seen them all. And the haunted animals, like Beauty, and the bad bugs, and the zombie bones.

Brenna would have doubted it all, but she had seen the ghost in the kitchen, and of course she had already known about some of the rest. "And your father has seen these— these manifestations?" she asked.

"Some of them," the child agreed. "But he doesn't really believe in them. Chris is afraid the bad saw will—"

"Will turn on your father, just as it did on Elijah?"

"Yes."

Brenna sat on the bed, shaking her head. "Why should any of this be occurring?"

"We think the Skunk Ape doesn't want us here."

The skunk ape. Brenna could not disparage it, for she shared that fear. But she continued the game, for she was learning things. "You think the skunk ape is conjuring ghosts to scare you away?"

Sue's brow furrowed. "We don't know. The ghosts don't try to hurt us; they're just there. But the zombie bones—"

"Your illness!" Brenna exclaimed, the game dissolving into reality. "Is that connected?"

The girl tried to avoid that subject, but Brenna persisted. "Look, Sue, you really did show me the ghost. I accept the fact that you're not making any of this up. You must trust me! If something is making you sick—"

The child capitulated. "Promise you won't tell Daddy?"

"Not tell him! Sue, if there is something hurting you, he *has* to be told!"

"But he might worry."

"Of course he might worry! He loves you! If you've been keeping something from him—"

"My fish died."

Brenna was startled by the sudden shift of subject, but followed through. "How did your fish die?"

"She got the icky patch on her scales, and it spread and spread, and she died. I buried her, down beside Pharaoh and Beauty."

"And how does that relate to your own illness?"

Slowly the child turned back the cover, then drew down one sock.

Her leg was a mass of discoloration. She had some kind of severe skin disease. "And when it finally spreads all over me, I'll be dead," Suzanne concluded.

"But you couldn't have caught a fish disease!" Brenna protested, appalled. "Diseases don't—they aren't contagious from fish to man!"

The girl merely looked at her legs. That was answer enough.

"And you believe that the skunk ape sent this disease to kill you, so you wouldn't live here anymore."

Gravely, the child nodded.

"And you hid this from your father, so he wouldn't worry?"

Again the nod.

Brenna was in a quandary. She had elicited the child's confidence, and felt obliged not to violate it. But this definitely called for medical attention.

"Will you let me phone a doctor, if I don't tell him about you? To find out what kind of disease this might be? I can't just let you go on like this! Perhaps there is some simple home treatment that will make you better."

"Nothing will stop it," the girl said forlornly.

"If nothing does stop it, then we'll have to tell your father. We certainly aren't going to let you die!"

Suzanne shrugged.

Brenna left her and went downstairs. She phoned her own doctor, and described the symptoms. In short order she determined that it wasn't impetigo, eczema, poison ivy or any other standard rash. But what *was* it?

"You know, if I were a vet," the doctor said, baffled, "I'd swear you were describing a fish disease. We had a pet goldfish once that—"

Brenna hung up the phone, feeling faint.

When Chris returned from school, Brenna braced him immediately. "I talked with Sue, and she told me all about the ghosts. She showed me the ghost in the kitchen. She thinks the skunk ape is doing it. What do you say?"

"You *believe*?" he asked incredulously.

"Chris, I was here before, remember? When Beauty tried to break into the house. The skunk ape terrifies me! But we've just got to get through, so I want to know everything you know about it, so maybe we can do something before someone is seriously hurt."

"Like Great Uncle Elijah?"

"Yes. We don't want anyone else to be killed like that."

"That saw—" he said.

"We don't have to touch it. It can't hurt anyone if it isn't started running."

He nodded, reassured.

She made supper, and took a tray up to Sue. The girl seemed more cheerful. She ate, but her heart wasn't in it.

At 8:00 P.M. Joshua phoned. The children had been expecting it, and jumped at the sound of the ring. Brenna let Chris answer, while she went upstairs to fetch Sue.

She paused at the doorway, for she saw a bug on one of the child's thin arms. The ghost insects—they didn't need *that* manifestation! Then she saw that it was not a bug, but worse; it was a new spot of that discoloration. It really was spreading.

She said nothing, and helped the girl get down to the phone. The two children passed the phone back and forth, delighted to be in touch with their father. Brenna stayed clear; there was so much she preferred not to say at this time. She was doing her job; the children's evident welfare attested to that, and that was all Joshua needed to know.

But she could not escape it. "Daddy wants to talk to you, Brenna," Chris said, holding out the phone.

She accepted the instrument. "Yes?"

"There's something they're not telling me," he said. "Is something wrong?"

What could she say to that? "We're getting along well enough."

"I did not expect evasion from you, Brenna."

And of course she was guilty. But Sue was watching her, and she just did not feel free to discuss the illness. "I saw the ghost."

His tone hardly changed. "Which one?"

"The kitchen ghost. Irma Pease. But you know, she's not dead."

"I suspected. The rape victim isn't dead either. They seem to be a lingering presence, and harmless."

"But if there can be a living ghost, there may also be—"

"The skunk ape," he finished. "This may be foolish, but I would feel easier if you stayed inside the house after dark."

"We will." She experienced a surge of warmth, appreciating his understanding. She knew that he refused to believe in the supernatural, and that had been part of what had driven her away, before. His unbelief, which tacitly made her out to be a fool. His superior attitude. But things had happened in the interim, and he had seen what she had seen. What did a rational person do, in the face of the irrational?

"I'm sorry to have gotten you into this," he said. "I hoped that there would not be any trouble during my absence."

"There wouldn't have been," she admitted. "But I talked to Sue, and when she said she could show me the ghost—"

"Skepticism can be dangerous," he said, trying to laugh.

"But I can see that you are taking care of my children, and for that I sincerely thank you, Brenna. I know what a sacrifice it is for you."

Her pulse was pounding at her breast. "I love you, Josh."

Then, appalled, she hastily hung up. What had she said!

Both children were gazing at her. Brenna flushed. "I don't know why I said that," she told them awkwardly. "I didn't know I was going to say it."

As one they turned to ascend the stair.

"I didn't mean to say it!" she cried after them. "I have no interest in—" But that was a lie. She had been desolate after she walked out on Josh, and had cursed herself for her fear without being able to conquer it. Until now, maybe.

They proceeded on up, the boy helping his sister.

Brenna's vision blurred. The tears were flowing down her cheeks. She cursed herself for her transgression. What had come over her? Certainly the children didn't want her encroaching on their territory. She was just here to baby-sit!

Her resolve firmed. She would simply have to apologize. She stepped up the stairs, her mind bubbling with explanations and retractions.

Chris stood at the top, evidently having gotten his sister safely to her room. He stared down at her, expressionlessly.

Brenna fell to her hands and knees, clinging to the stairs. Her tears redoubled. "I'm so sorry, so sorry!" she sobbed.

The boy bent to touch her head. "It's okay, Brenna. It happens to us too. Even to Daddy."

She lifted her face. "It happens?"

"You know. The feeling. We understand."

She shook her head in wonder. "I'm supposed to be taking care of you, and here I am sobbing on the stairs! I'm usually a practical woman."

"You can't help it," he said. "None of us can, when it

takes you. Any li'l thing can set it off, and it just goes and goes. But it passes. You just got to be steady."

"You mean—like the ghosts," Brenna said. "An effect of the house." Now her prior experience with Josh was coming clear; she had surprised herself by setting out to seduce him. She had had the notion—and then suddenly gone ahead and done it. Then she had gone into a tizzy when the skunk ape looked in. She was still terrified by that notion, but now she had a better basis to understand it.

"Yeah. We were afraid you'd laugh."

"I'm not laughing, I'm crying."

"Yeah."

"But I suppose the truth did come out. I didn't mean to say it, but I guess I do love your father. It happened so suddenly—"

"Yeah."

"But that doesn't mean I'm any threat to the two of you. I wouldn't ever—"

"It's okay, Brenna. We like you. Daddy likes you too. That's why he brought you here."

"To baby-sit you two," she said quickly.

"That too."

"But how could you know—did he ever say—?"

He shrugged. "We just know."

And she knew that they did know. Josh had wanted her to interact with his children, here in this house, and she was doing that. They had gotten along great before, and now their mutual understanding had progressed to a point that would have required weeks elsewhere. There was, indeed, something about this house.

Ghosts, emotion, and the skunk ape. And violent death. Was there, indeed, some unifying principle? Something that didn't want them here, that shoved them this way and that, trying to make them go away? If the sight of a ghost didn't do it, and a surge of uncontrolled emotion didn't do it, then did the bones start animating out in the pasture, and did the monster ape prowl around, squatting on branches and peering in?

But emotion cut two ways. If a surge of hate were to come, could mayhem be far behind? Those deaths—

Brenna's tears evaporated. She was coming to a kind of understanding that she didn't like. There could be danger indeed, here, and not necessarily from any skunk ape! It would be better if they all got out of this house.

She got back to her feet. The boy had returned to his room for the night. Suzanne was already asleep, her arm thrown up across her face as if warding off some threat—but the spot was on it, and looked larger. The threat was already upon her!

Nothing could be done tonight. Not with the darkness outside, and no car. It was Tuesday night, and Mom was off at an evening program, so she couldn't drive down anyway. Brenna felt a twinge of guilt; she should have been home now, keeping the kids in line. But this emergency had pre-empted that.

But tomorrow she could do it. She could phone Mom to pick the three of them up. It would be an imposition, and the crowding would be terrible at home, but it was better than staying here. She could leave a message for Joshua Pinson.

Tomorrow. By daylight. That would be best.

She made herself ready for sleep. But as she lay on the bed, her eyes strayed to the window that overlooked the porch. Was the skunk ape prowling out there, trying to look in? She tried to tell herself that she was being foolish, that the skunk ape had never actually hurt any of the family, that she had reacted hysterically before, because of the way the house was, and there probably wasn't really any danger. For the sake of the children, she had to hang on. But it took her a long time to get to sleep.

*   *   *

But in the morning Sue was worse. Brenna considered,
and concluded that it simply was not safe to try to move her.
They would have to remain here, at least for a while. Maybe
Sue would strengthen in a few hours, and then they could do
it. Nothing bad had happened in the night, so maybe they
could tide through here all right. That would really be best.
She did so want to do a good job, to conquer her fear of the
skunk ape, so that Josh would be pleased, and . . .

She required herself to face her true feeling, again. She
had wanted to settle into a good situation: a nice house, a
good man, good children, security. With a family that would
truly appreciate her. She had figured that love would come,
and that would be nice, but the situation had to exist first.
But the truth was that things were happening out of turn.
What she had said on the phone, however unintended, was
accurate. She was just about in love with Joshua Pinson. She
wanted to be with him, as she had been before. That was the
real reason she was fighting so hard to get past the skunk
ape. The real reason she didn't want to call Mom. To be
here, successfully, when he returned, if she possibly could
manage it. He wanted her; she knew it. He had called her; he
had begged her to come. But she had to prove out. That was
part of the rules of this game. This game the adults played.

On top of everything else, this was Halloween. Who could
guess what spooks might manifest for this occasion?

Sue now had spots on both arms, and on her back. The
blight was spreading at an alarming rate. Probably it would
be best to call an ambulance and take her in to the hospital—
but Josh had forgotten to sign an authorization, and Brenna
lacked the authority to commit the child on her own. In
addition, it would represent a betrayal of Sue's confidence,
and Brenna knew she could not do that. They would just
have to hang on until Joshua returned. Anyway, she hadn't

said anything to Chris, and had helped him get ready and go out to the school bus; she couldn't leave until he got back in the afternoon.

Or was she rationalizing? She so much wanted to make it through without any big disturbance that would turn Josh off! Maybe she was making a mistake. Still, in two days he would be back; that really wasn't so long.

At midmorning the first rumble occurred. The house shuddered on its foundations, and seemed to settle slightly.

Brenna had heard that the sensation of an earthquake was the most alarming one a person could experience. She believed it. They *had* to get out of the house!

"It's the Skunk Ape!" Sue shrieked. "We can't go out there!"

Brenna stood still, aghast. Could it be? She had assumed it was ground motion, but—

The house shuddered again. It felt as if something huge were shoving at a wall.

She peered out Suzanne's window, which overlooked the north porch, but could see nothing but the main trunk of the Tree. She crossed to the master bedroom and looked out the south window, but there was only the huge lateral branch of the Tree. Still, there were large areas she could not see.

"I'll go down and look," she said.

"No!" Sue cried weakly. "I don't want to be alone!"

Brenna waited. After a while the child slept, and Brenna went downstairs. Apparently it *had* been a tremor of the earth, though those were extremely uncommon in this region, and it was over. The house did not appear to have sustained any damage.

Chris arrived home in the late afternoon. "About Halloween—" he began.

"Do you really want to go out alone tonight?"

He shuddered. "No."

That night the house shuddered again. It seemed to sway on its foundations like some wallowing ship, tilting one way, then the other, and finally settling back into place.

Brenna found herself in her nightrobe, standing by Sue's bed, with Chris crowding in behind her. She turned on the light. "Maybe we should just stay here for a while," she said, keeping her voice calm. She didn't want them to know that she was as frightened as they were.

The children were quick to agree. They sat on Sue's bed, waiting, but the house remained stable. Finally they separated and slept, uneasily.

The next day was the first of November. The patches on Suzanne's arms were larger, and one was starting on her neck.

One more day! Brenna thought. One more day until Joshua arrived home. He would know what to do.

Neither the radio nor the television had any mention of local tremors. That meant either that she had somehow missed the notices—or that there had been no tremors. If no tremors, then what? That was the alternative she dreaded.

The house shook several times as the hours passed. Brenna went out and made a quick circuit of the house and tree. The ground seemed to have been disturbed in places, with ridges of earth showing, but she could make out no special pattern to it. She looked for footprints and found none. If the skunk ape had been here, its feet left no imprint. Unless the thing scuffled out the prints . . .

Increasingly, the situation did not make sense. Harmless ghosts, malignant bones, and a monster ape that wasn't quite here? Uncontrollable surges of emotion, and a spreading illness? Huge branches bent out of position, and a house that shook? If there was a common theme here, she could not fathom it. If something really wanted to be rid of the human occupants of the house, why were its attacks so varied and peripheral? Why kill a pony and a fish and a dog, and attack a child, while sparing the others? Or, if Elijah and Old Man Foster had been victims, why them and not Josh or Brenna herself?

She returned to Suzanne's room. "I really didn't see anything," she said. "But let's work this out. I don't want to frighten you, but—"

"Daddy says ignoring a problem doesn't make it go away," the girl said. "Anyway, I'm already scared."

"Then see whether you can figure this out," Brenna said. "Let's say that there is something that doesn't want people here. Something that maybe can kill, but sometimes doesn't. Why would that be?"

"To scare us away," the girl said promptly.

Brenna nodded. "Do you think it could have tried to scare Elijah, and when he didn't scare, it killed him?"

The girl nodded affirmatively.

"And Old Man Foster was snooping about, so it tried to scare him, and then killed him?"

"Yes."

"But does this make sense? For example, why does the ghost in the kitchen just stay at the sink? Why doesn't she fly at us and yell 'Booo!'?"

Sue smiled. "That's funny!"

"And the skunk ape. Why does it just walk around and shove, but not punch its way in to grab us? *That* would scare us!"

"Maybe it's not very smart," Sue volunteered.

"Like the ghost," Brenna agreed. "But your illness—I am ready to accept that it is somehow caused by the house. That it killed your fish, and now is killing you. But doesn't that mean that if you go away from this house, you will get better?"

Sue's face lighted with realization. "Maybe so!"

"So as soon as your father returns, we'll see about taking you somewhere else for a while, and see how you are. Your fish died, but that's no sign you will; *you* don't have to stay here."

"That would be so nice to believe," Sue said.

Throughout the day there were irregular tremors, most of them slight. Brenna didn't know what to make of it. Perhaps some slight settling of the foundations. If one of the roots of the tree had died, leaving a weakness . . .

Chris returned in the afternoon, happy because the following day, Friday, was a student holiday, and because Josh should be returning.

They wrapped up the chores and shut themselves in the house before dark. So close to the end, they did not want to invite any problems.

In the night it rained—and the house was taken by a much stronger tremor. Brenna leaped out of bed, turned on the light, and hurried across to the children's rooms—and the power failed. "Chris! Sue!" she called, alarmed as the shaking continued. "Are you all right?"

"It's starting again!" Chris cried.

Downstairs, something crashed. Nefertiti yiped.

Brenna reached out and found Chris's hand. "Tomorrow we'll get away!" she said. "Right now we just have to wait."

They felt their way into Sue's room. Soon they were on the bed, huddled together, as the house rocked about them. It was definitely worse this time, and it went on and on. They could feel the tilt as the house shifted. Again Brenna struggled to conceal her fear. She wished she were anywhere but here!

"The Skunk Ape's trying to tear it down!" Chris said.

"The house shook in the daytime," Brenna said, "but I saw no monster." Yet it was distressingly easy to believe.

"It just wasn't close enough!" he said.

"Sue and I agreed that it just wants us out of here," Brenna argued. "It's trying to scare us. Tomorrow we'll go, and we'll be all right."

"But what about Daddy?"

"We'll wait for him."

"But he won't go. He likes the Tree."

"Well, it's a nice tree, Chris. I like it too. But something doesn't like us, and until we know what it is, and how to deal with it, we had better stay clear."

"Maybe the Skunk Ape likes the Tree!" Chris exclaimed. "It wants it for itself!"

"That must be it," Brenna agreed. "It couldn't stop Elijah from building the house, maybe because there were too many workers and machines, but when Elijah tried to live in it, the skunk ape struck directly at him. Now it's warning us, and we'd better go."

"Daddy won't go," the boy insisted. "He'll fight it."

To that she had no answer. She was very much afraid that Chris was right.

Chapter 19

It was raining as Josh returned, with some showers heavy. He had tried to phone, to let them know he might be delayed by the weather, but could not get through. The phone appeared to be out, and that gave him a queasy feeling that did not diminish as he drew near.

A tree was down across the road, a third of a mile from the house. It was rotten, but too big for him to move. He would have to saw it out later; meanwhile, he parked the bus and trudged on through the rain.

At three in the afternoon he reached the house—and paused in dismay. The ground around it seemed to have been chewed up, and the tree was strangely different, as though the major branches had shifted again.

Again? Had the skunk ape been back at work?

At least the house seemed to be intact. He hurried toward it. "Hello! Anybody home?" he called.

In a moment the door burst open and Chris charged out. "Dad!" he cried, rushing up for a hug. "We've got to get out of here!"

Now Josh saw Brenna at the door. Her hair was disheveled and her face was drawn. With her was Sue, who looked worse. What a contrast to his last return!

"Where is your car?" Brenna asked tersely. "We have to leave immediately."

"There's a tree across the road," he exclaimed. "What's the matter?"

"We'll have to talk," she said. "But right now Sue's very ill, and we all have to get away."

"But what—?"

Brenna turned back Sue's long sleeve. The child's arm was splotched with brown. "She needs help. But first we have to get her out of here. She can't walk far; maybe you can carry—"

"Sue, what happened to you?" Josh asked, appalled.

"The Skunk Ape's trying to kill me," Sue explained faintly.

"It's been shaking the house all night!" Chris said. "It's the last warning! We've got to get out!"

"I really don't believe—" Josh started, bending to pick up his daughter. But she whimpered, and he knew his grip was painful. She really was worse, and carrying her, besides being slow, clumsy, and tiring, might do her more damage that he cared to risk. Yet obviously she couldn't walk, either.

He thought fast. "There's a tractor. It can go anywhere through the forest. We can put her on that, and I can—" He broke off again, for Sue was clinging to Brenna. The two had evidently become very close.

"I guess I could drive that," Brenna said. "I could take her to the nearest house with a working phone, and call an ambulance—"

"No!" Sue cried weakly.

"Or maybe call Mom, and wait till she got there, and— where's the nearest house on a different line? The phone's been out, here, and I don't know—"

"Across the tracks," Josh said. "But—"

"Well, if there's a road—"

"There's a path that a horse can use, and a road a little farther north that the tractor could navigate—I suppose that would be best. But the nearest house—" He didn't want to have Brenna go to Pip's house, but didn't want to give his reason.

"Okay, I'll take her there. Maybe that will be enough, and we won't have to call anyone else."

"Enough for what?" he asked, perplexed.

"To be far enough clear of the skunk ape."

Not that again! But it was evident that Brenna and the children had had a harrowing experience, and this wasn't the moment to discuss all the details. "Then I'll take Chris down to the bus, and you drive Sue across, and we'll meet at—at Philippa Graham's house. That's the first one you'll come to."

She nodded. He went to the tractor, uncovered it, and started it. There was no trouble; it was another good machine. He brought it around, quickly reviewed the controls with Brenna, and helped her get on. Then he lifted his daughter and set her on the seat in front of Brenna. Sue seemed weak and hardly conscious; her illness had worsened horribly during his absence. And the blotches on her arms— when had this manifested? This dramatic new development alarmed him more than he cared to show, lest he add to the child's misery. And what was this about the skunk ape trying to kill her? Once again, hell seemed to have broken loose during his absence.

Brenna started the tractor moving slowly, following the road. He gave her hasty additional instructions, making sure she wouldn't get lost. There were only two forks, so it should be all right. Soon the young woman and the child were out of sight.

"Well, let's go, Chris," he said. "You can explain everything on the way."

The boy had Nefertiti on the leash. "The Skunk Ape's been shaking the whole house!" he exclaimed. "Brenna checked around but couldn't see it, but last night it got real bad!"

"Brenna was nervous about the skunk ape before," he said cautiously. He wanted to get the story without spreading any further alarm.

"The Skunk Ape gave her the shakes, and she was crying," the boy said excitedly. "Sue showed her the Kitchen Ghost, and then the Skunk Ape came and ripped out the phone and the power and shook the house all night, and it's going to kill us if we don't get out."

They were passing the gravesites, cutting toward the road. "Let's see if we can't cover the territory in more detail," Josh said, still trying to project a calmness he did not feel.

"Dad, it was terrible! I thought the whole house was coming down! The Skunk Ape kept circling around and around and shoving and shaking, and we were all really scared. But it was just a warning, we decided. We knew we had to get out as soon's we could, so it wouldn't kill us like it killed Old Man Foster."

They continued walking toward the bus, and gradually Josh got a picture of what had been happening during his absence.

Slowly the tractor wended its way along the road. The rain had made mush of the sugar sand of the back trail, forcing her to travel carefully, but her minor detours had put her into rougher ground. Sue, too weak to walk, had started whimpering; the bumping was abrading her skin and putting her in increasing pain. Brenna actually felt some of that pain herself, in an empathy that was becoming stronger. Suspecting that the worst of the ride was ahead, she had made a snap decision: to turn back and get a pillow to protect the girl from this violence. It meant going into the house alone, and she didn't like that, but she really had no choice.

So here they were, back a few minutes after leaving. Josh and Chris, of course, would be at their bus by this time, starting south down Forest Drive. They had forgotten the kittens and chicks, but those should be able to forage by themselves, and of course food had been put out for them.

There was no tremor at the moment, which was a relief. She parked the tractor, set Sue down beside it, and hurried inside. Now if she could just avoid the kitchen ghost—

The ghost appeared. "Darn it, get out of here!" Brenna cried. The ghost vanished.

She charged up the spiral stairs and into Sue's room. And froze. The entire bed was covered with dark bugs.

Brenna caught up the upstairs broom. "Get *out*!" she screamed, and slammed the broom down on the bed. The bugs vanished. They didn't scurry away, they simply ceased to exist. They were of course ghosts. "You don't need to try to frighten me away!" she muttered. "I'm already going!"

She grabbed the pillow and top blanket, bundling them together. Then she went to the master bedroom to fetch another pillow.

Something outside caught her eye. She paused to peer out the window.

The huge lateral branch was moving, like a monstrous tentacle.

Brenna blinked. No, of course it was merely the wind!

She took the pillow and jammed it into the bundle. Then she hurried down and out.

Sue was waiting, sitting on the ground. Brenna set a pillow on the front of the seat, and held the other to her stomach. She draped the blanket about the girl, then hauled her to her feet. It was tricky getting onto the tractor without dislodging the pillows, but Sue cooperated as well as she could. The

whole arrangement seemed impossibly clumsy, but the girl
was more comfortable than she had been, and would be
shielded from the shocks of the ride.

Another tremor began, shaking the tractor. The gound
seemed to writhe about them. Brenna was torn between alarm
and curiosity. They had thought the skunk ape could be
stomping about, but there was no sign of anything. The
ground seemed to be shaking itself—but only in the vicinity
of the house. So it *was* an earth tremor—but an extremely
limited one.

She started the motor and nudged the tractor forward,
turning it toward the road that bore north and away.

The ground immediately ahead rippled. A root broke the
surface, twisting like a snake.

Brenna goosed the motor. The tractor leaped forward, the
wheels throwing up sand and crunching over the root. In a
moment they were out of it and on firm ground, accelerating
away from the house. "We're *going!*" Brenna called.

She turned east on the trail, and glanced south at the
house. The rain was worse now, making soup of the chewed-up
ground around the house and tree, and wind was gusting
through the big branches, making the tree seem to struggle
like a conscious thing. The limbs seemed to be at odd angles,
growing closer to the house than before, as if trying to grasp
it.

Then the brush and forest hid the view, and she had to pay
attention to her business. The pillows seemed to help; Sue
was not hurting as much.

This empathy with the child—how had she achieved that?
Of course she had to help a person in need, but it seemed to
be more than that. She seemed actually to feel Sue's feelings.

The rain pelted down, soaking the blankets and pillows,
and now Brenna felt the coolness of the wet blanket about her
shoulders. About Sue's shoulders.

What is this—telepathy? she thought to herself.

And Sue replied: "Oh, sure, Brenna. Chris and I do it all the time."

Brenna almost drove off the road. "You can actually hear my thoughts?"

"Not exactly. Mostly your feelings. That's why we know it's okay for you to marry Daddy."

Brenna kept the tractor on a steady course, but her mind was reeling. "But I promised to—to work it out with you and Chris, before making a decision!"

"Yes. But we think you can love us too."

Of course she could! But to have her thoughts read—!

They were coming to the tracks, where the cut leveled out just enough to make it possible for the tractor to get across. But Brenna didn't want to risk it with the bundled child; the steep bank was too treacherous in this rain. She would have to take the machine up, then carry Sue.

She stopped at the top of the bank overlooking the rusty tracks. Rather, the bed where the tracks had once been; for a moment she had imagined actual tracks there! The cut dropped down to them, then up on the other side. "I'll have to set you down here, and ride the tractor across," she explained. "Then I'll carry you to it, and we'll resume the ride at the far bank."

Sue did not protest. Brenna set her down, worried about the increasing chill from the water. She would have to do this as quickly as possible, and get the child to warmth and dryness.

She mounted, then goosed the motor and roared down the bank. The loose dirt caused the wheels to skid and slew, and she had to fight to maintain her course. Then she bumped across the tracks at an angle, glancing south along the weedy length of them.

And saw a headlight.

Now she was across, and grinding up the bank, the wheels throwing sand back at a horrendous rate. But her momentum helped, and in moments she fought the machine to the top and brought it to a halt.

She dismounted and started back down the bank, her feet sliding. The loud honk of an approaching train made her literally jump, so that she lost her balance and had to wind-mill her arms as she slid-stumbled down to the tracks.

A *what* on the *what*?

The headlamp was brighter now, cutting through the rain and mist, and around it loomed the dark shape of the engine. *A train was coming!*

But that was impossible! These tracks did not exist! The ties had been removed, and small trees were growing in the roadbed.

Now the ground shook with the approach. "Sue!" Brenna screamed, and lurched across in front of the train. Somehow it was in her mind that the child might stumble down into it and be killed.

Then she was up the bank and clutching the little girl to her, pillows and all, while the train roared by behind her. "Oh, Sue, I was so afraid—if anything had happened to you—"

"I guess you do love me," Sue said.

Brenna held her close and sobbed.

"It's all right, Brenna," Sue said. "It's a ghost train."

Brenna turned to look at it—and the train vanished.

"It hurt the Tree," Sue explained. "So it's a ghost."

"A ghost," Brenna echoed, numbed.

"Whatever hurts the Tree, it remembers."

A phenomenal realization dawned. "The Tree! *It* projects the ghosts!"

"Yeah. When that woman poured that burny stuff down the drain—"

"To unclog it—and it got into the septic tank and damaged the tree's roots. And the train—"

"It carried bad things, or something. The mining—"

"The old mine could have affected the water table," Brenna said, working it out. *That* would affect the Tree! The trains were associated with the mine, so they became part of the traumatic memory. Just as people did things to the ground and the water and the environment, affecting the Tree, becoming enemies. "A telepathic Tree! Projecting visions into the minds of intruders, frightening them away!"

Then she remembered the churning ground around the house, and the tremors, and the way that root had writhed out of the ground. The Tree—the Tree had done it all! It wasn't limited to illusory effects. It was trying to destroy the house!

"We'll have to tell your father," Brenna said. "But first we have to get there. He'll be waiting for us."

She picked up the child and staggered down the bank. There was no sign of the passage of any real train; the weeds were undisturbed, and there were no tracks. But what an impressive ghost it had been!

A train. Not a ghost, but a vision—spawned by the mental power of a thing that only *looked* like a tree. A thing that had killed more than one man, and now sought to finish the matter by destroying the Pinsons' house.

"Its leaves are funny," Sue said. "Chris tried to look them up in a book, but they didn't match, quite. They're flat."

Brenna remembered. The Tree's little leaves *were* flat, while those of a true live oak were spoon-shaped.

She finally reached the top, panting, and set Sue on the seat. She tried to start the motor—and could not. The rain had shorted it out.

"I can fix that," she said. She had learned a few things

from her car-crazy brothers. "I can dry off the distributor cap." She set Sue on the ground and got to work.

And suffered another revelation. "If the Tree is doing all this—then *it* must be the source of your illness!"

"But I like the Tree!" Sue protested.

"Honey, you may like it, but it may not like you. The way it was with Beauty. It may be trying every way it can think of to get rid of the people there, and it's trying illness on you. But it won't be able to hurt you when you're away from it."

"But we're away from it now, and I'm still sick," Sue pointed out.

"Obviously we're not far enough away. If it can project a ghost here, and make us telepathic and highly emotional, it can make you sick. We don't know its range. But the effect has to weaken with distance, and this may be near the limit. Certainly there *is* a limit."

"Then I don't have to die," Sue said, her hope strengthening.

Brenna replaced the dry cap and reached out to hug her. "You don't have to die, dear."

The little girl started to cry, letting down what remained of her guard. Brenna held her close, letting the emotion take her. There was no longer any doubt: she could be a mother to this child.

Josh crossed the tracks and hurried toward the house, worried. Brenna and Sue had not arrived at the Graham house. Something must have happened to them on the way. He should have insisted that they all go together to the bus, having Brenna and Sue ride the tractor while he and Chris walked beside it, but in the confusion he hadn't thought of it. Pip had not been home, and perhaps that was just as well. So he had left Chris and Nefertiti with Mr. Graham, Pip's father, with a hurried explanation, and set out on foot along the path. He would go to the house, then retrace their tractor route until he found them. They might have had trouble at the tracks; there was no nearby place to cross them on the level, and in this rain there could have been an accident—

The Tree!

Suddenly it came to him, like a thought from outside. All these effects, that they had tried in vain to attribute to the skunk ape—they were from the Tree! A Tree that somehow projected visions of terrible things, of ghosts and bugs and walking bones. To frighten intruders away. And when that didn't work, it took stronger measures, such as turning a power saw against its operator, or causing a child to sicken unto death.

Josh paused, appalled on more than one level. How could he suddenly know all this? And if it could be true—then the Tree was killing his daughter!

He resumed his motion, his mind working as hard as his body. Everything was falling into place. It was much easier to believe in a telepathic entity, even a tree, than it was to believe in the supernatural. An entity that protected itself from molestation by driving away intruders, and by killing those who persisted. That much he could understand. But when the human victims were the members of his family, his understanding hardened into something else. He could understand a rattlesnake's need to live its own life, but if that snake threatened his family, it forfeited its right to be left alone. It was simply a matter of whose security was to be enforced.

As he heaved into sight of the house, he was amazed at the change in it in just the past half hour. The branches of the Tree seemed to have wrapped around the house, as if trying to choke it, and steam hissed up from the wet soil. The smell was terrible. He had caught that odor before, when he sought the skunk ape; now he realized with horror that it emanated from the Tree itself. The Tree was moving its branches and roots, attacking the house from above and below, and the heat was the result of its enormous effort. The whole house was shaking. No wonder Brenna and the children had been terrified; they had escaped the house hardly too soon.

But where were Brenna and Sue now? Could the Tree have reached out to get them at a distance? What was the limit of its ambience? Certainly it could conjure tangible-seeming bones in the pasture—

And there those graves were now. The soil of all three of them was stirring, and the bones were poking up. He knew it was only a vision—but he remembered how determinedly those bones had opposed him before. The Tree was acting to prevent his approach!

But not quickly enough. Josh ran by before the bones were clear of the soil, and proceeded on toward the Tree.

The thing was really working on the house. The branches were almost touching in several places, and the big lateral limb was curled almost around the entire south side. Vapor rose from it, adding to the mist associated with the rain. Only the ponderosity of the branch had prevented it from crunching into the house, which could hardly withstand that pressure. But soon—probably within the hour—that curling motion would be complete, and the house would be doomed.

But first he had to be sure of his daughter. He started to skirt the Tree and house, giving both a wide enough berth to be sure he could not be physically touched. Then he heard the hoof falls. The ghost pony bones were getting up speed, and by the sound of it they would readily be able to catch him. He cast about for some kind of weapon, if only a fallen branch.

The animal came into view—and it was the tractor! Brenna was riding it. This was no ghost! He had somehow taken its sound for that of the ghost animals, or the Tree had masked it in this fashion, but could not conceal the sight of the reality.

Or could it? After the manifestations he had seen, he could not be sure of anything, here in the ambience of the Tree. It could be the bones, in different form, sent to lure him out.

No, he had to risk it. He stepped out and waved.

Brenna saw him. She came in close, and she was genuine. "Josh! I wanted to tell you—the Tree—"

"Where is Sue?" he barked.

"She's at the Graham house, with Chris and Mr. Graham. We got delayed—the ghost train—the tractor shorted out—but we got there just after you left. So I came across to warn you—"

"That the Tree is responsible for all these effects," he concluded, his anger increasing. "I suddenly realized that, as I approached."

"The telepathy," she agreed. "We realized, and you must have picked up our thought. But I wonder why the Tree should—"

"And look at that thing now!"

"It's going to crush the house!" she exclaimed, a note of hysteria sounding.

"After trying to kill my daughter," he agreed grimly. He was trying to keep a rein on his emotion, but the thought of Sue sickening and dying made that almost impossible. "And all the time I thought it was such a nice tree—just as my Uncle Elijah must have, until it killed him."

"Sue's safe now," Brenna repeated. Then she put a hand to her mouth, caught by a new doubt. "Unless its power reaches all the way across the tracks! We really don't know its limit. I'm trying to be rational. It must thin out, getting weaker, but it did reach to the tracks, and that other house isn't that far beyond—"

"I can stop the attack on her," he said, finding a certain exhilaration in the contemplation of a way to strike back. "The same way I can save the house. By cutting down the Tree."

"Yes," she agreed. "I always liked the Tree myself. But I guess it also has its dark side. This thing is dangerous." Her mouth had tightened. "But if it is to be done, it has to be done right now, before it takes out the house."

"The saw's right there in the shed. It's got gas in it, though it needs sharpening. It's a brute of a thing; I should be able to cut through several smaller branches before refilling it. Enough to get that alien Tree away from the house."

"But that saw—"

"Is the one that killed my uncle," he finished, understanding her thought. "But he didn't understand the nature of the threat. I do." He started toward the shed.

"Josh, I don't like this at all!" she cried, following him. "This Tree has been mostly quiet before, but now it's fully aware. It's telepathic. *It knows what you're doing.*"

"But it can't move fast enough to stop me," he said. He knew that in other circumstances he would stay well clear of anything like this. But his house and family were being attacked, and his rage bore him on. "I can prune it back enough to stop it for now, and then we can hire a crew to rip it out by the roots."

"But it strikes through the mind!" she persisted. "I saw those pony bones walking, and if it animates the skunk ape— Josh, that thing terrifies me! Can't we just go away from it?"

"I'm not going to run from it!" he retorted.

She was silent. He glanced at her face, and saw how frightened she was. The Tree had driven her away before; why had she come back now?

Because she loved him. As she had said on the phone; now that made sense. The telepathy made it quite clear. But right now he had no chance to sort out his own feelings; the threat was too immediate.

Now they entered the shade of the Tree. Each huge trunk seemed like the tentacle of the world's largest squid, and the whole seemed overwhelmingly menacing. But Josh knew it couldn't move its branches or roots quickly.

The shed was partly collapsed, as if the Tree had shaken it

in an effort to destroy the dread saw. But Josh wrenched open the door and saw the machine in the corner. Menace radiated from it, and the red oil seemed brighter.

But now he knew that the saw wasn't haunted. It was the projection of the Tree, trying to scare him away from the one weapon that could destroy it. All he had to do was take up the saw, and make sure it did not twist free of his grasp, and cut exactly where he intended to cut. The proper concentration should suffice despite all the Tree's ghosts.

He reached for the saw—and it growled, then roared into life. Josh rocked back. *He hadn't touched it!* The thing had started on its own, and now was menacing him with its chain.

No. That was impossible. It had to be a phantasm. The Tree could fool with his perception, but not with physical things. Not that way. All he had to do was ignore the seeming animation and take hold and command the saw himself.

He reached again—and the saw twisted in place and oriented its bar on him. Again Josh hesitated—then reached on. His hand touched the moving chain—and the animation stopped. He had overcome the illusion.

He hauled the saw in to him. It was cold and quiet; it had not been running. Illusions could not stand exposure.

He carried it to the big lateral branch on the south side of the house, as that was the most immediate threat. Suddenly that branch looked larger. How could he possible saw through it? But he reminded himself that this saw had a lot of brute power, and evidently the Tree feared it, so it must be capable of doing the job. He would start at the narrowest point of the branch that he could reach from the ground, sever that, then move down to attack a thicker section. It would be a big job, but he should be able to do enough to protect the house. At least until more drastic measures could be taken.

Brenna was nearby. "Josh, I'm afraid," she said, and her

fear was manifest as the telepathic effect carried it to his own mind. ''The way Elijah died—''

''I'm on guard against that,'' Josh said, though his knees felt weak. When he started up the saw, so that it really was going, and the Tree tried to cloud his awareness of reality— could he be sure that what he cut into was the branch?

He shut out the thought. All he had to do was start it and cut into the branch directly before him. Maybe the Tree would try to make that branch look like his own leg, but he knew that it wasn't. And once he started the correct cut, the Tree would be helpless. He could do it, and he *had* to do it.

He set the heavy saw on the ground, directly before the section he meant to cut. He fixed the location of the branch in his mind. It was about chest high, two feet in front of him. No matter what he seemed to see or hear, that was exactly where he would cut.

The ground shuddered. More steam ripped from the sodden earth. The roots were struggling, building up their heat, but they could not get him. Not in time.

Josh pulled on the starter cord. It drew out smoothly, and the motor did not catch. He let it rewind, and pulled again. Nothing. He pulled a third time, reminding himself that the Tree could not hypnotize a machine into nonperformance. This time the motor coughed.

On the fourth pull the motor spluttered into life, and died. On the fifth it roared into full life.

Josh lifted the saw and got his proper grip. Wind riffled the leaves of the Tree, and the branches seemed to reach toward him, but they could not touch him. He oriented the saw on the branch ahead. The teeth of the chain spit out clots of red oil that splattered against the wood.

He held on firmly and brought the chain into contact with the wood. It bit in, and a white line formed.

There was a scream. But Josh ignored it and bore down, cutting into the bark.

Chapter 20

He had finally realized that the Tree was a threat to his house. It could project ghosts and move its branches. Suddenly the array of peculiar effects made sense. So he was taking direct and immediate action, as was his wont: he was cutting it down.

But the saw twisted in his hands and came down on his own left leg. Too astonished to be afraid, he watched the blurred chain rip into the flesh of his left thigh. His own hands were guiding it, yet he could not wrench it away or release the trigger. His muscles were locked into the action, independent of his will. The chain sliced through the great muscle and nicked the bone. Then it stalled, as gouts of flesh clogged it.

The blood pumped out, bathing the chain and bar and his knee and the lower part of his leg, and pooling on the ground. He watched it, knowing he had to staunch the flow. He forced his clenched fingers to release the brute saw, and it fell beside his foot, its motor still running, trying to get the chain moving again. He tried to grab his wounded leg, to hold it together, but the blood sprayed out across his hands.

Then the depressurization reached his head, and he lost consciousness.

331

He was dead—yet still aware. How could that be?

He cast about—and found himself walking along the road leading in to the estate. He was coming to borrow the Pinson saw, to take out the fallen branch.

Joshua Pinson wasn't home, but it was probably okay to borrow the saw anyway. He opened the shed door and reached for the red machine.

He heard something in the brush to the side. Suddenly he was nervous. Suppose there was something there—like the Skunk Ape? Some folk pooh-poohed the notion, but he was sure that monster lurked around these parts. For one thing, there was the smell, especially around the big tree. Nothing ordinary produced that awful odor!

He smelled that odor now. Apprehensively, he looked— and there it loomed, half again as tall as a man, dark and shaggy, and the terrible smell pushing out from it. The thing he most feared, in all its horror: the Skunk Ape!

He tried to run, but the thing pursued with giant strides. In moments he was panting, his breath rasping. He fell, and the monster loomed. He scrambled up, his heart beating as though it would burst. In a few more steps the ape was upon him, its massive paw swinging down. He screamed, and fell, and clutched at his chest as the monster landed crushingly on him. His last thought was horror that his old flesh was about to be consumed by this abomination.

He was dead again, but still aware. Again he cast about, seeking to make sense of it.

He was running, fleeing the pursuer, his bosom heaving with the exertion. Maybe in the shade of the tree he could be safe.

But the pursuer caught up, and spun him about, and ripped off his blouse, exposing his breasts. Rough hands grabbed at the feminine flesh, and a rough face came down to force a

kiss. He screamed, but no one heard, and in a moment he was
borne to the ground, his dress yanked up.

"Oh, no, *no!*" he sobbed, but then the terrible thrusting
came, and the sharp pain, and the worst was happening. He
fainted.

Unconscious, but aware. And *female?* Raped beneath the
spreading branches of the Tree . . .

This was absolutely impossible! Some kind of continuing
nightmare. He cast about.

He bounded over the brush, running fleetly. In a moment
he would be past the Tree, hidden by it, safe.

The dread sound sounded. Pain sprang into his gut, and he
crashed to the ground. He tried to rise, but his legs would not
work properly, and his hooves only scraped the ground.

The Hunter tromped up, a figure of absolute terror, walking on his two hind legs. Something glinted in his paw. He
loomed close, the glint thrusting forward. It cut into the
throat, and the blood gushed out and awareness ended.

Again, dead; again, aware, despite the loss of awareness.
Each termination led into another scene. Casting about for
understanding didn't help, it merely led to more of the same.
This time he did not cast, he considered.

He had been cut by the saw and bled to death—without
remaining dead. He had been attacked by the Skunk Ape,
and died again, without remaining so. He had been raped. He
had been shot and had his throat slit by a hunter.

He had shared the ultimate horrors of four different enti-
ties. Three were not himself. He was not a deer, or a woman,
or an old man borrowing a piece of equipment at the Pinson
place. That had been Old Man Foster.

He had shared Foster's death. Foster had seen the Skunk
Ape—which creature Josh had alrady determined did not
exist. The manifestations of the Ape had in fact been the
Tree.

But Foster had *seen* the Skunk Ape! It had killed him! How could that be?

No. Foster had died of a heart attack. There had been no exterior mark on him. He had clutched at the pain in his chest as he fell; the Ape had never touched him. It had to have been a ghost.

A ghost. And the Tree could conjure ghosts. It must have conjured the Skunk Ape, literally scaring Foster to death.

But how had Josh shared that experience? He had not *seen* Foster die, he had *felt* it. He had shared Foster's last thoughts. That was considerably more than the conjuration of a ghost. Josh had *become* a ghost. The ghost of Foster.

And the ghost of a deer, killed under the Tree by a hunter.

And of a woman caught and raped.

And—of his Uncle Elijah, killed by the saw.

But how could he experience these things? He knew of them all, but these were no direct memories of his. The details, the thoughts, the sheer realism—these were true events, not imaginative re-creations. He had experienced them in their fullness; he *knew*.

All of them had happened in the vicinity of the Tree. The Tree had powers. It could move its branches; it could conjure ghosts. It could project the illness of a dying fish to a little girl. Could it also put a man's awareness into the minds of ghosts?

Elijah! he thought, focusing on his uncle.

He had finally realized that the Tree was a threat to his house . . . Suddenly the array of peculiar effects made sense. So he was taking direct and immediate action, as was his wont: he was cutting it down.

But the saw twisted in his hands . . .

Josh found himself playing through the death scene, exactly as before. Every motion, every sensation, every thought was identical. He had no free will, only the illusion of it.

Deer! he thought.

He bounded over the brush, running fleetly . . .

There was no doubt of it. These experiences, like ghosts, could be conjured at will. All of them were associated with the Tree. The Tree had to be what was doing it.

The Tree had taken over his consciousness.

He had tried to destroy the Tree, and the Tree had opened on him a new dimension of conflict. How could he prevail, if the Tree had such power?

Surely he *could* prevail, he told himself. He had prevented the Tree from making the saw twist in his hands to cut into his leg. It had tried, but his will had been stronger. Elijah had not been prepared, so Elijah had died, but Josh had been ready. So the Tree was trying another way. But the Tree would have killed him, if it had been able. Now it was trying to scare him into a heart attack, as it had Old Man Foster. But he was no old man; he was young and healthy. He had not been scared to death.

Surely his body was still standing there, sawing the branch, while the battle was waged for his mind. All he had to do was return to his body, and the victory would be his.

Josh! he thought, but nothing happened. He remained— where?

He did not know. He was isolated, with no input from his senses, as if suspended in warm water in a dark tank. The Tree had locked him in limbo.

Yet he could move. He could enter the experiences of ghosts.

He experimented. *Pharaoh!*

He woke, smelling something. Nefertiti remained snoozing on the other rug. He stood under the broken window, catching an interesting whiff . . .

He sniffed again. Yes—that was definitely the odor of

Pony . . . As he thought of it, the smell grew stronger. Now he heard the hooves. The stupid horse was coming again!

He knew his duty. He leaped at the window . . .

Josh followed the experience through to the finish. Now he had the confirmation: the dog had attacked a wandering cow, and had been gored. Josh had been unable to alter any part of Pharaoh's final experience, but his broader human perspective had enabled him to recognize signals that the dog had not. Pharaoh had perceived the walking bones, but they had been another ghost, masking the reality of the cow.

The Tree had used illusion of sight and smell to kill the dog. And it had recorded the episode, as authentically as any video camera could have.

Video camera? What instrument could record the thoughts and emotions too?

The Tree was no camera. It was more like a complete laboratory, that absorbed the total experience with absolute fidelity. Not even the most sophisticated computer system could do that!

Computer system: now there was a concept he was equipped to handle. He earned his living by devising compatible systems for companies. Obviously the Tree was no computer, yet it could have some computerlike properties. After all, what was a computer but an extremely unsophisticated brain? The living organisms routinely performed tasks whose complexity baffled the best computers. The chemistry of even simple plants—

And the Tree was no simple plant! It was an unknown species that could do one thing that no other tree could do, deliberately moving its branches, and one thing no other living creature he knew of could do, telepathically affect the minds of others. Could it also compute?

Obviously it could store experiences, for it had put him through the replay of several. That meant it had to have an excellent memory, items of which could be summoned on a selective basis. That was very like a computer, whose storage of information was on a tape or disk, using magnetic or laser patterns. A great deal of information could be stored on a so-called hard disk—the complete text of ten or a hundred full-length novels, depending on the megabyte capacity of the disk. Yet the complexity and detail of the information stored by the human brain was of an entirely different order; soft living flesh remained the best computer ever known.

Consider the Tree as a living computer. If an animal could do it, why not a plant? Consider the cross section of the trunk as a hard disk. If the finest machine disk were that diameter, it would have the capacity of a small library of books. But the Tree was three dimensional. Suppose the heartwood were used not only for support, but also for information storage: in effect, several thousand thin disks stacked vertically. What would its capacity be?

His mind began to strain at the concept. But it seemed reasonable to assume that much of the printed knowledge of man could be stored in such a column, assuming the other assumptions were correct. Certainly it could accommodate the scenes he had experienced. It didn't matter whether it had flat disks or vertical fibers; the capacity was there. So it was theoretically possible. Since it was also actual, because he had experienced a sampling, he was ready to accept that this was the way the Tree operated. It had enormous memory.

But not the other devices of an animal. It had no eyes, no ears, no hands. Therefore it had no need of the peripherals of computer or brain: the control mechanisms to operate the printer, modem, the organs of sight, hearing, and rapid loco- motion. How did it get all that information?

There was the rationale of the telepathy. The Tree simply read the minds of passing creatures, recording their experiences. It didn't need senses of its own, when it could borrow those of animals within its ambience.

Ambience—there was an operative concept. Obviously the telepathic power of the Tree extended some distance outward, diminishing by the square or the cube. Its effective limit might be out near the railroad tracks, and its greatest power would be right at the trunk.

But the Tree did not merely read minds, it projected back to them. Surely it required more energy to project than merely to read. Probably its awareness extended relatively far, but its projection was restricted. So the Tree might know that a man was coming from a mile away, but not be able to project any images farther than a quarter mile out, and the full feedback might not operate beyond the actual area shaded by its foliage.

Even so, the house was within that ambience. Thus ghosts.

More than that, he realized. Projections did not have to be merely visual or auditory. They could be emotional.

Suddenly it was clear why his emotional control had been so erratic here! When the rooster had been killed, he and the children had gone into a deep depression. That would never have happened ordinarily; the bird had not meant that much to any of them. But if the emotion of something else had been projected to them—

Why would the Tree record and project emotion?

The answer burst upon him. *Self-defense!*

The Tree could not defend itself physically. Not against a man wielding an ax or saw. It could move its branches and roots, but far too slowly for that. Yet obviously it had an instinct of self-preservation. So when directly attacked—it used emotion to drive away the attacker. This could operate in several ways. It could project fear, either as raw emotion or as a vision of some fearsome thing. But how would it judge what would frighten an attacker? The image of a wolf might frighten a rabbit, but not another wolf. Or it could simply use feedback. It could draw whatever concept was frightening from the attacker's mind, and animate that as a ghost. That must have been what happened to Old Man Foster, who feared the Skunk Ape.

But Foster had not come to attack the Tree. Why had it killed him?

The question keyed in the answer. Foster had killed the rooster, within the ambience of the Tree. The terror and agony of the rooster had been recorded, and the horror of those who saw the deed. That horror had lingered for days, as Josh well knew. So when Foster had come again, the association had come with him. He was a creature that killed in the vicinity of the Tree, therefore to be distrusted. Feedback had done the rest; Foster's own apprehension had been animated, and his own rising fear had been amplified and fed back to him, and his heart had given out.

The question had keyed the answer. Josh fixed on that. The Tree did not simply select scenes to project; they had to be evoked. Foster had conjured his own horror. Josh had conjured Foster's death scene, as well as that of his Uncle Elijah, and the deer, and the rape of the girl, and Pharaoh's death. Like the computer, the Tree was largely passive. Ask it the right question, it produced the memory.

To a human occupant of the house, that could be frightening. Josh had thought of a woman—and there in the kitchen a woman had appeared. The ghost.

The ghost. That woman had not died, had not even been close to death. But she had inadvertently hurt the Tree, so it remembered. It did not understand, it just remembered. With perfect detail. The Tree did not have the reasoning power of a man; it only reacted to protect itself, in the only way it knew. Had that woman returned, it would have known her, and—

Was that why it had resolved to destroy the house?

The question evoked only confusion. There was, it seemed, no file on the destruction of the house.

Now look, Tree, Josh thought emphatically. *Elijah attacked you, and you fought back by distorting his control of the saw so that it sawed his limb instead of yours. I attacked you, and you fought back by making my mind captive within your ambience. Both simple defensive reactions; I grant you that. But I saw you attacking the house. Your branch was wrapping around it, and your roots were shaking it. Why?*

His more detailed thought succeeded in conjuring the answer. Suddenly he found himself staring into a sinkhole. Water had washed out a hollow in the ground, forming a nether pool; then the water had seeped down, leaving a cave. Then more water had come, and the cave had started to collapse. The Tree grew above that cave. It had acted desperately in self-defense, changing its roots to find new anchorage, and moving its branches to achieve new balance. The house was above the sink hole too. To save itself, the Tree also had to maintain the equilibrium of the house. For three days it had struggled to do so.

Josh was appalled. All this he saw not as a vision, but as a perception of density and flow and unbalance; his human comprehension rendered it into terms he could more readily grasp. The Tree only knew that its support had been eroded, and it had reacted as it did to a storm, adjusting its configuration to withstand the assault. But Josh had seen it as an attack on the house. *He* had reacted negatively to what he did not understand, exactly as the Tree had.

Yet the Tree had tried to kill him, by turning the saw against him. It had tried to kill his daughter, by rotting her to death. Could he forgive that?

No—it had tried to drive him from the saw, by making the saw seem to attack him. Actually, his own concern about the

saw had done that; the Tree feared the saw, but Josh's mind
had conjured its haunted operation. And Elijah—he saw now
that the Tree had not tried to kill him either; it had merely
used the feedback to make the handling of the saw seem
wrong, to get it *away from the branch*. Elijah's determination
to keep cutting had caused the accident, and he had died. The
Tree was responsible only for the feedback; it did not know
exactly how that feedback would affect the subject. Usually it
caused such confusion that the subject simply fled the ambience of the Tree, and then of course the feedback abated.
Those who had experienced this effect usually stayed clear of
the Tree thereafter. There was really no malice in it, for the
Tree lacked such emotion of its own. The emotions it projected were recordings of those of other creatures, not its
own. Merely data files. A computer did not understand the
significance of the files stored in its memory or of those
summoned to its "conscious" awareness; it merely did as
directed. The Tree was more like that than like a thinking
human being. The illness of the girl had been only continuing
feedback; she had seen the fish die, and assumed she would
die similarly, and the Tree had automatically fed back that
emotion, strengthening it.

The Tree was not a monster. Not an enemy. It was just
trying to live and let live. It lacked initiative; like a computer, it only reacted to input. It recorded the horror of a
hunter killing an innocent deer—and caused the next hunter
to kill himself, by using feedback to reverse the target. It
caused a pony who hated children and who had been attacked
by dogs to spin out of control, emotionally, and to strike out
madly, and hate itself, and die. And the dog who had attacked the pony, imprinted in the memory file, suffered later
feedback that led it to a fatal decision. Not because the Tree
hated either the pony or the dog, but because it hated vio-

lence near itself, and used its defensive feedback on the sources of it.

But the feedback could be beneficial, too. As when two people made love, or a single person sought to think things out. Or when a child was lost, at the fringe of the ambience. And it could reverse the feedback-illness of a child, and make her well again. If somehow it could be directed to do so.

But because man did not understand the Tree's nature, it was in peril. It could protect itself from animals by feeding back emotions and images. It could survive high winds or shifting ground by rearranging its branches or roots. This was not lightly done, because it required intense heat to soften the living wood, and rapid, selective growth to force a branch or root into a new configuration; it could not be done at all when the sun was shining, because there was no adequate way to dissipate that heat before it killed the wood. In darkness, or during rain—then it could be accomplished.

But the brain of a human being was far more complex than the Tree could handle, and so its defensive mechanism was imperfect. Sometimes it reacted as if threatened, when it was not, as with Old Man Foster. Sometimes it was unable to divert the man's attack, as with Josh. For now he knew that his present state was not the result of any planning by the Tree, but of its explosive reaction to the cutting of the saw. Its telepathic impulse had intensified so much that it had swamped Josh's consciousness, and made him part of it. The ultimate feedback: incorporation.

And if he did not escape, he would die. Not in a pool of blood or from heart failure, but from loss of mind. His body would go into coma, while his mind became no more than a data file within the storage of the Tree. The Tree's last defense had been its best: it had conquered Joshua.

No! He had a life to live, children to raise. He could not suffer mental decapitation! He could not become another ghost! Yet how could he escape this monstrous labyrinth of emotional files?

There had to be some key to his survival. He was locked within the mentality of the Tree. Could he assume control of it? How? How could a mere file take over the computer?

Where was the "I" of the Tree? Where the self? The perception of identity? He had to break out and take over the main program, so as to develop the authority to free himself. Was that possible?

There was only one acceptable answer: he had to *make* it possible. Of all the creatures to interact with the ambience of the Tree, he was surely the one best fitted to do this.

As with a computer, he programmed it: *I am the Tree.*

His consciousness expanded. He became the command program. Now he could perceive the energy being received by the leaves—low, at the moment, because of the overcast and rainy day. He could feel the moisture at the roots. He was *aware.*

He was the viewpoint. Now the entire story of the interactions within the ambience of the Tree was clear. All the animals and people who had suffered unusual experience or emotion here. Including Elijah, who had liked this region, and had squirreled his haphazard wealth in crannies and underground, maintaining a mental map—that the Tree had dutifully recorded. Even Elijah's memories of his acquisition of the property, starting with a survey of the land and a tax auction. All there to be evoked from the comprehensive data files at will.

Josh's own thoughts were on file, as he first drove the bus into the wider perceptive ambience of the Tree. The thoughts of others, when he was absent, as the consciousness devolved on the dominant intellect of the ambience: that one that was most alert or intense, whether man, pony, dog, or fish. They were not separate creatures, they were aspects of the Tree's awareness. The entire story of the Tree was available—from the proxy viewpoints of its ambience.

The Tree had no true consciousness of its own. It drew upon the dominant consciousness within its range. That, recently, had usually been Josh's own. The Tree merely waited and watched, and assumed the reality of that consciousness. It could not reason by itself, could not truly understand. Because it was a plant, it was largely quiescent.

Which was still one stage beyond a computer. A machine did not feel. The Tree did. The Tree was alive; it tried to protect itself by using the feelings of the creatures who might otherwise hurt it. As it had used the aggressive thoughts directed at it by Patience Brown, automatically channeling them back to her and the two dogs, so that the interaction between them distracted the woman from her ire with the Tree. The Tree had not planned this; it was merely the automatic reaction, the manner that any thought directed against itself invoked the feedback mechanism. *She* had become the object of hostility.

And Josh himself had evoked another aspect. He had really liked the Tree, but had seen the need to prune its branch so as to let more sunlight in on the solar collector. The Tree had picked up the thought, recognizing the danger, but since there had been no hostile intent the feedback had not been invoked. Instead the Tree perceived it as a natural threat, such as the potential damage caused by a storm—so it had shifted the position of the offending branch to enable it to avoid that threat. Again, no reasoning was involved, only the criteria of Josh's mind: *here* the branch was in danger; *there* it would be safe. The enormous heat of that effort had provoked misunderstanding, and started Brenna's feedback syndrome, driving her away. Trigger and response, as with a computer.

And, like a computer, it could be enormously useful to man. Telepathy, within its ambience—what a dream! Complete understanding between minds. Projection of thoughts, three dimensional images, not really ghosts. Phenomenal memory storage. Experience, feeling replayed in full detail, such as ideal lovemaking. Protection from predators of any nature: Josh could make the tax assessor flee in panic merely by visualizing him as an attacker! The prospects were mind numbing. If more trees like this were grown—

No. No more could be grown. He knew this, because he was of the Tree.

Why? His human mind demanded a reason that the Tree had never had the initiative to seek.

The Tree surely knew, but did not know how it knew. But it was the only one of its kind remaining, and there would be no more. That much was certain.

Josh did not accept that. He probed for the rationale. The memory file of the Tree was enormous. He tapped into it randomly.

It was cold—too cold for the leaves to operate properly. The minds of the animals showed that the monstrous sheet of ice was coming close. The Trees to the north had perished before it, and now this valley too was slowly turning chill. It was a perpetual winter, too cold to grow leaves, so the sunlight could not be harvested. The Tree had existed on its own resources for a decade, but now the cold was worse and its bark was too thin. As the savage winter intensified, the Tree was finally closing down growth; by spring it would be dead.

Josh reverted to his own consciousness. His critical mind considered the memory. Sheet of ice? Not here, surely! Where had this occurred?

Again, the thought keyed the answer. It had happened in a section of the world he recognized as Siberia, between ten and a hundred thousand years ago. The record of the seasons was there, to be tediously read when properly keyed: every winter, every summer, every growth ring, for these changes were important to the Tree.

But that long ago, on the far side of the globe? How was this possible?

He sampled another random scene.

The grass fire was coming. There had not been one in several years, and the brush had piled thickly. This time a fierce wind whipped the flames high and fast. There had been a drought, weakening the Tree, and now this terrible fire was apt to be too much for it to withstand. The last bird was leaving.

Josh was back. He checked the time and place, becoming more proficient at triggering the information. Place: central North America, the spreading grassy plains. Time: fifteen to twenty million years ago.

Fifteen to twenty mil—that was the Miocene Epoch! Yet the count tallied; the years were all there.

There was no way it could be the same Tree. Both sample Trees had been dying, for one thing. This was evidently a record of the terminal impressions of other Trees of this species. How, then, could their memories be here? The ambience did not extend around the globe, but only in the immediate vicinity of each Tree.

He explored, and found the answer. The birds! They nested in the Trees, they consumed parasites of the Trees. They migrated from Tree to Tree, and left when one died. Their most recent memories of past Trees were read and recorded by the Trees to which they flew. Thus the record continued: the specific final scene, and the tabulation of seasons and weather patterns recorded by that Tree. The birds did not know they did this; they merely felt most comfortable in the ambience of a Tree, and their minds provided this service simply by being present. The birds were the wider senses of the Trees.

Josh followed up on this, evoking additional memories relating to the interaction with the birds. They also enabled the Trees to propagate, by eating the fruit and depositing the undigested seed in some place far enough removed to be clear of the ambience of any established Tree. Thus the Trees constantly spread to new territories.

But where were those birds today? They had declined as the Trees did, for they could not survive well beyond the ambience. They required the Trees' protection of their nesting sites. They could feed elsewhere, but reproduced effectively only in Trees. The Trees' mechanism of feedback defense served the birds too; they were immune to it themselves, but other creatures were not. Other creatures were not afraid of the Tree, but the feedback mechanism tended to disturb them, so they generally departed before long, and predators departed faster than the less aggressive creatures. As the more difficult climate limited the range of the Trees, the birds declined, and that caused the Trees to decline further. At last only one species of compatible bird remained, and a few Trees—and then that species of bird had become extinct.

Now there was only one Tree remaining, as far as current information went, and no bird to carry the information or the seeds. Thus the Tree was about to follow the bird into extinction.

Josh focused more specifically on the bird. The Tree did not visualize it in human fashion, but he was finally able to work it out. It was a large woodpecker—the kind man called the Ivory Bill. Extinct for several decades.

And so at last he understood the tragedy of the Tree. He *was* the Tree. Still he could not escape it. The program in charge of a computer was still only a program. He might live the rest of his life as the Tree—and when the Tree died, so would he. He could not even explain to his children. The Tree was doomed, for after this it would surely be cut down, by a crew of men like the one that had built the house: too much for its defenses. He had merely exchanged one demise for another.

The irony was that it didn't have to be that way. The Tree did not have to die. It could be saved—if only he could win free of it and return to his natural body. To protect it the way only an independent, committed man could. The man Elijah had not quite been. His uncle had come to understand the capabilities of the Tree, without grasping its underlying nature. He had seen it as a threat. Josh no longer had to guess at Elijah's motives; he could read them directly from the file. Had the Tree been able to explain . . .

My kind can substitute! he thought. *We can do consciously what the bird did unconsciously. We can take and treat and plant and nurture the seeds. We can propagate your species, and protect it from harm.*

The Tree did not follow his logic, for it was not a logical entity. But it was aware of his emotion and his motive. He was no longer an attacker. He had become, in its awareness, a woodpecker. An Ivory Bill.

That was the final key.

Now his consciousness expanded further, embracing the whole of the present ambience of the Tree. There was no further reservation. He found the two human creatures within that ambience, with their unmanageably complex minds. Minds that complemented the Tree's enormous memory, that provided the capacity for direct physical action and reasoning. Immeasurably superior symbiotes—now that they understood.

He touched the woman's mind, and found there her burgeoning love for him—a love he now realized he shared. She had seen him go rigid, and had quickly turned off the saw so that it could not hurt him. Practical girl! She was horrified by his loss of mind, but did not know what to do about that. Appalled, she was waiting, unable either to save him or to give him up.

The Tree is our friend, he thought to her.

Then he touched his own mind, and his consciousness returned to it without vacating the ambience of the Tree. He stood, and turned, setting down the saw. "Brenna," he said.

"Josh—you are all right?" she asked with an abrupt surge of hope and relief. "I heard—I thought—"

We are one with the Tree, he thought to her. *History is ours. Telepathy is ours. Love is ours.* He held out his hand.

She stood as if dazed. "What?"

He spread the awareness of the Tree to her mind. Its real nature was abruptly open to her.

Her mouth fell open as she felt the ambience and realized the enormity of the implications. What had seemed like horror was transforming into the greatest opportunity mankind could imagine.